W9-CAN-910
from Collection

DAMNED IF YOU DO

ALEX BROWN

Library District No. 1
Louisburg Library
206 S. Broadway
Louisburg, KS 66053

PAGE STREET YA

THIS ONE'S FOR ME.

Copyright © 2023 Alex Brown

First published in 2023 by
Page Street Publishing Co.
27 Congress Street, Suite 1511
Salem, MA 01970
www.pagestreetpublishing.com

All rights reserved. No part of this book may be reproduced or used, in any form or by any means, electronic or mechanical, without prior permission in writing from the publisher.

Distributed by Macmillan, sales in Canada by The Canadian Manda Group.

27 26 25 24 23 1 2 3 4 5

ISBN-13: 978-1-64567-999-8
ISBN-10: 1-64567-999-3

Library of Congress Control Number: 2022948998

Cover and book design by Laura Benton for Page Street Publishing Co.
Cover illustration © Pollyanna Dee

Printed and bound in the United States

Page Street Publishing protects our planet by donating to nonprofits like The Trustees, which focuses on local land conservation.

CONTENT WARNING

ALCOHOLISM, CHILD/SPOUSAL ABUSE, DEATH OF A PARENT, SOME GORE

CHAPTER ONE

IN WHICH MY POP QUIZ SWIMS UPSTREAM AND DIES

HELL HATH NO FURY LIKE AN AP LIT TEACHER SCORNED.

It wasn't that Ms. Fairchild had a personal vendetta against me. At least, as far as I knew, she didn't. But somehow, she always sensed when I hadn't done the reading. And then she'd gleefully unleash a pop quiz on the whole class, as if she was punishing them for my mistakes.

I stole a glance at the clock that ticked mercilessly over the door. Fifteen minutes left. Enough time to fail this thing with flying colors.

Wonderful.

"All the devils are here," Veronica said, bridging the gap between us. The ghost of a smile danced across her face. Sunlight caught in her hair, revealing the fact that it was actually a deep, dark brown instead of completely black. Like mine.

"Yeah," I said, a little too lost in how her fingers lightly brushed the top of my hand to understand what she was saying. But the crisp snap of the pop quizzes being shuffled at the front of the classroom brought me back to my doom-filled reality. I nodded over to our teacher. "If by 'devil' you mean Ms. Fairchild." She hovered at the front of the classroom, clutching my imminent demise in her hands.

I gripped my pen tightly as Veronica's light brown eyes met mine. My best friend tilted her head, tucking her hair behind her ears as she handed me a pencil. "It's from *The Tempest.*" I stared blankly at her. She shook her head, frowning. "Cordy, you told me you did the reading."

I groaned. "The cue-to-cue ran long. We had issues with sound and lights all night. I'm lucky I got any kind of sleep."

"I thought we weren't allowed to be in the theater past eleven?"

"Maybe if this was a normal Tech Week," I replied, letting out a long sigh as I waved the thought away. "But this is a Barry Buchanan Original. He needs everything to be perfect for his playwriting debut."

Sal perked up at that, turning around in their chair. They flashed a smile at us as they said, "Barry's lucky I was there to fact-check his first draft. Wildly inaccurate to what life looked like in 1922. And I fixed up some of his dialogue, too. As a treat."

"There will be *no talking* during the quiz," Ms. Fairchild snapped. She cast a pointed look in our direction.

"Sorry, Ms. F," Veronica said, as Sal turned back around to face the front of the class. "We're just excited for the play, is all."

"The play's the thing," Sal said.

Ms. Fairchild's expression softened as she rounded out the line. "Wherein I'll catch the conscience of the king."

"*Hamlet*!" I shouted, unable to stop myself, Sure, I was about to fail this pop quiz on *The Tempest* because I hadn't read a word of that thing. But I wasn't completely useless.

Ms. Fairchild shook her head. Her platinum blonde hair fell in disappointed waves over her shoulders. "Yes, Cordelia. That's *Hamlet*. Hopefully, you're equally as well-read on *The Tempest*, as that's our focus for the next few weeks."

My face warmed as uneasy murmurs spread through the class. I hated having everyone's attention focused on me. That was part of why I loved being a stage manager—I could help make the show a success, and if I did my job right, nobody knew I was there. But being called out in front of the whole class was too much.

Not that I'd ever let Ms. Fairchild know that. I shot her a sheepish smile and replied, "*Hamlet*? *The Tempest*? What's the difference?"

Our teacher sighed. Poor Ms. Fairchild. AP Lit pop quizzes were the only things she had in her life to look forward to. She clung to the stack of them so tightly like she worried that letting them go would cause everything to float away. "You'll have ten minutes to complete this quiz," she said, finally looking away from me and addressing the class. "Good luck."

Sal slid the last few quizzes onto my desk. I wanted to ask them when they had time to do the whole homework thing when they were also trapped in the theater well past midnight, but as soon as their pencil furiously scratched away at the quiz, I knew it wasn't worth breaking Ms. Fairchild's *No Talking* rule.

Sal wasn't the only one going to town on their quiz. The whole class filled in their answers with ease. I was the only one who didn't get the memo. I grabbed a quiz from the pile and passed the other two behind me in what hopefully seemed like a casually cool gesture. In reality, I probably looked about as panicked as I felt inside.

I didn't want to fail this thing, but I hadn't left myself any choice. I wasn't a straight-A student. Or a straight-B student. Most days, I did the bare minimum when it came to school—dancing through life with the right amount of Cs to get by. Academic un-achievement had kind of become my calling card ever since high school started. Except for English. I'd always done well in that class. Until last month, when we returned from winter break, I let my last good subject fall completely to hell.

It wasn't like I really had a reason—I'd simply found better things to do that didn't involve studying. Like falling in love with Veronica but not being brave enough to do anything about it. And somewhere, deep down in my soul, I cared about my failing grades. But that part of me was buried under so many layers that it might as well have been tossed into a bottomless pit. No telling when I'd be able to get it back. If I ever could.

I bit the inside of my cheek, scribbling a hasty answer about devils being here (thanks, Veronica!), and then closed my eyes as my ten-minute time limit slowly slipped away. I prayed to the Pop Quiz Gods, trying to summon any other Shakespearean tidbits from the corners of my largely abandoned cobweb-filled mind.

I didn't want to look *completely* hopeless. Then Ms. Fairchild might feel bad for me and reach out to my mom, asking if everything was okay at home.

For the record, things *weren't* okay at home. But my teacher didn't need to know that. No one aside from Veronica did. And even she didn't know the worst of it.

A poster of a cat hanging onto a branch with its front paws sat on the wall over Veronica's head. The text under it read, *Hang in there!* It was supposed to be motivational.

It wasn't working.

Veronica hummed the opening number to *Our Demon Town* next to me, tapping out the rhythm on her desk with her pencil as she wrote what I assumed were correct answers. After last night's cue-to-cue—strictly a rehearsal for everyone on the tech side of things to get on the same page—our first real run-through would happen after school. As one of the leads, Veronica had a lot of heavy lifting to do.

I did, too. The stage manager's job was to keep everything moving smoothly, especially during Tech Week. I wasn't good at many things—like telling Veronica how much I loved her, AP Lit pop quizzes, or any kind of math—but I was damn good at running a show.

"That's all the time you've got," Ms. Fairchild said as she stood. "Please pass your quizzes forward."

I sighed. Folded the paper up to hide my shame. Tapped Sal on the shoulder. They leaned back, their hand flailing wildly around as they waited for me to surrender to the inevitable.

I hastily shoved my quiz in their hand, watching as it made its way up the row and joined its brethren on the journey to the front of the room. The way the quizzes moved reminded me of those nature documentaries that followed salmon as they tried swimming upstream. Some fancy-sounding British dude would narrate the journey, reminding everyone watching that not all the fish would survive.

Maybe some would get eaten by bears, be too tired to keep swimming, or wind up bashed really badly against some rocks. The method didn't really matter as much as the result: they'd all come to a tragic end, in their own way.

My quiz suffered a similar fate as it hurtled from person-to-person, hand-to-hand, surging from the back of the classroom to the front. Fighting with its last breath until it reached its final destination, where it would die—alone, unremembered, and a complete failure.

There were times when I wondered if my quiz and I had that in common.

The bell rang so loudly that I jumped in my seat.

"Whoa, there," Veronica said. She grabbed my arm, steadying me. "You okay?"

"Tired," I replied, so I didn't have to lie to her. The lack of sleep was getting to me.

Before I left the house this morning, I couldn't stop staring at the white shag carpet in our living room. A small burn mark in the corner. It'd been there for a while, but I couldn't remember how it'd gotten burned in the first place. Most days, I ignored it.

This morning I spent at least thirty minutes watching it.

"Ms. Fairchild?" Sal called out, vaguely audible over everyone else hastily shoving copies of *The Tempest* in their backpacks.

Our AP Lit teacher looked up from meticulously arranging her stack of pop quizzes.

"Yes?"

Sal rocked back on their heels, running a hand over their hair before resting it on the back of their neck. "I just, uh, wanted to thank you for helping me with the script. I asked Barry if you could have a comp ticket—"

Ms. Fairchild smiled warmly, holding her hand up. "Oh, no. I've already bought my ticket for opening night and *refuse* to go for free. But tell ya what—we can give the comp to someone in class as a prize. Maybe whoever scored highest on today's quiz?" She looked over Sal's shoulder, her icy blue eyes meeting my gaze. "Who do you think that would be, Cordelia?"

Everyone aside from Sal, Veronica, and I had cleared out of the classroom by then. I don't believe in God, but at that moment, I was ready to drive over to St. Gertrude's and thank them myself. The last thing I needed was twenty-five people to know that, academically speaking, I was living on a prayer. It wasn't exactly news to Sal or Veronica. They'd both tried to help me, but I'd simply chosen to get wrapped up in the spring production rather than whatever fresh hell Shakespeare rained down on us this time.

"Not me," I said, swallowing a small cry for help. But my mouth was too dry to make a sound.

Veronica squeezed my hand. "That's our cue to leave," she said, smiling at Ms. Fairchild.

"Definitely," Sal added. They threw their backpack on and pulled on their emerald-green sweater. It complemented their dark brown skin. They turned around, gesturing to the front of their crew neck. My hands twisted together as the question, WHAT WOULD YOU WISH FOR? screamed at me in large block letters on Sal's chest. It was our cast and crew gift for the spring production—and a pretty effective marketing campaign since the show depicted the demon deal that *allegedly* founded our town almost one hundred years ago.

That question was at the heart of so many things in Ruin's End. But it didn't mean I had to like it. Or answer it.

"Hey, Ms. F," Sal said, heading to the door. They gestured to their sweatshirt. "Got an answer? What would be your secret Deal Day desire?"

Ms. Fairchild kept her gaze trained on me. "I'd wish for everyone to come prepared to class."

I looked down at the ground. My face warmed as I opened my mouth to respond. "I—" I started to say, but Veronica swooped in with a light laugh, saving me from further embarrassment.

"I'd wish for some coffee before our eight-hour tech rehearsal," Veronica interjected, looping her hand around my arm. She grabbed Sal's hand, too, and dragged us both out of the classroom. "Bye, Ms. F!" Veronica said, kicking the door shut behind us.

Sal wrenched their hand out of Veronica's grasp. "You didn't have to rush us out of there."

Veronica pulled me closer. "She was making digs at Cordy."

I sighed. "She was just saying what we all knew: I bombed that quiz."

"Well. I didn't like her tone," Veronica huffed.

"She probably didn't mean anything by it," Sal added. "I think she wants us all to do our best. She's probably disappointed in Cordy, is all."

I let out a low laugh as the class change happened around us. "Gee, thanks."

Maybe Sal was right, and Ms. Fairchild saw me failing to

reach my full potential, or whatever it was that teachers were always pushing their students to do. If she *was* disappointed in me, it was a damn shame. I'd rather she was angry. I knew how to deal with that. Disappointment was something else entirely.

"I was just kidding," Sal said, nudging me playfully with their elbow. "Ms. F. is probably just projecting her insecurities onto you, since you have friends, and she doesn't."

"Ouch," I replied, putting a hand over my heart. "That hurt me."

Sal shrugged. "My keen insight into the human psyche got me a full ride to Emerson this fall. It's not my fault I'm a psychology prodigy, a badass director, *and* devastatingly gorgeous. Some people are just born lucky."

"Sal, your story will inspire generations," Veronica said as she turned to me, smirking. "What would your Deal Day wish be? World domination? Millions of adoring fans?"

Sal winked at her. "Why would I wish for something that's already destined to happen?" Sal turned to me, gesturing to their sweater. "Cordelia Scott, as *Our Demon Town*'s stage manager, you're contractually obligated to tell me what you'd wish for on Deal Day. Or what you *did* wish for, if you've already tried it."

I rolled my eyes. *Wishing* was such a sugar-coated way to put it. We all knew what it really was, but no one ever wanted to say the words out loud. We called it Deal Day because we were a town full of unoriginal people who were foolish enough to believe that it was a real thing in the first place.

Conveniently, it was also in the Deal Day rules that there'd only be one bargain per year. *And* that the dealmaker couldn't talk about it, lest their pact be broken. It was about as harmless as playing the lottery for everyone who didn't believe it. But, sometimes, suspicions arose in town. Someone would get a promotion shortly after Deal Day, or their great-aunt Margaret would die and leave them a huge fortune. The timing could've been purely coincidental—but it was enough to keep the legend going. And, year after year, as we got closer to Ruin's End's birthday, people asked themselves what they'd wish for if they were chosen.

Sometimes they answered honestly. But, if I had to guess, the things they told themselves they'd wish for were different in theory than in practice.

It was always easier to lie to yourself than to someone else.

I sighed. "You mean what would I try to make a deal with a demon for?"

They both looked at me expectantly. I had to say something, so I smiled sheepishly as I gave a fake answer. "I'd like to finally understand what an imaginary number is."

Sal nodded sagely. "I still don't get why Mr. Jackson's so obsessed with them."

I laughed as the five-minute warning bell rang. "That's why it's my wish. Mr. Jackson has to love them for a reason."

They both nodded, looking satisfied with my answer. I didn't like lying to my friends, but some wishes couldn't be shared.

"Ah, it's almost lunch," Sal said, walking backward down the hallway. "I'll see you both at tech. Don't be late!"

"A stage manager is never late," I called out. Sal waved, vanishing as they rounded a corner. The crowd thinned as everyone scrambled to get to their next class. A locker squeaked shut somewhere in the distance.

"My wish still stands," Veronica said, with a mischievous

smile. "Wanna ditch lunch and get coffee before rehearsal starts? My treat."

I laughed, pulling her closer. It took everything I had to stay standing and not melt into the ground. "I thought you'd never ask."

CHAPTER TWO

IN WHICH WE GO INTO THE WOODS

I SHOULD'VE TOLD SAL AND VERONICA THAT MY WISH already came true. When I was younger, I would've done anything to send my father away. I didn't care where he went. All I knew was he couldn't stay in Ruin's End.

When I was ten, he left right after Deal Day. He was in such a hurry to get away from us that he left all his stuff behind. Mom couldn't go through his belongings without breaking down, so I handled it, recruiting Veronica's mom to help me drive his clothes—and whatever else he owned that wasn't alcohol—to the thrift store.

No one in town really cared that much when he left. They all knew what he did to us. But they were either too scared or too indifferent to intervene. Except for Veronica and her family.

I spent way too many nights at her house, avoiding my father when he drank too much and became a monster. She'd seen the bruises. The way I flinched whenever a car backfired, or someone popped a balloon close to me. She'd always squeeze my hand or yell at whoever decided that bursting a balloon was the best way to get rid of it.

It was nice to have someone who knew some of my deepest, darkest secrets and didn't run away. But there were still times when she treated me like I was on the verge of crumbling if something went wrong. She'd rather pull me away from a situation—like confronting Ms. Fairchild about what she meant—than let me handle it myself.

The night before my father left, Veronica and I tried the Deal Day summoning ritual. I'd waited all night for a demon to arrive and help me magically solve my problem. But I didn't get any help. I went home the next morning, defeated, knowing that another Deal Day would pass by without my wish coming true.

But if I'd known what I'd come home to, I never would've left Veronica's place.

"Cordy," Veronica called, her voice drifting down from somewhere in front of me. It was unreasonably quiet in the woods. No birds chirping, or squirrels running around the trees. But the way my best friend's voice lilted and chimed was enough to fill the silent void between us.

"What?" I shouted back at Veronica, wincing at the sharpness of my reply. It cut through the quiet. An unwanted disturbance on a brisk, sunny day.

Veronica paused, slowly turning around. "What?" she shot back.

I didn't want to keep shouting the same word back and forth at each other like we were playing a game of Ping-Pong across the world's largest table. I jogged closer to her and regretted that short burst of physical activity almost immediately as icicles stabbed their way down my throat and into my lungs. Winter was, truly, the worst season.

I stopped a few feet away, coughing as I caught my breath. "I was just answering you. What's up?"

"I was singing," Veronica replied, squinting at me. I moved a little to my left, so I wasn't standing right in the sun. "Not talking."

I shook my head. "You said my name. I heard it."

"No, I didn't. I was going back over the opening number." She smirked. "Maybe you heard the aswang that lives in the woods." Veronica wiggled her fingers in my face. "Don't let her lure you into the trees—then she'll suck the marrow out of your bones and bleed you till you're dry!"

I laughed nervously, swatting her hands away. I didn't need a reminder of the monster that haunted my childhood nightmares adding more stress to my already-existing heartburn—even if that was how Veronica and I became friends in the first place.

Veronica's parents and my mom came over from the Philippines at around the same time. Before we were born, they hung out together, bonded as some of the only Pinoys in town, and traded scary stories with each other about aswangs, the manananggal, Diwata—monsters they'd grown up searching for every time the sun went down or looking for over their shoulders, just in case something was watching them, waiting to strike.

After we were born, Veronica's mom kept the tradition alive. She'd tell the two of us those stories whenever I slept over. Which was pretty much every night, since Mom didn't want me staying alone with my father when she worked at the hospital.

I'd always thought things would be better after my father was out of the picture—and then he did something so unforgivable that he moved to Florida to avoid dealing with it.

I got my wish.

But instead of being happy that he was gone, I felt empty. Hollow. Like I'd been the one who did something wrong. Not him.

"Very funny," I said, taking another long sip of coffee, forcing away the memory of the last time I saw him. I flinched as Mom's scream tore through my mind. Gripped my coffee cup tighter. "Thank you for using my irrational fear of the aswang against me."

Her smile fell away. "Hey," she said, pulling me back toward her. "I was just teasing—"

Before she could wrap me in a hug, though, something crashed through the trees in front of us, screeching. I jumped, accidentally flinging my drink into the air. It hurtled to the ground, breaking apart where the lid met the cup, spilling bitter brown liquid all over. Coffee splattered everywhere, making the woods look like a crime scene where the victim was my one small bit of happiness. Dustin Jones lay a few feet away, clutching his stomach. He was practically suffocating from laughter.

"What the hell?" Veronica spat the question out.

"That was my coffee, asshole," I growled.

Veronica marched over to me, handing the coffee cup back to me.

Dustin has what I like to call Gaston Syndrome, because he had it built up in his puny, unimaginative brain that Veronica only rejected him because she was playing hard to get. And ever since that fateful day in freshman year, he pursued her relentlessly. Whenever we had a new round of auditions, he pulled all of the strings that his family had, coercing his way into lead role after lead role.

It wouldn't have been a big deal—if his family wasn't the center of our whole town. After all, it was Dustin's great-grandfather who allegedly made the deal that founded Ruin's End in the first place.

Dustin sat up once he finally had time to breathe. "Don't have a conniption, Scott. My brother's coffee isn't that good," he said, still laughing. In one sentence, he'd called me by my last name (which he knew I hated) *and* insulted The Coffee Spot (which was the best café ever *and* owned by Blake Jones, who was the only decent member of his family).

Dustin's bid to be nominated for Most Likely to Die Alone Because He's the Worst continued. "You should've seen the look on your face as I jumped out at you. Absolutely priceless. You actually thought I was an aswang. Whatever that is."

"Fuck off, Dustin," I said, picking my empty cup up from the ground. "If you ran into an aswang, you'd piss yourself."

"They're viscera suckers," Veronica said, her face twisting into sinister storyteller mode. She got that from her mom. A knack for dramatic storytelling ran in their blood. "They won't just drain the blood from your body. They'll go after your bone marrow, too." Veronica picked up a big stick as she moved closer to him. "But that's not the worst part. They're shapeshifters. *And* they can mimic voices. Lure you into the trees pretending to be someone you love. And then, when your guard is down"—she shoved the stick into the ground, right between his legs, narrowly missing a spot that would've replaced his laughter with screams of pain—"they strike."

Dustin raised an eyebrow, looking at the stick that was less than an inch away from disaster. "Doesn't seem that bad to me."

I rolled my eyes. An aswang would make short work of a fool like Dustin Jones.

Veronica crossed her arms. She sighed heavily, her breath misting in the cold air before it dissipated. "You can't still be mad that Jesse got the lead over you."

Fire burned in Dustin's bright blue eyes. "Of course I can. He's playing my great-grandfather. It was literally a role I was born to play."

I couldn't help but laugh. "*Or* talent finally won out over your parents' *generous donations* to our theater program."

"Please," Dustin said, pushing himself off the ground. "Jesse Smithe only won the role because I was sick during auditions. He's destined for the ensemble. Not leading man material at all."

Slow-clapping rang out around us. Dustin froze, a deer caught in headlights.

"Wow," Jesse said, as he walked through the trees. "It's nice to know how you really feel about me."

Jesse Smithe was infuriatingly handsome. Dark brown hair, bright green eyes. Tall enough that it mattered. And a sprinkle of freckles perfectly Jackson Pollocked across his beautiful, chiseled face. Veronica always looked at him like he was a work of art. I hated him for that.

"Not that I'm sad to see you," I said to Jesse, "but what are you doing here?"

"I saw him at The Coffee Spot," Veronica chimed in. "What'd you get?"

Jesse tipped a small cup in our direction. "Hot chocolate.

Not much of a caffeine person. Sounded like you needed a bit of backup here."

"Well, we don't." I bristled. Veronica cleared her throat, nudging me. I added, "But it's the thought that counts, I guess," more for Veronica's sake than mine. Or his.

"Can we get back to talking about *me*?" Dustin whined. "Do you really think Smithe is Ryeland Jones material when I'm standing right here?"

"Oh yeah," I said, at the same time Veronica added, "Duh."

"Well," Dustin said, casting a glance over at Jesse. "I'd be careful, Smithe. Good looks can only get you so far."

"You would know," Jesse shot back, sneering. "Tell me, do you have a personality at all? Or is that something your parents had to buy for you, too?"

Dustin launched himself at Jesse.

Three things happened as Dustin tried to tackle him.

First, Dustin's arm pulled back in slow motion. It was like he was wading through molasses. Eventually, he stopped moving entirely. And everyone else did, too.

Everyone aside from me.

Second, a branch snapped in half somewhere nearby. Which shouldn't have happened if nobody but me could move.

Third, the distant crackle of a flame licked through the air. With it, my name, spoken by a voice I hadn't heard in seven years.

My heart pounded; it was the only sound filling the silence. Adrenaline spiked through my body, screaming at my legs to move. Run. Go anywhere but here.

But then the world sped back up again before I could move. Dustin came *this close* to hitting Jesse, but our play's leading man sidestepped him, sending him sailing into nearby bushes.

As Dustin sat there, stunned, two figures emerged from the trees, watching the chaotic scene with wide eyes.

Well, one of them had wide eyes. The other looked kind of amused.

The stunned one was easy enough to recognize—I'd spent hundreds of hours with our theater teacher. Probably knew him more than I did myself, most days.

Barry was in his usual outfit: a respectable maroon sweater, light brown dress pants, and loafers that didn't need to linger on the icy grass for too long, otherwise, they'd get soaked. Our theater teacher stood with his hands on his hips, squinting at us through chestnut-brown eyes. "What, in the name of the Yankee Candle Semi-Annual Sale, is going on here?" he asked.

I opened my mouth to reply, but Jesse cut me off. "A small disagreement. Nothing to worry about." Jesse's eyes drifted over to the other man. Maybe it was my imagination, but even though the new guy had at least twenty years on Jesse, it still looked like he shrank under Jesse's gaze.

Barry was dressed properly for winter, but the guy next to him was one of those weirdos who put on shorts as soon as the temperature squeaked a little above thirty degrees. He wore a short-sleeved graphic tee that had a picture of a coffee cup with an angry face saying, *Don't talk to me until I've had my first me!*

"Ah, there she is," he said, tearing his gaze away from Jesse. The coldness in his eyes thawed as he focused on me. "The woman of the hour. Cordelia Scott."

"And you are?"

"This," Barry replied, frowning as he adjusted the beanie that covered his closely cropped hair, "is our newest guidance counselor, Fred Williams." His gaze drifted over my shoulder to Veronica and Jesse. "You two," he snapped at them, "come with me. And bring Mr. Jones, too." He waited for Jesse to retrieve Dustin from the bushes and led them away without another word.

"Where the hell are they going?" I asked, immediately wincing at my tone. If Barry was introducing me to a guidance counselor, it couldn't mean anything good. Maybe Ms. Fairchild already graded my quiz and knew how badly I'd bombed it. If she went to the principal—or worse, Barry—then I might have to answer for my shortcomings.

Which would have been fine any other week. Really. But with our first tech rehearsal only a couple of hours away, I couldn't afford to get distracted. Or guilted into doing better.

Normally, this would be the kind of thing Veronica could help talk me out of. She wasn't here, though. Just me and a thirty-something-looking man wearing shorts and a graphic tee.

"They'll be fine," the guidance counselor said, once Barry, Jesse, Veronica, and Dustin disappeared through the trees. "I'd be more concerned with where *you're* going, young lady."

"Oh yeah? And where's that?"

He smirked. "My office. It's time to talk about your future."

He gestured to the school, waiting for me to go first. I didn't want to move. But it was clear from the way he watched me that I didn't have much of a choice.

CHAPTER THREE

IN WHICH I RE-LEARN AN UGLY TRUTH

MR. WILLIAMS'S OFFICE WAS THE KIND OF PLACE WHERE nothing was holy, and everything was so ugly it was kind of pretty. It was like someone walked into a Michael's—without any taste whatsoever—and selected whatever random odds and ends they could get their hands on. Then they threw it all in a blender and called it a day.

A Maleficent figurine sat on his desk. Which would be weird enough, if it wasn't for the fact that it was a Precious Moments Maleficent. Her face was softened and unnervingly angelic. She held her staff up in the air as if she was going to cast a cute curse on every unsuspecting fool who sat in the chair across from the guidance counselor.

A *Live, Laugh, Love* sign was positioned on the wall right above the guidance counselor's head. Tears welled in my eyes. I couldn't tear my gaze away. It burned.

Thankfully, the poster next to it was less tacky. It was a cat dangling off a branch—an exact duplicate of the one in Ms. Fairchild's classroom. That sweet little kitty did nothing to help as I tanked my pop quiz. But the one in Fred's office didn't have the *Hang in there!* caption.

Cat-tion?

Instead, the words *Oh, Shit!* were right under the nearly falling feline. Relatable. I pointed up to the poster. "You sure you're allowed to have that in here? Wouldn't some parents find that language . . . uh, objectionable?" I didn't care about what it said. I actually found it kind of funny. But I knew what some parents—like Dustin's mom—were like. White. Rich. And weirdly sensitive about what their kids were exposed to, when they didn't take the time to get to know them at all.

Fred leaned back in his chair, looking up. His dark blond hair hung off his head like stalactites clinging to the top of a cave. If he went back any further, he might've tilted his chair and fallen onto the floor. But he held himself up—as if by magic—and shrugged. "What's so wrong with encouraging people to live, laugh, and love?"

I sighed deeply, putting my head in my hands. "Can we just get this over with?"

"Of course. Miss Scott, please tell me why, exactly, you requested this appointment?"

"I didn't. You did."

"Wrong!" he said, hitting the top of his desk. The little Maleficent jumped up. "Barry did, actually. And Ms. Fairchild. And your principal, whose name I don't recall."

"Thompson."

He shrugged. "Sure, we'll go with that."

"So, this is like, what? An intervention?"

"Do you need one?"

"No."

He shrugged. "Then it's not an intervention."

I crossed my arms, squinting at him. "You sure? Feels like it is if a bunch of people have been talking about me, and now I'm in some random guidance counselor's office, ready to receive some bogus advice about how things get better when you have no idea how bad they actually are." I paused, adding in a "No offense," even though it was clear that I meant it.

Mr. Williams sighed. "Is this how you always treat people who want to help you?"

"I do if they're just wasting their time and pretending to care. Find some other charity case out there. Maybe you can get Dustin Jones to be less of an ass."

"You think you're a charity case?"

"I'm sure Principal Thompson filled you in. My dad moved to Florida seven years ago after he tried to kill me and hasn't tried to talk to us since. Not that I'd want him to."

To anyone else, it might've felt weird to say something so heavy in such a cold, clinical way. But facts were facts. I didn't need a deal with a demon to make my father go away. Just a murder attempt.

Fred righted his chair, sitting back at the desk like he was supposed to. He steepled his fingers together, resting his chin on the top of his hands. "Is this why you've given up on yourself? Because your father . . . *left*?"

"Are you my therapist now?"

His nose wrinkled in disgust. "I'd never care about human emotions enough to do that."

"Human emotions?"

"Answer the question, Cordelia."

"I didn't give up on myself."

"That's what Barry, Ms. Fairchild, and your principal believe."

"Well, they're wrong."

"Are you sure about that? Do you think they don't see you spinning your wheels? Stuck, without any direction whatsoever? You've dug yourself into quite a deep hole, Miss Scott. One more failed quiz and you'll be relieved of your stage-managing duties."

I tried swallowing, but my mouth was too dry. "What?"

"Principal Thompson and Ms. Fairchild wanted you to be removed immediately. Barry persuaded them to keep you on, but there were conditions attached. You'll have to get your grades up in AP Lit. And there will be some structural changes to how this production will go."

Nausea roiled through my stomach.

"I'll be stepping in to lend a hand," Mr. Williams said. "Barry will work with the student director and the actors. And I'll oversee the backstage crew. Make sure you're not getting too overwhelmed with your extracurricular responsibilities."

The new rules hung in the air as a faint, ticking clock filled in the silence between us.

"But it's Tech Week," I said, scrambling for a way out of this and finding none. "I'm under a lot of pressure."

"Which is *exactly why* I'm here to help you."

I swallowed. "Okay, so if I make it through Tech Week and get my grades up, will all of you leave me alone?"

"I'm afraid it doesn't work like that."

"Why not? That's what you all want, right? For me to get my shit together?"

"That might be what the others want. But I need something else from you, I'm afraid."

Anger rose in my chest. "Oh yeah, what's that?"

His smile widened enough to make the Cheshire Cat jealous. "Your soul."

"What?" The word came out cracked. And about two octaves too high.

"I'm just kidding," he said, waving the thought away with a quick laugh. "Let's talk about your father. You said something that troubled me, earlier."

"What, that he tried to kill me? Is that really what you want to talk about, Mr. Williams? Ruin's End's least-guarded secret?"

"Call me Fred, please. And yes. I'd like to know more about what happened between you and him."

"Sorry, *Fred*, I don't think we're really at the tragic backstory level yet."

"Whatever you want to share."

I glared at him, blinking furiously to keep tears from forming in my eyes. "Mom came home before he could do it. She stopped him. He ran. We tried telling the cops, but they didn't believe us. He grew up here and was friends with them. Bullshit, but what can you do? He's gone now, and he's not coming back."

"You're sure about that?"

"Yes."

"And you're certain your mother saved you that day?"

I hesitated. I wasn't. But that was the thing about painful memories—it was easier to tuck the real thing away and put something else in its place. "Does it matter?"

"Yes."

"Why?"

The clock ticked a few more times. When Mr. Williams spoke this time, his voice was small. "You really don't remember, do you?"

"No," I said, fighting back the anger boiling in my chest. "And I don't know why you're bringing it up—"

"There's a white shag carpet in your living room," Fred interrupted me. "It's a dreadful, unfortunate thing to have. But you do."

Bile clawed up my throat. How the hell did he know that?

"In one corner of that ugly rug," he continued, "there's a small singe mark. If you didn't know it was there, you wouldn't see it. But you can't stop staring at it, can you? You haven't been able to take your eyes off it for seven years, trying to figure out how it appeared. *Why* it was there." His eyes met mine. "Am I correct?"

"Yes." My reply came out as a whisper. The air in his office was too stale. Thin. No matter how much I breathed, I couldn't get enough oxygen into my lungs. A scream raced through my mind, but I pushed it away, just like I'd done thousands of times before.

"Your mother didn't save you that day, Cordelia Scott. *You* did. When you summoned me."

"Summoned?" It was like someone reached into my chest, wrapped their long, clawed fingers around my heart, and squeezed it. I folded over in the chair, trying to breathe.

"Summoned," Fred repeated. He waited until I gathered myself together, moving Maleficent to the other side of his desk as I slowly sat back up. "Oh, fuck it," he said, frowning. "Your father isn't in Florida, Cordelia. He's in Hell. Put him there myself seven years ago. I'm a demon, by the way. You're welcome."

He dug around in his desk, bringing out one of those annoying little horn things people use at birthday parties and when they're super drunk on New Year's Eve. He blew into it, making a whiny *brrreh* sound as he threw a handful of confetti at me. "Surprise!" he deadpanned.

Seriously? I'd told him about how my father tried to kill me, and all he could do was turn it into a joke?

"Wow, you're super bad at your job," I said, staring him down. "Thanks for treating me like a punchline. Way to make me feel even worse about my life." I glared at him, adding, "Asshole."

Fred placed the little noisemaker on his desk, frowning at me. "This isn't a joke, Cordelia. It's the truth."

My heart pounded so loudly that Fred could probably hear it, too. "Right. You're a demon. And my father isn't in Florida. He's in Hell." I pushed back out of the chair. Stood up. "Well, this has been fun, but I have actual things to do that don't involve celebrating my childhood trauma. Really excited to see you get fired for this." I rushed to the door.

"Wait," he said, as my hand fell on the doorknob.

"No," I snapped back.

Cordelia, Fred's voice rang out in my head. *I'm asking you nicely. Please. Sit down.*

I slowly turned to face him. He smirked, tapping his temple. *I'd like to finish our conversation, if you don't mind,* he said, again, in my head.

"Ha, mind!" he said out loud, hitting the top of his desk again. "Do you get it, Miss Scott? It's funny because I was in your head." He tapped his temple.

He watched me sit with a smug smile on his face. I wanted nothing more than to punch it away. But I didn't really know how to hit things, and he'd probably just do some more weird Jedi mind tricks on me again, so instead of lashing out, I folded my hands in my lap and glared at him as I asked, "How in the hell did you do that?"

He tilted his head. Looking at me the same way a bird does right before it plucks a worm out of the dirt. "Hell has *everything* to do with it, actually. Told you before, little one. I'm a demon." He paused. "Cordelia, can we be honest with each other?"

"Uh, sure?"

"I'm kind of hurt that you don't recognize me. I changed your life! Thought I'd get a little more respect. Or a thank you, at least."

My hands twisted together as the faintest memory of a scream tore through the back of my mind. "We've never met before today."

Fred leaned back in his chair. "Is that so?" he asked as the angry coffee cup graphic on his t-shirt glared at me. "You truly mean to tell me that you can't remember *ever* gazing upon this ruggedly handsome visage?" As if to punctuate his point, he waved his hand around his face in a circle.

"Nope," I said, popping the *p* sound for further emphasis. "Sorry, can't say I know what you're talking about." Said the liar to the Maybe-Demon with the Precious Moments Maleficent sitting on his desk.

"Ah. Well, perhaps *this* will jog your memory."

The lights in the room dimmed as smoke drifted in from under his desk. It filled the small space quickly. I held my breath, not wanting to inhale whatever the hell that was, but had to give in eventually because oxygen was, sadly, something I needed. But the smoke didn't smell like it was supposed to. No earthy, woodsy quality to it. It didn't even have that manufactured burned scent that came with fog machines.

This was something else entirely.

Fred was shrouded in dark gray smoke. His eyes—which now glowed bright yellow—pierced through the semi-darkness as they watched me. It was hard to tell, but the faint silhouette of antlers sprung from the top of his head.

Oh, *shit.*

He *was* a demon. And, even worse, he was telling the truth. Against all odds, the town's legend was real.

Sure, I might've meant it when I did the summoning ritual with Veronica seven years ago, but I didn't think anything would happen. There were clear rules in place for anyone foolish enough to try it. First, only one day a year can you make your demonic bargain: the anniversary of the town's founding. Hopeful dealmakers would perform a small ritual, ask for what they wanted, and then wait to be blessed by some unknown force.

The night before my father disappeared, Veronica and I stumbled through our chosen ritual song—"Call Me Maybe"—laughing and not taking any of it seriously.

Neither of us ever tried the ritual again. I figured we'd grown out of things like that. Silly rumors that had no truth to them. But now, I knew the truth.

I'd spent seven years convincing myself that my father left of his own free will. He didn't. It was something I chose for him instead.

I made a deal with a demon and sent my father to Hell.

My shoulders tensed. I took a few deep breaths, almost tearing the chair's arms off as I steeled myself to face the demon that left a small singe mark on our white shag carpet rug when he sent my father to Hell. "What do you want?"

"Oh, I think you already know the answer to your question, Cordelia Scott," he replied. A low growl—and the screams of the eternally damned—mixed in with his guidance counselor voice. "I did you a favor. Now it's time for you to return the gesture. In kind."

I bit the inside of my cheek to keep from screaming as the past collided with the present. I wasn't supposed to be in the room when it happened. The demon tried to keep me away as he killed my father, but I didn't trust him. Thought he might help my father escape. Or let him off the hook, just like the cops had every time we called them for help.

The demon was true to his word, though. He skewered my father. Opened up a wound from his collarbone to his stomach and then burned him alive. He screamed as the living room filled with light. And then, our tormentor was gone.

I'd done a good job at hiding all of that away. Pretending that my father really *had* just moved to Florida. But that tiny burnt spot on the carpet was always there, waiting for me to remember exactly what it meant.

It took a few months for Mom to notice it. When she finally asked about it, I told her that I'd accidentally set the rug on fire. She took it as me lashing out, angry that my father left without a word. After that, she never pressed the subject further. I hid what I did from her. And from myself. Had to. It was the only way I'd make it through each day without feeling like the world would come crashing down any second. Punishing me for the decision I made.

I was right about the punishment part. Just didn't think it

would happen before I graduated from high school.

"What's the favor?" I asked, sounding braver than I felt. All I wanted to do was curl up into a ball and cry.

Fred's yellow eyes gleamed with an ancient hunger. "I need you to trap a demon," he said, patting the Precious Moments Maleficent on the head. "In this."

CHAPTER FOUR

IN WHICH I LEARN THE TERMS OF OUR USER AGREEMENT

LAUGHTER BUBBLED IN MY THROAT, PUSHING ITS WAY out before I could stop it. "Sorry," I said, when I could catch my breath and get a word in. "You want me to do *what*?"

Unlike me, Fred wasn't amused. His eyes narrowed at me through the smoke. "Trap a demon in this cute little tchotchke. I don't see what's funny about any of this."

"Who am I supposed to put in there?" I finally got out, after my laughter died down. "You?"

"Of course not. That would be ridiculous."

"And none of this is?" I gestured at him. "I didn't know you existed until five minutes ago and now you want me to, what, pick up a Bible and start chanting things in Latin? Cut the Maleficent in half and shove a demon inside of it?"

"What I did for you was not a simple task. Upholding

your end of our bargain won't be, either. This is not a joke, Cordelia."

Yeah, sure. *What he did for me.* I scoffed, leaning back in the chair and crossing my arms. The memory of watching my father die had been such an easy thing to forget. Trauma was funny like that—or that's what my therapist said. Back when I was still seeing her, anyway. She told me that sometimes when bad things happen it can be so difficult for someone to process the event that they tuck it away in a far corner of their mind until they're ready to work through it. Or they can keep it repressed. It really depended on the person and the situation.

She was fully supportive of me throwing that day into my Trauma Box and never taking it out again if I wasn't ready. So, I did, and things were fine until a demon disguised as a high school guidance counselor forced me to open the damn thing up. It was bullshit. I'd been doing just fine for seven years pretending that after my father tried to kill me—and failed—that he left Massachusetts and moved all the way down to the end of the East Coast out of shame.

What I'd hidden from her—from myself—was that he didn't go willingly. He died because I wanted him to. I knew I wouldn't be able to survive if he stayed alive. I was so desperate to see it happen that I was willing to trade anything for it.

It was kind of funny, in a sad way. Everyone in Ruin's End was so obsessed with making a deal with a demon, but no one talked about what happened when that demon came back to collect.

"What if I don't do it?" I asked, glaring right back at him.

"I'm afraid you don't have much of a choice," Fred replied, smoke still swirling around his bright yellow eyes. My father's scream as he was gutted from his abdomen to his collarbone tore through my mind. It dented one of the walls I'd put up seven years ago. My fingers wrapped around my sweater, pulling at the thick strings.

"Why not?" I asked, hoping I didn't sound as frayed as I was starting to feel.

Fred sighed. "As you've hopefully pieced together by now, the rumors are true. Your town was founded by a deal with a demon almost one hundred years ago—and he's been here ever since, becoming more powerful with each bargain he makes. *That's* who I need you to trap. If he's not stopped, things will only get worse."

"Got any specifics in there? Or are we stopping with vague threats?"

"It's not a threat," Fred said, steepling his fingers together. "It's a promise."

"Right. And why would you care?" I asked, crossing my arms as I leaned back in the worn leather armchair. "You're a demon. Don't you want power, too? Are you trying to take it from the other guy? Am I caught in the middle of some supernatural *Game of Thrones* shit?"

"I don't want his power. I simply want to stop him."

"Sure. And you're *simply* doing this out of the kindness of your cold, dead heart."

Fred scoffed. "I'm just as alive as you are. My reasons for asking what I do are none of your concern, little one. But I hope you'll believe that I'm not on his side. I don't want him to be more powerful. I want him to disappear."

Well. I couldn't argue with that. It was how I felt about my father when I summoned Fred to send him away. Still, something felt . . . off about this whole thing, aside from the fact that Fred was a demon posing as my new guidance counselor.

"Why can't you do it yourself? Is there some kind of demon law that forbids it?" I asked half-jokingly.

"Something like that." Fred drummed his fingers on the desk, humming a few bars of "Call Me Maybe" before he continued. "Tell me, Cordelia—how have you liked living in Ruin's End?"

That was definitely a loaded question. Most days, I hated it. Growing up in the same place as my father—going to the same schools or movie theaters he did—was not my idea of a good time. The constant reminders of someone who was supposed to have my best interest at heart—but who could never love me the way he was supposed to—weighed me down more and more every day. And that was *before* I remembered that I sent him to Hell.

I wasn't going to tell the demon any of that, however. Instead, I said, "It's not fun."

"Precisely," Fred replied, his bright yellow demon eyes burning. "You humans believe that the town was created because of a bargain, but that's only part of the truth. Ruin's End was designed to be a hundred-year-long experiment. You're all nothing more than whiny, desperate little guinea pigs."

My voice shook as I asked, "What kind of experiment?"

"The demon who founded this town relies on bargains to accumulate power. Rather than traveling and making deals with humans, he decided it'd be much easier to get this power if all of his bargains were in one place. If, at the end of the hundred years, his experiment is deemed successful, then towns just like yours will spring up all around the world. You can see why this might be an issue."

I frowned. *Issue* was an understatement. Everyone in Ruin's End who believed in the whole demon thing thought that deals were, ultimately, good things. That they could change someone's life for the better. But that wasn't what happened to me. Now that my father was gone, I was safe. But my guilt warped into depression. Mom could barely look at me if we were in the same room, and most people in the town still thought my father was a fine, upstanding citizen. There were whispers that my mother and I drove him away, and we lied about him trying to kill me. If it weren't for us, one of their favorite sons would've stayed.

I raised a hand, making eye contact with the antlered shadow monster that sat across from me. "What makes his experiment a success?"

"He needs to strike his one-hundredth bargain during your town's one hundredth year of existence."

"And he hasn't made the deal yet?"

"Of course not. Your town's anniversary hasn't happened."

Sweat slicked my palms. I wiped them off on my pants. "So that part of the legend is true? Deals can only be made on Deal Day?"

"Yes. Though that's such a horrible name for it, isn't it?" Fred winced. "Deal Day. How tacky."

"You realize that our one-hundredth *Deal Day* is in a week?" I asked, placing an unholy amount of emphasis on our town's holiday.

Fred bristled. "I do."

"And you didn't bring this up sooner because—"

"I was trapped. Shortly after we struck your bargain, I was shoved into this—" He picked up the Precious Moments Maleficent and shook it like a bell before setting it back down. "As if being captured wasn't bad enough, I was stuck inside something cute."

I squinted at him. "How'd you get out?"

"I don't know."

"And you want me to trap the other demon in there."

"Yes."

"How do I do that?"

"I also don't know."

"But it happened to you? Weren't you paying attention as you got sucked into that?"

"Being trapped and doing the trapping are two entirely different things," he snapped.

I put my head in my hands, groaning. "Can't I just ask a priest to do an exorcism? It works in horror movies. Sometimes."

"Ah yes, that's an excellent plan. And while you're at it, be sure to tell them about me." The demon shook his antlered head. "The Catholic Church is nothing more than a useless bureaucracy that's seen its fair share of corruption. We don't need to get them involved. We can handle this on our own. Besides, exorcisms aren't real. Just another lie they've made up to make you humans think you have control over the unknown."

"You're using a whole lot of 'we' here."

That, of all things, seemed to catch him off guard. He scoffed. "Are *we* not a team?"

"No, we're not. And I'm not trapping a demon inside a Precious Moments Maleficent."

"Not with that attitude."

"Not with any attitude." I cleared my throat, glaring at him. "You're a guidance counselor. Aren't you supposed to be encouraging me to study more or be a better student? Not asking me to chase demons around, tank my grades, get me kicked off the show, and, I don't know, maybe getting me killed!"

Fred clicked his tongue. "I'm disappointed in you, Cordelia Scott. You were much more ruthless as a child."

I tore my gaze away from him, angrily staring down at my feet. "You think I sent my father to Hell because I was *ruthless*?" Rage shook my voice, but I held it steady. Tears filled my eyes as I continued. "Do you know what it's like to have your father's hands around your throat, wanting to scream but not being able to as you watch the world fade away? Knowing that if he squeezes a little harder—chokes you for a few seconds longer—there won't be anything left of you?"

Fred replied so quietly that I wasn't sure I'd heard it. "He wasn't quite my father, but he was close enough. And that's *why* we need to work together, Cordelia. The demon who created this town is very powerful. Divided, we don't stand a chance. But if we work together, we can destroy this experiment and spare more people from making ruinous bargains."

I glared at him. "Why can't you just say the other demon's name?"

"Names hold power. There are some things we can't share freely, even if we'd like to."

"Cool. Helpful." Bitterness laced through my voice. "So, all I have to do is figure out how to trap a super powerful demon into that cute figurine in a week. Otherwise, I'll be dooming humanity to live in Demonville forever?"

"Yes."

"Great," I said, biting back a slew of curses. "Seems super manageable."

It was hard to tell, on account of my demonic guidance counselor's face looking like a Nightmare Deer, but it felt like he was smiling.

"Excellent," he said, extending a Nightmare Hoof toward me. "So, Cordelia Scott. Do we have a deal?"

I swallowed, reaching out toward him. Before I could wrap my hand around his hoof, however, I batted it away. "Fuck no, we don't have a deal!" I yelped, jumping out of my chair. "I'm not gonna try to fight some super strong demon and die just because you can't talk out your issues. And even if I *did* have some kind of death wish, we're about to start Tech Week. Do you know how stressful that is? I can't get distracted when I have to ensure everything is ready for opening night!"

The demon gaped at me. "But—"

"No," I said, injecting a pretty impressive snarl into my voice. "I'm sorry you were trapped, and I'm sorry that other demon's an asshole, but this is way too much to process. I can't do it. I'm done."

Wait! Fred called out in my head. But I'd already thrown open the door and raced out of his office.

Had he seriously expected me to take all that in and agree to a plan that would, most likely, result in me dying before I went to prom? Well, maybe I was exaggerating a bit. Calling it a *plan* was giving Fred too much credit. It was more of a proposal. A loose idea.

Trap a demon in this Precious Moments Maleficent, Cordelia. It's the only way to save others from making the same mistake you did, Cordelia. You owe me because I banished your father to—

"Hell-o, Cordelia," Barry said, as I rounded a corner and crashed into him. "How was your meeting with Fred—er, Mr. Williams?"

All I wanted to do was scream. But that would probably make Barry send me home, and no way I was gonna miss our first tech rehearsal.

"Fine." I squeaked the word out and cleared my throat, trying to recover. "Great. We talked about a lot of stuff. Really changed my perspective on what I've been doing with my life for the past seven years."

Barry beamed. "Excellent. And what about your future? Did he talk to you about that at all? Is your whole life planned out now?"

I grimaced. "Oh, don't worry, Barry. Fred *definitely* has a plan for me."

It just wasn't a good one.

"Wonderful," Barry said, clapping his hands together. "Well, I'm looking forward to seeing him work with you on this production. It looks like you two have already made quite the team."

Oh, damn. Fred dropped so many fun nuggets of information during our meeting, that it'd completely slipped my mind that my academic shortcomings gave him an excuse to be around me. He'd be breathing down my neck all of Tech Week, trying to convince me that working with him was a good idea.

Awesome.

I nodded meekly at Barry, forcing a smile. "We're definitely something!"

"And on that note," Barry said, looking at his watch, "it's

almost time for our first tech rehearsal. I *love* Tech Week. Don't you, Cordelia?"

I opened my mouth to reply, but a voice from down the hall cut me off.

"I certainly do," Fred said. I stiffened. Barry smiled as Fred continued. "I can't wait to see the show come together. From what I've heard, this will be a production to *die* for."

CHAPTER FIVE

IN WHICH THERE'S A FUN SURPRISE

FRED WAS RIGHT—SOMEONE WOULD PROBABLY DIE during this production. If I wanted easy money, I'd bet on Dustin. Out of everyone onstage, he was still the worst actor. And the only one left calling for his lines, even though we were a week away from opening night.

And our town's one-hundredth Deal Day, but I wasn't trying to think about that.

At least we were almost to the end of our eight-hour tech rehearsal, and nothing outright horrendous happened so far. I'd stage-managed show disasters that were way bigger than this. Like sophomore year's production of *Sweeney Todd,* when the two leads came down with food poisoning—ironically enough from eating the cafeteria's "mystery meat pies"—and they had to be replaced with ensemble members who weren't understudies because Barry hadn't cast any understudies. That was the first time Veronica was the lead in one of our shows.

She killed it. Figuratively, of course.

Then junior year with *Grease!*, which was a total downgrade from *Sweeney Todd*, but Barry was in a retro mood that year. For some reason, Barry added a dog to the show. Just for the finale. The small, yippy little pupper had one job: cross the stage and run into Veronica's arms. But instead of doing that, Jake the Dog caught the glint of a trumpet down in the orchestra pit. He dive-bombed off the stage, plunging a good twenty feet down.

Thankfully, the conductor caught Jake before disaster happened. But it was enough to make the Animal Rights Club try shutting down the production. Instead of throwing away all of our work, we made a deal with them: no more real animals in our shows ever. That satisfied them enough. They crawled back into the shadows after that, and we never heard from them again.

"Cordy," my assistant stage manager, Ashley, said into my headset. "Dustin's going way off-script here."

I tightened my grip around my third cup of coffee. Of course he was. Still bitter that Jesse got the lead role over him, Dustin did his best to sabotage the process every step of the way. He spent all last week calling for every line when he'd been totally memorized the week before. All because he'd wanted to play his great-grandfather, Ryeland Jones, who *allegedly* made the deal with the demon that created the town. Unfortunately for Dustin, that role went to Jesse.

Dustin was stuck playing the demon.

He *should* have been singing his villainous "I Want" song. The musical number would let the audience know what Dustin's demonic character was after, which, in Sal's script, was more or less sucking the life force out of everyone in town.

Our protagonist, Ryeland, didn't know this was the demon's agenda. His reasoning for agreeing to the bargain was pretty simple: he wanted to *be someone*. And, with a whole town that he created, he could be.

Even though I knew the truth—that the demon side of the founding wasn't a life force–sucking thing at all, and it was more of a power play—I wasn't going to tell Sal. Other than the fact that I'd sound a little too bonkers with my new demon knowledge, there was no point in re-writing the show now. Not when we were so close to opening night.

And anyway, certain people in our cast could barely function with the material they *had* spent months memorizing. Dustin, for example, was standing in the middle of the stage, in a spotlight that wasn't his, reciting the "To be, or not to be?" soliloquy from *Hamlet*.

Badly.

"Hold!" Barry yelled. "What, in the name of Stephen Sondheim, do you think you're doing, Mr. Jones?" His voice rang out loud and clear. I had no problem picking out every overly enunciated word from backstage.

"Someone's maaad," Leon, the soundboard operator, sang into the headset.

I rolled my eyes. "Use this thing for official purposes only," I hissed.

"Sorry, boss," he shot back. "This is a once-in-a-lifetime event. Can't pass it up in silence."

"He's right," Ashley chimed in.

I groaned. "Not you, too."

"Shhh!" Ashley said, unable to hide the glee in her voice. "Barry's really going for it."

And he was—which was something I never thought I'd see in my life. It was like Barry shoved his hand in Dustin's chest, ripped out his heart, and then threw it down into the orchestra pit.

Even though Dustin would never admit it, we all knew there were two reasons he was always cast. The biggest one: the donations his parents made every year were enough to fund our shows completely. The best one: The Coffee Spot—his older brother Blake's business—provided all of our catering for Tech Week.

Barry was a little eccentric, but he was also pretty practical. If we lost Dustin, we lost his parents' money and The Coffee Spot's free meals.

Dustin's presence in our lives was a small price to pay for the delicious sandwiches, salads, pastries, and coffee that Blake's business provided. Besides, Blake had it worse: he had to live with Dustin in their family's reclusive McMansion tucked away in the middle of the woods.

Some weird part of me longed for the days when Dustin was my biggest problem. Now, unfortunately, there were way bigger fish to fry.

Throughout the night, I kept my distance from my demonic guidance counselor, even though he kept making appeals to *see things his way*. But stage managing the production provided a solid distraction from the fact that a few hours ago, during our dinner break, I passed the salt to the demon that gutted my father from collarbone to abdomen and sent him to Hell, where he'd be tortured for the rest of eternity.

I didn't want to think about what I'd done. And, for the most part, I was succeeding. But then we'd pause a scene to fix someone's mark, or adjust a lighting cue, and Fred would strike.

Now that's *what I call entertainment!* Fred chimed in my head. *Is theater always this fun? I should've been doing this all along!*

I grimaced. Anyone close enough to see me would probably think it was because Barry's diatribe was still going and not from a demon sitting in the audience. *There's, uh, less yelling most of the time,* I replied.

A shame, Fred said, *Barry seems to be having a blast.*

I shook my head. *At least one of us is.*

Oh, come on, little one, Fred replied. *Some part of you is enjoying this as well. Admit it.*

No. I crossed my arms. *Wouldn't this be a good time for you to convince me to join the dark side, or whatever?*

Fred sighed. In my head. *I have no idea what that means. If you're referring to the noble cause of trapping my rival in the figurine version of an adorable witch, it's not dark at all. Merely the right thing to do.*

That's what you think, I shot back. *I have other things to focus on. Find someone else.*

I can't.

Why not? I didn't mean to scream the question back at him, but I did. *You were a little sparse on the details earlier.*

The details don't matter, he shot back.

I had no idea if he could see it, but I flipped him off in the darkness. *They do if I'm the one risking my life.*

It's simple: demons can't harm other demons. Humans can. We've been counting on your kind to fight our battles for us since the beginning.

So, I'm a means to an end?

"That's it!" Barry shouted as Dustin stomped off the stage.

"We're calling it a night. I'll see all of you tomorrow morning."

"But we still have to get through the last few scenes," Sal said.

"Which we'll start tomorrow's rehearsal with," Barry said. "That's a wrap, everyone. Go home and get some rest."

"Boss?" Leon asked uneasily over the headset.

"You heard Barry," I replied. "Back to pre-show settings. House lights up. Full lights backstage."

As soon as I said it, I regretted it. It should've been an easy enough adjustment to make after four years of going from a blackout to a flood of lights, but it still made me stagger back a few steps and put a hand in front of my eyes.

"Blake isn't supposed to pick me up for another hour," Dustin whined. "He's gonna kill me for making him leave before The Coffee Spot closes."

"Be sure to tell him *why* he's being summoned early," Barry replied. "You have one job, Mr. Jones. Learn how to be a team player or you're out of the show."

"Opening night's in a week," Dustin shot back. "You can't find anyone to fill my shoes. There's not enough time."

"It's happened before." Veronica walked out onstage, glaring at Dustin. "Remember sophomore year?"

Dustin scoffed. "Whatever." He grabbed his bag and stormed out of the auditorium. The door slammed behind him.

Barry cleared his throat after a few seconds of silence. "I apologize for losing my cool a bit tonight, everyone. Even with our . . . *difficulties* . . . we had an excellent first tech rehearsal. I'm proud of this production, and I hope you are, too."

"We are," Veronica replied. The cast and crew murmured in agreement.

"Hear, hear!" I called out from backstage.

How touching, Fred said in my head.

Shut up, I replied. Maybe telling a demon to shut up was a bad idea. But he was being annoying.

"It's gonna be a great show," Veronica said. "This is a good sign, right? A perfect Tech Week would mean a disastrous opening night, remember? We're gonna knock this thing outta the park."

"She's right," Jesse added. "I'm proud of all of us."

Uneasy applause followed. Fred snorted in my head.

"Thank you all for your support," Barry said. "Now, go home so I can, too."

After about thirty minutes, there were only a few of us left in the theater. Sal and Veronica were talking to Barry. Fred was backstage, helping me do final checks and lock the doors that led to our workshop and out to the parking lot.

The demon hadn't tried to talk to me—in my mind or otherwise—since I told him to shut up. When we were done backstage, he gave me a nod and went back into the auditorium. He pulled Barry away from Sal and Veronica right as I walked down the stage right steps.

Sal and Veronica drifted toward me, trading conspiratorial looks.

"We have a plan," Sal said, barely holding back a wide grin.

"We know who'll replace Dustin if we have to," Veronica added.

"Good," I replied. "Don't tell me, though. I wanna be surprised."

"My favorite students," Barry called out to us. "Oops," he said, dramatically putting a hand over his mouth. "Don't tell anyone I called you that."

Sal gave him an exaggerated wink. "It's our little secret."

"Good," Barry replied. "The newest member of our thespian troupe, and guidance counselor extraordinaire, Mr. Fred Williams, has graciously volunteered to help Cordelia finish locking up. I need some Me Time tonight. Gotta catch up on *The Bachelor* so that I can be fully present for day two of Tech Week tomorrow. I suggest you all get some rest as well. If tonight was any indication, we're all going to need it."

Fred led Barry up the center aisle to the back of the house. "I'll be back, Cordelia," he said. The doors creaked shut behind them.

"Think anything *interesting* is happening with those two?" Sal asked, waggling their eyebrows.

I gagged. "Ew. I hope not."

"Why?" Sal asked. "What if they make each other happy?"

"Fred is—" I started to say, and then caught myself. "A little dramatic."

Veronica shrugged. "So is Barry."

"Yeah." Sal nodded. "Hey, V, can I still get that ride home?"

Veronica smiled at them. "Sure. But could you give me and Cordy a second first? There's something I need to talk to her about."

Sal smirked. "Sure. I'll be in the lobby. Find me when you're ready."

My hands slid into my pockets as Sal walked up the aisle and out of the auditorium. I wasn't sure I could face Veronica—not after remembering that I'd sent my father to Hell—but I didn't have much of a choice. I wanted to tell her everything and nothing at the same time. She was with me when we did the summoning ritual, after all. Maybe she'd understand what I'd done.

Or she'd hate me for choosing someone's fate for them.

Veronica waited until the door closed behind them to ask, "Are you okay?"

"I'm fine." The lie slipped out of my mouth too easily.

"No, you're not. I saw your face after Dustin scared you earlier. I'm worried about you. You can talk to me, you know. I'm a good listener."

"I know." My gaze met hers, desperately trying to sell the lie. "But I'm fine. I'll be okay."

"Cordy, if that reminded you of your dad—"

"Veronica," I said firmly. My hands squeezed hers, cutting her off. "If I need to talk about anything, you'll be the first one I go to. But that was just Dustin being Dustin. Compared to my father, he's harmless."

The theater's muted fluorescent lights highlighted dark flecks in her light brown eyes. She watched me for a few seconds, opening and closing her mouth as if she was trying to figure out what to say. Finally, she sighed and let go of my hands. "I know when you're not okay." She frowned. "I'm here when you need to talk."

She turned and walked away without another word. I grabbed onto the top of a nearby chair, gripping it tightly as the lobby door shut behind her. She was right, of course. I wasn't okay. But I couldn't tell her why. Demons being real was already hard enough to believe—I couldn't tell her that it worked when we tried summoning one on Deal Day. That I got my wish the next day, and she didn't. And, when I did, it created way more problems than I anticipated.

Veronica couldn't get involved in any of this. And she wouldn't. All I had to do was keep her in the dark for a week. And then, hopefully, it would all be over.

I sat on the edge of the stage, my feet dangling over the twenty-foot drop to the pit. Why did this demon bullshit have to happen during Tech Week? I wasn't sure I could keep this whole show *and* myself together.

A loud crash broke through the silence. I jumped, running backstage in the direction of the sound. A harsh wind was coming from outside, slamming the workshop door over and over again.

I swallowed. Fred locked that door. I watched him do it.

"Hello?" I called out, like every poor unfortunate soul in a horror movie. "Is anyone there?"

Wind rattled the door again. I swallowed, slowly backing away from it.

Heat and the faint crackling of flames rose behind me. I wiped small beads of sweat off the back of my neck, turning around to run, but hitting one of the set pieces instead.

It was the entrance to Ryeland's home. I stared at the door, opening it slowly. Smoke charged in, surrounding me. Flames licked the side of the door, quickly spreading throughout the side of the fake house.

"*You . . .*" a voice inside the flames snarled. A cold chill raced through my body. I knew that voice.

I opened my mouth to scream, but nothing came out.

"You did this to me," my father said.

The fire roared. A hand reached out of the flames, clawing at the air as it reached out for me. Dread filled the cracks in my bones that anger couldn't reach. It was impossible. He shouldn't be here.

Tears filled my eyes as smoke invaded my lungs. I ran past the hand, still grasping at air, and snatched up one of the fire extinguishers we kept backstage. I pulled the pin out of it and screamed as I doused the tiny inferno with way too much white foam, desperately trying to get my father away from me.

The fire—and the hand—disappeared.

I walked over to the burnt set piece, crumbling down next to it—but it wasn't burnt. Ryeland's house looked just like it always had, only now its dark blue paint was covered in white foam.

Laughter bubbled in my chest. It wasn't real. None of it had been real. I hadn't seen a fire. Or heard his voice. Watched his hand try to grab me. Everything was fine. I was—

A sudden pulse of pressure cut the thought off cold. My father wasn't in the fire anymore. But someone else was here with me. Holding my shoulder.

CHAPTER SIX

IN WHICH THE OTHER DEMON MAKES A MOVE

"YOU OKAY?" JESSE SMITHE ASKED. HIS GREEN EYES widened as I whirled around to face him.

"Of course I am," I said, setting the fire extinguisher down. "Why wouldn't I be?"

"Well, I heard you scream, and then found you going all Smokey the Bear back here."

My gaze drifted back over to where the flames had been. "There was a fire. I tried putting it out . . ." I *thought* that was what I saw. But then I sprayed it with the extinguisher, and it was like it hadn't been there at all.

"You saw a fire?" Jesse asked.

"Didn't you?"

"No. Maybe we should sit down, Cordy. It's been a long day."

I nodded, letting him guide me down the steps into the front row. "What're you still doing here, anyway? I thought you went home a while ago."

"I forgot my lunch box," he replied. "Need it for tomorrow. I'm bringing snacks for everyone, remember?"

Distantly, I did. But our Tech Week Snack Schedule wasn't quite at the top of my mind for obvious reasons.

"Do you wanna talk about it?" Jesse asked.

"About what?"

"The whole imaginary fires thing?"

I bit back a laugh. If I wasn't going to tell Veronica about how the literal fires of Hell slithered onto the stage and I heard my father's voice—saw his hand reaching out for me—there was no way I'd ever tell Jesse.

He'd moved to town a few months ago. I didn't think he was anything to write home about, but lots of people in the theater department swooned over him. I couldn't blame them for that. He was magazine pretty, talented, and not an asshole. But that didn't mean we were friends. This might've been the most we'd ever spoken to each other.

"I'm good," I replied. "Thanks, though."

"Then, can I say something?" he asked, shifting to face me.

"Sure."

"Has anyone ever told you that you're beautiful?"

Out of all the things I was expecting the lead of our play to say, that definitely wasn't one of them. "Excuse me?" I asked, my voice a couple of octaves too high. It sounded like I'd sucked all the helium out of a balloon.

"You're beautiful, Cordelia Scott," he said, reaching out to caress my cheek.

I shot up out of the chair. "Oh. Well. Thanks?"

"No, thank *you*. You're so gorgeous. It breaks my heart a little more each time I look at you." He gave me a look that would've melted anyone who was into him. But I wasn't.

What a weird compliment. I was cute, sure, but I wasn't earth-shatteringly good-looking. And something felt off about his tone. I'd spent enough time around my father to know he was saying the words, but he didn't mean them.

"Cool," I said, backing up the center aisle toward the door. "That's uh, flattering, but I'm—"

"Cordelia," Fred's voice snapped from behind me. "What's going on here?"

Jesse's face lit up at that. He slow clapped. "Mr. Williams. How nice of you to join us."

When Fred and Barry found us in the woods, I thought I saw the guidance counselor shiver when Jesse looked at him. I figured I was reading into things, but now I wasn't so sure.

Whatever color was left in Fred's pale face drained away.

Walk toward me, Cordelia, he cautioned, slowly, in my mind. *Slowly.*

What's happening? I asked.

Not now, he replied.

Jesse's smile widened. He was as happy as a shark swimming through chummed water. "I was giving our dear, sweet Cordelia a few compliments. I think it's important to tell people how you feel about them. Don't you? After all, you never know when they'll be taken away from you. Life is so fickle sometimes."

"You should go home," Fred replied coldly. "It's a little late for *kids* to be out here. Alone. Wouldn't want you to miss curfew."

Jesse nodded. "You're right. I'd hate to break the rules." He snatched his lunch box from a nearby chair and pushed past me. "Good talk," he said as he walked by Fred.

My demonic guidance counselor jumped, stumbling into a row of chairs behind him.

Jesse turned to me and winked. "See you tomorrow, Cordelia." He walked out of the theater. The doors shut behind him. Their echo was the only thing that broke through the silence.

Fred slowly untangled himself from the chairs. He stood up straight, brushing himself off. "I told you to walk toward me," he said, his voice still cold. "You didn't listen."

I crossed my arms. "You didn't tell me why. What the hell was that? You're scared of a high school senior?"

Fred barked out a laugh. "That's not a teenager, little one. There's nothing human about that boy." He paused, letting the silence linger around us.

If Jesse wasn't human, then—

"*He's* the other demon?" I didn't mean for that to come out as a shout, but it bounced around the auditorium's brick walls, announcing my revelation to anyone who was around to hear it.

Fred winced. "You don't have to be so loud about it."

"Why didn't you tell me?"

"I was waiting for the right time."

"To bring up the fact that my best friend is sharing the stage with a monster?" My hands balled into fists. "What if he hurts her? Or anyone else in the show?"

"He won't."

"You can't guarantee that."

"I can," he said, watching me. "*We* can. If you trap him, he'll never be able to hurt anyone again."

"Right. And how do we do that?"

He looked down. "No idea."

It was my turn to laugh. "Then what's the point? We're screwed."

"Giving up isn't an option. There are more souls at stake than yours, Cordelia. The sooner you get this through your head, the better."

I blinked. "What do you mean, 'more souls'?"

"Whenever you make a deal with a demon, part of your soul is sent to Hell."

He said it in such a matter-of-fact way that it didn't feel real.

"What?" I asked.

He pointed down. "A piece of your soul is in Hell."

"Are you serious?"

"As the grave," he replied. "This wasn't how I wanted to break the news, but you ran out of my office before I could tell you."

I slid into a nearby chair. Put my head in my hands. Fred's footsteps were the only sound in the theater.

The chair next to mine squeaked as he sat in it. "I hoped you'd take this news a little better—"

"You stole a piece of my soul when I was ten," I snapped, looking over at him. "And sent it to Hell. What do you want me to do, thank you?"

"I didn't *want* to take it," he snapped back. "It was a contractual obligation. An inevitability. I couldn't banish your father without it."

"How do I get it back?" I asked, quieter than I thought I'd be.

"You finish the deal," he replied. "Do what I ask—what is *right*—and your soul will be returned to you."

"Since when does a demon care about doing the right thing?"

He considered the question for a few minutes. "Sometimes terrible things happen because that's the way life goes. But if a terrible thing happens that's your fault—that you could've prevented—well, you'll spend the rest of your life trying to make up for it."

His thought hung in the air around us. Was that how I'd feel if I didn't agree to his plan? If I let more demon deal towns pop up? What did it say about me if I could've stopped other people from making my mistake—from condemning their souls to Hell—and I sat by and did nothing?

What did it say about me that a piece of my soul had been in Hell for seven years, and I hadn't realized it?

"Jesse," I asked, shifting in my seat, "can he make me see things?"

"No. He has other abilities, but illusions aren't one of them."

"Oh."

"Why?"

"Just wondering."

"You don't have to lie to me, Cordelia."

I didn't want to talk about what I saw backstage, but he was the only person who might have the answer I needed. "I think I saw Hell." The words were barely a whisper as they crept out of my mouth. "There was a fire backstage, and a hand reaching out through it. And I heard—" I paused, swallowing back bile as it clawed its way up my throat. "My father was *here*. How was he here?"

Fred sighed. "Human souls are fascinating things. If they're intact, you have no idea what's happening around you. But as soon as a little piece chips off, it's easier to drift between realms. Think of it like this: right now, some part of you still feels a connection to him. There's a little string leading from you to where he is. He can't use the string to get out, but there are moments where he can tug on it, just to let you know he's there."

"So . . . every time I looked at that burn mark on the rug—"

"He was pulling on the string," Fred replied somberly. "And he'll continue to do so until your connection is severed."

I blinked back tears. "How do I make it stop?"

"Finish your bargain. Trap my rival. Bring your soul back from Hell. *That* is how you end this. Now," Fred said, standing. He held his hand out to me. "I'll ask you again. Will you help me, Cordelia?"

Taking his hand was the only way to fix my problems. So, I did. "You've got a deal."

CHAPTER SEVEN

IN WHICH FRED AND I DISCOVER A PROBLEM

"WHAT'S HELL LIKE?" I ASKED AS A BITTER WIND gusted around us. It was almost midnight. Only two cars were in the parking lot, and they were right next to each other. I'd hoped we'd be able to part ways once we got out of the theater, but clearly, Fred had different plans. I wasn't sure if it bothered me, or if I was relieved. Part of me wanted space to work through everything. But the rest wanted answers to so many questions.

Fred shivered. "Depends," he replied. "Hell is deeply individualized. If this"—he gestured around us—"disgusting display of pollenated air would augment a human's torment, then that's what the place decides to be. But if getting lost in a desert is more existentially terrifying, it can be that, too."

"Hell's what you make of it?"

"In a sense."

I swallowed, dreading the answer to my next question. "People who make deals with demons . . . what's it like for them. Down there?"

"You don't have to worry about that."

"If it's where I'm going—at some point, anyway—I kind of do. It's not like you were clear on the terms when we made the deal."

"Hell won't be an issue for you."

A fire that threatened to burn me from the inside out rose inside my chest. Seven years ago, I agreed to something I didn't fully understand. *And* I just remembered I'd done it in the first place. Vague answers weren't going to help me.

"What will happen when I die, Fred? Or if I fail? Or if I fail before I die?" I threw my hands up into the air, holding back a frustrated scream. "Part of my soul's in Hell. You said the only way to get it back is to trap Jesse, but what if I can't? What if he kills me before I have the chance?"

"You don't want to back out of our arrangement, do you?"

"No. Yes." This time, I really did scream. "I don't know. You threw a lot at me with the whole 'your soul is in Hell' thing. Add in the fact that my father can now show me how much he's burning up down there, and I can't stop thinking about what's waiting for me on the other side."

"That'll be between you and my boss. If that's even where you wind up."

"I *did* get you to murder my father—"

"Who was a horrible example of a human being. From my perspective, you did the world—and yourself—a favor."

"Doesn't feel like it most of the time."

Fred laughed. A harsh sound that bounced around us on a cloudy night. "You got rid of one problem and more popped up. That's life, little one."

"But—"

"I'm a demon," he said, holding up a hand. "Not your fairy godmother. I can't fix everything for you."

"That's not what I want."

"Then what is it?" he snapped.

It was a fair question even if he asked it in a shouty way.

I wasn't sure how to answer. It's a lot to process learning that the only way to repay my debt is trapping the town-founding demon. Then there's my newfound Hell-O-Vision, the severed piece of my soul, and the fact that failing another pop quiz would get me kicked off the production. The cherry on top, of course, was that this was all happening during Tech Week. It would've been too much for anyone who *did* have their shit together. And I one thousand percent didn't.

I'd gathered all of my frantic feelings in a jumbled ball, holding them tight in my fists like strings being yanked away in a billion directions by forces that had more power than I could ever imagine.

I was a tiny ant caught in the middle of some demonic cosmic power struggle. But my feelings still mattered even if Fred didn't think so.

When I answered his question, the words came out slowly. Carefully. I needed him to understand what was happening to me. Not give him an excuse to brush it all off.

"I don't know," I replied. "This is . . . it's too much, Fred. My brain hasn't really caught up with everything that's happening. You waltz in here, become my new guidance counselor, and want me to keep pretending everything's normal." Tears welled in my eyes, but I fought them back. "But it's not, and I don't know what to do."

A flock of birds burst from the trees and into the air. They cawed and screeched, filling the awkward space between us. Fred started to take a step toward me but stopped. The smoke drifting out from under our cars warped into a thin, misty veil. "I . . ." His voice trailed away. He cleared his throat. "I'm sorry if I threw a lot at you, Cordelia. We really do have a lot of work to get you used to all of this, but"—he exhaled—"it will all wait until tomorrow. You should go home. Rest."

It was a good plan. I wasn't sure my legs would hold me up for much longer. But I needed to know something first. I wouldn't be able to sleep until I heard the truth.

"Fred?"

"Hmm?"

"What's happening to my father . . . down there?"

He sighed, looking up at the moon. "I don't know."

That wasn't the answer I was expecting. "What?"

"I don't know," he repeated. "It's different for everyone, remember? Lucifer's the one who figures it out and we all do his bidding. At least, that's how it was when I was there."

"So, after you sent him to Hell, you didn't like . . . pop down there to check on him? Make sure he was still there?"

Fred's eyes flashed in the misty moonlight. "Where else would he go, Cordelia? He's dead."

"I know."

"He can't get out and he'll be tortured for the rest of eternity."

"Okay."

"I don't have any more details than that."

"Fine."

"That doesn't sound fine."

My breath fogged up the air as I pushed my luck. "Why

didn't you go down there? You could've made sure there weren't any complications—"

"Hell isn't something that you can simply walk into," he said, interrupting me. "It's not like the Super Bowl."

I blinked. "You can't just walk into that either?"

He waved the thought away as the flock of birds circled back around, nesting in nearby trees. "There are certain conditions that need to be met."

"Which are?"

"Nothing you need to worry about at this moment."

"Yeah, sure." I crossed my arms. Glared at him as the wind whipped around us. "I don't see any reason to give me more information on how Hell works."

Fred groaned. "It's been a long day. I don't know about you, but demons get tired, too. Can we save the questions for tomorrow?"

"Fine," I said, not satisfied by that answer.

"Fine," he parroted back.

I fumbled around in my bag for my keys. Before I could find them, though, my knuckles brushed Mom's rosary.

Interesting.

I had no idea how to hurt a demon.

But I had a theory.

"Hey, Fred," I said, yanking the prayer necklace out of my bag. "Catch!" I lobbed the rosary at him as a lone bird cawed behind me.

Fred's hand instinctively went out. It closed around the beads. "What did you—" was all he could get out before he screamed. He dropped the necklace. Smoke rose out of his hands. The putrid smell of burnt flesh filled the air.

"Oh, shit," I said. Unfortunately, that was out loud and not just in my head. That worked? Seriously?

Fred peeled back his gloves. The rosary seared a hole right through all of its layers. "Congratulations, Cordelia," Fred growled. "I'll be burned there for the rest of eternity. Hope that felt good."

It kind of did. I wasn't proud of it, but an odd sort of release sang through my bones as soon as the cross burned through his clothes. If Fred could get hurt, so could Jesse. Maybe this wasn't such a hopeless cause, after all.

Fred's eyes glowed again. "Bring your little blessed necklace tomorrow," he spat. "But if you try that again, I'm going to—"

A bird cried out behind me, cutting off Fred's threat. Air rushed down on me as it flew past my head. It was fucking huge. At least as big as me. It looked like some kind of vulture, but I'd never seen anything like it around Ruin's End before. It had bright, fiery red eyes. Dark brown feathers that shone in the moonlight. A beak with a tipped snout that was sharp enough to rip a hole through flesh. And it was heading straight for Fred.

Before I could figure out what to do—or even move—the vulture's talons dug into Fred's shoulders. The bird hauled him up. He screamed. Not that he was airborne for long. The bird dropped him on top of his car. He bounced off, slamming into the ground as his car alarm blared to life. I had no idea if injuries actually mattered to demons, but if they did, he definitely would've broken a few ribs.

"What the hell is that?" I yelled at him. "If you're trying to get back at me because of the rosary thing—"

"I am being *attacked*, Cordelia." He stood, wheezing the

words out. He was doubled over. Held onto the side of his car like he was about to collapse. "Do something!"

The vulture landed between me and Fred. It slowly stalked toward him. Its feathers fell off, molting away with each step. Slimy gray skin replaced them. Its body stretched as if some invisible hand tugged it. Long, claw-like arms extended out where its wings used to be. It stood on two legs, crossing the distance between them in less than a breath. It still had a beak—and it came dangerously close to ripping out Fred's eyes.

"Little one," Fred said, as the monster stood in front of him. "I think you should—"

The monster didn't let him finish. It tossed him into a nearby lamppost that was tall, sturdy, and made entirely of rusted iron. Fred crumpled to the ground. He was still breathing. But he wouldn't be waking up anytime soon.

The creature turned to me. Its eyes were no longer red. Instead, they were inky black.

I ran to Fred's car, grabbing my rosary. My hand shook as I held it out in front of me. Adrenaline tore through my body, amping up every sensation as the monster crept closer.

The shapeshifting creature growled. It was an odd mix of clicks and snarls. I held my breath as it bent down on all fours and crawled toward me. Its limbs were too long for its body. Disjointed, disconnected movements pushed it across the empty, unforgiving parking lot.

It stood up when it got to me. Long, dark hair framed its face. Its beak fell off, giving way to a set of fangs that jutted out of its mouth. My startled reflection stared back at me in its pitch-black eyes—but it was upside down.

A small scream slipped out of my mouth. The world spun around me. I scrambled back, trying to get away, but the monster reached out, holding me in place with its long claws.

Well. Fuck. I knew exactly what this was.

Shapeshifting. Upside down reflection. This monster haunted my nightmares ever since I was a kid. It looked a little different from what I imagined, but somehow, I was being held down by an aswang.

The monster from Mrs. Dominguez's stories was real.

Right in front of me. Snarling.

Pissed.

My heart raced. I opened my mouth to scream, but nothing came out.

The aswang was just a made-up monster used to warn people about real terrors that lurked in the dark. But then the damn thing tilted its head, like a predator regarding its prey, and it didn't matter if it was in my nightmares or in real life.

I could die, just like I had in every dream where it chased me around. Its fangs would clamp around my throat and rip it out.

I bit the inside of my cheek, holding back a scream as the aswang's face got way too close for comfort. Its nose raked up the side of my face. My heart sank as it snarled.

If I was smarter, or braver, or better in any way, I would've wriggled out of its grasp and hauled Fred out of there while I had the chance. But the aswang's gaze seared into mine accusingly. Like this was my fault, somehow. It screeched. Recoiled away from me, running away on all fours right for the trees. Before it made it into the woods, it turned into a jaguar. Its sleek patterned fur shone brightly under the moon. It looked back at me. Bright red eyes searing in the darkness.

It sank into the tree line. Vanishing.

My mouth hung open. "Was that real?" I asked, not expecting anyone to answer.

Fred groaned as he tried sitting up. "Extremely."

CHAPTER EIGHT

IN WHICH I HATE ON ANGELS BECAUSE THEY DESERVE IT

I BARELY SLEPT. WOKE UP IN FITS AND STARTS THROUGH-out the night, always screaming as the aswang that chased me around in my nightmares finally caught up to me and tore my throat out with its teeth. Each new dream happened in a different place. Sometimes I was at school—in the theater, or the parking lot, or I was in the woods, on my way to The Coffee Spot. The last time I let it kill me, I was on the beach, running and slipping in the sand as waves calmly slid onto the shore.

As the aswang sunk its sharp teeth into my neck, my father laughed.

I was out of bed before the sun came up. Made a giant pot of coffee. Didn't bother adding any cream, even though I usually couldn't stand drinking it black. I sat at a chair behind the counter. Stared at our off-white wall, still covered in a bunch of random drawings I'd made when I was a kid, and waited for something to happen.

An hour later, I got a text from a number I didn't recognize.

Cemetery. 7 a.m.

Mom walked into the kitchen before I could reply. I was too deep into my existential crisis hole to wave, which was fine since she was too focused on ignoring me to notice. She stopped at the fridge, holding onto the handle as if it was the only thing keeping her steady. Still in her scrubs. The same tired, vacant look in her eyes that she always had after a twelve-hour shift at the hospital.

I cleared my throat. She froze, gripping the handle so hard that her tan knuckles paled. Her jaw clenched as she went through a series of calculations in her head, trying to figure out if it was worth it to acknowledge my existence. I wanted to help her arrive at a conclusion sooner. Give her a magic formula that would fix everything. Show her that I was still someone worth caring about.

Instead, I just sat at the counter, watching her. Years of silence and distance created a chasm between us that was too hard to cross.

Neither of us really knew what to do. We sat there in a quiet stalemate, frozen as a storm raged around us.

After Fred killed my father, Mom found a note that Fred forged. I thought it was real at the time—another way I'd tricked myself into believing that the demon deal never happened. The note said that David Scott had enough of both of us. He went down to Florida. Had no plans to return. We could keep the house, though. And sell off his possessions.

Where he was going, he wouldn't need them.

The handwriting in the goodbye note was close enough, except for a small difference in the way he dotted his *I*'s and looped his *O*'s. She didn't believe it was real, at first. But I did. I refused to think anyone had written it other than him. Maybe that made her suspicious of me.

Maybe that was what planted the thought in her head. Maybe that was why now, whenever she looked at me, she probably saw a monster. Someone who could make her father mysteriously disappear without batting an eye.

"Hey, Mom," I said, slowly waving at her. I was desperate to break my curse and have her see me as a person again. Not a terrifying, bloodsucking shapeshifter like an aswang. Just her kid. "How was work?"

I asked it every time, trying to create a small spark of conversation, even though we both knew she couldn't really go into any details. As a nurse, she couldn't exactly broadcast everyone's medical business. Not that she'd be the type to gossip, anyway. She wasn't like Dustin's mom, who spent her days collecting secrets and weaknesses like they were Pokémon.

"Fine. Nothing too exciting." She slowly turned her head in my direction. A ghost of who she used to be.

I cleared my throat. "Opening Night is this Friday. Veronica's the lead."

"That's nice," she replied. Her eyes focused at a spot above my head.

"I think it'll be a good show. You should come see it, if you can."

"Sure . . ." Her voice trailed away as she opened the fridge.

"Ah," I said, as she took in the mostly empty shelves. All that was left in there were a stack of fake cheese, a half-used package of deli turkey, and five cans of Coke. “I meant to go to the store last night, after rehearsal, but I had to stay late at school.”

“Oh.”

“Sorry.”

“It’s fine,” she replied. But it didn’t feel like it.

“Okay, well. I’ve got some stuff to do. So, I’m gonna go, if that’s okay.”

“Of course,” Mom yawned, closing the fridge. “I’m about to go to sleep anyway.”

I wanted her to ask where I was going. What I was doing. I wanted her to scream at me, or cry. Say that it should’ve been me who went away instead of my father. I wanted her to have one single opinion—*any* opinion—rather than none at all.

She didn’t have to care, but a little curiosity wouldn’t have killed her. Instead, she turned away from me, shuffling out of the kitchen and down the hall to her bedroom.

And that was the end of that.

I sighed. My phone buzzed with a text from that same unknown number.

Bring a weapon, little one, it said. *Preferably something sharp.*

I saved Fred’s contact info into my phone and walked over to the kitchen knives, frowning. Learning to fight with a paring knife seemed kind of boring.

I didn’t know why I’d need something sharp to trap a demon, but if fighting was involved, I wanted to do it with some style.

There's only one cemetery in Ruin's End. Our town had been around for centuries, and somehow, they never ran out of grave space.

I hadn't spent a lot of time there. Death wasn't something I'd dealt with—Mom's family was back in the Philippines and my father's parents died before I was born. The only death I'd ever faced was my father's, and that was too new to process. It wasn't like I could start publicly mourning him, anyway. Not when I was the reason he wasn't around.

When he died, he was alone. Unloved and unremembered.

I didn't want to suffer the same fate, but a voice in the back of my mind wouldn't stop comparing us. He'd done horrible things to my mother and me. In return, I did a horrible thing to him.

We weren't the same. We never could be.

But there were moments—short, brief bursts of lucidity when he was sober—when he'd sob and scream and quietly whisper about the things his father did to him. And how he was sorry—he was so sorry—about how he got when he drank. He wanted to try to be better. He promised he'd stop. For us.

And he did. Every now and then, until something went wrong. He'd lose a job, I'd fail a test, Mom wouldn't listen to some small thing that he said, and all of his sorrow and regret would melt away. Whomever he'd been before warped and twisted into something unrecognizable. And we'd begin again, spinning around and around in a cycle that only ended because I summoned a demon.

I didn't want to be the one who made the decision. But then his hands wrapped around my neck, and he wasn't letting go, and I knew that it was either going to be him or me.

I chose me.

By the time I sent my father to Hell, he wasn't a person anymore. To me, he was a monster that needed to be slayed. And maybe doing the slaying made me a different kind of monster in my mother's eyes.

And mine.

I hadn't found a way to live with any of that, yet. But I wanted to. I needed to. I had to prove that I wouldn't hurt people as carelessly and casually as I hurt him.

I exhaled as I crossed under the cemetery's entry gate. It was a tall, arched, wrought-iron barrier. An angel sat on top, keeping watchful guard over the place. Whenever we'd drive by it when I was younger, I'd get this sinking feeling in the pit of my stomach. Like the angel had something to judge me for. That its rusted gaze harbored some resentment toward me.

Whenever Mom dragged me to Mass, the priest always talked about Heaven and Hell and how one couldn't exist without the other. He clarified that God and angels were good, and the Devil and demons were bad. But the ones who were supposed to answer my prayers never did. I'd almost given up—until Fred appeared. He offered to help me. Didn't hide who he was.

If demons were really *that* bad, an angel would've shown up and stopped it. They could've scared Fred away or reminded me that it wasn't worth condemning my father to Hell if it would cost me my soul.

Obviously, that didn't happen.

Angels weren't coming to save me. They didn't then, and they wouldn't now.

Whatever. I flipped the angel off as I walked under it. If

those winged, heavenly assholes *did* exist, I hoped all of them saw that.

Fred paced near the entrance. "You're late," he said, smiling as I held my finger up to the statue. "But I'll give you a pass this time. It's what he deserves." He gestured up at the angel. "Righteous bastard."

"Do you know him?"

"Unfortunately. Did you bring something sharp?"

"*Uh*, yeah." I patted the sheath hooked into one of my belt loops. Slowly took my mother's kalis out of it. Technically, it was my grandfather's, and his father's before that, but Mom was the one who brought it with her when she moved here from the Philippines.

The blade, longer than my arm, curved and twisted, like the imprint a snake leaves winding through dirt. My fingers ran along the slight bump of the intricate designs carved generations ago.

Fred's eyes widened. "*Oh*, this looks fun. This would definitely do a lot of damage on its way out."

He wasn't wrong. A regular sword is basically like any old knife. Getting stabbed sucked, but it isn't the worst. With something like my kalis, though, the curved blade worked like the serration of shark's teeth: cutting, tearing, and causing all sorts of chaos as it's ripped out of someone's body.

I'd only used knives for cooking. And I was never much of a fighter. But holding the kalis just felt right. Like it was a weapon I was always meant to wield.

"So," I said, gritting my teeth as I got into some vague imitation of a fighting stance. "How does this help with the whole demon-trapping thing?"

"We'll get to that, but—put your sword down first. We need to talk about something."

"It's called a kalis."

"Great. Well, *kalis* or not, you're going to wear yourself out if you keep trying to hold that pose. Relax. For now."

I sighed, using what little strength I had to wedge the blade into the dirt at my feet.

Wait. I was in a cemetery.

Panic fluttered in my chest as I checked to make sure I hadn't just shoved my kalis into a grave. The ghost of someone's grandmother would never forgive me if I disturbed her eternal slumber.

We were in the middle of the cemetery's central path, though, so if anyone *was* buried down there, I could at least pretend they weren't.

Fred slow-clapped as my internal dilemma came to a conclusion. "If you're done with whatever that is," he said, probably regretting choosing me as his demon-trapping champion and not some actually well-adjusted person, "you need to know some things about the enemy before we begin your training."

"I thought you were going to teach me how to trap a demon?"

Fred shook his head. "And I told you that I have no idea how to do it."

"So why are we here?"

"If you think that Jesse will simply stand there and let you shove him into the Maleficent without a fight, perhaps you're not as bright as I gave you credit for."

"Fair point." I chewed on the thought for a moment. "Jesse—why do you think he's possessing a teenager? Couldn't he have possessed an adult, like you?"

Fred sighed, leaning against the side of the Jones's mausoleum. "There's no possession involved. Jesse and I are our own entities. That's *why* you have to trap him. We're too old to be killed, and there's no body to force us out of. The only way to incapacitate us is with this—" He dug around in his satchel, pulling the Maleficent out. He held it up in the air, shaking it.

"Right. I get that," I replied, even though I definitely didn't. "But why is he in school?"

Fred shrugged. "He still needs to make his one-hundredth deal. Perhaps he's eyeing one of your classmates as a possible candidate."

"Isn't that a better use of our time? If we can figure out whom he wants to make a deal with, we can convince them not to take it."

Fred's eyebrows rose up into his hairline. "Do *you* have time to question your entire student body? The teachers? The staff? Everyone wants something, Cordelia. It would be impossible to know who he's going to pick."

"Fine. We can't predict the bargainee, so we need to take him down. Offense over defense. Makes sense." Mostly.

"One thing doesn't, though," Fred said, with a frown. "The creature we encountered last night . . . do you know what it was?"

"Yeah." My voice was an octave too high. It was like someone plucked the monster right out of my nightmares and set it loose in our high school's parking lot. "An aswang. It's kind of like a mix between a vampire and a witch, but it can also shapeshift. Mimic voices. Loves to suck blood—particularly from pregnant ladies—"

Fred held up a hand. "I get it. Thank you."

"You're welcome?"

"Now, in your studies of this creature, did you come across any way to kill it?"

I frowned. "No. I didn't really study it. It's not like they have a class on Filipino folklore at school."

"Then how did you learn of such a beast?"

"Veronica's mom always had stories about them. Tried to ask my mom about it, once, but she doesn't really talk about that stuff."

"I see. Well, your first homework assignment is to figure out how they're vulnerable."

He seemed to be putting a lot of emphasis on the aswang when a whole-ass demon was running loose. "Do you think Jesse and the aswang are connected?"

"It's . . ." Fred's voice trailed away. He sighed. "It's complicated. I can't say for sure, but I think so. Turning people into monsters is kind of his thing. He loves doing it. Hasn't stopped for centuries."

My mouth became drier than a desert. "Sorry? You said you think he *turned someone into* an aswang?"

"That's my theory, anyway."

"But why wouldn't it be anything else? Isn't there some kind of Christian monster he could've used?"

"Like what?" Fred asked, his tone a bit more mocking than I would've liked. "A demon?"

"Well, no. Unless that's a possibility?"

"In rare cases, yes. But that's not what's happening here." He paused, leaning on a tall tombstone. "Besides, religion isn't really a thing that matters when it comes to making monsters. It's more . . . what someone chooses to believe in."

I shook my head. "You think a random person just *decided*

to become an aswang? For fun?"

It wasn't like an aswang was something everyone knew about. Not like a ghost. Or vampire. Hell, even a Chupacabra was more popular. It was such a specific monster to create. My teeth chattered as I pulled my jacket a little tighter. Veronica's mom and mine knew the stories. It could be one of them. Or my best friend.

But that was impossible. It couldn't be Veronica.

She wasn't a monster.

"I do," Fred replied. "Which is why you need to find some way to stop them, too."

Anger twisted my words into a snarl. "Great, anything else? Maybe I should figure out how to fight an angel, too, while I'm at it?" I laughed, a jagged sound with edges that wanted to tear through my skin. "You seem to have a lot of demands for someone who *just* found his way out of a figurine a few days ago."

"Time is of the essence, Cordelia."

"And whose fault is that?" I snapped. "We have less than a week to figure out how to trap the other demon and you don't even know where to start. Seems like pretty slim odds to me."

Fred shrugged. "I've had worse."

"But why me?" I snapped. My voice rose to a shout before I could stop it. "Why is this my problem? There've been a hundred years of demon bargains in this town, but I'm the only one who can stop it? Why can't you find someone else?" I stared at him, blinking away the tears that pooled in my eyes.

Fred sighed. "Because there *is* no one else. Don't you see? Don't you understand? Our deal was never supposed to happen. The experiment's rules were very clear: one deal per year, for a hundred years."

I swallowed. One deal per year—and Fred wasn't the demon who founded Ruin's End.

"There were two bargains," I said, looking up at him. "You broke the rules."

"I did," he replied. "You want to know why I picked you, little one? Here's the truth: even at a young age, you were able to stand up for yourself in a way that I couldn't. And I'm sorry that my help wasn't quite what you were expecting—that you've lost part of your soul, and now I'm asking something impossible of you. But I do believe that we can figure out how to stop this. Together."

I scoffed. My breath vaporized in the air before me as I crossed my arms. "Yeah, well, you're giving me too much credit. I'm nothing. No one. Sorry to disappoint."

"You are many things, Cordelia Scott. But you're not disappointing."

"Tell that to my mom."

"Your summoning was different from the others," Fred continued, glazing over what I just said. "I've seen countless bargains throughout history. Usually, people only think of themselves. Their successes. They're willing to trade their soul away for a shot at getting the thing they've always longed for, no matter the cost. But you . . . your cry was so urgent—so terrified—that I knew I had to help you."

"So, I *was* a charity case."

"No," he shot back. His voice was firm and full of fire. "You had the strength to do what I could not: kill your father."

"*You* killed him."

"Only because you asked me to. And now, I need your help with someone who was very much like a father to me.

He has to be stopped," Fred said softly. "This is what he does. Luring people into a bargain but finding some way to twist their desires. Turns them into a monster. Once that happens, someone's humanity falls away, piece by piece. Day by day. But we can right all the wrongs he's ever created once he's trapped. Ensure that his dream of gaining more power at humanity's expense ends."

A few birds scattered from nearby trees. Fred shrunk away from them. I did, too. It was too early for the aswang to make an encore appearance. I hadn't even finished my coffee yet.

At least I had a sword, in case it did. Though I had no idea how to use it.

"You said you'd help me," Fred continued. "But to do that, I need you to trust me. Can you do that?"

I wanted to. I *had* to. But I wasn't quite there yet. "Maybe one day," I replied.

Fred nodded, checking his watch. "Good enough. Now, we have a little bit of time before rehearsal. Are you ready to learn how to disarm a demon?"

"Uh, I guess?"

Fred smiled like a wolf about to take down its prey. "Wonderful."

CHAPTER NINE

IN WHICH I COMPARE A NUN TO A HAUNTED DOLL

I HAD AN HOUR BEFORE I NEEDED TO BE AT THE THE-ater, which was good because I'd already started to get so sore from training with Fred that I was moving slower than normal. Freshly showered, I pulled into a parking spot, lingering outside one of my favorite places in town to avoid: St. Gertrude's Catholic Church.

Even before I met Fred the first time, religion wasn't really my thing. Sure, it seemed nice for other people. Mom was into it enough to keep slipping a rosary into my backpack, no matter how many times I tried to hide it around the house. But I never really liked the idea that humans had taken the 'Word of God'—whatever that even meant—and imposed our own biases and beliefs on it. We distilled it. Warped and twisted it until God said exactly what we needed them to. And then we used that as a weapon. A way to justify hating anyone different.

It wasn't like that all the time, of course. But I'd seen enough to know that I'd never go to church willingly ever again.

This is why I lingered on the church's front steps, trying to convince myself to cross the threshold and go inside. I didn't think I'd burst into flames as soon as I set foot on their decades-old maroon carpet, but the possibility—even if it was small—screamed in the back of my mind.

The Catholic Church had never felt like a particularly welcoming place. Especially for me—a biracial kid whose mom was only devoted to that religion because Spanish conquistadors colonized the Philippines centuries ago. They burned my ancestors' beliefs to the ground, slowly indoctrinating us until everything felt so normal that we paid them without a second thought when they collected money from us every Sunday.

And, of course, I was super gay. Catholicism was slow to catch up to a bunch of other religions—if it ever would. People like me were still pretty high up on the sinners list. Public Enemy Number One. Lots of parishioners thought I deserved to rot in Hell just because I had feelings for my best friend, who wasn't a dude.

But where I went after I died wasn't their call to make. If God—or something else—existed out there, I hoped I'd be judged by my actions and not by who I was in love with.

I took a deep breath, exhaling as soon as the white tips of my Converse touched the carpet. I wasn't swallowed up in a sudden burst of flames.

At least I had that going for me.

St. Gertrude's wasn't the flashiest house of worship, even though Dustin's rich-ass family was here weekly. On Sundays *and* Wednesdays. If they had their way, the ancient insides of this church would be gutted and replaced with state-of-the-art everything. But I liked it the way it was. Kind of stuffy. Paint that used to be bright white but yellowed a bit with age. Dusty old curtains frayed at the seams.

Even though I avoided this place like the plague, I let Mom drag me here every Christmas and Easter for Mass without too much of a fight. It was my small peace offering. The only way I could show her that I cared.

For the rest of the year, though, I only stepped foot in St. Gertrude's when I needed something. Unfortunately, that was what brought me here today. I wasn't going to confess to a priest or anything like that. But I'd found out demons were real less than twenty-four hours ago. This was the best place I could think of to figure out what that meant.

The familiar aroma of incense and stale air wafted around me as I moved farther inside the church. A few parishioners walked into the main room. They paused at the door, dipping their hands in the holy water bowls and kneeling as they crossed themselves.

"Is there anything you need to confess, dear?" a nun asked me. She was a lot younger than the nuns I remembered. Probably wasn't older than thirty. She wasn't wearing a habit, but her black hair was pulled back into a neat bun. Freckles scattered across her light brown skin.

"Sorry?" I squeaked. She couldn't have known about my deal with Fred, but what if it was easy to read on my face? Was I that bad at hiding what I'd done?

"The confessional," she replied, gesturing to a booth in the main room. "If you need to pop in there, I can find someone to assist you."

"Oh, no. I don't need to sit in that thing—" I caught myself before I dissed the confessional too hard. "I was on my way to a pew. Got a few questions to ask . . . uh . . . the Lord. You know how it goes."

"Isn't that nice?" she asked, to no one in particular. Or maybe it was to God. Either way, I stood there, smiling uncomfortably.

"Yeah. Super nice," I replied. "Well, thank you for your time, Sister—?"

"Annabelle."

I grimaced. "Like the doll in *The Conjuring*?"

"I'd like to think I had the name long before the doll existed, but . . ." Her voice trailed away as she shrugged. "Can't outrun the damn thing now." Her eyes widened. She slapped a hand over her mouth. "Whoops! Do me a favor and don't tell the big guy upstairs about that one."

"God?"

She chuckled. "Oh, no. Father Marcus. He lives in the rectory above the church."

This officially won the award for the weirdest conversation I'd had in the last twenty-four hours. Which was saying something, since I also found out I'd banished my father to Hell.

"*Um*, sure," I replied. "It'll be our little secret."

She winked conspiratorially at me. "Wonderful. Well, I don't want to hold you up. I'm sure we'll meet again—I'm sorry, I didn't catch your name?"

"Cordelia Scott," I replied, holding out my hand. "Nice to meet you, Sister Annabelle."

I hurried away from her, trying to keep what remained of my dignity intact. That wasn't the most embarrassing conversation I'd ever had, but I *did* just compare a nun to a possessed doll and tell her that I was here to ask God a few questions. I hadn't been in this place for five minutes and already made a fool out of myself.

I rushed over to the Family Room, which drew way too much attention to myself. I peeked through the open doors. While Mass was happening, anyone with small children who might squirm or make a scene crammed into the Family Room. It had a decent view of the main area, where rows and rows of pews faced the stage, waiting for the priest to deliver his homily. Inside, an exhausted mother tried convincing her toddler to sit still in the pew while her husband stood a few feet away, having an animated conversation with a nun. His wife shot daggers at him as he ignored her.

I shrugged sympathetically at her as I walked by. I wanted to go in there and say, *Men, am I right!?* like I was a middle-aged white lady at brunch, but it was best not to linger. I didn't need to be kicked out before I had the chance to make sense of everything that was happening.

I stopped in the doorway to the main room. Didn't bother doing the good old holy water Dip and Kneel when I entered. Just walked to one of the pews in the back and scoped the place out.

There were still a few hours before Saturday afternoon Mass, but that didn't stop little pockets of people from scattering around in the pews. Other than me, there were about fifteen of them all in various states of prayer. A family of three, a few couples, some loners like me. All asking God for help that would probably never come.

Giant stained-glass windows filled with religious icons lined the walls. St. Francis held a lamb. St. Patrick chased snakes into the sea. Angels looked, well, angelic, erring more on the beautiful people portrayal of God's celestial messengers than the thousand-eyed nightmare creatures from the Bible.

A priest—who hadn't been there for Christmas Mass last year—stood near the stage at the front of the room. His brows furrowed in concentration as he argued with a taller, blonder version of Dustin.

Blake Jones, owner of my favorite coffee place and the least awful member of his family, was having a heated argument with a priest.

Interesting.

Blake was at St. Gertrude's almost as much as my mother. They were both so devoted that I didn't think a thing on this earth could spur them to publicly argue with members of the clergy. And yet, here I was, witnessing history in the making.

I scooted out of the pew, creeping closer to their conversation, and pretended to be very into whatever was happening in the Noah's Ark stained-glass panel as I strained to hear what they were harshly whispering about.

I lingered for a few seconds but couldn't make out anything.

To paraphrase Sister Annabelle: *Damn!*

A large bowl of holy water sat a little closer to them. I moved over to it, pretending to do an appreciative sweep of the church's inner architecture. Exposed wooden beams snaked across the vaulted ceiling. St. Gertrude's was almost as old as the town itself—and it looked the part, aside from the awful maroon carpet that lined the floors. That was probably a regrettable remnant of the '60s.

I sidestepped the bowl until my back faced Blake and the priest. Before I walked into the church, I slipped an old cup from The Coffee Spot into my bag. It was the only thing I had in my car that could hold a little bit of holy water. I figured it was a good thing to have, just in case. I had no idea if it actually would work, but if the rosary could burn Fred, then it was worth a shot.

I took the cup out of my bag. Popped the lid off. And dipped it into the bowl while Blake scoffed.

"You aren't listening," Blake snapped. "We have a problem."

"We do," the priest replied. "You're in over your head, son. It's best to leave some things alone."

"I just need to figure out how to stop it. I've been researching sigils, and—"

"Sigils aren't foolproof," the priest said, as something cold and wet crept up my arm. "Blessed weapons, on the other hand—"

"Um, miss?" someone said, tapping me on the shoulder. "Your sleeve is getting wet."

"What?" I asked, looking down. "Shit." Well. Fuck. My eyes widened as I brought my free (and dry) hand up to my mouth. I swore. Out loud. In a church. Plus, that random parishioner was right; my whole right arm was soaked. I'd been eavesdropping so hard I hadn't noticed that I'd plunged the whole thing right into the bowl of holy water.

The priest cleared his throat. "We can continue this in my office, if you'd like. But we shouldn't discuss these matters so publicly. You never know who's listening."

Wow. That was rude.

"But—" Blake tried protesting.

"I'll meet you there." The priest's voice was gentle, but firm.

Blake muttered something that I couldn't understand. He rushed past me, a blur streaking past the corner of my eyes.

I turned, watching him go.

"Miss, I'm afraid we don't allow any outside beverages here," the priest said, from behind me. "Even if The Coffee Spot makes a mean mocha."

"Ah, sorry," I said, whirling back around. I tipped the cup to him. Every muscle in my body stiffened, but I tried to play it off. "I was about to head to my car anyway."

Great. I was kicking myself out of the church before I had the chance to process anything.

"Allow me to escort you."

"Oh no. It's totally fine—"

"Please. I insist." He used the same tone from when he sent Blake to his office. It sounded like a request, but carried an edge to it. The insinuation that I didn't really have a choice.

I shrugged. "If you really want to."

He gestured to the door, eyes darting down to my soaked arm. He kept pace with me as I made my way outside. Maybe this was an opportunity. I didn't have to say that I *knew* a demon, but this priest could have an idea about how to trap one.

"So," I said, trying to sound as casual as I could. "Are you new? Haven't seen you around before."

"Oh, yes. How rude of me. I haven't properly introduced myself. Father Marcus Bennett. Nice to meet you." I nodded as he continued. "I arrived a few weeks ago. Father Mahoney tried making it through another winter here, but it was too much for him to handle. I replaced him right after the new year. He's out in California now. Endless sunlight does wonders for a weary soul."

I nodded. As a frail, ninety-year-old-man, Father Mahoney probably didn't have much longer to live. I didn't blame him for trading our cold, dark winters for whatever was happening on the West Coast. "Good for him," I said.

"Indeed. And what brings you to St. Gertrude's today, Miss—?"

"Scott."

"Miss Scott. Ah. So, you're Amalia's daughter."

"Yep."

"The one who said, and I quote, 'If I want to talk to God, why would I need some old white dude with bad breath to do it for me?'"

On the inside, I screamed. On the outside, I cleared my throat and very calmly said, "Well, that was heavily paraphrased. But yeah. Church isn't really my thing."

"And yet, you came to one because you seek guidance."

A string pulled tight in my chest. I looked up at him as we stepped onto the parking lot. "How'd you know that?"

He gestured to St. Gertrude's. "It's what we're all here for, isn't it? Forgiveness, guidance, compassion, meaning. Everyone's searching for answers to their questions."

He wasn't wrong about that. I took a sip from my coffee cup out of pure habit. My eyes widened when lukewarm holy water filled my mouth. I gagged. *No.* People's hands had been in there.

"So," he said, as I stopped in front of my car. "What would you like to know?"

I threw the passenger's side door open and put the cup in a cup holder. Wrenched the lid off. Spit the holy water back into it. And cried a little on the inside.

I closed the door, smiling up at the priest. In the two seconds it took me to re-join the conversation, he'd put on a Red

Sox hat. I had no idea where he was keeping that thing in his priest robes, but hopefully he couldn't tell that I was in serious need of heavy-duty mouthwash from accidentally drinking stale-ass, finger-flavored holy water.

I'd tried to play this thing like someone else. A capable person who could lie without accidentally drinking a cup filled with demon-repellent juice. I could keep lying. Pretend that I was only here to socialize. But we only had six days until a bunch of demon towns started popping up all over the world. No point in beating around the bush.

"How do you trap a demon?" I blurted out.

His eyes bugged out of his head for a second before he smoothed his expression into one of calm composure. "Excuse me?"

"Theoretically, if someone wanted to do it . . . how would they?"

Father Marcus sighed. "Did Mr. Jones put you up to this?"

"Dustin? Why would he—"

"No," Father Marcus said, "Blake. He's in my office, waiting for the same speech I'm about to give to you."

I blinked multiple times. Looked down at the ground. What the hell was Blake Jones doing? And how did he know about any of this?

"Blake wanted to trap a demon?" I asked.

"Worse. He wanted to *kill* a demon. Which, even if it could be done, is a dangerous task. There are powers at play that are greater than you and I can comprehend. It's best to leave them alone."

I could *comprehend* them just fine. But he didn't need to know that.

I nodded. "But what you're saying is, a demon *can* be trapped? Or killed?"

"Do you have a demon problem, Miss Scott?"

"No," I lied. "Just doing a report about the town's founding. For school."

"School's changed quite a bit since my day."

I laughed nervously. "Consequence of living in Ruin's End. We're all a little obsessed with demons."

His eyes narrowed. "Well, please include in your report that, if demons *were* real, they're not meant to be meddled with." He tipped his Red Sox hat to me. "It was nice to meet you, Miss Scott."

"Wait," I yelled, as he walked away. I ran to catch up with him. "I've found lots of stuff on . . . Google. Something about a . . . sigil?" This was a flat-out lie. If I wasn't already going to Hell for sending my father there, then I was *definitely* getting on the list for telling the priest I'd heard about that through the internet, rather than five minutes ago when I was eavesdropping on his argument with Blake.

Father Marcus stopped, turning to look at me. "Sigils can hold demons in one spot. Convenient for disposing of them, if you know how to do it."

"And, theoretically, if demons are real," I said.

"Yes. Theoretically, of course."

"But then what happens after they're trapped?" I asked, throwing all of my chill out the window. "Is that what a blessed weapon does? It kills the demon, or traps it—"

Father Marcus held up a hand, cutting me off. "Ah, so you *were* listening in on our conversation, Miss Scott." He sighed heavily, dragging his hands down his face. "I shouldn't have let that slip to Mr. Jones. Or you. A blessed weapon is a dangerous thing. It can do what you're asking. But power always comes at a price."

He leaned in a little closer. A cold wind gusted around us, sending a chill down my spine. "So, I'm going to ask you again, is there anything you need help with?"

Part of me wanted to tell him—to have someone to confide in who could make me feel less alone. But I already judged myself enough for what I'd done. I didn't need a priest knowing. Especially one who was on a first-name basis with my mother.

I laughed, barely concealing how close I was to a nervous breakdown and slapped the priest on the shoulder. "I'm okay, Father Marcus. Thanks for answering my questions."

As if sent from the Heavens above, my phone's alarm went off. Thirty minutes till I needed to be at the theater.

"Don't want to hold you up any longer," I said, jogging backward to my car. "Good luck with Blake."

"Any time, Miss Scott," he called out. "And don't be a stranger. I'm more than happy to help with your . . . report."

I threw the car in reverse, stopping to say, "Thanks! Break a leg at Mass!"

"That's not how it works," he shouted as I drove away.

St. Gertrude's slowly faded out of view. My grip tightened on the wheel.

I had no idea who this priest was—and I didn't trust him as far as I could throw him. I'd only go back to him if I got desperate. But maybe he was onto something with that whole blessed weapon thing. Hopefully Blake would be able to get some more information out of him—and I could use him to see what he knew. After all, I was a regular at The Coffee Spot and hadn't killed Dustin yet. Blake liked me. Maybe he'd help me figure things out.

I frowned as I turned a corner, getting on the long stretch of road that led from St. Gertrude's to the school.

I only had six days to save my soul. Hopefully that was enough.

CHAPTER TEN

IN WHICH VERONICA RUNS AWAY

NO MATTER HOW MANY TIMES WE TRIED, WE COULDN'T get this scene right.

Totally not a big deal at all—it was only one of the most pivotal parts of the show. Everyone had it down before we added in the lights, sound, and fake fog. But some of that sweet, sweet dry ice must've gotten into Jesse's possibly demonic brain and muddled it up. He'd been ad-libbing for the past hour.

And the ad-libs weren't good.

I still wasn't sure how I felt about the fact that a demon was the lead in the school's play. That he'd been sharing the stage with Veronica all this time and I hadn't known it. If I was being completely honest, some small part of me didn't believe it. Or refused to.

Fred painted his rival as this dangerous entity that wanted to spread Demon Capitalism all over the world. But other than weirdly hitting on me last night, Jesse Smithe had been a pretty standard white dude. Not a genius or as funny as he thinks.

The only thing out of the ordinary was that, out of all the guys at our school, he was uncomfortably attractive.

If I was a pettier person, that might have been all the proof I needed. As Jesse continued to stumble through terrible ad-libs, though, I wasn't convinced.

"Return my sister, foul creature!" he shouted at Dustin.

In *Our Demon Town,* Ryeland's sister (and Dustin's great-grand aunt), Eloise, was played by Veronica. During this scene—when Ryeland and the demon finally make their deal—Eloise was somewhere off-stage, trying to find a way to stop the deal from being made. She didn't trust that the demon had her brother's best intentions at heart. And, since Dustin's character had spent most of the play sucking the life force out of Jesse's character, she was probably right.

Even though Ryeland thought the demon was holding his sister hostage for collateral, Jesse still got his line wrong. Our town's founder was supposed to pretend that he *wasn't* suspicious of the demon. His plan (as demonstrated in the previous song) was to go through with the deal first and worry about his sister after the fact.

A real family man, that one.

As long as Jesse kept deviating from the script, he'd force Dustin to flex his improv skills. Which was never a good idea.

Dustin shook his head, laughing. "Dude, seriously?" he asked. It was quiet enough that only I could hear it, since I was standing right off-stage. He cleared his throat, taking a step toward Jesse. "I don't have your sister. If you can't find her, that's your fault, Ryeland."

I let out a sigh. Okay, that wasn't as bad as it could've gone—

"And," Dustin continued, puffing out his chest. "I don't

appreciate the accusation that I'm doing anything sketchy here. You keep insisting that we make this deal. Do you want to do this thing or not?"

I groaned, putting my head in my hands. None of that sounded like something a theoretical demon in the 1920s would say.

"Of course I do," Jesse proclaimed. "When we're done, Ruin's End will exist. I'll pay any price to leave my mark in the world." It was close enough to what was actually scripted for the conductor to pick up on his cue. The music started, sending a melody that was frenzied and triumphant throughout the theater.

Jesse was supposed to sing his first line after sixteen bars. But those bars came and went without him joining in.

"Did he forget to go?" Ashley, my assistant stage manager asked.

"What do we do?" Leon added.

I sighed. "We keep going until—"

"Cordelia!" Jesse snapped. The orchestra came to a screeching halt. "Let's do this again."

"—that happens," I said, finishing my thought.

Sal's voice drifted in from the house. "That's not your call to make, Jesse."

"It *is* when I missed my cue, Sal," Jesse barked back.

Veronica scoffed, poking her head out from backstage. "If you miss your cue, you just keep going."

"Cordelia," Barry called. "Come out here, please."

I groaned, moving around the scrim and giant red velvet curtains that were drawn backstage. I shielded my eyes as I stepped out onto the stage. Leon decided to put a spotlight on me. I flipped him off as I stood upstage right, looking out into the house. "Yeah?"

"What do you do," Barry asked, "when someone other than the director tries to give you direction."

I blinked. "*Uh*, ignore it?"

"Precisely," Barry replied. "And Jesse, what do you do if you mess something up? Do you get flustered and stop the whole show, or do you find a way to make your mistake work in your favor?"

Jesse shrugged. "I do what feels right in the moment."

Dustin snorted. I bit down on the inside of my cheek to keep from screaming. I wasn't sure what I hated more: that Dustin was having a good time or that Jesse was being extremely disrespectful.

I'd been doing shows since my freshman year, and no one had ever stopped a rehearsal who wasn't the director. Especially during Tech Week.

"All right, everyone," Barry said, keeping his voice level. "It's almost 6 p.m. anyway. Let's pack it up. I'll see all of you tomorrow. Except." He paused, letting the uneasy silence linger around us. "Mr. Smithe, Mr. Williams and I would like a word with you outside."

Dustin's "Oooohhh," carried throughout the auditorium. Ashley shushed him.

"Thank you for your hard work today, everyone," Barry continued. "We'll pick up from this scene in the morning."

Chatter rose and doors opened and closed backstage as the actors walked out through the wings and into their dressing rooms. Instruments clattered back into their cases in the orchestra pit below us. The house lights went on revealing Barry and

Fred standing next to each other, chatting animatedly, while Sal looked down at the script.

Fred's shoulders were stiff—if Jesse really *was* the other demon, he must not have been excited about talking to him. Even if it was in a vaguely authoritative manner.

You gonna be okay? I asked in my head. I wasn't sure if he could hear it. Or why I was asking the question. But I did it anyway.

If you hear screams, they'll most likely be from me, Fred replied.

Not comforting, I shot back.

Fred and Barry's conversation ended right as Fred looked at me and said, *I wasn't trying to be.*

"Let's go, Jesse," Barry said.

Jesse winked at me and then skipped down the stage right stairs, into the house.

"What's up with him?" Sal asked.

"Did he wink at you?" Veronica added.

I shrugged, nervous laughter bursting out of my mouth before I could stop it. "Definitely what it looked like." Warmth rushed to my face. Damn. I was blushing, but not because I was into Jesse. It was embarrassing. I'd lived my life under the radar—at home, at school, and especially when it came to romance—and now here was a conventionally attractive guy (who was a demon, but no one else aside from my guidance counselor knew that) winking at me in *public*!

The freaking nerve.

And, to make everything worse, he did it right in front of Veronica. It didn't matter that looking at her made my heart pound way too fast and my palms get all sweaty. Or how, if she asked me to leave Ruin's End with her right now, I'd forget about this whole demon business and run.

Veronica was the only person who knew the real me—well, most of the real me, anyway. She held all of my secrets. Understood my insecurities. Didn't see my weaknesses as flaws or use them against me. She cared about me. And that was how things were going to stay. She couldn't know about my deal with Fred—how I'd basically murdered my father. Keeping her out of that world was the best way to keep her in my life.

I wasn't going to lie to her, necessarily. I just wouldn't tell her everything that was happening.

"Do y'all want to hang out after Cordy's finished closing up?" Veronica asked.

Sal shook their head. "Wish I could, but I've gotta go fill out a few more forms for Emerson—trying to get some fancy private school on-campus housing." They paused, frowning slightly. "Think I'll get a cool roommate?"

Veronica laughed. My face warmed more than before as the sound danced around the theater. "No one will be as cool as you, Sal. But maybe they'll be a close second."

Sal's frown flipped into a smile. "That's all I ask! Catch you tomorrow." They grabbed their bag and walked out of the auditorium with a few of the ensemble members.

Veronica's hand fell on my shoulder. A fire blazed at that spot. "Need help wrapping things up?"

I nodded, gave her instructions on what to do, and then checked in with my stage crew. After Leon closed out the tech booth, Ashley reset all the props, and Veronica checked the dressing rooms for stragglers, the last thing I needed to do was lock everything up.

I breathed deeply as I slowly walked back on the stage.

When I tried doing this yesterday, I wound up with Hell-O-Vision. I wasn't ready to see my father again. Even if it was a glimpse of his hand, and even if he was in Hell, and even if he had no way of coming back, it was still too much.

I didn't want to be reminded of what I'd done to him, or what he'd done to me. The sooner I could put this all behind me, or forget about it completely, the better.

But there was a non-demon piece of this whole puzzle that still didn't make a lot of sense. Fred said that Jesse loved turning people into monsters—and it was likely that someone who made a deal with the other demon was the aswang that attacked us in the school parking lot.

Why would Jesse need an aswang, though? To run interference? To try trapping Fred back in the Maleficent—or kill him?

And who was the aswang, anyway? Anyone in Ruin's End could've made the deal, but not a lot of people knew about that specific creature. There weren't a lot of candidates.

That didn't mean any of my options were good.

The monster I'd encountered last night was either my mother, my best friend, or her mom.

I needed to start crossing people off the list.

"You good?" Veronica asked from behind me.

I jumped, throwing my elbow into a nearby set piece. Pain arced across my arm. "Yeah," I said, rubbing at the place where a bruise would eventually bloom. "Got a little lost in thought."

"What were you thinking about?"

"You," I said, before I could stop myself. My eyes widened. I clamped my hand over my mouth, thankful that I hadn't turned around to face her as warmth rushed back up to my cheeks.

Awesome. Way to play it cool.

"Me?" she asked, a hopeful note ringing in her voice. Or maybe I was reading into it because I wanted there to be a hopeful note in her voice.

I was definitely overthinking it, but the solution to my problem was pretty simple.

If I couldn't figure out who the aswang was—and stop them from helping the other demon—then I wouldn't be able to trap said demon in Fred's Maleficent. And if I couldn't do that, then I'd either get murdered by Fred's rival for trying, *or* I'd lose a piece of my soul to Hell for forever.

This was kind of a damned if you do, damned if you don't situation.

There was a chance, though, that I wouldn't be alive six days from now. I couldn't tell Veronica how I felt—I was still too afraid of what would happen once she rejected me—but maybe I could express it in a different way while still getting the answer I needed.

My fingers curled around the edge of the set piece. I could talk in circles all day. Convince myself that it was a good idea to look into Veronica's eyes—to see if my reflection was upside down or not—or that it was a disastrous one.

The worst-case scenario: my best friend made a deal with a demon and turned into a monster.

The best-case scenario: she didn't, and I thought she was capable of stooping down to my level.

The life-altering, world-ending scenario: she didn't, and she'd be so close that, if she wanted to, she could lean in and kiss me. Or maybe I could kiss her.

My hands shook as I let go of the set piece. I stamped out the small bit of hope that bloomed in my chest. That last one wasn't ever going to happen. Veronica deserved someone who didn't let a demon solve her problems for her.

Besides, she liked me as a friend, and that was all we were to each other. Friends. Nothing more, nothing less.

"You still want to hang out after this?" she asked.

"Sure," I replied, taking a few steps closer to her. It was now or never, dammit! "We just have to do one thing first."

"What's that?" she asked as I bridged the gap between us. We were less than a breath away from each other now. Her lips parted slightly. I swallowed. It wasn't like I was looking at her lips, or anything. They were just there. In front of me.

Parting.

Slightly.

Well, damn. Never might have been the better option, but I really wasn't opposed to the now.

I tucked a loose strand of hair behind her ears. Grazed her cheek with my thumb as I pulled my hand away. Her eyes drifted down to my lips. No way this was actually happening. I wasn't sure when I started breathing way too fast, but I couldn't stop it. Or how sweaty my forehead was getting. It was like I'd just tried to run a mile, but I hadn't moved at all.

I needed to get even closer. Which, under any other circumstance, would've been anxiety-inducing enough. But now I had to do it without giving anything away.

I leaned in, stopping when our noses touched. Her arms wrapped around my waist. An alarm bell screamed through my mind. We were getting terribly close to the life-altering, world-ending scenario.

"Cordy. I have something to tell you." Her eyes fluttered shut.

Wait.

Goddammit.

Her eyes fluttered shut.

If this moment happened at any other point *before* I found out that demons existed, I would've died of happiness on the spot. But if she was the aswang, she could just be doing this to distract me. Maybe it was real. Maybe it wasn't.

I needed her to open her eyes.

"Yes?" I asked, as one of her hands moved up my back and wound into my hair.

"I'm—"

"Am I interrupting something?" There was definitely a smirk in Jesse's voice.

Veronica's eyes popped open. It was only a split second, but I got my answer.

My startled reflection looked back at me. Right side up.

Relief coursed through my veins as Veronica jumped away from me. But something else, too, disappointment that we were interrupted when the thing I'd dreamed about for so long was *finally* going to happen. A mischievous smile spread across Jesse's face.

"No," Veronica said, looking down at the floor. It was only one word, but it shattered my heart into a million pieces. "Cordy and I were just heading out."

"Like . . . on a date?" The smirk in his voice fell away, only to be replaced with a cruel sharpness. "Didn't know you two were a thing. How . . . cute."

Veronica opened her mouth to reply, but she snapped it shut before she said anything. Her cheeks were as red as mine felt. She pushed past Jesse, not bothering to answer him.

"What's up with her?" Jesse asked.

I didn't reply, either. I bolted out through one of the side doors, leaving Jesse behind as I frantically tried to find my best friend.

CHAPTER ELEVEN

IN WHICH I RUN AWAY

I DIDN'T KNOW IF I COULD SALVAGE THINGS WITH Veronica. It was my fault for even trying in the first place.

I'd spent most of my life being comfortable as a coward. I wasn't much of a fighter—the only time I ever stood up for myself, I wound up sending my father to Hell. I thought I was fine never really trying for anything again. Even if that meant hiding my feelings from Veronica.

But now, she knew. There wasn't a way to get out of what I did. How I pulled her close. Wanted her to kiss me. How maybe she would have, too, if Jesse hadn't interrupted us.

A brief flash of her ruby red jacket flew into the woods.

"Veronica!" I yelled, running down the school's steps. "Wait up! Please!"

She disappeared through the tree line. I swore, pushing myself faster. The muscles in my legs cramped, but I didn't stop moving. Next time they forced us to run the mile in gym, maybe I'd run for more than a quarter of the first lap.

Branches cracked up ahead. She must be slowing down because I sure as hell wasn't speeding up.

"Veronica!" I shouted again. "We need to—" Her red jacket appeared out of nowhere. I barreled into her. She slammed into the ground, taking me with her. "—talk," I said, pinning her to the ground.

Oh, *no*.

I got up, not wanting to linger on top of her. Offered my hand and helped her up. I waited for her to brush her jacket free of some dirt before I said, "Look, about what happened backstage. I'm sorry if I did anything I shouldn't have."

She didn't reply right away. Seconds stretched into eons as the silence widened a gap between us. "Like what?" Veronica finally asked.

"I didn't mean to—I hope that didn't embarrass you. When Jesse found us, I mean . . ." My voice trailed away. This wasn't how I was hoping this discussion would go.

I would've sold my soul to have her wrap her arms around my waist. Pull me close. Whisper that she loved me just as much as I loved her. But that wasn't what she said.

Veronica sighed, looking down at the ground. "I know what you're afraid of."

The faint crackle of flames flitted through the air. Heat rose up from the ground. I tore my gaze from Veronica, just in time to find fire springing up in a solid line between us. My heart pounded in my chest as I jumped back.

No. He didn't need to come back right now. I couldn't split my focus between Veronica and my father.

"You do?" I tried ignoring the hurt in Veronica's eyes as I moved away from her. The line of fire grew up to our knees.

"You think you're just like him," Veronica replied sadly. If she could feel the warmth coming from the flames, or see them at all, then she'd know why all I wanted to do was run. It wasn't because of her at all. It was him. "But you're not your father, Cordy. You're not a bad person. You're allowed to be happy, you know."

I wanted to believe her. But I'd spent my whole life terrified that I'd turn into a monster, just like him. And now, knowing I was the reason he died—well. I wasn't sure what that made me.

I swallowed, taking another step away from her. A small breeze blew by, carrying my father's laughter with it. "I don't think happiness is in the cards for me."

The flames rose higher.

"She's wrong about you," my father's voice called as the wall of fire blocked Veronica completely from view. *"We both know it."*

I took another step back.

"I'm sorry," I shouted.

Veronica Dominguez didn't belong in a world full of monsters and stolen souls and fires that only I could see. She wasn't the one who still had to pay for what she'd done.

I wanted to tell her everything. But I was so scared of losing her once she knew what I'd done. Would she hate me as much as I did, when she learned the truth? How would she react to the fact that I sold part of my soul?

She deserved someone better. Someone who could love her unconditionally. Who'd stand by her no matter what. Someone who was brave. Who wasn't destined to become a monster.

"I'm so sorry," I said. I'd never meant anything more in my life. "I can't do this."

And then, I did the only sensible thing left. I ran.

I wasn't really paying attention to where I was going, or how I wound up in the school's parking lot. Some part of my brain must have taken charge while I ugly-cried a lifetime's worth of tears and commanded my feet to bring every sad, pathetic molecule in my body to the car.

I dug around in my bag for my car keys. Dry heaved a bit. Fished them out and let them dangle in front of my face like a carrot on a stick.

I needed motivation to keep moving. Otherwise, I'd collapse into a puddle of shame and regret and never get up.

I could've told her how I felt—maybe even learned how she felt, too.

But I didn't. I just stood there and let it happen while the flames of Hell crept up through the ground and my father reminded me that I wasn't worth loving.

After an eternity of crying, I'd gotten to the point where my body was incapable of making new tears. I was a tumbleweed getting pushed through the desert of life—completely dried out and useless.

My heartbeat pounded behind my sore eyes. I rubbed my temples, pushing myself to move faster through the empty lot.

I pulled my coat tighter as I walked. Footsteps sounded behind me. I stopped. They did, too. I started up again, pushing myself a little quicker. I passed by a red pickup truck. Used the rear-view mirror to see if anyone was following me. The blurred outline of an emerald-green coat followed.

My jaw clenched. Only one person at school was audacious enough to sport a pea coat *that* obnoxiously green when it wasn't even pea coat weather to begin with.

I rounded on my shadow, grabbing a fistful of a thick wool as I slammed Dustin Jones into a nearby car.

A glass bottle clattered to the ground as he laughed. A familiar smell filled the air between us. Burnt wood. A hint of sweetness. Something sinister bubbling just underneath the surface. I didn't need to look at the bottle he dropped to know that he'd been drinking my father's favorite type of bourbon.

"Come here often?" Dustin slurred.

I grabbed the bottle and moved us both behind the truck. I had no idea where she was, but I didn't want Veronica to see us. Or anyone else for that matter. If Dustin was caught with alcohol on school grounds, he'd probably get kicked out of the show. There was already enough to deal with during Tech Week. I didn't want to lose Blake's goodwill and all of The Coffee Spot's food donations if Dustin was out of the picture.

The petty side of me wanted to drag him back into the school. Plop him down right in front of Barry and Fred. Get him kicked out, free food or not. But seeing him like that—clutching the half-gone bottle of poison that changed my father into a monster—made Dustin seem more human than he had his whole life.

"Have you been doing this since rehearsal ended?" I asked.

He winked sloppily at me. "Before."

"How much did you drink?"

He leaned in way too close to my face. "Enough."

I recoiled, letting him go. He laughed again. Slid down the side of the truck and fell to the ground in a weirdly graceful way.

He snatched the bottle out of my hands, tilting it to me. "Spring Break," he said.

"That was one month ago, Dustin."

"Doesn't matter." He tipped the bottle to his lips. I snatched it away before he could drink more. *"Boo,"* he said, toppling over.

I rolled my eyes. "Okay. Get up, Jones. I'm bringing you home."

"No!" He snapped up. His eyes weren't glazed over anymore. They were painfully alert. "Just . . . just bring me to Blake. My parents can't know."

I crossed my arms. "Why not?" I didn't owe him any favors. If his parents got mad at him for drinking at school, that was his problem. Not mine.

"I can't mess up again," he said, reaching for the bottle. I held it out in front of him, tipping it so the liquid slowly started sloshing out onto the pavement. Dustin sucked in a sharp breath. "Stop," he hissed. "That's mine!"

"Not anymore. Belongs to the parking lot now."

"You always ruin the fun." He pouted.

"That's me. Cordelia Scott, professional fun ruiner."

That made him laugh. Which made me laugh—until I realized what I was doing. I stopped, clearing my throat. "Right," I said, hoping he didn't notice that. Or the abrupt, cheery change in my tone. "Well, I don't know about you, but the last ten minutes of my life were a complete disaster. I need to get the hell away from here. If I take you to Blake, can you pretend that this never happened?"

Dustin swayed a little. "Was gonna ask you the same thing."

"Great," I said, holding my hand out to him. "Then we have a deal."

He took it. "*Yup!*"

I pulled him up and immediately regretted it. His palms were way too sweaty. I slung his arm over my shoulder to prop him up and slowly led him to my car. Did my best to keep us hidden from any prying eyes as we moved.

I pried open the passenger's side door, shoving him into my car like he was a bag of trash that needed fitting into a bin.

"Why are you helping me?" he asked.

"Because it's the right thing to do," I lied.

I gently closed the door. Stood outside of my car for a few seconds longer and sighed.

If I did a good thing for bad reasons, did it still count? Or was it something in-between?

Not that the answer mattered. I needed a distraction from what happened with Veronica, and to put as much distance between the fire in the woods and me as possible.

Life gave me Dustin Jones when I needed him the most, and I wasn't going to waste it. I could use him to get close to his brother. Ask him a few questions about the sigil thing he was arguing with Father Marcus about. Persuade him to tell me everything he knows.

And finally solve my demon problem, once and for all.

CHAPTER TWELVE

IN WHICH I DON'T TAKE THE FREE COFFEE

ONE OF MY MOST MUNDANE NIGHTMARES FINALLY CAME true: I was stuck in a car with Dustin.

"So," I said, tapping on the steering wheel. "You drink bourbon often?"

He stared straight ahead. "No."

"Right. Thought you were more of a *chug a few beers till you pass out sloppy drunk at Liz Knight's New Year's party* kinda guy."

He sighed. "I thought you were taking me to my brother. Not analyzing my bad PBR choices."

I winced. "PBR? Dustin, we need to talk about your taste."

"We're not friends, Scott. We don't need to pretend. Just drive."

Heat finally started to drift through the car. "Fine," I said, throwing it in reverse. I might've been kind of petty and hit the gas a little too hard. "Let's go."

Dustin groaned as I peeled out of the parking lot. I smiled.

If I had to suffer through his company, he was going to enjoy it just about as much as me.

He was right. We weren't friends. But I needed him to talk, and what better time to do it than when half a bottle of Redemption ran through his veins?

"So," I said, slowing down at a red light. "How's Blake doing?"

Dustin scoffed. "Better than ever. It's annoying."

I didn't reply. It was easier for him to keep going if I stayed quiet. And there wasn't much I could add anyway. If I dropped the demon card too early, he'd laugh his way out of the car.

"Figures, though," Dustin continued, talking through the silence. "He gets everything. The Coffee Spot. Mom and Dad's respect. Serotonin. And I'm just . . . here. Second best to a weirdo."

My hands tightened around the steering wheel. "Second best? Since when? You get everything you want."

"Not everything."

I snorted. "Sure. Like your parents didn't buy your way to Kenickie last year."

"Okay. Maybe they did. But it's not like anything happened because of it. I could play Veronica's boyfriend in the show, but she wouldn't give me the time of day outside of it."

All of the tension coiled tightly in my chest sprang loose. It was hard to keep my voice steady. "That's your takeaway? Veronica wouldn't date you, so your life is sad?"

"I don't even know why I tried," he continued, not seeming to hear what I said. "It's not like she ever noticed me anyway. Or you."

Oh, fuck no. There was no universe in which Dustin and I were on the same level. Where he could understand even the smallest iota of what I was going through.

I slammed on the brakes. We both were thrown forward, though his was a little more violent, since he hadn't braced for it. "That's not true. I—it was different for me," I snapped. "Get out. Now."

He blinked. "What?"

"Out, Dustin!"

"No." He turned to face me. Crossed his arms over his seatbelt. "I don't know why you're so mad. You've loved her longer than I have. And what do either of us have to show for it?"

I shook my head. "We're not the same."

"No. You're worse. I know I'll never have a chance with her. I've accepted it. But you . . . the way she looks at you is different. Like the world would stop spinning if you weren't right by her side."

"Yeah, well, I wouldn't be too sure about that." I paused, blinking back tears. Cleared my throat, desperately searching around for a change of subject. "Didn't know you were a poet. What you said was kind of beautiful."

He burped. Classy. "What can I say? Bourbon brings out the thinker in me."

"How did you get that stuff, anyway?"

"What? Redemption?"

"Yeah."

He hiccuped. "I don't know," he replied, smiling. "Ask a priest."

I groaned. Put the car back into drive as we continued down the road to The Coffee Spot.

"Was I that obvious?" I asked, not daring to look at him. "About being in love with her, I mean."

"It's not really a secret. Hasn't been since middle school."

"Great."

Silence settled between us. It made a nest, all cozy and warm as it sucked up the heat from my car. How long had Veronica known how I felt about her? I knew I wasn't good at hiding it, but I didn't think someone like Dustin would be able to pick up on it. He was always too into himself to notice what anyone else was feeling. I must have practically been waving an *I love you, Veronica!* flag every day for the last handful of years.

And, if she *had* known how I felt, why had she never tried talking to me about it? Was I just misinterpreting things, or was she going to tell me that she loved me, too, if I hadn't run away?

I bit the inside of my cheek, fighting back tears. It was hard enough to drive with waterworks blurring my vision. I didn't need to make everything worse by crying in front of Dustin.

"Um, are you okay?" he asked when a traitorous tear slipped down my cheek.

I thought I'd already gotten them all out, but they must have been waiting for exactly the right moment. I pulled over as the deluge started again. Couldn't wipe them away fast enough.

Dustin cleared his throat. "Maybe I should drive."

I squinted at him through the tears. "You were just chugging bourbon in the parking lot ten minutes ago."

"I was *sipping* bourbon. It's not a drink that should be chugged."

I laughed, startled by the sound. It was like I'd slipped into some weird alternate universe where I wasn't compelled to punch him in the face every time he spoke.

"Cordy," Dustin said, reaching out as if he was going to pat me on the shoulder. He pulled back before he could. Like he'd thought better of it. "Maybe this is the bourbon talking, but . . . if something happened, you could tell me."

"Why? So you can use it against me later?"

Hurt flashed in his eyes. He leaned away from me. "You really think I'd do that?"

"There hasn't been a lot of proof otherwise. You said it yourself: we're not friends." I paused, twisting the knife further. "You're an asshole. In case you haven't noticed."

It was Dustin's turn to laugh. "You sound a lot like Blake, you know. He's always trying to get me to be better."

"Well, are you?"

"Am I what?"

"Trying to be better."

"No," he replied, without hesitation. "Why would I do that?"

If I could've torn the steering wheel off and thrown it at him, I would have. "Do you know how lucky you are to have someone looking out for you like that?" I wasn't yelling at him, but I was in the neighborhood. "I wish I had that. Instead, all I get is—" I caught myself.

All I got was a father that I sent to Hell, and a mother who struggled with the fact that I existed. Veronica had been the most supportive person in my life, and I'd just run away from her without any sort of explanation.

I shook my head. "Never mind," I said, turning back onto the road. "You wouldn't understand."

"I guess you're right." He paused, tapping on the passenger's side window. "It's just . . . it's so hard to be his brother, you know? He can't do anything wrong, ever, even when he's being weird about all this demon bullshit—"

I gripped the steering wheel tighter. "What?"

Dustin threw his hands up in the air. "Blake's obsessed with that ridiculous rumor about our family founding the town. He's always been like this. Gramps—when he was alive—he'd spend every Deal Day with Blake trying to summon that damn demon. I figured it would stop after he died, but Blake kept going.

"When he's not at work, he spends all his time at the library, researching God only knows what. He thinks it's all *real*, Cordelia. And *he's* our parents' favorite kid. Can you believe that?" Dustin laughed. "I could go out and prove that demons *aren't* real, and I'd get in trouble for ruining Blake's dreams. How's that fair?"

It wasn't, but I didn't want to tell him that. Dustin Jones was a lot of things, but I never thought sad would be one of them.

We didn't talk for the rest of the drive. Thankfully, we only had to endure about five more minutes of painful silence before I pulled into The Coffee Spot's gravel-filled parking lot.

I hadn't even put my car into park when Dustin threw his door open. "Thanks for the ride, Scott," he said, getting out of the car. "I'd say it's been fun, but—" He slammed the door shut and walked inside the café.

I rolled my eyes. "You're welcome, asshole." I sighed and followed him.

I wasn't expecting Dustin to offer up his family drama so freely, but I was glad he did. Now, at least, I knew what to shoot for when I talked to Blake. It would be easy enough to convince him that Jesse was the demon who founded the town with his ancestors—and that, in order to save us all, he needed to go. Hell, maybe he'd be kind of mad at Jesse for never appearing when he and his grandpa tried to summon him.

I took a deep breath, stepping inside.

The Coffee Spot's aesthetic could, unfortunately, best be described as *woodsy hipster chic*. Blake Jones spared no expense when creating his ode to high-end, expensive, gentrifying big city cafés. Well, really Blake's *parents* spared no expense in bringing their son's vision to life, but who was keeping track, anyway?

The main room's wide-open space could be cleared out and used for different events. During the first week of each month, beleaguered Coffee Spot employees put all the furniture away and pulled out a small stage for Monday Night Karaoke. It was mostly just theater and choir kids from our high school who showed up, since anyone who also wanted a side of alcohol with their karaoke had actual bars to go to. But we all loved getting on that makeshift stage and singing, and Blake was more than happy to give us a space to do it. He even let us host fundraisers for our productions there, to help offset the cost of costumes that we might not have the budget for.

The barista counter was also in the main room. It was a little farther away from the door so that they didn't freeze every time someone opened it in the winter. Quirky art lined the walls, usually switched out every couple of months. They always made sure to highlight a local artist, which was pretty cool.

The side room was a little more rustic than the main room's sleek, contemporary leanings. A small fireplace always stayed lit in the winter. And there were old leather armchairs that were easy to sink into. I'd fallen asleep in them a few times. Mostly trying to do homework.

Dustin slunk down a small hallway that led to Blake's office.

His brother watched him from behind the counter, shaking his head as he poured out two shots of espresso.

"I suppose I have you to thank for that," Blake said as Dustin disappeared behind a door.

"Yeah. He didn't want to go home, so—"

"He came here." Blake sighed. "Getting wasted in the school's parking lot. *While* he was supposed to be here for a shift. I knew I shouldn't have left him alone."

Well. I wasn't expecting that. "You knew he was drinking?"

Blake nodded. "He's been touch and go lately. He was doing better, actually, until yesterday. When I came home last night he was already passed out. Went through a whole thing of scotch." Blake winced. "I don't know how he drinks that stuff. Never could stand the taste of it, myself."

I wondered that about my father a lot. He always had a cup of something strong by his side, and refilled it all night until nothing remained in the bottle the next morning.

One time, when he was asleep on the couch, I took his half-drained cup of Redemption off the table and tried it. Just to see what all the fuss was about. But the bourbon stung my mouth, even though I only took a small sip. It clawed its way down my throat. Acid stripping it raw. I dropped the cup. Held my breath as I waited to see if that small sound was enough to wake him up.

When it did, I ran into my room, locked the door, and hid under my bed.

I didn't sleep that night.

I shook my head, sighing. Dustin and my father weren't the same. Yet. But he was definitely on his way. "He needs help, Blake. If he keeps going like this . . ." My voice trailed away. It was like my body refused to let me say the words out loud. Just in case my father could hear them from Hell.

"I know. My parents won't listen to me. I'm trying. I really am."

"Well. If you ever need anyone to yell at him about it, I'm around."

Blake chuckled. "I might have to take you up on that." He gestured at the espresso bar. "Pick your poison, kid. It's the least I can do after you rescued him from making things worse."

My fingers drummed on the counter. I didn't come here for free coffee—even though it *was* pretty tempting. It was now or never to convince him to help me.

"I've got a question for you," I said, trying to sound as casual as possible.

"Shoot."

"When I was in St. Gertrude's this morning, I heard you talking to Father Marcus—"

"Cordelia." My name was nothing more than a warning as he tried interrupting me. I kept going. Once the floodgates opened, they couldn't be closed.

"—and you said something about a sigil—"

"Please stop."

"—and when I asked him about it, he said your question had something to do with demons. So. I want to know what you know."

Blake dragged his hands down his face. "You should leave this alone."

I shrugged. "Sorry. Can't do that. A literal life is at stake."

His eyes widened. "What?"

I made a big show of sighing. "Look, I'm not supposed to

tell anyone this, but those rumors about the town's founding are true." I leaned in closer as righteousness brightened his eyes. "Something bad is in Ruin's End. Has been for almost one hundred years. And I need your help to get rid of it."

An odd sort of fire—a mixture of excitement and hatred—burned in his eyes. "A demon?" he asked.

I nodded.

A feral smile pulled at the corners of his mouth. "How do I find it?"

"I need to know that you'll help me, first."

He blinked a few times, forcing his expression back to something more neutral. "What're you after?"

"Well . . . Father Marcus was a little light on the 'how to trap a demon' details, so I was hoping you'd know."

Blake ruffled his tousled blond hair, frowning. "You want to trap it?"

"What would you do?"

His mouth formed a grim line. "Kill it."

Well, damn. Father Marcus was right. Blake really wanted to kill a demon.

"Wait," I said, holding a hand up in the air. "How would you do that?"

"I wasn't sure until this morning. Father Marcus says the key is to use a blessed weapon. He knows how to make one, but he won't do it. Not even after I made a generous donation to St. Gertrude's."

For once, someone existed that a Jones couldn't buy in this town. That earned Father Marcus a few respect points—though it was still pretty annoying that he knew how to make a blessed weapon and refused to do it. Something existed that could solve my problem—potentially save my life, if it came to that—and the priest wasn't going to help.

"Did you find anything else on the blessed weapons?" I asked. "Did you Google it one day, or—"

"Even if I did," he said, cutting me off, "I wouldn't share it with you."

"But—"

"I'm sorry. You're trying to mess with things that are ancient. Powerful. Whatever you're thinking of trying, don't."

"You sound just like Father Marcus," I snapped.

"Good," Blake replied. "Focus on Tech Week. Leave the demon hunting to me."

I bit the inside of my cheek. I couldn't let him push me out. There wasn't enough time for a setback. "Okay," I said, leaning in closer to the counter. "I'll tell you who it is—and stay out of your way—*if* you promise to find a way to kill the demon."

Killing or trapping, it didn't make much of a difference to me. Fred wanted Jesse out of the way. Even though he said there wasn't a way to kill him, maybe he was wrong. Or he lied. That wouldn't be too shocking. Fred wasn't doing any of this out of the kindness of his heart.

Or maybe Fred *was* telling the truth, and trapping Jesse was the only way. If Blake was willing to help me, I wasn't about to go against his wishes. I'd be pro-demon killing until that plan failed.

"Why does it matter so much to you?"

"It just does."

Blake held my gaze. "Let's say I *had* been researching blessed weapons independently. And I *would* like to see a certain demon wiped off the face of the earth. I'd need a few days to get everything together, but then, in theory, I could help you. And I'd need to find the right sigil, or course, which would take time. Time that I *could* have." He took a sip from his cup. "*If* you tell me who it is."

"I will, when you're ready to go."

"Now, or no deal."

"I'm not the one who's been obsessing over this."

"How'd you know that?"

"Dustin told me about your grandfather."

Blake frowned. "That's family business."

"Did it ever work?" I asked, laying one too many cards on the table. Fred probably wouldn't approve. And I wasn't sure I did, either. But Blake and his grandfather tried summoning that demon every year on Deal Day. Maybe he'd seen or heard something that would be helpful. I needed every bit of information he had if I was going to make it out of this alive.

The fire that'd burned in Blake's eyes quickly extinguished. "It did. Too well."

"What do we have here?" Dustin chimed in, sitting down next to me before I could ask Blake more about his grandfather. Impeccable timing, as always, Dustin. "If it isn't my favorite brother and my least-favorite stage manager, conspiring against me."

I glared at him, wishing we hadn't gone through such an abrupt subject change. "You wish I cared about you enough to conspire."

Dustin hiccuped. Blake slid him a cup of black coffee and then looked back at me.

"Cordelia and I were just talking about church," he said, holding my gaze. "She's going to stop by this Sunday. You should too, Dustin."

"Yeah," I added, playing along. "Seems like it'll be an interesting time."

Dustin's gaze darted between the two of us. "Okay. You're both acting weird. What's up?"

"Nothing." I pushed away from the counter. "I should go."

"I'll think about what we discussed," Blake called. "You should, too."

I waved at him without looking back. I even made it a few steps to the door before Dustin yelled out, "Wait!" I paused. Slowly turned around. He walked toward me, holding out his phone.

"We need a picture," he said.

"I think I'm good," I replied.

"Oh, come on," Blake said, from behind the counter. "What could it hurt?"

I grimaced. "Other than my pride?"

But Blake's distraction worked. Dustin slipped next to me, holding his hand above our heads and taking a selfie before I could stop him.

"Don't post that," I said, even though it was at a really good angle.

Dustin booped me on the nose. "I'll do what I want." His breath still reeked of bourbon.

I winced. "Well, I'd say it's been fun, but . . ." My voice trailed away as I hurried out the door. I slid into my car. Turned the key in the ignition. And laughed.

Blake hadn't agreed yet, but he was going to. When he was ready, I'd have no problem leading him to Jesse. There'd be no need for me to trap him if he was already dead.

That was one problem down. But the aswang was still out

there, threatening to ruin my plan. I needed to get some solid intel on it—and I knew exactly where to go to get it.

Hopefully I'd also be able to talk to Veronica while I was there.

CHAPTER THIRTEEN

IN WHICH I DIDN'T SEE THAT ONE COMING

I COULDN'T FIND ANYTHING ON 'BLESSED WEAPONS,' no matter how many Wikipedia rabbit holes I fell down. I should have gone straight to Veronica's house to apologize to her and ask her mom about the aswang. But all the demon lore I *did* find was so damn compelling that it was hard to put my phone away. Even though reading a bunch of articles on such a small screen was causing a bit of a pressure headache behind my eyes, it was totally worth it.

The first thing I learned: Catholicism didn't have a monopoly on vanquishing demons. That was what they wanted you to think.

There were different styles and exorcism traditions from all over the world. One of the things they all had in common was repeated chanting and prayer. The words were usually from some kind of holy book, though they weren't required all the time. It did seem like some kind of training was consistently involved in performing the ritual. Not that any of that helped me.

I didn't need to drive a demon out of someone. I needed to trap it.

It would've been nice if all I needed to do was find someone to perform an exorcism. If that was even a real thing, anyway. Fred said it was something the Catholic Church made up, but with all the information on it from different places and cultures, it couldn't all be fake.

I found a few things about sigils—which were kind of like demonic cages. Someone could, theoretically, incapacitate them inside of a sigil in order to buy time to complete their ritual—like shoving a demon into a Precious Moments Maleficent, perhaps.

But I still had no idea how to do that. I didn't think it was too much to ask for a recipe-style blog post that would tell me how to jam a demon into a cute porcelain figurine, but apparently, I'd need some divine intervention for that miracle to happen.

I bookmarked more entries for later and switched over to my contacts, selecting Veronica's name. I wanted to jumpstart an apology and give her a heads-up that I was coming over. But instead of picking up, it rang until voicemail.

I hung up without saying anything.

Gravel crunched under the car as I slowly pulled out of the parking lot. Would she forgive me for running away from her? I needed to try.

When Veronica and I were little, Mrs. Dominguez told us scary stories whenever I spent the night at their house. It was the perfect distraction when we were too young to look for Broadway bootlegs on YouTube. Mrs. Dominguez *tried* starting out with the glossed-over, Disney version of fairytales where everyone had their happily ever afters, but, even then, I'd already seen enough to know that good guys triumphing over evil just wasn't how the world worked.

If heroes existed, they weren't in Ruin's End. Otherwise, I wouldn't have made a deal with a demon in the first place.

Luckily, Veronica's mom was able to read the room. She switched tactics and told us stories she'd grown up with. Monsters that were passed down from generation to generation and the ordinary people who were forced into reconciling with extraordinary, terrible things.

Her stories always made me feel less alone.

I would've given anything to go back to that time. When I hadn't doomed myself to working with a demon or ran away from the only person I promised to never abandon.

I didn't want to do it, but I wasn't sure I had another choice. Veronica said I deserved happiness, but she had no idea who I was. Who I could become.

What if I turned into someone like my father? I didn't want to lose control. Couldn't bear the thought of continuing the cycle of violence that plagued my father's side of the family for generations.

An eerie green glow filled the air around me as the light finally changed. I turned off the gravel road in the woods and onto the main road. Trees pressed in from both sides, standing in silent judgment as they looked down on all the choices I'd ever made.

I drove slower than usual. The sun set behind me, casting an odd shadow on the trees as I moved. I sighed. Turned the radio on.

Nothing but static.

I toggled through stations, shifting my focus from the road ahead to the rear-view mirror every few seconds. No one else was around. Just me, my car, and a forest that felt a little more unwelcoming than usual.

Static continued crackling. I frowned. I'd never had a problem picking up a signal here before.

It swelled, getting louder and louder even though I wasn't messing with the volume. Sweat slicked my palms as I reached out to turn the radio off. Before I could mute it, though, it turned off.

Silence cut through me like a knife. I eased up on the gas. Pulled over to the side of the road. Took a few deep breaths and reached a shaky hand out to turn the radio back on again.

I pressed the button.

A saxophone blared in the middle of a jazz solo. I hit the button again. Taylor Swift. Ugh. Again. Talk radio. Gross.

I sat there for what felt like an eternity, flipping through channels and not getting a second of static. I turned the radio off and put my head in my hands.

My aswang-filled nightmares hadn't let me sleep much last night. Maybe that—along with the compounding pressure of everything that was rapidly going wrong in my life—led to whatever the hell that was.

"You're losing it," I said aloud to no one, really bringing the sentiment home. I tried calling Veronica one more time before I pulled back onto the road, but it went to voicemail after a few rings.

Fine. She wanted to avoid me. Horribly relatable, since I also wanted to avoid me.

But I owed her an apology, and I'd be much harder to dodge

when I was sitting in her living room, talking to her mom.

An Instagram notification flashed on my phone. I clicked on it, and I had to resist the urge to throw my phone as far into the woods as I could.

"Goddammit," I muttered.

Dustin had posted the picture he took of the two of us in The Coffee Spot. The caption read:

LOVED HANGING WITH MY NEW BEST FRIEND @CORDYMANAGESLIFE AT THE BEST PLACE IN TOWN @THECOFFEESPOT

He just *had* to tag me in it. I switched over to text him, typing *Take that down before—*

When another notification popped up.

My heart sank. Veronica liked the picture.

I put my phone down. Rested my head on the steering wheel. And screamed.

The damage was done. Now, Veronica probably thought that as soon as I ran away from her, I ran right into Dustin's arms, which . . . ew. That was the grossest thing ever. But he really made it seem like we were having a good time, when in reality I'd had a surprisingly bearable one. Leave it to Dustin to make a vanity post that wound up getting me into even deeper shit.

No use in putting it off any longer. I *really* needed to talk to her.

I turned back onto the road; jaw clenched with determination. I'd find a way to fix everything. Starting with my best friend.

I drove for a few more minutes in silence, checking the rear-view mirror every now and then. Nothing. Trees behind me. Trees in front of me.

As I shifted my attention back to the road, one of the shadows moved. It wasn't a slow, graceful kind of thing. It was jagged. Sharp lines and edges. It moved in a disjointed way, hovering above the trees before it dipped down close to the ground.

The shadow flew closer to me. Its silhouette took shape in the rear-view mirror. Vagueness melted into details as its bright red eyes watched me. Dark brown feathers ruffled in the wind.

I gripped the steering wheel tighter. The aswang was back.

I swallowed the scream that wanted to escape.

The aswang cried—a vulture's shriek—as it rose up into the sky.

"Shit," I said, as I lost sight of it. I had no idea where it was or what it was going to do next, but it probably wasn't good.

Last night, it attacked Fred and me in the school parking lot. No one else was around to see it then, but if I could get it to a place where more people were, maybe it would leave me alone. Or I'd have witnesses to verify that a monster was trying to run me off the road.

It shrieked again from somewhere overhead.

A large shadow covered my car, darting forward. The vulture flew down to the road, folded its giant wings back, and stood there, its angry gaze burning through the darkness.

I didn't think about it as my foot slammed down on the gas. Even though I barreled toward it in my mom's ancient Toyota Camry, it didn't move. Or blink. It just sat there. Watching. Waiting to see what I would do.

In my nightmares, it killed me before I got the chance to kill it. But here, in reality, it wasn't in control. I was. My heart pounded a frantic rhythm as my pulse resonated through my whole body.

I could end this. Right here, right now. Take the aswang out so I only had one demon to worry about.

But I'd already killed my father. I wasn't going to do it again. Whoever the aswang was, they made a deal with a demon, too. They made the same mistake I did.

I took my foot off the gas. Slammed on the brakes.

The car turned, reacting to the sudden change in momentum. My tires screeched. The smell of burnt rubber filled the air. I wrestled the car back for control, coming to a stop right in front of the aswang. I was so close that I could make out the small details in its features. How the vulture's feathers shone deep purple in the sunset. The small bit of humanity tucked away in its pitch-black eyes.

I blinked, leaning into the steering wheel to get a better look. The aswang's eyes had been bright red when I was far away, but they changed as I got closer.

And now, I was too close. A chill scraped its way down my spine. If I hesitated for a second longer, I would've killed them.

The aswang-vulture tilted its head. Straightened up, opening its wings. I couldn't stop a gasp from leaving my lips. It was bigger than me. Another impossible thing that I had to accept as part of my new reality.

It flapped its wings. The air it pushed away was strong enough to straighten my car out. I was back on the right side of the road. All I had to do was hit the gas to move forward.

The aswang rose into the sky.

Just as suddenly as it appeared, it was gone.

I exhaled. And maybe cried a little.

I could have killed someone. But I didn't.

And in return, it seemed, someone didn't kill me.

When I got to Veronica's house, the light was off in her bedroom window. I sighed. Maybe she was out on a drive, trying to sort through everything that happened.

In better times, when I wasn't the cause of her problems, it was something we'd do together. But I'd tried calling her again as soon as I parked and this time it went straight to voicemail. Whatever she was doing, she didn't need me around to ruin it.

I walked through their front lawn, marching up the steps like I was about to attend my own funeral. If she wasn't there, I'd wait for her to get home. Talking to Veronica was my top priority. But I also needed information about the aswang, which meant I'd be able to wait for Veronica for as long as it took. Once I got Mrs. Dominguez to tell me one story, she could keep going until the sun came up.

My hand hovered above the door. I could turn around and go home without talking to anyone. Come back when there was light outside, and I'd had the chance to sleep this horrible day away. But I was already here. And, if I'd learned anything from a demon coming back to collect on a bargain I made seven years ago, avoiding my problems didn't make them go away.

I knocked on the door. It was a jarring sound that broke through the calm night around me. A clap of thunder that came before the storm.

Mrs. Dominguez opened the door. She smiled as her dark brown eyes met mine. "Oh, Cordy, hi! Come in, come in. You don't want to linger outside and catch a cold."

I walked past her, trying to return the smile. That was always her big thing. Even if a slight chill invaded the air, Mrs. Dominguez always worried that we'd get sick if we were out there too long. This usually embarrassed Veronica, but I thought it was nice. It showed that her mom cared. That she was around enough to notice if something went wrong with her daughter.

Sometimes, I wondered if my mom would have the same brightness in her eyes if she hadn't married my father. If her ability to feel joy or happiness died the day she decided she loved him. I'd be lying if I said that looking at her didn't hurt. It wasn't fair, sometimes, to have this example of what a happy family could be. It was something I envied. A thing I knew I'd never be able to have but still wanted desperately.

"Thanks," I said, peeling off my coat and shoes once she shut the door behind me. The smell of thin, fried dough and veggies and pork wafted around me. My mouth watered. She made lumpia.

"Veronica's not here," Mrs. Dominguez said, pulling me into a hug. Hopefully she couldn't feel how strongly my heart pounded as I looked into her eyes, searching for my reflection. "Did you need her for something?" she asked, as I exhaled.

It was the right side up. She wasn't the aswang.

But Veronica also wasn't home. Relief mixed in with disappointment. That explained the light off in her room.

"Oh. No. Actually, I needed to talk to you," I replied. Now that I knew she wouldn't turn into a monster and eat me, I could ask her everything.

Mrs. Dominguez guided me to the table. "Would you like some water? Lumpia?"

"No thanks. I'm fine."

"Well, *I'm* going to get some lumpia." She marched away. I tapped the table while she was gone, taking in all of the pictures of Veronica lining the walls. A lot of them included me. We were at the beach, going to Homecoming dances, sitting by campfires, or greeting people after one of our shows.

We were happy. Or, at least, Veronica was. My smile never reached my eyes.

"Okay." Mrs. Dominquez set a plate of lumpia down between us. She took one of the rolls in her hand, dipped it in some sweet chili sauce, and bit off half of it. "What's going on?"

"Well . . . I'd like to know more about the aswang."

"You? Who are you, and what have you done with my favorite stage manager?"

I rolled my eyes. "It's for a school project, Tita Rosalind. We have to re-tell an old folk tale. I thought this would be a fun one to do."

Veronica's mom was practically beaming. I knew that evoking the ancient Filipino naming convention of Tita would be enough to keep her distracted. She always wanted me to use it, but even after all these years, it felt like something I wasn't entitled to because we weren't related—even if using it was a sign of respect. But Titas weren't dictated by blood. They could be chosen, too. "You've come to the right place, beh! What do you need for your project?"

I hated lying to her. But the truth wasn't a possibility. And it was safer this way.

"It can turn into things, right? Like a big bird or a cat?"

Mrs. Dominguez—Tita Rosalind—nodded. "The aswang can take many forms. It can also be a pig or a dog—when it's an animal, its eyes glow red. Pretty creepy, right?"

"Yeah." I laughed nervously. "Pretty creepy."

"The worst one, though, is when it's almost human. But not quite close enough."

I swallowed. "And its skin . . . when it's . . . kind of human. It's gray and slimy? Like there's an oily film stretched across it?"

"That's what some of the stories say. My lola was fond of that version, so that's what I passed down to you and Vero."

I grabbed a few of her homemade lumpia, taking a delicious bite out of one as the room spun around me. It was one thing to believe that the monster from my nightmares was real. But now I confirmed it. The monster that attacked Fred and the vulture that messed with me on the road were the same thing: an aswang.

"How would someone stop it?" I asked, after I'd devoured more lumpia.

Tita Rosalind leaned back in her chair. "Ah, that's a little tricky. There are ways to ward against them—like making a special oil out of coconut. But killing them isn't easy. They have to be stabbed in the middle of their back with a bolo knife. Or, sometimes, magic prayers can be used to freeze the aswang in place so that someone can hack it into pieces." She laughed, hitting the table. "It's a good thing they don't *actually* exist, huh? They'd be tough bastards."

"Hah. Yeah," I replied, not sure what else to say. Even if I wanted to get close enough to stab it, the aswang was still a person. Killing was out of the question. I cleared my throat. "If someone wanted to freeze the aswang by praying . . . do you know what they'd say?"

She shook her head. "My lola never got into specifics in her stories. I tried asking her once, but she said those secrets died long ago." She leaned in closer, winking at me. "I think she didn't want to make me brave enough to go into the woods, alone, to spout some nonsense at the air."

"But do you think it could work? Theoretically?"

"Hmm?"

"A prayer to stall the aswang. If I—if *someone*—found an incantation, would it work?"

"Maybe." She shrugged. "What kind of report did you say you're doing?"

"I—"

The front door opened at that moment, saving me from another lie. Veronica walked in, stopping at the threshold of the living room when she saw me. She wasn't Casual Veronica. Her long brown hair had been braided and her makeup was subtle but gorgeous. She must be trying to impress someone. She peeled off her red leather jacket and sat it on top of the couch. Stared daggers at me as she asked, "What are you doing here, Cordy?"

I blinked, too distracted by how well she pulled off her winged eyeliner. "Uh, I needed your mom's help on a school project." I cleared my throat. Twisted my hands together. Swallowed back a scream as I added, "I'd also like to talk to you about earlier. If I can." I shoved a piece of lumpia into my mouth to give myself something to do.

Veronica scoffed. "There's nothing to talk about."

"Oh, I think there is," Tita Rosalind said. "How was your date, Vero?"

I coughed, choking the lumpia down. "Date?" I asked as

silver dots danced in my vision.

"Not a date." Veronica shrugged. "We were just hanging out."

"He seemed like a nice boy," her mom said.

"Sorry?" I asked.

"What was his name, Vero? Jacob? John?"

"Jesse," Veronica and I said at the same time.

"Seriously?" I asked.

Veronica crossed her arms. "Seriously. Do you have a problem with that?"

Anger forced the words out of my mouth before I could stop them. "Yes."

"Why?" she asked, tears pooling in her eyes. "It wasn't planned or anything. After you left, it kind of just . . . happened."

My heart sank. This was my fault. Veronica was in danger, but I couldn't tell her Jesse was a demon. So, instead, I said, "I don't think he's a good person."

Veronica crossed her arms. "Yeah, well. Takes one to know one."

It was something I thought about myself all the time. But it was different to hear her say the words out loud. Veronica Dominguez didn't think I was a good person.

She was right.

"Vero," her mom snapped. "That was rude. Apologize."

"No," I said, before Veronica could reply. "I . . . I've gotta go. Hope your date went well, Veronica. Or hangout. Whatever. See you at school. And thanks for the help, Tita Rosalind. I'll let you know if I have any more questions for you." I ran out of the house, holding back tears.

I'd deal with what Veronica thought about me later.

If Veronica wasn't the aswang, then I had no idea why Jesse was trying to spend time with her. But he was putting her in danger.

And that was something I couldn't let him do.

CHAPTER FOURTEEN

IN WHICH I TRY KICKING A DEMON'S ASS

EVEN THOUGH JESSE HAD ONLY LIVED IN TOWN A FEW months, I'd been to his house before. A couple of weeks ago, I dropped him off after he grabbed food with Veronica, Sal, and me. He didn't have a ride back, so, being the good Samaritan that I was, I helped him out.

If I'd known then that he was a demon and would try stealing my best friend, I would've made him find his own way back. Maybe he could use whatever powers he had to fly himself home or some weird shit like that.

He probably didn't even live in that house. Or it wasn't real.

I ground my teeth together as I turned onto his street. I ran away from Veronica to keep her out of danger. And now here he was, hanging out with her like everything was normal and he wasn't involved in the same deeply fucked up mess that I was.

All I wanted to do was talk to him. Try reasoning things out. Get him to understand that I didn't care what happened to me, but Veronica needed to be left out of it. I'd already sold my soul to Fred, so I couldn't promise that, but I was willing to do whatever it took to make sure she was safe.

I parked in front of his house, digging around in my bag for my mom's rosary. Slipped it around my neck and let out a small sigh of relief when my hand brushed against the kalis's hilt. I barely knew how to use it, but I was glad I had it.

The old Victorian house that Jesse lived in didn't exactly scream, *Demon Mastermind sleeps here!*, but maybe that was part of his plan. Lure you into a false sense of security with a fun, multicolored paint job on ancient wood paneling, welcoming turrets, and a quirky cow mailbox situated at the foot of a decently long driveway.

My hand shook as I rang the doorbell. The sound bounced around inside the house, lovely and pleasant and not at all demonic. The door swung open and a tall man who looked like Jesse if he'd been aged up about twenty-five years smiled down at me. Same casually swooped-back brown hair. Bright green eyes you could get lost in. Even the freckles on his face looked almost identical.

"Hi there," the man said, politeness oozing out of him in an entirely unhuman way. "Can I help you?"

"Oh. Yeah." My face warmed as he watched me. I looked down at the ground, half to sell the embarrassment of the moment, and half to cover the blush steadily creeping up my cheeks. It wasn't because his dad was ridiculously beautiful. He just seemed like an okay parent and aside from Veronica's mom and dad, I hadn't met a lot of those.

Too bad I was here to beat up his demonic spawn. If Jesse even was his son. I had no idea how new demons were made.

Or if this guy was another demon, helping Jesse sell the lie that he was actually a person.

"I'm one of Jesse's classmates. Cordelia," I continued, kicking at some dirt on their porch. "I was wondering if I could speak with him? I've got a question about, um, a group project we're doing together. I was going to just text but . . . my phone died, and your house was on the way home, so I figured this was quicker . . ." My voice trailed away. My hands twisted together as I waited to see if he bought it.

Jesse's dad smiled. "He just stepped out to run to the store but should be back soon. Would you like to come in? You can charge your phone here while you wait."

A few minutes hanging out with Jesse's Fake Dad wouldn't kill me.

Probably.

"Yes. Thank you," I said, as I stepped through the front door.

The outside of the house didn't really match what was inside. Instead of more quirky, out-of-place furniture, everything in the house was sleek and modern. If the façade of the house looked welcoming, the setup inside gave off the impression that no one really lived there. Everything looked as if it was perfectly positioned to appear in a catalog. Or one of those Vanity Fair photoshoots that made rich people look even richer.

"Would you like anything to drink while you wait?" Jesse's father asked.

"I'm fine, thank you." No way in hell was I gonna drink anything I didn't prepare when I was there. I'd read enough thrillers to know that you never sip from a glass of anything when you're in potentially hostile territory.

Jesse's dad nodded. "Of course." A cuckoo clock ticked somewhere in the background. "There's an outlet in the wall next to you, if you'd like to use it for your phone."

"Oh, right!" I laughed. Made a show of searching around in my bag. "I don't think I have one in here, actually. Could I borrow yours?"

Jesse's dad moved to a nearby desk, plucking a spare charger and handing it to me. "So, Cordelia, are you in the show with Jesse? I met another friend of his tonight. Victoria, maybe?"

I smiled so hard that it hurt. "Veronica." My voice was about two octaves too high.

"You'll have to forgive me, I'm so bad with names."

"No problem."

"This is my son's first leading role. He's so excited."

I shifted in my seat. Didn't seem like that when he auditioned. "Oh, cool. Happy for him," I replied, even though I didn't sound like I meant it.

"Who do you play?"

"I don't act. I'm the stage manager."

"What's that like?" His eyes lit up in a fascinated way. Pain wound its way through my chest. I'd never seen my mom look that interested in anything I did.

"Well—" Before I could answer, their front door swung open.

"Dad," Jesse said, setting a grocery bag down. "And . . . Cordelia? What're you doing here?"

I made my saccharine smile even sweeter. "I had a question about our group project. And, uh, my phone died so your dad was letting me charge it here."

Jesse's eyes fell on his father. "How kind of him," he said, but it didn't sound like a compliment.

His dad chuckled. "It's like I always say. You've gotta help others, 'cause you don't know when—" He stopped mid-sentence, completely frozen. His mouth was open as if the words were lingering on the tip of his tongue. Which they probably were.

Jesse's eyes glowed bright red. Fear turned my blood to ice as he stood in the hallway, watching me. Adrenaline made every muscle in my body scream to run. But I couldn't let him see that I was scared. I wouldn't get what I wanted that way. "What are you *really* doing here?"

"I just want to talk," I replied, voice steadier than I felt.

"About what?"

"Veronica," I replied, maybe a little too quickly. I nodded at his dad. "What'd you do to him?"

"Don't worry. Manipulating humans' physical forms is tedious work, but it doesn't hurt anyone unless I want it to. And, as long as you keep playing nice, it'll stay that way."

"Is he even a real person?"

"That's for me to know, and you to wonder." The demon smirked. "It's interesting, though. Given your complicated history with father figures, I didn't think you'd care what happened to this one. Not when you were so reckless with your own."

I bit down hard on the inside of my cheek to keep from screaming. "I didn't have a choice."

"Is *that* the lie you've been telling yourself? Does it make you feel better? Help you sleep at night?" He stepped closer to me with each question. I stayed rooted to the spot. Not because he froze me in place, but because I wasn't going to back down.

Rage rose and fell with every breath. "It does, actually. I feel great about it."

"Another lie. But I guess that's what you do, isn't it? You really *are* just like him, you know. You lie and you hurt the people you care about. It's all you're good for."

Tears pooled in my eyes. My hands shook, aching to reach into the bag and pull out my kalis. "I'm *nothing* like my father."

Jesse's head tilted. "Who said I was talking about him?"

Before I could ask him what he meant, the front door burst open. It bounced open and closed a few times until Fred strode through it, slamming it shut.

"Cordelia," Fred said, every ounce of playfulness drained out of his voice. "Get behind me. Now."

"Oh, I don't think that's necessary. We're just talking, *Mr. Williams*." Jesse chuckled, saying Fred's name in a mocking tone. "No need to blow things out of proportion."

"Cordelia—" Fred started to say, but he was cut off. Frozen in place, just like Jesse's dad. Fred's eyes were wide. They darted back and forth between Jesse and me, the only things that could still move.

Run, Fred's voice frantically screeched in my mind. *Now!*

Maybe listening to him was the smart thing to do. But I'd come here for a reason, and I wasn't going to leave before I saw it through. I turned my back on him, facing Jesse. "Leave Veronica out of this." My voice was steadier than I thought it would be. "Or else."

Jesse's smile fell, but only for a moment. Then he tossed his head back and laughed. "Or else what?" he said, in between howls. "You're going to trap me? Is that what he's told you to do?"

"Don't listen to him—" Fred started to say, but then his voice abruptly cut off. His mouth moved, but no sound came out.

"That's enough out of you," Jesse snapped. "I don't know how much our newly-minted guidance counselor has told you, but I wouldn't trust anything he says. He's always played the victim. Blamed everyone else for his problems when he was the only one at fault."

I tore my gaze away from Fred, focusing on Jesse. "I thought demons couldn't hurt each other," I said quietly. It was the whole reason I was going on an absurd quest to trap Jesse in the first place.

Jesse smirked. "Taking his voice away does no harm. There are always loopholes. The sooner you learn that, the better."

I glared at him. "I'll be sure to write that one down."

Jesse took another step toward me. He was way too close. He reached out, brushing my cheek with his thumb. "I'm sorry that you entrusted your soul to such a pathetic excuse for a demon. You really do deserve better."

I put my hand on his, holding it as I looked into his bright red demon eyes. "You're right," I said, moving his hand off my face. I made sure it hovered right above my collarbone. "I do." I slammed his hand down right on the spot where the cross on my mom's rosary sat, hidden underneath my sweater.

Jesse screamed, pulling his hand back. A burn mark seared neatly into his palm.

"Nice trick," Jesse said, shoving his cross-burnt hand in his pocket. "But I've got them, too." He gestured to Fred. "I'll let you in on a little secret: demons don't care about humans. We never have, and we never will. So, if you think that demon over there is your friend, you're in for a rude awakening."

It's not true. Fred's voice was soft and strained in my head, but it was there.

I tried moving, but concrete solidified in my veins. Every muscle in my body was too heavy. My heart beat a frantic rhythm in my chest, the only thing working the way it should.

"Ah," Jesse said, standing close enough to see the individual freckles on his face. "I don't think I've made myself clear. I can hurt anyone I want at any time, Cordelia. Aside from you. Isn't that fun?"

I strained against the extra weight holding me in place. He was right; I wasn't in pain. Just . . . weirdly frozen. There had to be a way to break free.

"Your little human friends have remained untouched for now, but if you continue down this path—if you listen to this sad excuse for a guidance counselor—then I'll have no choice. Don't make me do anything I wouldn't want to do."

"I don't know," I said, still trying to break free of his hold. "Sounds kind of tempting."

Jesse's gaze drifted back over to Fred. "I see why you chose this one. It's hard to break her spirit, isn't it?"

Fred couldn't reply, but he looked at Jesse with murder in his eyes. Dark smoke appeared under his feet, wrapping around him. Somehow, Fred broke free enough to send a streak of blue fire hurtling toward Jesse. I wasn't sure what it would do since they weren't allowed to hurt each other. But I never got to see what would've happened, because Jesse put it out with one breath before it could touch him. Like he was blowing out a birthday candle.

Jesse's smile widened. "I was hoping you'd do that." He snapped his fingers, and white smoke popped up where Fred was, completely enveloping him.

The weight that held me down lifted, just in time for the smoke to clear.

Fred's human form vanished. The Nightmare Deer took his place, standing where he used to be. But he looked different from when we were sitting in his office. White makeup with a red line through the middle encircled his bright yellow eyes. A round red nose sat on top of his deer snout. And a curly wig of firetruck red hair sat atop his head, between his antlers.

Confetti fired from right above him, raining down as Fred the Nightmare Deer crumpled to the ground.

"Don't worry, Cordelia," Jesse said, as I rushed over to Fred. "I didn't wound him. Unless you count his pride. But just think—if I can break another demon so easily, what could I do to a pathetic little human like Veronica?"

He wanted a reaction from me, but he wasn't going to get it. I helped the Nightmare Deer to his feet and dragged Fred out of the house without another word.

"I'm sorry," Fred said, as I guided him down the driveway. "I put you in danger. This is all my fault."

"No." I opened my passenger's side door, doing my best to jam all of him into the seat. Jesse watched us from his window. He smiled, giving me a small salute. I turned away from him, focusing on the broken demon sitting in my car. "It's mine."

CHAPTER FIFTEEN

IN WHICH I FIGURE OUT WHAT I WANT

I DROPPED FRED OFF AT HIS HOUSE. HE'D TRIED CHANGING back to his human form but was having a rough go of it. After an hour of failure, he sent me home.

I drove home, waiting until I parked my car before I let myself feel anything. Back when I was seeing a therapist, she told me that pushing aside emotions in the heat of the moment was a way to cope with situations happening around me. That the trauma I'd experienced had re-wired my brain into survival-mode every second of every day, even when there wasn't a threat around me. It was exhausting constantly looking for dangers that weren't even there and stashing away all my emotions for a time when I could feel everything all at once. I hated it.

But I had no idea how to change it.

I let out a deep breath, resting my forehead on the top of the steering wheel, closed my eyes for a few seconds in a halfhearted attempt to hold back tears, and then, when I knew I couldn't fight it anymore, I gave in.

I cried.

Too much was happening. It was the understatement of the year, but it was true. Yesterday, I was failing a pop quiz and had no idea what I was going to do with my future. Now, I wasn't even sure I'd *have* a future. In six days, I'd have to face off against a demon who seemed impossibly powerful.

Jesse was just as much of a monster as my father. I'd only been able to banish the latter to Hell because he'd almost killed me. Was I doomed to repeat that again? Could I only act on something if I was near death? And what if that demon pushed things a little too far? He could kill me before I had the chance to kill him.

I wiped away at tears that clouded my vision. Despite what Jesse thought, I wasn't a murderer. I didn't like what I'd done. Hell, I'd spent the last seven years willfully forgetting it. Trying to move on. Start fresh. But I couldn't avoid it anymore. If I kept carrying this secret around, it would destroy what was left of my soul.

I sniffled, grabbing my phone. Sent Veronica a text. And didn't bother to stop the tears as I waited to see if she'd reply.

Twenty minutes went by without any word from her. My eyes, sore and dry from crying too much, still trickled with a few tears every now and then. Inside out, my body decayed, no matter what I did, I'd always be rotten. Maybe Veronica knew that, too, and that's why she didn't answer me. Maybe—

Someone tapped on the driver's side window. I jumped, jerking back when the seatbelt stopped the movement. I'd meant to unbuckle it—it wasn't like my breakdown sent me driving anywehere—but I'd been too busy crying to remember.

"Sorry," Veronica's muffled voice said through the window. "Can you let me in?"

I nodded, unlocking the car. Veronica opened the door. She slid into the passenger's seat, handing me a box of tissues. We both sat in silence for a few seconds before I said, "I was an asshole. I'm sorry."

"I appreciate that," Veronica replied, looking straight ahead. "I got the kind you like, by the way. The ones with aloe in them."

"Thanks," I replied, though the word sounded funny with my stuffy nose.

"How long have you been crying in your car, Cordy?"

"Too long."

"Are you going to tell me what's wrong now?"

"I can't." I wanted to, but how would she react when I gave her all the details? Some things I could share, though. Even if they were vague.

Veronica sighed. "Then why am I here?"

"I shouldn't have gotten mad at you earlier. I'm sorry. But Jesse . . . you shouldn't hang out with him. He's not who he says he is."

"Are any of us, really?" She didn't look at me when she said it, but her words cut through me just the same. She kept staring straight ahead as she said, "I'm sorry, too. I don't think either of us handled it well. I was . . . I don't know. Mad, I guess. You wouldn't even hear me out about the Jesse thing."

"I didn't want to. I don't know if I want that now, to be honest."

"Then what *do* you want?" she asked, finally looking at me.

"I need you to tell me that I'm a bad person."

Silence lingered between us. Veronica's expression softened. She reached for me, as if to brush a tear off my cheek, but pulled her hand back. Disappointment shot through me. Things had changed between us, whether I wanted them to or not.

"I don't think you're a bad person," she said.

"It's what you said earlier."

"I was mad at you. I didn't mean it."

"But what if it's true?" I asked, hating the tears welling in my eyes. Veronica had seen me cry loads of times. She was the only person I ever did it around. But this time was different. I'd put up a wall that I never thought would be there. At least, not with her. "What if I did something terrible, and now I have to pay for it?"

"Like what?"

"I can't—" I started again, but I cut myself off with a sigh. "It's . . . it's my father. I'm worried that he might come back. From Florida."

Veronica's hands twisted together. "Did he reach out to you?"

"Kind of."

"We can go to someone for help. The police, or—"

"The police aren't going to do anything. They didn't then. Why would they now?" Especially when he came right out of the fires of Hell.

"So, what do we do?" Veronica asked.

"I don't know. I thought I did, but—but what if I made the wrong decision? What if I wind up doing more harm than good?"

What if I wind up like him?

That was what I really wanted to ask her. But I was too scared to let the question live outside of my mind. Once I spoke it aloud, it wasn't my fear anymore. It was something the universe could twist around and use against me.

The air weighed heavily between us. Veronica shifted in her seat. "Cordy, did—did something happen before he left? Is that why you think you're a bad person?"

I didn't answer her, but she knew me well enough to know that my silence was a yes.

She cleared her throat. "Well, if you ever want to talk about it, I'm around." Her hand slid on top of mine. She squeezed it. "I meant what I said in the woods, earlier. You're not like him."

I shook my head. "I am." That was easy enough to see. I had no problem hurting her—running away before we could really talk about anything.

Veronica pulled her hand away, taking all of the warmth with her. "You're so much more than that. One day, I hope you'll believe me."

"Maybe."

She ran a hand through her hair. "I don't know what it'll take to convince you."

I shrugged. I didn't either. There were differences between my father and me—I knew we weren't exactly the same person. But a part of him hadn't been a monster, once. Maybe he faced the same choices I had and decided to go a different way. Or people in our family were doomed to repeat these mistakes, over and over.

"What do you want from me?" Veronica asked again.

I thought the answer was for her to confirm my worst fear: that no matter how hard I tried to be a good person, I'd wind up like him. That I was just as rotten and irredeemable. But that wasn't it. I wanted something from her that she couldn't give me: absolution.

Fred had been right all along. I needed to find a way to forgive myself for what I'd done. I had no idea how to do that, but maybe talking to Veronica about it—even in vague terms—was a good way to start.

"I just want to be your friend," I finally said, meeting her gaze.

Sadness drifted through her expression, but only for a second. She nodded. "We're friends. You don't have to worry about that."

"No matter what?" I asked.

She smiled at me. "No matter what."

I wanted to believe her. But the smile didn't reach her eyes.

CHAPTER SIXTEEN

IN WHICH I LEARN FRED'S TRAGIC BACKSTORY

THE NEXT DAY, I TRIED TO MAKE SURE FRED WAS OKAY, but he wasn't answering any of my calls or texts. Veronica and I sent a few memes back and forth, but whatever walls I'd put up around her, she must've done the same for me. Something felt different about the way we talked. Something strained. I hated it, but if that was how I could keep her out of my demon-laden mess, then I had to do it.

Dustin hit me up, trying to hang out, but I decided that spending the day reading through *The Tempest* so I didn't bomb another pop quiz was a better idea. Shockingly, it paid off on Monday. This time, I knew all the answers.

Every now and then, homework became a necessary evil.

I also spent the last dregs of the weekend looking up some more demon lore whenever I got bored with good old Willy Shakes. I still couldn't find any details on what a blessed weapon was, but Blake was (theoretically) handling that and the sigil thing anyway, so I abandoned that pretty quickly. I wound up looking at more exorcism rituals, just in case some small clue lay hidden in them about trapping demons.

While I was glad that I got a little bit of research out of the way, I couldn't help but feel like I was up shit's creek. It was Monday, and we were already on our lunch period. Deal Day, coming faster than I thought, would be here Friday, and so far, all I had to show for it was a demon mentor who wouldn't talk to me and Dustin's post about us hanging out, which had fifty likes so far. Awesome.

At least I had a fix for one of my problems. Since Fred's actual job was sitting down and having a conversation with me, I could force some kind of a check-in with him. Maybe he ghosted me because of how ashamed he was about being turned into a clown in front of me. Or that he hadn't been able to change back into his human form that night.

I hated admitting it, but I missed his Jedi Mind Trick and how he'd randomly say something snarky about little chaos fires that popped up during rehearsal.

So, I ditched lunch, twisting my hands together as I sat outside of his office door. I wasn't sure what to say. Or if I should be, like, comforting or whatever. But the way everything went down at Jesse's house was not okay—and it also wasn't his fault. I didn't know why he needed to know that, but he did.

The door slowly creaked open. "Oh," Fred said, peering through the crack. He was back to being human again but sported a retro pair of Ray Bans. "It's you."

"You say that like it's a bad thing."

He sighed. "I suppose this was inevitable. Come in."

I slunk into his office, sliding into the chair across from his desk. The little room was just as chaotic as it had been before, but everything in there felt slightly more depressing. The Precious Moments Maleficent looked like she was on the verge of adorable tears. Fred's framed *Live, Laugh, Love* picture shined dully under the school's harsh fluorescent light. Even the *Oh, Shit!* cat dangling off the poster's branch seemed close to just letting go of the damn thing.

"So," I said, watching him as he sank into his chair. "What's with the sunglasses?"

Fred pulled them down, looking at me with his Nightmare Deer eyes. "Can't go around scaring everyone, can I?"

"I guess not. But you're human again. That counts for something, right?"

"What do you want, Cordelia?" he said, with an edge to his voice.

"I just want to know how you're doing."

He rolled his eyes. "I'm *fine*. How are you?"

"I'm wondering why you're lying."

"I'm not."

"Oh, right. Silly me. I must've missed the part where Jesse put you in a terrible clown wig to embarrass you."

Fred forced a smile as he nodded. "The hair would've matched my outfit today."

It wouldn't have. Fred's bright orange graphic tee—with Smokey the Bear saying *Only YOU can prevent forest fires*—looked like something a hipster threw up in the middle of a fever dream.

"Fred, what Jesse did to you—"

"Doesn't need to be discussed," he said abruptly. "We should focus on your task. Not on me. We're running out of time. And, it seems, the closer we get to the day, the stronger he gets. Terribly unfair, but that's always been how he operates."

"—he wanted to humiliate you—" I tried saying, but he barreled on without listening to me.

Fred focused his gaze on the top of Precious Moments Maleficent's head. "You're only being nice to me because you feel pity."

"No. I'm telling you the truth. Jesse manipulated you. Embarrassed you. If you feel ashamed—"

"I don't," he snapped.

"Okay, well, on the off chance that you do, it's completely normal. Jesse's an asshole. And when you're ready to talk—when you're ready for me to help—you know where to find me."

Fred frowned. "You're only offering to help because I'm forcing you to."

"Well, yeah. That's how it started. But after Jesse's house last night, I—I don't know. I guess I see things differently now."

I meant every word and hoped it was the right thing to say. I barely slept last night, and aside from my pop quiz in AP Lit, hadn't really paid attention in any of my classes today. I'd been too busy turning over Jesse and Fred's conversation in my head. How horrible the other demon had been to my fake guidance counselor. He made Fred feel pathetic and small just because he could.

I had experience with someone like that. Fred sent him to Hell. I still wasn't sure how to repay the demon for changing my life, but I figured getting rid of Jesse would be a good step toward being even.

Fred sighed. "I think it's time for you to go to rehearsal." I figured he'd get mad again or break down or show *some* kind of emotion, but he'd put a mask of cool indifference on and refused to take it off. I wanted to pick that Maleficent up off his desk and throw it at him.

"We should talk about it," I said, crossing my arms.

"No."

"Why not?"

"Because I don't want to."

"You're being stubborn."

"So?"

"So, it's annoying. God, you're acting just like—" I caught myself, not daring to finish the thought. He was behaving exactly like *me* whenever Veronica tried talking about anything serious. It was frustrating. Infuriating to not be able to discuss what he was going through. But maybe I could get through to him, somehow.

I glared at him. "We're not done here."

"How did you put it before?" he asked, as thin gray smoke rose up around him. "Ah yes, that you weren't some charity case to be helped. Well, I'm not, either. What you saw in that house was shameful. I was weak and was adequately punished for it. I trust we'll never speak of this again."

"But—"

"Go to class."

"No—"

A wall of flames burst into life on top of his desk. It blocked my view of him. Fine. He could be as stubborn as he wanted. But we weren't done talking about this.

"You're not weak," I said, sitting back in my chair. "And I'm not leaving."

The flames lingered on the desk for what seemed like an eternity. I didn't yield, though. I refused to get out of the chair until he put the fire out and talked to me.

He gave up after a few more minutes, lowering the flames, and exhaled loudly when he saw me. "You're still here?" he asked.

"What part of 'we should talk about this' was so hard to understand?" I shot back.

"I seem to recall you saying we weren't at the tragic backstory level yet."

I shrugged. "That was a few days ago. Things change."

"Fine," he replied, shaking his head. "If I tell you, you'll leave me alone?" He chuckled. "It would appear our roles have reversed, little one. Maybe I've taught you something after all."

I rolled my eyes. "I wouldn't go that far. But hey, I'll tell ya what: if you share your tragic backstory with me, I'll go to class."

"You can't skip calculus, Cordelia."

"Calculus won't matter if I die on Friday, Fred."

He leaned back in his chair, pinching the bridge of his nose. "You aren't going to die."

"I know. Because you're going to tell me *exactly* who I'm up against." It was hard to keep the smugness out of my voice. I patted the top of the Maleficent's horned head. "I can't win if I don't understand who I'm fighting. I need to know what he's capable of. Every last detail."

"I . . . " His voice trailed away, but only for a few seconds. "You're right." He waited for me to reply, but I didn't. He sighed as he continued. "I had a favorite human, once. Demons—we can't have kids, but she was like a daughter to me. Dolores. She was smart. Curious. Dreadfully stubborn. We didn't always get along, but I would have moved Heaven and Hell for her. Tried to, in fact. Didn't work out well."

I shifted in the chair. "What happened?"

"She was young when I first met her. Early twenties. She thought she could change the world, so I made a deal to help her do it. But the price she had to pay was too steep. She couldn't go through with it. She refused to uphold her end of our bargain. And I . . . I didn't have the heart to make her. She was the first deal I'd ever made, and I didn't understand—I didn't know—that there would be consequences."

"Jesse," I said, slowly. "He's that consequence?"

He dabbed at the corners of his eyes. "I did everything I could to hide her. Keep her away from him. But he found her anyway and gained her trust. He made Dolores doubt me. And then, before I could intervene, he turned her into a monster."

I nodded. First Dolores, now the aswang. How many monsters had Jesse left in his wake throughout the years?

"Jesse's stronger than I am," Fred said. "I learned a lot about being a demon from him. He taught me that humans were only ever a means to an end. And I believed him, until Dolores. He couldn't accept that I'd changed, so he changed her. She was never the same after that."

My hands flexed, balling back into fists. The other demon took someone Fred cared about and hadn't stopped tormenting him since. I knew what it was like to not be able to escape someone who only wanted to cause you pain. How it seemed like there was no way out, so you either fought like hell to make your own or sank so far down you couldn't come back from it.

"What happened to her?" I asked, even though I dreaded the answer.

"I tried staying with her, but she got away from me. She turned into someone I didn't recognize. And she . . . well.

She did horrible things. All the carnage—all the destruction—it's my fault. If I'd never made a deal with her in the first place, she would've lived a normal life. Not one filled with pain and suffering. She truly could've changed the world. Instead, the world changed her."

My hands twisted together. "Oh."

"I tell you this," Fred said, clearing his throat, "because I need you to understand that I'm scared, too. The demon we're facing is dangerous."

"I know."

Sadness filled his eyes as he looked away from me. "I don't think you do, little one. I'm sorry that I ever got you involved. I shouldn't have been so selfish."

I narrowed my eyes. "What?"

"I couldn't protect her. I won't be able to keep you safe, either."

"I don't need you to do that," I replied. "I need you to help me."

"No," he said, the softness in his expression falling away. Firm and immovable resolve stared back at me. "I still have a few days to figure this out. Forget everything I've told you, Cordelia."

I wanted to scream. Instead, I sat there and said, as calmly as I could, "Can't do that. I need that piece of my soul back, remember?"

"Oh, yes. That." Fred lazily waved his hand. Flames sprouted at my feet, winding up my legs. I recoiled, scooting deeper into the chair. Unlike when my father appeared, though, I didn't feel any heat from this fire despite the fact that it covered my whole body.

Ice-cold fingers wrapped around my heart, squeezing it so tight it was close to bursting. I wheezed, looking up at Fred through tear-filled eyes. He sat there, rigid and unmoving as I doubled over from the pain. Something sharp as a shard of glass slid into my chest.

I opened my mouth to scream, but no sound came out.

A bright flash of white light filled Fred's office. And then it and the fire faded away, leaving only the two of us.

"Consider your end of our bargain fulfilled," Fred said, bitterly. "Congratulations, Cordelia Scott. You just got your soul back."

CHAPTER SEVENTEEN

IN WHICH I DO WANNA MISS A THING

THE THING ABOUT GROWING UP WITH MONSTERS IS this: sometimes, when you wish them away, another one swoops in and takes their place.

And it's not always who you think it's going to be.

Sometimes, the monster is you.

I got my soul back from Fred and he let me off the hook. He wanted me to walk away from everything—to let him handle it on his own—and a big part of me wanted to let him.

Every decision I'd ever made had served only one purpose: survival.

I sent my father to Hell, and forgot about what I did, because that was the only way I could keep going. I thought it would help me feel whole. Fulfilled. Happy.

But even with my soul back, I still felt empty. I wanted to let the whole thing go. Put it behind me and forget about everything all over again. Run away from my problems, just like I'd always done before.

The problem with running away though was, eventually, you'd get tired. Worn down. Your muscles would ache, you'd need a break, and you'd stop. And that's when everything could catch up with you.

That's when you figured out who you really were.

I did a monstrous thing. So far, I'd let it define me. If I kept running, it would keep happening. But there was another way. I could help Fred. Stop the other demon from making more towns like Ruin's End and gaining more power every time he took a human soul.

Maybe I was wrong, earlier. I didn't need to forgive myself for what I'd done. I had to stop thinking of *just* myself, and care about what would happen to everyone else if Fred failed. Or I did.

"You sure you don't need to talk?" Sal asked, as everyone onstage scrambled back to their starting positions at the top of the song. We had a shorter tech rehearsal today, so they were hanging out backstage with me, wincing as the chaos unfolded around us. "You don't look too good."

"I'm fine."

Sal sighed. "Look, I saw that Veronica and Jesse—"

"They were just hanging out," I said, maybe a little too quickly. "They can be friends . . . I guess." They really couldn't be friends. But I couldn't get into any of that, so I sat there, seething, instead.

"Well, I know that you and Veronica are . . ." Their voice trailed away. "I'm here if you ever need to talk."

I reached over and squeezed their hand. "Thanks, Sal. Sorry I fell off the face of the earth this weekend. There was, uh, a lot happening."

"Like hanging out with Dustin?"

"You saw that?"

"The whole school saw that."

"Oh. Great."

Sal laughed, hitting me lightly on the shoulder. "Don't worry. Everyone knows that Dustin is tragically straight and that you're well . . . you know." They gestured to Veronica. "Already taken."

Warmth rushed to my face. "I don't know about that. I kind of messed things up."

Sal shrugged. "You'll work it out."

"Maybe. How was your weekend? Did you get a cool place at Emerson?" I asked, desperate to change the subject.

"Oh yeah. I got a spot at the Paramount Center. We went into Boston to scope it out. They've got a black box theater in there! How cool is that?"

"That's amazing! I can't wait to visit you!"

They beamed at me. "I'll get us front-row seats at all the hipster one-man shows. How's your post-graduation plan going?"

I winced. Before I learned about my demon deal, I hadn't put much thought into it. After, I had the excuse of not knowing whether or not I'd make it past this Friday. But now, if I *did* decide to walk away and leave Fred on his own, I could start to think about the future. *My* future. "I'll let you know when it exists."

"All right," Barry said, standing in front of the stage and mercifully bringing our conversation to an end. "We're going to try this one more time before we end early tonight. Take the time you need to rest. Just because we're releasing you in time for Monday Night Karaoke doesn't mean you *all* have to pile into The Coffee Spot in a few hours. You still have a long week ahead of you. Understood?"

Mumbles of agreement rippled through the cast.

Barry put a hand to his ear. "I can't hear you."

Choruses of *got it*s, *yeah*s and way too enthusiastic *woo*s followed.

"Much better," Barry said.

Sal and I exchanged a glance. Despite Barry's warning, at least half the cast had already talked about cramming into The Coffee Spot after rehearsal to let off some steam. I wasn't sold on the idea that one could de-stress from a musical by singing karaoke, but traditions were traditions.

Hopefully, that would be the fun portion of the night. To get there first, though, we'd all have to keep suffering through the most cursed Tech Week I'd ever been a part of.

We'd been stuck on this song for way too long. What should've been a simple number where everyone in the town sang about what they'd wish for if they had a chance to change their lives, had quickly devolved into a continuous train wreck.

For the fifth time in an hour, our frantic actors moved around the stage like they'd had too much to drink. It was like they'd all forgotten their choreography, the lyrics, and their harmonies all at once. They knocked into each other—and the wall, sometimes—as they tried finding their next mark.

The only ones who weren't making fools of themselves were Jesse, Veronica, and Dustin. Maybe it was because the three of them were seniors and had a good idea of what they were doing. But some of the juniors who'd take over once we graduated were acting like they didn't know stage left from stage right. And it was even worse for some of our first-timers.

Sara, one of the freshmen in the ensemble—an amazing singer who, unfortunately, didn't have the same control over her legs as she did with her voice—stumbled right into Jesse as she made a cross to the other side of the stage.

"Sorry," she said, so loudly that it cut Dustin off mid-phrase.

Jesse broke character, patting her on the shoulder. "It's okay," he replied. That kind gesture cost him a crucial line, which snowballed and threw everybody else off. Every muscle in my body tensed. He shouldn't be on that stage, pretending that he's just a normal kid when he made Fred a living meme the other night. He could do the same thing to everyone around him with a simple snap of his fingers.

Dustin stormed upstage, ripping his bowler hat off as he stood right at the edge. He yanked his hand back then threw it forward, launching part of his costume into the house. Only, the hat didn't make it that far. Instead, it drifted down into the orchestra pit below. Cellos and violins came to a screeching halt.

"Dustin Jones!" Barry yelled from the front row. "That'll be detention!"

Dustin shrugged, stomping away backstage to the dressing rooms.

"Well," Barry said, from the darkness that was still covering the audience. "I think that's a sign that we're done for the day. Get some rest, all. We'll pick it up from here after school tomorrow."

Groans bounced around the ensemble as they all slowly shuffled off-stage.

"House lights up," I said into my headset. Nothing happened. "Leon?" I asked, a little more impatient this time. He usually responded within a few seconds. It'd been at least a minute now. "Leon, what are you—"

Feedback from a microphone rang out through the theater. I stumbled onto the stage trying to figure out what was going on. I put a hand over my eyes, shading them so I could look up at the tech booth in the balcony. Leon smiled, waving down at me. He gave me a thumbs-up.

I frowned at him. "What are you—"

The opening notes of an instrumental Aerosmith's "I Don't Wanna Miss a Thing" cut me off. The track drifted through the air as Jesse walked onto the stage holding a microphone.

"This one is dedicated to a special lady." He turned to me, holding his hand out. "You know who you are."

Oh, no. I swallowed back the bits of cafeteria lasagna I'd had at lunch. I was wrong before. Veronica theoretically confessing her feelings for me wasn't the world-ending, life-altering, worst-case scenario.

This was.

I had no idea what the hell he was doing. Or why. But nothing good could come from it.

"I could stay awake, just to hear you breathing," he sang, flourishing it with a high note at the end, just like Steven Tyler does in the song. *"Watch you smile while you're sleeping. While you're far away and dreaming."*

"Cordelia," Barry snapped, fighting to be heard over the music. "What, in the name of Steven Tyler's sweet falsetto, is happening here?"

I threw my hands up in the air in defeat. "No goddamn idea," I replied, as Jesse belted out the song's chorus. Everyone wandered in from off-stage, watching the scene unfold in front of them. Jesse crossed in front of them. Toward me.

I backed away from him, right into a set piece. My heart

pounded. Adrenaline raced through my body, urging my legs to run. But I couldn't move.

Electricity jolted through my body, forcing me to stand still. The weight that made it impossible for me to move when I was trapped in Jesse's house returned.

Jesse waltzed up to me, making a meal out of the whole damn thing. I stood there, helpless, as he slowly reached out and took my hand.

Fred, I screamed in my head, because my mouth wasn't cooperating at the moment. *A little help!*

Veronica walked back into the theater right as Jesse brought my hand to his lips. Anger sent my blood into a boil. That manipulative bastard.

He wanted her to see this.

I had no idea what kind of twisted game he was playing but hitting on me after I'd seen what he was capable of was a hundred kinds of fucked up.

As soon as his lips brushed my skin, the weight lifted. I yanked my hand away, pulling it back before I put as much power as I could into swinging it forward, right into his cheek.

The slap rang out through the auditorium, drifting over the music for a few blissful seconds before the sound died away.

"That's detention," Barry yelled. "For Mr. Smithe and whoever's up there running sound—"

"Leon," I said.

"Leon," Barry repeated, waving up at the booth. His ire turned toward me. I shrunk back. I'd done a lot of annoying things to Barry over the years. And sure, there were times where he was frustrated. But he'd never actually been *mad* at me. "And you, Cordelia. You'll join them as well."

It was like he stabbed me through the heart. "What? I didn't do anything wrong!"

"You *hit* me!" Jesse cried out, like it had actually hurt him.

"There's more where that came from," I growled.

"Cut the music," Barry yelled up at Leon, drowning our argument out. The last few notes of the song hung in the air around us.

"Sorry, Barry," Jesse said into the mic. "The things you do for love, right?"

Oh, hell no. I wasn't going to be a part of whatever messed-up game he was playing with Veronica. I snatched the microphone from him. "Fuck you, asshole."

I shoved the mic into Barry's hand, running out of the theater as tears pooled in my eyes. I'd been so worried about how he could physically hurt everyone that I hadn't planned for him to pretend to be in love with me in front of the whole cast. If Veronica thought that I liked him, too, after I'd just told her I didn't trust him—no.

All I wanted to do was talk to her about this. Clear the air. But I wasn't sure I could undo the damage while Jesse was still around, adding more to the pile.

I passed Fred's office. His door was shut. "Thanks for nothing," I screamed, hitting it. He hadn't even tried to do his weird mind message thing with me when I needed help. I was trying to support him, and now he pretended I didn't exist. If he'd been there, he could've stopped the song from happening. Or had my back when Barry assumed I also had something to do with Jesse's little show.

If I stood by and let him, Jesse Smithe would ruin my life. I wasn't going to let that happen. Fred might've been determined to stop Jesse on his own, but I'd find another way, in case he failed.

I couldn't do it alone, though. I needed help.

I threw the school's doors open, charging out into the parking lot. Dustin's bright green peacoat was almost to his car. "Wait up!" I called out to him.

He stopped, lingering half in and half out of his car. "What now, Scott?"

"You going home?" I asked, jogging up to him.

"Yeah. Gotta pick some stuff up for karaoke. Why?"

"I'm coming with you," I said, sealing my fate. All I'd ever done was run. Avoid my problems. It was time to face this one head-on. With or without Fred's help.

Dustin raised a dark blond eyebrow. "At least buy me dinner first," he said.

"Gross," I replied, shoving him in his car. "I just slapped Jesse. I have no problem slapping you, too, Jones."

Dustin's mouth hung open. "You really did that?"

"Got detention for it."

For the first time in his life, Dustin Jones genuinely smiled at me. "Well, what're you waiting for? Get in!"

I'd say agreeing to hang out with Dustin was like making a deal with the devil, but that would be giving him too much credit. Still, if he'd let me into his house, I could probably convince him to help me go through his brother's things.

I hurried around the front of his car, sliding into the passenger's seat. Blake didn't want to tell me what he knew, but maybe I could find something in his room.

Only five days left until Deal Day. If I was going to do this without Fred, I'd need all the help I could get.

CHAPTER EIGHTEEN

IN WHICH REGINALD DOESN'T REPLY

MOST HOUSES IN RUIN'S END WERE NORMAL. OR unremarkable, depending on how you looked at it. Basic one- or two-story homes that looked like generic neighborhoods from any movie. Apartment complexes that belonged everywhere and nowhere at the same time.

But the Jones's McMansion was different. Cold, modern architecture greeted us as we rolled up to their cobblestone driveway. Sleek lines separated the gabled roof from the third story. Each side met at such a steep angle that one could easily be impaled on its point. During the day, the dark gray paint covering most of the massive house gloomed drearily at anyone unfortunate enough to see it. At night, with barely any lights on the outside, it looked like nothing more than a massive black hole in the middle of the woods.

If this was a horror movie, someone like me would *definitely* get murdered in this house.

The driveway curved into a semi-circle. Dustin parked right in the middle of it.

"Don't you need to leave room for your family?" I asked.

He got out of the car, gesturing to the space around him. "They've got plenty of room. Besides, my parents are out of the country till Thursday, and Blake's at The Coffee Spot. No one's around to care about what I do."

He tossed it out there like it was a joke, but the sadness in his statement stuck with me. I never thought I'd have anything in common with Dustin Jones. And yet, here we were, two people who only ever wanted their families to notice them.

"Are you coming in?" he asked.

"Oh, yeah. Sure." I got out of the car, closing the door softly behind me. Dustin hummed one of the songs from *Our Demon Town* as he walked up to his front door and unlocked it.

If the exterior of the McMansion was all sleek, dark modern lines, the inside looked like it was pulled right out of *Clue*. A grand staircase cut most of a long hallway in half. There were doors to either side. More than there probably should've been, considering only four people lived in there.

A giant chandelier, only rivaled in size by the prop one they used in productions of *The Phantom of the Opera*, hovered over the staircase. The crystals that dangled at the bottom taunted us as we walked under them. As if they dared me to stand right under them, just to see what would happen.

The occasional taxidermized animal lined the walls. Mostly deer heads. Ew. But there was one door that had a whole-ass bear standing guard. I grimaced at it, walking a little faster.

"Your house is weird," I said, as Dustin led me further down the hall.

He shrugged, opening another door. "What house isn't?"

Dustin stepped aside, and I walked into a room that was as big as our school's library. The study was lined with books from floor to ceiling. Almost like that library in *Beauty and the Beast.* But the walls of books weren't the thing that caught my eye.

I wish it had been that simple.

A group of comfortable reading chairs sat in the middle of the room. Which would make sense, for a study. What was baffling—and slightly terrifying—was that those chairs were surrounded by a pack of wolves. They weren't alive. Thank *God.* Like the deer and the bear in the hall, these animals had been stuffed and mounted, but they looked as if they could easily jump out and attack us anyway.

Dustin's behavior started to make a little bit more sense. This house didn't exactly scream 'stable living environment.' He stood next to one of the wolves, absently patting its head.

"So," he said, in a completely normal tone that didn't convey how odd all of this was. "I'm flattered that you wanted to hang, but I don't really know what you're doing here."

I blinked, holding back a laugh. "You probably should've asked me that *before* you let me walk through your front door."

"Maybe I just love a good mystery."

"Or you didn't want to be alone."

Dustin gasped dramatically, putting a hand up to his heart. "Ouch. Cut me right to the core there, Scott. But I think we might be after the same thing. You don't want to be alone, either."

I glared at him. "Maybe. But there was another reason I wanted to be here."

"What's that?"

This was either gonna go my way, or I'd get laughed out

of Dustin's McMansion. "I need to get into Blake's room," I replied, holding my breath.

"How come?" Mischief brewed in Dustin's eyes. "Don't get me wrong. I love a good breaking and entering as much as the next troubled rich kid—especially if it involves my brother. But his room is boring. All he's got in there are boring business books, old journals filled with the town's history, and a fish tank."

"I—" I closed my mouth. I slumped down into a leather armchair that was precariously positioned between two snarling wolves. If I couldn't tell Veronica the truth, when she was the one person I trusted more than anyone in the world, how was I supposed to drop the demon bomb on Dustin? "I need to learn about the town," I said, skating as close to the truth as I dared.

Dustin scoffed. "Like . . . Ruin's End?"

"Yes."

"Don't tell me you've bought into my brother's conspiracy theories." Dustin dragged a hand down his face, groaning. "There's no such thing as demons."

"How do you know?"

Dustin absolutely lost it. He doubled over with laughter, holding onto one of the wolves so he didn't fall down. While he picked himself back up, my gaze drifted behind him. A wall-mounted shadowbox with a long, old quill inside peeked into view, but before I could get a good look at the strange relic, Dustin sat back up, obscuring it.

Finally, he gathered enough breath to speak. He clutched his stomach, wheezing, as he said, "Oh, come on. Do you really believe my family summoned a demon centuries ago and created the town? I think you've had too much caffeine for one day. They're not *real*." He pointed to the wall behind him.

"Blake thinks the quill we've got hanging up there signed a deal with a demon instead of some boring Prohibition-era papers. Don't tell me you agree with him—I thought you had more sense than that."

I sighed. Loudly. He wasn't letting me into Blake's room until I told him the truth.

Fine.

"I'm not joking," I shot back. "Blake's right. One hundred years ago, Ryeland Jones created Ruin's End with the help of a demon. And, every year, that demon makes one bargain with someone in this town on Deal Day. *That's* why I need to get into your brother's room. He knows more about this than me, but he won't talk to me about it." I paused, adding, "I can't stop this demon without your help," for good measure.

Dustin stared at me for a few seconds and then started laughing again.

Well, awesome. This was going about as well as I expected it to. It was a mistake on about a billion different levels. But I wasn't leaving until I got what I came for.

"Yeah, okay, sure," he said, still cackling. "If demons are real, then Santa Claus and the Easter Bunny are, too."

I rubbed my temples, fighting the stress headache forming right behind my eyes. "I think those are a little different."

"Speak for yourself. Those mall Easter Bunnies can be pretty terrifying. Definitely demonic." He turned to the taxidermized wolf next to him. "Can you believe it, Reginald? She says *demons* are *real*."

Reginald the Taxidermized Wolf, thankfully, did not reply.

"I don't care if you believe me," I said, once he stopped laughing to catch his breath. "Blake does. I think he knows something that might help me."

"Help you with what?"

"Trapping the demon." He didn't need to know about the whole killing thing. Trapping was much easier to digest.

"Why?"

I cleared my throat. Took a deep breath before I spoke again. "I know how this sounds, but I need you to go with it."

Dustin frowned, crossing his arms. "I'm still not convinced."

I pinched the bridge of my nose. The idea of helping people wasn't appealing to him. I had to switch up my argument. "Haven't you always wanted to know if Blake's right?" I asked, hoping this would work. "If he isn't—if this is all some made-up hocus pocus—wouldn't you want to hold that over his head for the rest of his life?"

He turned back to the wolf. "What do you think, Reginald?"

I blinked. "Do you . . . really think that thing's gonna talk to you?"

"Of course not." He shrugged. "But you believe in demons, so even if I *did*, you don't have a lot of room to judge."

I groaned. "Look, are we doing this, or are you going to keep wasting my time?"

"Okay, okay. God, learn to take a joke." He walked to the wall of bookshelves but stopped before he reached it. "Wait. If demons exist, then is God real, too?"

"I don't know," I replied. "I—"

"I'm just kidding," he said, as he busted out laughing again. "I really don't care."

I flipped him off as he turned his back to me.

"Demons are real," he wheezed, reaching up to one of the higher shelves. His hand lingered in front of one with gold writing etched into a navy-blue spine. He laughed as he tilted the book down.

He turned back around to face me. "Just so we're clear, I'm only playing along with this to prove Blake wrong. He won't be the favorite after I've thrown his life's work away."

The wall shifted silently. An opening just big enough for one person to walk through appeared where only books had been moments before.

My eyes widened as he stepped into it, vanishing completely. *Of course* Dustin Jones had a secret passageway in his weird taxidermy-filled mansion.

I'd figured there'd be more spiderwebs. But it was surprisingly clean. Other than a lack of creepy crawlies, the rest of the hidden tunnel was about what I expected it to be. Fake torches lined the wall in a dramatic kind of way. The manufactured light cast a dull yellow shine on the exposed brick walls. My hand traced our path as we walked. There was no room for imagination in this secret passageway. One simply just walked through the wall and kept going until they emerged victorious on the other side.

"How old is this house?" I asked.

"A little older than Blake," Dustin replied, still laughing. My hands balled into fists. At least someone thought that demons existing was funny. "Mom and Dad were *very* involved in its design."

"They put this here on purpose?"

Dustin shrugged. "Oh, no, the creepy tunnels that connect a bunch of rooms in the house were *totally* an accident." He paused, shaking his head. "Come on, use that big brain of yours. My parents thought it would be a fun thing for us to discover. Blake and I spent a lot of days playing some killer games of Hide and Seek in here."

Oh, yeah. I was right before. This place *definitely* wouldn't qualify as a stable living environment.

After what felt like an eternity, the tunnel finally tapered off. Dustin reached out, pushing the wall out and to the side.

Blake's room wasn't what I was expecting—but neither was the rest of Dustin's house, so it really shouldn't have been that much of a surprise. It was neat. Tidy. The kind of place that never really looked like anyone lived there. It was as if we'd walked into a model home and were touring someone's meticulous staging of what they thought a bedroom was supposed to be.

I figured there'd be some giant corkboard with articles pinned on it and red string bouncing around from one thing to the next. But it was well-kept. Almost precise in how normal it was meant to appear.

The tiny aquarium full of brightly colored fish was the only thing that seemed out of place. A small bit of life in an otherwise soulless room.

Dustin strolled over to the desk, slumping down into his brother's chair. Behind him, a dark, moonless night sky watched us from the window. "Well, here we are," he said, waving his hands in the air. *"Woo."* It was a deflated cheer. "What are you looking for, exactly? Ye Olde Town Charter?"

"I'm not sure yet."

"Great. Glad I put all of my Future-Favorite-Child eggs in your basket."

I nudged Dustin aside, going right for Blake's desk. I went through each drawer. I dug around in them but only found papers filled with enough accounting spreadsheets to make even the most seasoned tax professional cry. There had to be something I was missing. I scooped them all up, dumping them onto the floor.

"Oh, come on, I'm gonna have to clean that up. What the hell are you doing?"

"I don't know," I replied. My hand grazed the bottom of the drawer, brushing against a small cut out in the corner. "Maybe finding *this*." I pried it away. Held it up for Dustin to see. He took it from me, turning it over as I reached into the drawer again.

A small piece of paper sat inside. It was hastily torn in half. But from what we *did* have, it looked like Blake wrote down a number: one hundred.

"What does that mean?" I asked.

Dustin shook his head. "One hundred years of Ruin's End? You're the demon conspiracy theorist, right? What do *you* think it means?"

It could be anything. But if Blake was always at church, and he knew demons were real, maybe that narrowed the field down a little bit more.

I handed him the torn piece of paper while a giant bubble *blooped* in the aquarium. "Did Blake keep a Bible in here?"

"I don't know."

"Seriously?"

"What? It's not like I sneak into his room every time he's out of the house. Only Tuesdays and Thursdays."

Water bubbled furiously behind us. A pot that was about to boil.

"I think we should find a Bible. It might be a page number. Do you want to go—" I paused. The fish tank behind Dustin was filled with bubbles. The water slowly changed from clear to a deep red.

"Do I want to go where?" Dustin asked. I turned him around. "Whoa," he said, walking closer to it. "Did you drop food coloring in here when I wasn't looking? Kind of a mean trick to play, Scott—that could really hurt Blake's fish."

"I didn't do that."

"You sure? Maybe you wanted me to believe in the demon thing so badly that you decided to spice up your visit."

"I don't care if you believe me, I—" A harsh, metallic laugh cut me off as it scraped through the air. The crackle of flames sounded from the other side of the room. I grabbed Dustin's arm, wheeling him around so he had a clear view of what I saw: a fire slowly climbing up the frame to Blake's bed.

"You okay?" Dustin asked as I pulled him away from the flames. "The fish thing was funny for a second, but you're being weird now. This isn't cool."

"Do you see the fire?" I asked, hating how frayed my voice sounded.

"No. No, I don't. I think you should leave. Whatever you're doing is creeping me out. And not in a fun way."

"I'm not doing anything," I said, as my blood turned to ice.

"*It's always about* you, *isn't it*?" My father's voice crashed into the room, a rogue wave destroying anything that happened to cross its path.

I swallowed, backing up to Blake's desk. "No."

"No?" Dustin asked. "What's going—"

He didn't get to finish that sentence. The lights died, covering us in complete darkness.

Dustin applauded. "Wow, well done. Is Veronica helping

you out with this? Sal? You really had nothing better to do with your night than come here and mess with me?"

My hands twisted together. "I'm not doing this."

"*But it's happening* because *of you, isn't it? Why don't you tell him what you did to me, Cordelia? It doesn't matter what he thinks of you. Or does it?*"

A low growl filled the room.

Dustin stepped back. "This isn't funny, Scott."

"It's not," I whispered. My heart beat a frantic rhythm in my chest. Bile slowly rose in my throat, but I swallowed it back down. "We need to leave."

As if to punctuate my point, a light on the opposite side of the room burst. A shower of sparks rained down, exposing a shadowy silhouette of something that had to squat down to fit inside of the small space. The growl warped into a scream. The peal of metal folding in on itself, scratching and scraping until there was nothing left.

"You know how to make this right," my father added, as the flames grew higher. The wall of fire burned brightly, searing into my vision. *"You know what you have to do."*

"No." My voice was barely more than a whisper. "How are you here?"

"What?" Dustin asked.

Bright red eyes appeared where the silhouette's face should have been.

My stomach twisted into a billion knots. The aswang was here.

And so was my father.

Dustin grabbed my hand. "Do you see that?" he asked.

"The aswang or the fire?" I whispered back.

"What—"

The aswang roared, cutting him off. Screams threaded into the sound. Dustin winced, pulling me closer to the door. "Are you ready to run?"

But I didn't answer him. Couldn't. My father's light blue eyes stared back at me from the flames. *"Well? What are you going to do, kiddo?"*

The monster behind us roared.

I squeezed Dustin's hand. "Go."

He yanked me through the door to the secret passageway, screaming "What the hell is that?" as we darted through the tunnel and back into the study. He held his hand out for me, wrenching me into the room with him.

The light in the secret passage should've made the aswang easier to see. But it was still a sharp silhouette. Long lines, serrated claws, hard edges. Bones cracked behind us as it roared again. The sound morphed into something different this time. Not a vulture's screech, or a scream that sounded too close to being human. This was thunderous. Angry. Like a big cat was trapped in a small space with us.

My heart pounded. It wasn't just from our sprint down the passageway.

The aswang growled again. Dustin screamed. I joined him shortly after. Pushed him out of the way, getting a good look at the creature as I slammed the secret passage shut behind us.

I was right. It turned into a big cat. From the short glimpse I caught, it was a jaguar with bright red eyes and fangs that were ready to rip us apart.

Dustin stood there, watching the whole wall shake as the monster barreled into the locked secret passageway.

"Remember when you made fun of the aswang?" I asked, gesturing to the wall. "Still think it's a silly story now?"

Whatever color was left in Dustin's pale skin drained away. I tried pulling him into the hallway, but he didn't move. I bit back a scream. If we didn't move, we'd *both* get our throats ripped out by that thing, and that wasn't on my to-do list for today.

"Dustin," I snapped, shaking him. "Run. Now." Relief and adrenaline mixed together, filling my body with a strange cocktail of emotions as Dustin took a few steps back. I tugged him into the hallway, dragging him along as I broke into a run.

"That's not gonna hold it forever," I shouted between breaths. "We need to get to your car."

Something I said finally snapped him out of it. "How long do you think that wall will hold it?" he shot back, wrenching his hand out of my grasp as he took the lead. "How strong is that thing?"

It took Fred down without breaking a sweat. Telling him that wouldn't really help, though. "We should hurry," I replied. "Before—"

The aswang burst through the study door and into the hallway. Its roar shook the giant crystal chandelier hanging above us.

"Too late," Dustin said, grabbing my arm. "Move faster or it's gonna catch us."

As if to emphasize his statement, a side table flew past us and crashed into the wall.

Dustin groaned. "That's gonna be a bitch to explain to my parents."

"Whine later," I screamed, forcing myself to move faster. "Run now."

We ran past way too many taxidermized animals to count on our way out of Dustin's McMansion. Adrenaline pushed me forward. Once it wore off, every muscle in my legs would punish me for the rest of my life.

The night's fresh, crisp winter air hit me like a train when we stepped outside. Dustin pulled his keys out of his pocket, starting his Mercedes with one click.

Rich people.

We jumped into his car. He floored it out of his cobblestone driveway. The aswang stumbled out of his house, roaring.

"That was—" Dustin paused, catching his breath as we sped back to town.

"Terrifying? Straight out of a movie? Really weird?"

"—fucking awesome!" —he punched the air— "woo!"

"Seriously?"

A genuine smile lit up his whole face. Or the profile of his face, anyway. It was hard to see the whole thing from the passenger's seat. "You didn't tell me demons were so much fun."

I wanted to scream. "They're not. And that wasn't a demon, for the record. That was just the opening act."

Of course he'd think the aswang chasing after us was cool. He wasn't being haunted by the Hell-specter of a father he condemned to eternal damnation or having frequent nightmares about getting his throat ripped out.

I wished I lived in semi-ignorant bliss like him.

"Whatever. Doesn't matter what it was. That was so cool!" Once we got out of the woods around his house, he slowed to a stop at a light. "Wait. Where are we going?"

"Monday Night Karaoke," I said, checking the mirror to make sure the aswang—or my father—wasn't following us. Though I hadn't seen any sign of David Scott since we ran out of Blake's bedroom, the fact that I could see him at all was troubling.

Fred thought my connection to him existed because part of my soul was in Hell. But he'd given that back to me. I shouldn't have been able to see him anymore. And yet, there he was, reminding me that I was the one who sealed his fate.

Maybe Blake would have an answer to that, too.

"Do you seriously want to sing at a time like this?" Dustin asked, as the light turned green. "Damn, you really are a theater kid."

The urge to smack someone on the back of the head had never been stronger than in that moment. "No, Dustin," I replied, rolling my eyes. "I need answers from your brother. And I'm not leaving until I get them."

CHAPTER NINETEEN

IN WHICH I THROW A WISH IN THE WELL

I NEVER THOUGHT I'D WILLINGLY LET DUSTIN JONES drive me anywhere. But here I was, sitting in his car for the second time today, barely making it through yellow lights as he raced toward The Coffee Spot.

"You doing okay?" Dustin asked, breaking through the comfortable silence that I'd allowed to form around us.

I startled in the passenger's seat. "What?"

"You look like you're gonna throw up."

"I'm not."

"If you do, roll the window down and stick your head out of the car."

"Wow."

"What? It's easier to clean it off the outside than the inside." He said it like he'd had experience with this. I wasn't gonna go searching for that story.

I groaned as my phone rang. Veronica was calling me. A wave of nausea rolled through me as I stared at the name on my screen.

"You gonna answer that?" Dustin asked.

"No," I replied.

"You sure?"

"No."

Dustin whistled as we breezed through another yellow light. "Okay then. Anything you wanna talk about?"

Well, that was a loaded question. We could discuss how complicated things were between me and Veronica, and how they got even worse with what Jesse did at rehearsal. Or Fred's radio silence when I asked him for help. My father rising up from Hell to torment me, even though I got my soul back. The aswang that was still around. And the freaking demon I needed to trap in a Precious Moments Maleficent.

I crossed my arms, staring straight ahead. "You said it best yourself. We're not friends."

He swallowed. "No. I guess we're not."

"Why do you care, anyway?"

"I don't." He sighed as he finally met a yellow light that he couldn't beat. "But, if I did, I'd wonder how you got involved with the whole demon thing in the first place."

"What can I say?" I shrugged. "I watch a lot of horror movies."

"Right. An aswang just wrecked the ground floor of my house *after* you found a random number that my brother—who's always thought that our family *did* make a deal with some demons to create our town—just hid in his room and *that's* the best you can do?"

"Yes." Part of me wanted to talk to him about it. But the rest of me still wasn't sure I could trust him with it. This was the same guy who'd gotten his parents to buy his way into the lead of every show so that he could spend more time with Veronica. He'd ambushed me in the woods a few days ago and spilled my coffee without remorse.

Sure, we were chased out of his house by an aswang and made it out of there alive. But being through one scary thing together didn't mean every shitty thing he'd ever done was wiped away.

Whatever was left of Dustin's good mood fell away a little at my non-answer.

"You can't do that," he said, pulling into The Coffee Spot's parking lot.

"Do what?"

"Use me to get into my brother's room and then throw me away. I want in on whatever you're doing."

I frowned. "You don't exactly have a solid track record of being the most supportive person. And you were using me, too. I needed access to Blake, and you needed a friend. I think it's best if we go our separate ways now. Don't you?"

"Barry said I had to learn how to be a team player," Dustin said softly, as I opened the passenger's side door.

"What?" I lingered in his car.

"I can't change what I did," he said, looking at me. "Or how I acted. But maybe Barry's onto something—and Blake too, other than the whole 'demons founded the town' thing, I mean. I could be better. I could try."

I shouldn't have been suspicious. But I was. "Why would you want to do that?"

Dustin shrugged. "It's nice having someone to talk to who actually talks back. Reginald is fun, but he's kind of a dull conversationalist."

I laughed, in spite of myself. "Really? I would've thought Reginald never shut up."

We both laughed, then stopped abruptly when we realized what we were doing. It was weird and confusing. But not entirely repulsive.

Maybe that was what it was like to be vague friends with Dustin.

The wind picked up around us, ushering us inside. The Coffee Spot's warmth washed over me as we left the cold winter air behind. There weren't usually this many people on a Monday night in April, when the weather was slowly getting nice enough to linger outside without regretting the decision, but the long winter we'd endured must have gotten to everyone.

Despite Barry's encouraging reminder to get some rest, two-thirds of the cast, and most of the show's crew, were jam-packed inside. Three-quarters of our freshman choir—which was at least fifty people—were crammed into the small café as well. A crowd fought their way to the DJ's table.

I touched Dustin's arm. "Do you see Blake?" He had a good foot and a half on me, height-wise, so he had a way better shot of finding his brother.

"Nope. Not at the counter. I can check his office, if you want to check the back room."

"Got it."

The poor baristas manning the event gave each other uneasy glances as Dustin and I crashed through a few sopranos. A chill ran down my spine at the singers' murderous gazes. They did *not* like being moved aside. In that moment, it felt like if they could find a way to kill me and get away with it, they would have.

Sure, a demon and an aswang were terrifying, but a soprano would send someone to Hell and not feel guilty about it at all.

I scurried past them, desperate to not be taken out by the choir department's baby divas. Dustin's blond head threaded through the crowd a few feet in front of me. It was hard to tell, but the back room was open, allowing for a bit of overflow. Which the place definitely needed tonight.

I pushed my way past the karaoke stage, not bothering to look at who was up there as the opening bars to John Legend's "All of Me" started playing. The singer smoothly ran through the first verse. I froze. I'd recognize those dulcet tones anywhere.

"This one's for you, Cordelia," Jesse said into the mic.

My whole body stiffened as someone nearby sighed, "How romantic."

Dustin dry heaved. "Gross."

My hands balled into fists. He was still trying to pretend that we were something. Messing with my life for no reason, other than his weird feud with Fred.

Dustin grabbed my arm, dragging me away from the stage before I could jump up there and punch Jesse. "We can't talk to Blake if you get arrested for assault. Hit him *after* we get the intel. And maybe do it outside. Less witnesses that way."

He was right, but I kind of hated him for it. I tried spotting Veronica in the crowd—to explain that I had no idea what was happening—but she was probably swallowed up by the sea of unforgiving sopranos. I didn't like how we'd left things in my car—and, with Jesse weirdly declaring his love for me every five seconds, we were overdue for another talk. But I wouldn't be able to find her like this. There were too many people.

"Text me if you find anything," I said, moving toward the back room. "I have something I need to do."

"But what about our mission?" Dustin asked.

"Still important," I replied, waving him away.

Dustin disappeared down the hallway that led to his brother's office. I pushed through the crowd, getting into the back room as Jesse finished his song. Sal sat at a nearby table. They had on a light pink long-sleeved shirt, a silver vest, and black jeans. Matching silver bracelets hugged their wrists, clinking together as they flagged me over.

I shoved my hands into my pockets as I moved toward them. Between rehearsal and getting run out of Dustin's house by a demon, I hadn't changed out of my usual, boring school outfit of jeans and a hoodie. A quick glance in a nearby mirror revealed the horrifying fact that my dark hair was disheveled and out of place. I smoothed it down as I stopped at Sal's table.

"Cordy," they said, pulling me into a hug. "We weren't sure you were gonna show."

"Neither was I."

"You can join us, if you want. We just need to find you a chair."

Veronica's bag sat in the seat next to Sal. Jesse's was next to hers.

The good news: she was here, somewhere. The bad news: Jesse had time to tell her things when I wasn't around.

"I'm good," I said, even though I wasn't. "I'm actually looking for Blake. Have you seen him?"

"Nope. It's hard to find anyone in this crowd, though."

They were right. I'd gone back here hoping to find Veronica, but it was still impossible to pick anyone out. The back room wasn't as bad as the main one, but everyone in here was packed together like sardines. Humidity, the aroma of espresso, and messy theater kid hormones thickly filled the air.

"Thanks, Sal. I'll see you later."

"Hey, Cordy?"

"Yeah?"

"For what it's worth, I think Veronica really wants to talk to you. She doesn't seem mad. Just . . . really sad."

I nodded. "I really need to talk to her, too. I've gotta go, but—thanks. Really."

They winked at me. "Don't mention it."

"Veronica Dominguez," the DJ said. "Come on down!"

Well. That was one way to find her. I hurried out of the back room. Wove through the crowd on my way to the stage. Jesse stood off to the side, as if he was waiting for me.

"Cordy," Jesse said, grabbing onto my arm as Veronica walked up the steps and onto the stage. "Think about what you want to do here. I could make things very unpleasant for her."

Veronica pulled the mic off its stand, scanning the crowd. Her whole face lit up when she saw me, but it died down quickly as she caught Jesse holding onto my arm.

"This goes out to a special someone who deserves the world," Veronica said. "One day, maybe I can give it to her." Her voice rebounded around the room as the name of the song flashed on the screen:

"Call Me Maybe" by Carly Rae Jepsen.

Dustin groaned so loud I could hear it through the crowd. He hovered by the hallway near his brother's office, mouthing *Really? Right now?* to me.

The opening bars to the song started. A few scattered rounds of applause rippled through the audience. Butterflies slammed into my chest, almost as frantic as my heartbeat.

Veronica dedicated this song to me. We used to perform it all the time together when it first came out. We even used it on Deal Day seven years ago, when we tried summoning a demon, just like every other poor soul in Ruin's End. Thankfully, out of the two of us, I was the only one who succeeded. Otherwise, Veronica would've been turned into a monster.

Like me.

"That's my leading lady," Sal called from the back. Words flashed on the screen. Veronica cleared her throat.

I threw a wish in the well, don't ask me, I'll never tell, Veronica sang. *I looked at you as it fell, and now you're in my way.* She took a deep breath, continuing on with the first verse. *I'd trade my soul for a wish*—which was all too real—*pennies and dimes for a kiss, I wasn't looking for this, but now you're in my way.*

"Choose your next move carefully," Jesse hissed.

I yanked my arm out of his grasp. "Try something, and I'll find a way to rip your heart out," I growled.

He let go, smiling. "There's the fire I was looking for. Break a leg," he whispered in my ear. Typically, in the theater world, that was a way to wish someone good luck. But the way he said it, it sounded like a threat.

Or a promise.

How nice.

I meant what I said, though. I was done running. If this was Veronica's way of reaching out for me, I wasn't going to leave her alone.

I stumbled to the stage as scattered applause peppered the

crowd. I cleared my throat, leaning into the mic. Maybe this was a mistake. But there was no going back now.

I grabbed the other mic and sang, *Hot night, wind was blowin', where you think you're going, baby?*

She pulled me into a hug as the opening chords to the chorus swelled.

Hey, I just met you, we sang together, *and this is crazy, but here's my number, so call me, maybe!*

Whistles and cheers spilled through the crowd. Sal gave me a thumbs-up. If I knew how to levitate, I would've floated off the stage. I smiled, unable to contain the happiness that bubbled up in my chest.

And all the other boys try to chase me, but here's my number, so call me maybe!

The crowd clapped and cheered as we went into the next verse. Jesse disappeared somewhere around the second chorus, but I didn't care. Veronica and I were up there singing with each other. For a few blissful moments, demons and Hell and the aswang weren't filling me with anxiety. It was just her and me, together. The way it always should have been.

Before you came into my life, I missed you so bad, we sang. Veronica's hand slid into mine as I caught sight of Dustin. He wove through the crowd and to the back door, following someone taller and blonder outside.

Blake.

I stepped close to the edge of the stage. Veronica reached out, pulling me closer to her. She leaned in so she could get picked up by my mic.

I missed you so bad, she sang. *I missed you so, so bad.*

The back door swung shut behind Dustin and Blake. The

piece of paper with 'one hundred' written on it weighed heavily in my pocket. I was here to figure out what that meant. To find a way to trap a demon in four days without getting myself killed in the process. Not to stand on a stage and sing with my best friend. It didn't matter how much fun I was having, or that Veronica and I were finally on the same page about something.

Veronica was a distraction that I couldn't afford to have.

I missed you so bad, Veronica sang. *And you should know that—*

"I'm sorry," I said, regretting the words with my whole heart as the orchestra soared.

I jumped off the stage, pushing through the crowd. This was the second time in as many days that I ran away from her. A deep, unending sorrow tore through me as I made my way to the back of the café.

Hopefully she'd find a way to forgive me once I got my shit together.

I didn't mean to hurt Veronica. But I couldn't wait for answers any longer. Once Blake and I figured out how to trap Jesse, everything would go back to normal. I wasn't sure if I'd be able to explain everything to her, but once I could, I wanted to try.

The Coffee Spot's back door closed slowly behind me, muffling Veronica's solo karaoke run. All I wanted to do was turn around, charge up to the stage, and keep singing with her—but that was never going to happen. Not until I survived the town's one-hundredth Deal Day, at least.

The wooden porch creaked as I stepped onto it.

"Drop it, Dustin," Blake said, his voice carried over by the crisp spring wind as I crept forward. The two brothers stood about a hundred feet away, halfway between The Coffee Spot and the woods. "I'm not talking about this anymore."

I moved closer to their conversation. Blake's back was toward me, but Dustin met my gaze before settling back on his brother.

"Something attacked us in the house," Dustin replied.

"Us? Who else was with you?"

"Hi Blake." I jogged up to them, answering his question.

If there'd been a moon in the sky, its beams would have shone down on him. Cast him in an eerie glow. Made a spectacle of the bloom of angry red spreading across his pale face. But the sky held no moon. No light. His anger was a contained thing. Something boiled and stuffed into his sharp, precise movements as he pointed to The Coffee Spot.

"Go inside. This doesn't concern you."

"It does. We found the paper you hid, with the number on it—"

"I told you to stay out of it," Blake roared. It was a different sound from what I was used to. Not the kind that threatened to tear my throat out. Or the way my father's calm, menacing thoughts always simmered right beneath the surface.

No.

This was righteous anger. Judgment that sang through my bones as if it was handed down directly from God. Something Blake reserved for the monster that dragged his little brother into a world of demons and murder.

"I'm sorry." I couldn't look at him as I said the words. "I know you're mad. But we don't have time for that. I need answers—"

"You should have kept him out of it," Blake snapped at me.

"Demons are dangerous."

Dustin shook his head. "No, demons are awesome."

Blake opened his mouth to reply, but someone slow clapped behind me, cutting him off.

"You should listen to your little brother, Blake," Jesse Smithe said with a booming laugh. My blood turned to ice at the sound of his voice. "Demons," Jesse continued, "are definitely awesome."

CHAPTER TWENTY

IN WHICH DEMONS ARE DEFINITELY NOT AWESOME

I HAD NO IDEA HOW TO USE MY KALIS YET, BUT IN THAT moment, I wished I hadn't left my family's badass sword at home. Not that I'd be able to do anything with it, but damn. It would have made me feel better about staring down a demon with nothing but Blake and Dustin Jones to help me.

"What the hell are you doing here?" Dustin asked. An odd sort of fury flared up in his words. I'd seen Dustin lose his temper a lot, but this felt different. Like he wasn't necessarily in control. "Shouldn't you be in there, winning over the crowd? Letting them adore you for the perfect performer you are?"

I grabbed his arm. Pulled him behind me. "Chill out," I muttered. "Not the fight you want to pick."

"You should listen to her," Jesse said. "She seems to have a good head on her shoulders."

I wanted to scream. He was the reason my life was falling apart, and he was being such a smug asshole about it.

"Cordelia." Blake's tone was calm. Even. "Stop."

I froze. I'd taken a few steps forward, so that I was closer to Jesse than I was to Dustin. I backed up. I wasn't sure if I chose to do that, or the demon made me move. Either way, I was getting too close for comfort.

Blake moved in front of us. He pulled a small crucifix from his coat pocket, holding it up in front of him. "Your tricks won't work here, demon."

"Demon?" Dustin asked. I held onto his arm. Shook my head.

"Demon," Jesse confirmed. He ran a hand through his neatly tousled brown hair. "Sorry we haven't gotten to chat sooner, Blake. I know you've been eager to find me. But I had a few things to do first. You know how it goes."

"Unclean spirit," Blake said, stepping even closer to Jesse. The crucifix shook in his hand, but his voice held steady. Jesse took a few steps back as Blake continued. "In the name of the Father, Son, and the Holy Spirit, I command you to return from whence you came—"

Jesse laughed, cutting him off. "God has no power here. Only me. Besides, there's no leaving this thing." He held his arms out. "This is who I am. Or a version of myself, at least. You can try your little exorcism tricks until you're blue in the face. Not gonna make a difference at all."

"I know," Blake said, smirking. "You just weren't in the right spot yet." He took out a lighter. Clicked the small flame to life. And dropped it in the grass.

"Whoa," Dustin said, pulling me away from the fire that arced around Jesse. It spread in a circle, with small lines and symbols searing into the ground around him. "Blake, what the—"

Jesse cracked his knuckles, barking out a laugh as he dodged the flames. "How smart of you to try a sigil. You forgot one thing though, rich boy," he said, smirking. "Fires can be put out." He stomped down on some of the flames by his feet. Reached down and dug into the earth, throwing a handful onto more of the fire. "Next time you try to put me in a little cage, you'll have to do better."

Jesse looked over at me. "Can you believe this guy?" He waved his hand toward Blake, who started reciting the Lord's Prayer. "Still trying it, even though he knows it's useless. I can't be cast out of this body. I can't be contained." He gestured to himself. "I can't help it if I'm perfect."

"Perfectly fucked up," I muttered.

Jesse's ire turned to me. "What was that?" he asked sharply.

"Hallowed—" Blake said, cutting in before I could reply. But he didn't get to finish the next line. It was like an invisible hand picked him up and tossed him aside. He was nothing more than an old McDonald's wrapper that wasn't worthy of being thrown away properly.

Dustin winced next to me. He called out to his brother, trying to run over to him. But he'd have to pass Jesse to do it. I didn't trust the demon to let Dustin run by without getting hurt. So, I grabbed onto his arm and held him in place.

"That's better," Jesse said, turning his attention to us. "It's hard to concentrate with all that babbling. Wouldn't you agree?"

My whole body shook with rage. After everything he'd done, he was trying to be *friends* with me?

"Go to Hell," I said.

Jesse chuckled. "Oh, maybe one day. I have a friend down there that I've been meaning to visit. I think you know him."

Dustin stopped fighting me. "What's he talking about?"

"Not now," I muttered, backing us up. Jesse's words stung, but I didn't want him to see that he'd hurt me. I couldn't let Dustin find out what I did.

No one could know.

Out of the corner of my eye, Blake slowly pushed himself off the ground. All I had to do was stall Jesse until Blake started praying again. Then we could make a run for it.

I didn't like the idea of backing down without a fight. But I had no weapon and no idea how to trap him. If I wanted to make it to Friday, we had to run.

"Oh, I think now is the *perfect* time to discuss your past, Cordelia," Jesse continued. "Did you *really* think word of what you'd done wouldn't spread among my kind? It was an impressive thing for a child to do. Even if the demon who assisted you was subpar. Really, you should've come to me. You went through all that trouble of trying to strike a bargain with me on Deal Day, and instead you choose to work with my pathetic former apprentice."

"What's he talking about?" Dustin asked.

"I—" I started to reply, but Jesse's laugh cut me off.

"But now you have a chance to make everything right. We don't have a lot of time left before the next Deal Day. So, I have a proposition for you. I'd like *you* to have the honor of being my one-hundredth deal. You're the one that got away, after all."

"No thanks, asshole," I shot back. "I'm good."

Jesse clicked his tongue. "You'd be doing me a *favor*. You don't know how hard it's been for me—laughed out of all my demonic social circles because I lost such a powerful soul to someone else. You have the chance to right all of your wrongs. I want to help you with that."

"No," I replied, though it came out as barely more than a whisper. "I don't need your help."

"Oh, but you do," he said, summoning his own flames. They surged up, creating a wall between Blake and me, and died down in the blink of an eye. "You're an amusing one. So lost. Confused. You pretend to be so ashamed of what you've done, but some small part of you is also proud. Relieved. And would gladly do it again, if you had to."

I bit the inside of my cheek, taking another step away from the demon. He was right about one thing—if I had to do it again, I would. Even if my life hadn't been magically fixed when I sent my father to Hell, I still *had* a life. He was ready to take that away from me. Just like Jesse.

"I'm nothing like him," I spat back. "You're wrong."

Jesse's smile stretched too widely. "Face it, *kiddo*. You're a monster. Just like your old man."

Rage simmered under the surface of my skin, setting my whole body on fire. I lunged for the demon, striking out at the air only to be yanked back by a sweaty hand that wrapped around my arm. I snarled, trying to wriggle out of Dustin's grasp. My father used to call me kiddo all the time. He did it right before he tried strangling me.

That son of a bitch was taunting me.

"Leave them alone," Blake growled, moving between me and Jesse.

Dustin tugged on my arm. "We need to go."

"No," I snapped back. A few seconds ago, I wanted to run. But that wasn't going to help Blake. Or stop Jesse.

"Cordy," Dustin whispered, "you can't hurt him. Let Blake handle it."

I shook my head, anger giving way to adrenaline as my heart beat frantically. "I need to trap him."

"I don't know what that means," Dustin said, "and it doesn't matter. We're leaving."

He tried pulling me away, but I let go of his hand. Dustin broke into a run. He only made it a few steps before Jesse looked up, grinning like a wolf about to enjoy the hunt.

"Humans," Jesse said, as Blake kept loudly praying, "so predictable."

A shadow that'd been perched on The Coffee Spot's roof sprang to life. The silhouette of a vulture became sharper as it soared into view. I balled my hands back into fists, ready to fight the aswang.

But it wasn't flying toward me.

Dustin looked up, screaming as its talons sank into his shoulders. It picked him up, wings flapping furiously.

The aswang dropped Dustin a few feet from the ground. It was close enough that he wouldn't break anything, but he'd definitely bruise in the morning. He crashed into the dirt. Wheezed as he tried to catch his breath.

The aswang stood next to Dustin, as if it was guarding him. It stared at me with bright red eyes that matched Jesse's.

"Hey," Blake snapped, throwing the lighter at Jesse. "You don't remember me, do you?" Behind his back, Blake waved at me as he continued. "But I remember you. I was there the day you killed him."

A smile curled at the corners of Jesse's mouth. "Oh yes. Liam Jones. What a shame he passed away so suddenly. Sometimes heart attacks just" —he snapped his fingers— "happen."

Blake grabbed his chest, screaming as he crumpled to the ground.

"Do you *ever* shut up?" Jesse asked. He waved lazily at Blake.

The skin under his nose stretched out, covering his mouth. Blake's eyes widened as he looked at Dustin. His younger brother stood there, completely frozen, too terrified to even scream.

Jesse clapped. "That's what I like to see!" He knelt down next to Blake and Dustin. "Now, I need to teach one of you a lesson because I'm not allowed to touch dear, sweet Cordelia. At least, not right now."

What the hell did that mean? Maybe he'd learned his lesson from a couple of nights ago, and he knew I was wearing my mom's rosary.

The aswang shifted. Jesse continued as if he didn't notice. "So, which one will it be? The saintly Catholic Crusader who *really* thought he could avenge his dearly departed grandfather with a little bit of well-placed gasoline? Or the annoying brat who couldn't sing his way out of a paper bag?"

"Rude," Dustin muttered.

"Leave them alone," I yelled.

"Oh, Cordelia," Jesse said, smiling at me. "No. Not unless you agree to my proposal: become my one-hundredth deal, and I'll let them go."

Even if I believed he'd set them free—which I didn't—there was no way in hell I was going to make another deal. I'd just gotten the missing piece of my soul back. Besides, I didn't want to create more towns like ours. One Ruin's End was more than enough.

I flipped him off. He shrugged. "Suit yourself. I have an even better idea anyway." He turned to the aswang. "It's your lucky day, dear. Dealer's choice."

The aswang screeched. Folded up its wings as its red eyes darted from Blake to Dustin.

"No," I said, stepping closer to all of them. The aswang hadn't tried to hurt me yet. I could try to get through to whoever it was. "You don't have to do this," I said, moving closer to the monster. "I don't know who you are, but I think you might be someone like me. Maybe you didn't mean to get mixed up with him, but you did, and you think there's no way out."

The aswang tilted its head. Watching me. "You don't have to do everything he tells you," I said, almost within arm's reach of the thing. "Especially if you don't want to. There's always another way."

Jesse whistled. "Wow. How inspirational. It's not enough, I'm afraid. The clock is ticking, my shapeshifting friend. Choose a brother to dismember. *Now.*"

The aswang's gaze shifted from me to Blake and Dustin.

"I'm waiting," Jesse said.

The aswang blinked. Its red eyes turned pitch black. Its wings fluttered open. Wind gusted around us as it lifted up into the sky, flying away.

I waited until it was almost out of sight before I mimicked Jesse's whistle. "Looks like Blake wasn't the only one who talked too much."

Jesse glared up at the aswang's retreating form. "If you leave," he yelled after it, "our deal is off. You'll be stuck like that forever." The aswang paused for a moment, hovering above us. And then it flapped its wings, soaring over the woods.

I smirked. "Good help is so hard to find, isn't it?" My smug expression fell away when Jesse turned back to face me. He was smiling.

"You know," he said, wolf's grin distorting his handsome features, "you're right. Good help *is* hard to find. And I think you need a little extra encouragement to agree to my little bargain. So. I hope you'll *love* my next trick."

"What—" I started to say, but the ground shook beneath my feet.

"Oh shit," Dustin said, tightening his grip on my arm. He pulled me back as a huge chasm appeared in the semi-frozen grass, right where I'd been standing.

Fire erupted from the gash in the ground. Ice froze the blood in my veins.

The demon didn't need to hold me in place. Fear was doing a good enough job of that.

Jesse clicked his tongue. "I *wish* you could see the look on your face. It's priceless! I'm sure you know what's coming, so let's not delay the inevitable. David Scott," Jesse said, putting on his best game-show announcer voice, "Come on down! Or, up, I guess!"

Smoke rose up around the fire, obscuring it. A silhouette slowly rose up, illuminated by the flames. Orange eyes watched me from behind the inferno. They burned with a hatred that felt familiar. I'd carried the same feeling around in my heart for as long as I could remember.

"What is that?" Dustin asked, his voice coming out as nothing more than a whisper.

"My father," I replied.

Jesse applauded. "Very *good*! Gold star for you! Back from his unexpected stint in *Florida*, please welcome David Scott to our lovely little production."

The flames died down. My father stood in front of me,

looking exactly as he had the day he died. My heart pounded so loudly that it was the only thing I could hear. I took a few deep breaths, trying to steady myself, but I reached back for Dustin and held his hand.

This was impossible. The world spun around me as I fought to stay standing. Adrenaline shot through my body again, screaming at my legs to start moving.

I wanted to run. To collapse. Scream. Cry. Seeing him in glimpses was hard enough.

But now, he was here. He was *back*.

"I've made one big adjustment," Jesse said, gesturing to my father. "He's a bit stronger than before. If you want to get rid of him, a simple banishing won't do. I'm afraid you and your little demon friend will have to get a little more creative. That is, if your father doesn't kill him first. Or you could take my deal. The choice is yours, Cordelia Scott." Jesse paused, his gaze drifting over to Blake. "In the meantime, though, let's have a little fun. Hey, David? Could you take care of that one for me? The one with the skin covering his mouth. He's annoying me."

My father nodded, slowly moving toward Blake.

"No," Dustin screamed, trying to push past me.

It was as if the world had been moving in slow motion, only to snap back into place as Dustin broke free of my grasp. I reached out, holding him back as my father picked Blake up by his collar and shoved him against a tree. He held Blake there, and even though Dustin's older brother did his best to break free, he was no match against my father.

"We need to run," I said, pulling Dustin away.

"No!" Dustin shouted. "We have to help him!"

"We can't," I replied quietly.

"Now, pay attention," Jesse said, gesturing to Blake. "*Someone* has to learn that there are consequences to their actions."

My father pulled his hand back, as if winding up for a pitch. Threw it forward with so much force that it could've plunged straight through someone's chest.

And it did.

My father ripped Blake's heart cleanly out of his chest.

Dustin screamed as Blake slumped down the tree's trunk. Blood oozed out of Blake's open wound. His body twitched. His muffled screams died before they got the chance to make much of a sound.

Dustin collapsed, wailing. I tried to pull him back but couldn't move him.

Panic fluttered in my chest as my father stood above us. Smiling.

"Well," Jesse said, as my father dropped Blake's heart at Dustin's feet. "Looks like we're done here. For now, at least. Behave yourself, Cordelia. Otherwise, dear old dad might be disappointed in you. And you know what happens when he's disappointed."

My father knelt down next to me, lifting my chin so that I had to look him in his new, bright orange eyes. He didn't say anything. But he didn't have to.

I screamed. He let go of me, standing and striding over to the demon who raised him from Hell.

Jesse saluted me. "This has been *such* a fun time, Cordelia. I'm sure we'll meet again soon."

They walked into the woods, silhouettes vanishing in the darkness.

Dustin clutched Blake's lifeless body, crying into his brother's hair.

"I'm sorry," I said, but I wasn't sure if he could hear me over his sobbing.

I tried to hold Dustin's hand, to give him some kind of comfort, but he wrenched it away from me.

Blake was dead. My father was back from Hell.

And it was all my fault.

CHAPTER TWENTY-ONE

IN WHICH I TRY TO FIGHT A DEMON . . . AGAIN.

I TRIED STAYING WITH DUSTIN AFTER THE PARAMEDICS came, but he wouldn't talk to me. Not that I could blame him. I didn't want to talk to me, either. I wasn't the one who killed Blake. I didn't rip his heart out of his chest. But my father did, and now David Scott was back—and a demon—all because of me.

Because I didn't agree to be Jesse's one-hundredth deal.

Well. At least that was one mystery solved. We knew who he was targeting for Deal Day.

Me.

My hands twisted together as I waited for my ride to show up. If it were any other night, I'd be able to drive myself home. But my car was still in the school's parking lot and Veronica hadn't answered any of my calls or texts. I had to wait in front of The Coffee Spot in the dark like a sitting duck. I wasn't too worried that my father would try anything there, though. There were still too many people running around, trying to make sense of Blake's death.

Now that he was out of Hell, there were only two places he'd go: the hospital, to find Mom, or our home, to wait for me.

I wasn't going to take any chances.

I pulled out my phone, dialing the only number I'd committed to memory: Diane's line. She was the supervising nurse in my mom's hospital ward. When I was younger, I used to call Diane all the time to see when my mom was coming home—even though I always had her schedule memorized. My check-ins with Diane became less frequent after my father left, but I still did it every now and then to see how she was doing.

I held my breath as the phone rang once. Twice.

"Diane Johnson," she said, picking up on the third ring.

I exhaled. "Hey, Diane. It's Cordy."

"Cordelia!" she chirped, dropping her business voice and switching it out to something much warmer. "How are you doing, dear? Are you all right? It's a bit late to be calling."

"Yeah. I'm . . . okay," I said, not doing a good job of selling the lie. "How's my mom doing?"

There were two seconds too many of hesitation on Diane's end. As if she was weighing whether or not to ask me more questions. But that was the great thing about Diane. She never did.

Diane sighed. "I see her right now, actually. She's down the hall entering something into her workstation. Do you want me to pass anything along to her?"

"No," I replied, maybe a little too quickly. I took another deep breath, allowing relief to soften my heartbeat. "Keep an eye on her, okay?"

"I always do."

"Thanks, Diane." I hung up and put the phone back in my pocket and stared out into the dark expanse of trees around me. The light from The Coffee Spot's front porch extended a few feet into the tree line, but after that it was absorbed into a bleak nothingness.

Everything else might be falling apart, but at least my mom was safe. As long as she stayed in the hospital, there were security guards, other nurses, and doctors that could protect her—or provide enough of a public shield to deter him.

My father never did anything to us when other people were around. That would ruin his image. While it was still a possibility that he could try to get to her at work, it was way more likely that he'd wait for us both to get home and continue torturing us where he left off.

Unfortunately for him, I wasn't going to let that happen.

A sleek, black BMW sedan pulled up in front of me. Its tinted passenger side window *whirred* as it rolled down. Fred kept his sunglasses on despite the darkness outside. He tilted his head, looking over them to see me. His Nightmare Deer eyes caught mine before I looked away.

"Well?" he asked.

I ground my teeth together. After everything I'd been through, all he could say was *well?* He hadn't even been my first call for help. I tried to find Veronica and Sal, but by the time they dispersed the crowd at The Coffee Spot, they were both gone. Considering the way Fred and I left things, I was surprised he showed up at all. But if he was gonna be angsty about this late-night pickup, I wasn't sure I wanted his help at all.

I yanked the door open, got inside, and slammed it. Fred frowned, speeding away.

"Do you know what time it is, Cordelia?" he yawned. "I was just catching up on *The Bachelorette*—"

"Blake's dead." The words fell out of my mouth with barbed edges. I didn't think I'd be able to say it so easily. But there it was, plain as day. Well. Night.

"Who's that?" Fred replied, flatly.

It was like someone took a knife and carved out a hollow spot in my chest. The emptiness spread, sprawling out into the darkness around us. "Dustin's older brother," I replied. "He brought food to our tech rehearsals?"

"Oh," Fred said, hitting his forehead lightly, "the Catholic one."

I hit the dashboard. Blake was just murdered, and he wasn't taking any of this seriously. Maybe he still felt awkward about how everything went down at Jesse's house. Or how he acted in his office afterward. But that wasn't an excuse for how terrible he was being right now.

Anger simmered right beneath the surface of my skin. It yearned to break free. Rip me apart so that it had a chance of doing the same to Fred. He hadn't taught me how to fight a demon yet, but that was all I wanted to do. Lash out and burn the world down until there was nothing left.

"Cordelia—" he started to say, but I cut him off with a glare.

"Pull over," I said.

"No."

"Now!" I snapped, shoving him. It wasn't the smartest move. The car swerved a bit on the road. Thankfully, no one else was around. Fred sighed before he finally gave in and pulled over.

I threw the passenger's door open and bolted out of the

car—but Fred was quicker. He stood in front of me, watching. Waiting to see what I would do.

Well. There was no use in delaying things.

I stomped down hard on his foot. He grunted from the pain, stumbling back. There were a few decent-sized rocks lying around on the side of the road. I picked one up and lobbed it right at his head. He dodged it. It flew into the trees behind him. For the second time that night, I wished I had my kalis. I didn't know how to use it—and I wasn't going to stab him through the heart—but that didn't matter. I wanted to pretend that I knew what I was doing. Needed the illusion that I wasn't useless.

I did everything I could to make sure no one would die, and it still wasn't good enough.

I wasn't good enough.

Tears streamed down my face. I ran at Fred, blurred vision making that more difficult than it should have been.

"Cordelia," Fred said, firmer this time. He reached out. Grabbed my shoulders when I got close enough. He held me an arm's length away as he said, "Talking might be more productive than—"

But he didn't get to finish that sentence. I kicked out, hitting him right in his crotch. He doubled over. Let go of me as he wheezed from the pain.

My chest heaved. I fought to catch my breath as Fred fought to stay standing.

He held up his hands, surrendering. "Let's take some deep breaths. It's going to be okay."

I didn't want to chill out. I wanted to fight. But it was like as soon as he spoke, the mixture of rage and adrenaline coursing through my veins gave way to exhaustion. I was angry. Scared. And doing the same shit that my father did whenever he lost his temper. Instead of talking about my feelings, I was taking them out on whoever was around me.

I'd always promised myself I wouldn't turn into him, but maybe I was doomed to keep repeating his mistakes, no matter how hard I tried.

I tried to fight a demon on the side of the road—not because I wanted to, but because I didn't know what else to do. I needed to work through my emotions instead of punching and kicking them away. Trouble was, I didn't really know how to do that. I sank down to the ground, putting my face in my hands as tears leaked in endless rivers down my face.

Fred sat down next to me with a heavy sigh. "What else happened?"

I smeared the back of my hand across my face, sniffling. "You said he'd never come back." My voice was fractured. Broken into a million tiny pieces that I wasn't sure I'd ever be able to put back together. I couldn't stop the tears from falling as I stared at him.

Fred waited for me to elaborate, but the silence stretched on for too long. "Who?" he finally said, shifting a little next to me.

I wiped my nose on my sleeve. "Who do you think?"

"Oh."

"You *lied*." The words fell out of my mouth before I could stop them. Fred winced. I didn't mean to hurt him. But sometimes the truth did that.

"I didn't."

"You said he'd never come back," I repeated, my voice steadily rising. "But now he's here. He killed Blake. Shoved his hand in his chest and ripped out his heart." I paused, frantically trying to dry my face. "Jesse did it . . . he wants me to make a deal with him. Figured it would push me in the right direction."

Fred swore, too soft and too fast for me to catch what he said. He frowned, finally meeting my gaze. "I'm sorry. I should've foreseen that he'd want to go behind my back like that. When we made our deal, Cordelia, I thought your father wouldn't be able to come back. These kinds of things are usually permanent, unless . . ." His voice trailed away.

"Unless?"

Fred's mouth became a thin line. "What did your father look like tonight? What color were his eyes?"

"Orange."

Fred said something under his breath that I didn't understand. It felt like a curse in a language that humans were never meant to hear. He cleared his throat, standing. Offered me his hand as he said, "We need to get to your house. I'll stay with you tonight."

My heart sank. I hadn't stopped to think of what Jesse meant when he brought my father back. He said he'd made few a minor adjustments. Fred's reaction told me all I needed to know. It was a truth that I didn't want to face—but I knew I'd have to. Eventually.

I took Fred's hand, letting him help me up. "He's a demon, isn't he?" I asked, after I got back on my feet. Fred nodded. I held onto his hand, not daring to let him go. "How's that possible?"

Something broke a branch in the woods behind us. Fred's head whipped around toward the noise. His eyes glowed bright yellow, shining through his glasses as he gazed into the nearby trees. "We should get in the car," he said, pulling me back toward it. "And go home."

"But—"

"Now," he growled, throwing the passenger's door open. He cleared his throat, gesturing inside. "Please."

"Only because you asked nicely."

I slid into the passenger's seat. Fred jumped in the car, turning it back on before I had time to close the door. I didn't even have my seatbelt buckled before he sped away. The car beeped a few times until I finally took care of it.

"How did Jesse bring him back?" I asked, once the seatbelt alarm stopped screaming.

"There are two types of demons," he replied, scanning the road ahead of us more than someone normally would. "The ones who've been around since before the beginning of everything—like Jesse and me. We can't be killed, which is why I've been so determined to figure out how he trapped me. We're tough bastards to get rid of, unfortunately."

My fingers curled in my jacket pockets, twisting the fabric inside of them. "But that's not what my father is."

"No. Your father was a human *before* he was turned into a demon. And he's not really a *demon* demon. More like, a very strong human with some demon powers. Which makes things a bit more complicated."

"Great."

"Complicated, but not impossible," Fred said, as he turned down the street to my neighborhood. The streetlights were all out, casting the rest of the houses on my block in darkness. "The good news is, he *can* be killed. The bad news: he doesn't know the limits of his power yet. That makes him more dangerous."

"More dangerous than you? An actual, old-as-hell demon?"

Fred pouted. "I'm not *that* old."

"Could've fooled me," I joked, poking at his pride.

Fred bristled. "Regardless of my age, I've had a long time to master my abilities. Your father has not. He'll experience moments when he has bursts of strength, but they always come at a price. He won't be able to sustain that for long. Eventually, he'll crash and need to recover."

"Oh," I whispered.

"That's when you'll have to strike," Fred said, way too matter-of-factly. "Once he's made himself vulnerable, you'll need to strike him through the heart. That should be enough to kill him."

Bile burned in my throat. I swallowed it back, shuddering. "I can't do that."

Any sense of relief I'd had when we pulled onto my block faded away. Facing Jesse was terrifying enough—how was I supposed to confront the man who almost killed me and walk away from that alive?

"I'm afraid you don't have much of a choice." He pulled into the driveway. The car idled as we sat in front of my house. It was only one story, and the light gray paint on the siding was always peeling away. It wasn't the nicest house on the street. Or the biggest. But it was ours.

I opened the passenger's side door. "Weren't you forbidding me from helping you at lunch today?"

Fred rolled his eyes. "Oh, so *now* you listen to me."

"That's my secret," I said, getting out of the car and trying my best at keeping things lighter than I felt. "I'm always listening."

Fred laughed as I moved to the front door. I pushed it open, turning back to face him. As I did, a large shadow moved out from the darkened street behind us, standing right behind Fred. His smile faded when he looked at me.

"Cordelia?" he asked, as a monster watched me from over his shoulders. "What's wr—"

But he didn't get to finish his question. Instead, he was thrown through the front door and into the house. The aswang chased after him, ducking down to all fours. It broke into a run, galloping in a surreal, disjointed way toward him.

My heart raced as I ran into the living room. I grabbed my backpack, unzipping it, my palms slicked with sweat. I almost dropped the kalis as I raced after both of them.

I stumbled into the kitchen. The aswang and Fred were grappling, pushing the table aside as they got dangerously close to a long, tall window. I stood there, frozen, waiting to see if they would slam through it and break it, just like my father had.

A pang of ice shot through what was left of my heart. Even though David Scott wasn't in the house right now, I was just as helpless as I was before.

He came back to finish what we started.

Fred was right. I didn't have a choice. If I couldn't kill him, he was going to kill me.

The aswang wasn't my father. But it was still a threat. I winced as the aswang slammed Fred against the wall next to the window. I'd stood up for myself once before. But I wasn't sure I could do it again.

No.

I couldn't stand by and do nothing.

I gripped the kalis's handle tighter. Fire thawed the ice in my veins as I screamed. It was enough to distract Fred and the aswang. They both turned their heads to look at me, right as I tackled the aswang, forcing it down to the cold tile floor. The kalis dug into the monster's arm as we got tangled up in each other. A small cut appeared, dark red blood blooming from the wound. It mixed with the aswang's filmy gray skin.

A pang of regret shot through me. I hadn't meant to hurt them. I only wanted to get them away from Fred.

The aswang's pitch-black eyes widened as it looked at me. It screeched, not resisting as I clumsily pinned the creature to the ground.

My legs wrapped around the aswang's waist, holding it in place. I put the dagger up to the monster's throat, more careful with the blade this time. "Who are you?" I said, between ragged breaths.

The aswang blinked. Its eyes slowly changed. Inky black darkness gave way to the same light brown irises I'd stared into a few days ago, when I was desperate to prove that my best friend wasn't a monster.

I didn't know how I was wrong—or why—but the aswang's monstrous form changed, too. In a few blinks, I was sitting on top of Veronica Dominguez, pinning her to the ground.

Well.

Fuck.

Didn't see that one coming.

My mouth hung open as if it was waiting for my brain to catch up to everything.

Fred applauded behind us. "Well, I don't know what I was expecting," he said, kneeling down next to me. "But it certainly wasn't that."

"Hello, Cordy," Veronica said. Her gaze drifted down to my lips. A blush rose in her cheeks as her eyes flicked back to mine. "It looks like we've got a lot to talk about, doesn't it?"

CHAPTER TWENTY-TWO

IN WHICH SECRETS ARE REVEALED

"HOW IN THE HELL ARE YOU THE ASWANG?" I ASKED, accidentally squeezing her torso with my thighs.

Oh, wait.

I was sitting on top of Veronica. Well, not just sitting.

I was *straddling* her. In the middle of my kitchen.

Heat blazed through my body, sending crackles of flames licking up my spine. I jumped off her. Ran a hand through my hair, offering the other to help her up. "I don't get it," I said, as her hand slid into mine. "I did the eye test. My reflection was normal."

"The eye test?" Fred asked. Skepticism colored his question.

No. No, no, no. I'd forgotten he was there, watching this whole awkward exchange unfold. The only thing that would make this better was if the ground opened up and swallowed me whole. I'd even trade places with my father and take eternal torment over the embarrassment that twisted my stomach into a million knots.

I swallowed, forcing back the horrified, angst-ridden groan that wanted to escape from my throat. "It's one way to tell if someone's an aswang." I pulled Veronica up, scratching my head with my free hand. "But you passed. How'd you do it?"

"I knew you'd try that one," Veronica said, getting up to her feet. She squeezed my hand before she let it go. "I wondered if it was you—kind of planned for it, actually. Just in case." She looked over at Fred. "Sorry for attacking you. I wasn't sure if I could trust you."

Fred tilted his head, watching her. "What changed your mind?"

Veronica nodded at me. "Cordy trusts you. That's good enough for me."

"Really?" Fred asked, chuckling.

Veronica shrugged. "Yeah."

I held up a hand, butting back into the conversation. "Wait . . . Veronica, what did you mean when you said you wondered if it was me?"

"The other deal maker," Veronica replied, the smile slowly drifting off her face. "We did Deal Day together, once. Don't you remember?"

An icy grip coiled its fingers around my heart. It squeezed, sending a pain stinging through my chest. I sat down at the kitchen table, putting my head in my hands.

I *did* remember. The night before my father tried to kill me, I slept over at Veronica's house. We were bored and, since the last few hours of Deal Day were slowly waning away, we figured it was as good a time as any to test out our town's most infamous urban legend.

"But nothing happened right away," I said, looking up at

Fred. "We didn't see a demon that night."

Veronica nodded. "Jesse came to me in the morning, right after you left. I didn't want to let you go—and neither did my parents. Not with the way *he* was looking at you."

My father already had his fair share to drink when he picked me up that morning. Mom was stuck at the hospital, so he came to get me. He wasn't happy about it.

I glanced up at Fred. "Our deal happened shortly after I left, too."

Veronica swore under her breath. She grabbed a chair and swung it around the table to sit next to me. She took my hand, squeezing it as her eyes went from light brown to pitch black. "What happened?"

Fred cleared his throat, his gaze shifting from me to Veronica. "I think you two need to sort a few things out. When you need me, I'll be in the living room." He gave my shoulder a reassuring squeeze before he walked out of the kitchen.

My heart pounded so loudly in my ears that it was hard to hear anything else. Everything I'd bottled up for the past seven years slowly became undone. I was about to give her an answer she probably didn't want to hear. But I was done hiding the truth from her. She needed to know what I'd done. Then she could decide if I still meant something to her.

I let go of Veronica's hand. "He hated that he had to come pick me up. He, um. He was already mad, but he got worse when we got home. I was trying to do the dishes and I was singing. I thought I was doing it quietly, but I wasn't quiet enough, I guess, and then he came in, and I should've stopped singing but I didn't. I knew he couldn't stand it when I did it, but I didn't care." My voice wavered. Tears filled my eyes.

This time, I didn't try to hold them back. Veronica brushed them away as they fell down my cheeks.

"It's okay, Accordion," she said, wrapping me in a hug as she used her oldest nickname for me. "You're okay."

I shook my head, lightly pushing away from her as I sobbed. "I'm not. Don't you get it? It's all my fault. I should've stopped singing but something was different when he yelled at me. *I* was different. I didn't want him to tell me what to do anymore or scare me into obeying him. I couldn't stop doing something I loved just because he didn't like it. So, I sang louder. And then his hand wrapped around my throat. And the other one did, too. He squeezed so hard, it felt like my head was going to explode. I tried to breathe and wrench his hands off me, but I couldn't. The world started to go dark. I thought—" I paused, letting out a low laugh. "I thought, 'it figures this would be how it goes.' I tried to act tough for the first time in my life, and of course it was a mistake." I wiped the tears out of my eyes so I could meet Veronica's gaze. "And I thought I was dead, until . . ." My voice trailed away. I nodded toward the living room.

"Fred saved you," Veronica said, finishing the thought for me. She was crying, too. Whatever small pieces were left of my heart broke at that. I hadn't meant to make her cry.

I nodded, sniffling as I continued. "He sent him to Hell. That's where he's been all this time." My breathing picked up. It was fast. Too fast. By the time I could speak again, I was hyperventilating. Getting the words out between frantic gasps for air. "I'm sorry I lied to you. I didn't know—I didn't remember—"

Veronica's hands held both sides of my face. "It's okay," she said, rubbing her thumbs in circles on my cheeks. "Will you take some deep breaths with me?"

I nodded.

"Good," she replied, wiping her tears away with her sleeve. "Ready? Breathe in. Breathe out. And in. And out." We did that for a few minutes, until I'd finally calmed down. "Better?" she asked.

"Yeah. Thanks."

Silence lingered briefly between us. Then Veronica pulled her hands away from my face. It was like she'd taken all of the warmth out of the room with her when she twisted them together, folding them back into her lap.

I cleared my throat, not daring to look at her as I asked the question I didn't want the answer to. "Do . . . do you hate me?"

Veronica blinked a few times, watching me. And then she laughed. It wasn't a harsh, mocking sound. It was light. Surprised. A small flicker of an unexpected flame, dying down before it had the chance to catch onto anything. Her hand drifted under my chin, lifting my head up so I could look at her.

I thought she'd judge me. Be repulsed by what I'd done. But the only thing in her eyes was pride. I didn't understand it. I hadn't done anything to be proud of.

"Why would I hate you, Accordion?" she said, tucking a strand of hair behind my ear with her free hand. "You didn't do anything wrong."

"I did," I said, trying to keep my breathing steady so I didn't freak out again. "I killed him."

Veronica grabbed my hands, pulling me out of the chair and into a hug. "You had to," she said, stroking my hair. "If you hadn't—" Her voice broke. She let go of me, looking at me—seeing who I really was—for the first time. "I'm so glad I didn't lose you."

She didn't hate me. She still wanted to be my friend.

"Hey," Veronica said, wiping away more of my tears. "Do you want to know what my wish was?"

"Something Broadway related?"

"No." She smiled as she nudged my shoulder. "Though, thinking about it now, that would've been a good one."

"What was it?" I asked, not daring to meet her gaze. Veronica didn't hate me, but I still did.

She reached out, booping my nose. "I wanted you to be safe. I wished he'd go away. That nothing could hurt you. And then, when you told me he moved to Florida, I thought—I thought it was because of me. What *I'd* wished for. I wasn't sure what to tell you. Or how. But now . . ." Her voice trailed away, morphing into musical laughter. "I guess it wasn't me, after all."

My mouth hung open. Veronica gave up part of her soul to keep me safe. If I hadn't beaten her to it, she would've gotten my father out of my life. I wasn't sure I could love her more than in that moment. But I did, and I always would.

When I spoke, my voice was low. Soft. "You didn't have to do that."

"I know. But I did it anyway."

"And now you're a monster because of me."

"No," Veronica said, so sharply that it finally made me look up at her. "I chose this form. I figured something was wrong when the demon showed up again. He said the best way to keep you safe was for me to turn into something terrifying. So, I became the aswang. Or, at least, what I *told* him an aswang was."

"Hold on," I said, barely holding back a smile. "You got to custom-build your aswang?"

Veronica winked. "Turns out, Jesse isn't super familiar with anything outside of the Catholic Canon. Guess he thought researching other beliefs was a waste of his time, so I used that to my advantage. I'm not a real aswang. Just the idea of one."

My mouth dropped open so far, it might as well have hit the floor at that point. "You tricked a demon?"

"Tricked is such a strong word," she replied, beaming. "More like . . . I found a loophole."

My eyes darted down to her lips as warmth rushed to my face. All I wanted was to reach out and pull her close to me. Kiss her until all of this fell away and we were the only things left that mattered. But I didn't want to mess anything up, now that we were finally talking again.

Instead, I pulled my gaze away from her lips and said, "I can't believe you did all of that for me."

Veronica's smile faded away. "You would've done the same. I wish I'd done more, though. If I'd known that he tried to kill you, I would've changed the terms of my deal and murdered that asshole myself."

"You were ten," I shot back.

"So were you," she replied quietly.

"Well, if it's any consolation, you might still have your chance," I said, wincing a little. "After you flew away, Jesse . . . he brought my father back. Raised him up from Hell. And then my father killed Blake."

Veronica's expression hardened. Her irises shifted from brown to black again. "He's back."

I nodded. "I don't know what to do, Harmonica."

"Whatever it is, you won't be alone," Veronica replied. "I'll help you."

"And I will, too," Fred said, from the hallway. He wiped away some of his own tears. "I owe you that much. This is my mistake, anyway. If I hadn't interfered maybe things would've turned out differently."

Veronica looked over at him. "You're a lot nicer than the other one."

"Yeah, well," Fred said, shrugging. "Statistically, we couldn't all be assholes, right?"

Veronica's brows scrunched together as she considered this. "I guess not."

"Right then," Fred said, clapping once. "Anyone got a bright idea? Afraid I'm all out."

I nodded, slowly standing. "I do. I'm going to make a blessed weapon."

Fred scratched his head. "What the hell is that?"

CHAPTER TWENTY-THREE

IN WHICH I LIE TO A PRIEST

FRED WAS SKEPTICAL OF THE WHOLE BLESSED WEAPON thing. He'd never heard of it, but I figured that was because the Church wouldn't tell demons about something that could hurt them. He reasoned that the Church hadn't been the most forthright institution (to which I agreed), and that I shouldn't put all my eggs in this alleged blessed weapon basket. We stayed up most of the night arguing about it. We finally came to the conclusion that it was something worth checking into around 6 a.m. And that was when we all got the same text.

School was canceled.

Since Blake was brutally murdered next to The Coffee Spot while a bunch of students were inside singing karaoke, the powers that be wanted to give everyone time to process what happened.

The rest of Tech Week was also called off. The show wasn't in shape at all for opening night, but that was the next time we'd all be in the theater together. It felt weird to force everyone to sing and dance in front of a crowd on Friday. Maybe they thought our show would bring everyone together and that's why they were still making us go through with it.

Either way, now we had a few days to figure out how to trap Jesse before Deal Day.

Fred left shortly after our school's cancellation announcement. Veronica sat with me for a few hours after that. She paced around the house, looking out the windows, expecting to see my father standing there. Watching us. And I did, too, but I didn't bother checking.

Veronica went home to change and get a little bit of sleep. I should've been productive and tried doing more research on the blessed weapon. Instead, I sat in the kitchen, completely numb as I stared at the wall full of our pictures. Some of them were from when I was younger; ripped where my father had been or folded over to hide him.

We'd put some of those pictures over holes and scratches in the walls. Mementos of David Scott's temper flaring up.

A key turned in the front door. Adrenaline spiked through my body. Veronica and Fred weren't here to help me. It was just me, alone in an empty home filled with memories I'd rather forget.

I picked the kalis up from where I was storing it—on top of the small table I sat at—and stood at the entryway to the kitchen, waiting. The rush of blood and my heart's frantic beating were the only things I could hear.

There was no way my father had a key to the house. I knew it was impossible for him to be on the other side of the door. But I couldn't help gripping the dagger tighter. Crouching, so that I could charge down the hallway in a run if I needed to.

The front door slowly opened. Mom stood there, eyes

passing right over me for a moment, before she finally found me, stumbling back.

"Cordy?" she asked, stepping through the door. "What are you doing?"

"*Um*, research?" The words came out more like a question than a real answer. "For *Our Demon Town*. We're testing out . . . different . . . kinds of blades . . ." My voice trailed away. I lowered the dagger, standing up.

"And you were going to use our family's kalis in the show?"

"Oh, no! I wanted to show them what it looked like. It's a cool design."

She nodded. "It is," she replied, breezing past me.

If I reached out, I'd be able to touch her shoulder. I couldn't remember the last time she'd been that close. I sighed, heading back to the kitchen. Sat down at the counter, watching while she rooted around in the fridge.

I could tell her everything. How I sent my father to Hell, and how I was paying for it now. The fact that neither of us would be safe until I found a way to get rid of him for good.

How terrified I was that he'd find a way to kill me before I could finish what I started.

I wasn't sure if Mom would have the same reaction as Veronica. My best friend had always been on my side—she'd seen what living with my father had done to me—but Mom loved him, once. Married him. When he left, she broke into way too many pieces for me to pick up and put back together. If I told her what I'd done, it might shatter what was left of her. Ruin whatever chance we had of repairing what I'd destroyed.

Mom closed the fridge door. "Are you doing okay? You look tired."

"I'm fine," I said, unable to keep the lie going as tears pooled in my eyes. They slipped down my cheek, betraying everything I fought so hard to keep inside. "Blake—" was all I could get out before I dissolved into a puddle of uncontrollable sobbing. I couldn't tell her everything. I didn't *want* to tell her everything. And I never would.

Did that make me a horrible person?

"Oh, Cordy," Mom said, stepping closer to the counter. "I'm so sorry. Before I left work, I heard . . . it must have been awful, seeing that."

It was. But I wasn't just crying for Blake. So much pain happened in such a short span of time, and it was all because I'd been foolish enough to make a deal with a demon seven years ago.

I needed to know if that was the right thing to do.

"Mom?" I asked.

"Yeah?" She frowned. Probably assessing me just like she did with a new patient. *This one looks sad. She's too pathetic. We can't help her.*

I shook the thought away. "When Dad left . . ." I let my voice trail away. Tried to make the 'left' sound as innocent as possible. "Were you mad?"

She sighed. "That's a complicated question."

"I know. I just . . . I want you to know that *I* was mad." The words stung as they drifted into the air. We'd never talked about this before. I thought she'd run out the door as soon as I mentioned him. But she stayed. Her vacant expression finally giving way to firm resolve.

"Of course I was mad," she replied. "I was a lot of things. Still am, in case you couldn't tell."

"It's pretty obvious."

Mom winced. I did, too. I didn't want to hurt her like he had. And somewhere, deep down, I knew that what I said wasn't the same as anything he'd done. Still, the small voice in the back of my mind that loved to call me a monster couldn't help but compare us.

Mom drummed her fingers on the counter. "I could've done better. *Been* better. For you. But I didn't. I'm sorry."

I bit down hard on the inside of my cheek, trying to stop more tears from coming out. But the floodgates had already been opened. I couldn't do anything to stop them. I had another question I needed to ask her, but I couldn't find the courage to say the words out loud.

Did you wish I'd disappeared instead of him? Separately, the words didn't mean anything. Together, they had the potential to shatter my world beyond repair.

Mom yawned. "I'm tired. I'm gonna go lie down." She turned around, heading for her bedroom. Just like that, the spell was broken. The little bit of fault—of tenderness—that came out slowly faded away.

"Wait," I said, scrambling to block her way to the hallway. I needed to see her face. "Do you ever wish he was dead?" I asked, fingers twisting together as I waited for an answer. It wasn't exactly the question that haunted me for seven years. But it was close enough.

I wanted her to say that she had. She did. If she wanted him to die, then the choice that I made—and all of the terrible things that followed—would be worth it.

Justified.

Her eyes filled with something I couldn't stand to see. Pity mixed with regret. A little bit of guilt. I looked away as she replied.

"I don't know," she said slowly. "But it's okay if you do. We feel what we feel, and there's nothing wrong with that."

She stepped around me and closed the bedroom door behind her.

That was it, then.

It was kind of funny, actually. I'd tried to trick myself into believing that I sent my father to Hell to make both of our lives better. To fix everything he'd broken.

But I hadn't done it for her. Just for me.

That didn't mean I'd made a bad decision. Or that I wouldn't do it again if I had the same opportunity. Sure, I might have ripped a hole in our lives when I damned him to an eternity of torment—but he wasn't innocent.

I couldn't keep waiting around for someone to answer my questions for me. Or tell me that what I did was right.

There was only one way for me to make Blake's death count—to justify everything I'd done. It was finally time to stitch up the wound I'd opened up seven years ago. Find a way to stop the pain. Get him out of our lives, once and for all.

I had to go back to St. Gertrude's.

I pulled my phone out, texting Fred.

5 p.m. My house. Don't be late.

Fred sank into the shadows when he arrived, waiting and ready in case my father tried getting to Mom while I was gone. His bright yellow eyes stood out in the rear-view mirror.

It was a relief to know he was there. David Scott might be a demon now, but he was new. And hopefully no match for Fred.

As I drove down the road that led into the woods, a vulture screeched overhead. With Fred watching my mom, Veronica was tailing me. She'd be nearby in case anything went wrong.

I parked near the back of the church's lot. Sat there for a few minutes in silence, staring at the place that would either help me win this thing or royally screw me over. I *had* to leave with the blessed weapon if we had any shot of killing my father and trapping the demon he was working with.

I got out of the car. Quietly closed the door behind me. Pulled my coat tighter and took a deep breath as the church beckoned me closer. The setting sun hit the stained-glass windows, casting a warm pastel glow over cars in the parking lot.

Stained-Glass St. Francis holding that little lamb looked especially friendly. Like I could walk up to his artfully arranged figure and tell him everything I was struggling with. A one-sided confession that would get me absolutely nowhere, but hey, at least I wouldn't be judged.

"Do you need help, dear?" Annabelle asked.

I nodded. I needed more help than she could ever know. "Uh, yeah," I replied, sounding way calmer and more collected than I actually was. "I'd like to talk to Father Marcus. If he's free."

"I can bring you to him, but he doesn't have long."

"I understand. Thank you, sister."

"Not sister, dear," she said, pointing to her habit. "Novitiate."

"Ah. Right. Novitiate," I paused, deadpanning, "I definitely know what that means."

She smiled. "I'm training to be a nun. Haven't taken my vows just yet."

"Oh. So, you're like, a Baby Nun."

"That's one way to look at it."

"Why didn't you correct me before? I've been calling you Sister this whole time."

Novitiate Annabelle shrugged. "Have you heard the phrase 'dress for the job you want'? I like to think I was doing that, but with words instead of clothes."

She gestured for me to head into the church before her. The sunlight caught her face, sending streaks of purple and crimson across her dark features. She *definitely* won the award for Most Interesting Clergy Person of the Year.

Novitiate Annabelle led me to a hallway that held all the offices in St. Gertrude's. We passed door after door marked with names that I didn't recognize. Not that I expected to. I hadn't started paying attention to the clergy people in the church until recently.

One of the doors stopped me short. There were messages for Blake taped on the peeling beige wood. Prayers and well-wishes for his soul. Positive thoughts for his family. I paused in front of the impromptu shrine, biting the inside of my cheek to keep from tearing up.

"It really is a tragedy," Annabelle said. "He died so young."

I nodded, voice shaking as I said, "Yeah."

She placed a comforting hand on my shoulder and guided me forward.

Father Marcus's office was at the very end of the long hallway. Annabelle knocked, opening the door slowly after a gruff "Come in!" from the other side.

"Ms. Scott is here to see you, Father. She knows that you only have a few minutes to spare."

"Thank you," Father Marcus replied. "I'll see you soon."

Annabelle nodded as I slid past her. "Good luck." She closed the door before I could reply.

Did I look like someone who needed luck? It was kind of a weird thing to say, but it was also oddly comforting. Something told me she really meant it.

"Ms. Scott," Father Marcus said, gesturing to the seat across from him. The Red Sox hat sat on top of his desk, as did a stack of papers piled neatly in the corner closest to the window. The room was smaller than I thought it would be. Packed with books that overflowed from shelves onto tables and then onto the floor. Some of the books were thrown open, scattered and left on random pages.

Even though he had a fluorescent light overhead, it wasn't on. Two lamps filled the room with warm pools of light. The priest's pale skin stood out against his black robes. His light brown hair was cropped even shorter than it had been a few days ago.

I lingered in the doorway. He looked at me, still gesturing to the empty seat. "Sit. Please."

"Okay," I said, sliding down into the chair. The cushion was made of fake leather, and squeaked a bit as I settled into it.

"How can I help you?"

Well, it was now or never. No point beating around the bush. "I need a blessed weapon. Can you help me?"

He leaned back in his chair, watching me. "Let's say, hypothetically, that I knew the intricacies involved in making a blessed weapon. Do you? Are you aware of what you'll have to sacrifice in order to see this through?"

"Yes," I lied. I wasn't going to give him any excuse to turn me away.

"And you're ready to take on this burden?"

"Yes."

"Even if it will cost you a piece of your soul?"

I wrung my hands together, holding his gaze. "Yes." Hopefully there was more than enough conviction in my voice to convince him. He didn't need to know that I'd already given up a piece of my soul and gotten it back. Or that, even *with* my soul back, I didn't feel complete.

I thought it would change everything. But nothing happened.

If this was what I had to do to get rid of my father, I could live with this decision.

"I admire your enthusiasm, but I'm afraid it has to stop. If you keep going down this path, you could be hurt. Or worse—your soul could be damned for the rest of eternity."

Well, I was way ahead of him on that one. This argument wasn't working. I didn't want to have to play this next card, but if it would get the job done, I had to try. Under normal circumstances, I could muster up enough emotions to fuel a pretty convincing fake cry. But now, everything simmered just underneath the surface. I didn't even have to think about it. Tears pooled in my eyes as I looked at him.

"Did my mom ever tell you about what happened to my father?"

Father Marcus tilted his head, frowning. "Just that he moved to Florida."

"He didn't. He tried . . ." My voice wavered. I cleared my throat, not working too hard at being convincing. This bit, at least, wasn't a lie. "He wasn't a good person. And one day, he tried to . . . well. He did something horrible. And I made a choice."

I let the thought hang in the air. This was where I could reel him in. Once he came to his own conclusion, I'd be able to win him over to my side.

Father Marcus sighed. "I made a similar choice, you know. Years ago."

It took everything I had to not fall out of the chair.

"You did?" I asked, still not sure we were talking about the same thing.

He gestured around his office. "That's how I wound up here. I never thought the priesthood was for me. But after I fulfilled my bargain, I couldn't keep living in a world where demons existed, and I stood by and did nothing. So, I joined the Church. Learned how to get rid of them, *including* how to make the thing that kills them. *That's* why creating a blessed weapon comes with such a steep price, Cordelia. It's a powerful tool. If you choose to wield it, you'll be damning your soul for the rest of eternity."

If what he said was true—if he really *had* made a deal with a demon—then it made sense why he wanted to transfer to Ruin's End. Maybe he wanted to intervene and prevent more soul-stealing bargains from happening. I could use that.

I scooted to the edge of my seat. "All I want is for this to stop. Will you help me?"

"I won't let you surrender a piece of your soul."

"Please," I said, pulling my bag closer to my chest. "Blake died because of me. I have to make things right."

"But you could be killed, too, Cordelia."

"Then *help me*," I begged, holding his gaze. "*Please.* I'll do whatever you ask. I just . . . I really need your help."

Father Marcus looked away. "Desperation can be a dangerous thing."

"Not if it's supervised."

He frowned. Dragged his hands down his face before he

replied. "Fine. I'll create your blessed weapon. But you must promise me one thing."

"Anything."

The priest smiled, but it wasn't a comforting thing. Instead, it felt like I'd lain all most of my cards on the table, and he was still holding some back.

I'd thought I was playing with a winning hand. But I wasn't so sure anymore.

"What I'm about to do will break just about every rule the Church has." He leaned over his desk, steepling his fingers together as he said, "It's best if we keep this issue between us. Can you do that?"

I couldn't—not when Veronica and Fred were waiting to hear about how my meeting went. But I needed his help. And if I had to lie to get this thing done, I would.

"No one else will know," I replied.

The priest's smile stretched even wider across his pale features. "Wonderful. Then tonight, my dear child, you shall become a weapon of God."

CHAPTER TWENTY-FOUR

IN WHICH SOMEONE IS LISTENING

FATHER MARCUS WOULD HELP ME MAKE THE BLESSED weapon after Tuesday night Mass. He gave me the option of attending the service, but I didn't want to sit in those pews and pretend to believe in something that I didn't think existed. Sure, demons were real. But the other side of things—God and angels and all that jazz—I still wasn't sold on it.

Not that I was going to tell the priest that.

It was a little surprising that Father Marcus agreed to help—*without* the Church's permission. Maybe the priest thought I stood a chance. Or he was just as foolish as I was.

I waited for about half an hour after Mass finished before slowly opening his office door. I'd spent the whole service catching up on my reading for AP Lit. If I managed to survive my demon showdown on Friday, I figured it was a good idea to be prepared for a pop quiz as soon as school reopened. I wasn't sure what the future held for me, but for the first time since I could remember, I wanted to be there to find out.

The door creaked softly as I wedged it open a little wider and slipped out. I'd been stuck in that small office for way too long. A little exploring wouldn't hurt anything. Besides, St. Gert's wasn't that big. Father Marcus wouldn't have a problem finding me when he was ready.

I'd brought the kalis with me as an extra measure of protection—which wound up being useful, since a blessed weapon was created by linking one's soul to something that already exists. Or so Father Marcus said. According to him, the ritual we'd go through would take a piece of my soul and merge it with the kalis.

I left the sword in his office as I walked around. I didn't want to alarm any of the nuns or parishioners by walking around with a long, curvy blade. If someone caught me with it, they'd probably take it away. There was no way I'd let that happen.

Besides, I was in a church. There were plenty of things I could defend myself with if I needed to, like giant copies of the Bible or the small statue of a cherubic angel sitting in the corner of Father Marcus's office.

The halls—and the church's main room—were empty. That wasn't what usually happened after Mass. I'd only been around during Christmas Eve and Easter, but after the service families hung around and talked. Maybe people didn't want to linger after Blake's eerie death. There'd been no official ruling on what killed him, but there were already rumors circulating about a winged monster and how, perhaps, there was more truth to our town's founding legend than anyone thought.

Or people had better things to do on a Tuesday night than gossip in a church.

Either way, no one watched as I pulled the door to the church's main room open. I paced around the cluttered space, winding through the pews. The only things keeping me company were the stained-glass images that cast colorful patches of deep purples and red all around me.

Stained-Glass St. Francis and his little lamb's judging stares seared into me. It was uncalled for. I hadn't done anything wrong.

Lately.

Sure, I was going to forfeit a piece of my soul again. I had no idea if I could get that back. Or what would happen to me if I died without a whole soul. But if I didn't give up that part of me—if I let my father and Jesse roam free—then I was condemning so many other people to a worse fate.

I wasn't going to be Jesse's one-hundredth deal. Hopefully, the blessed weapon would be more than enough to get rid of my father. Giving up my soul to do that—instead of giving a demon more power—was the right thing to do. But that didn't make it less terrifying.

I needed reassurance. Someone to lie to me and tell me that everything would be all right in the end. But there was no one around to help me now. Just me and my own thoughts, spiraling down into an endless, angsty abyss.

I didn't want to sit out in the open and gather my thoughts. Then anyone would be able to see how much of a mess I was. The confessional beckoned to me, promising a small space where I could mope in peace.

I darted over to it, shutting the door behind me so hard that the whole booth shook. Normally, there would be a priest sitting on the other side of the window, ready and waiting for me to talk about my sins. But Father Marcus was occupied preparing for whatever the blessed weapon ritual was. So, I was all alone.

It was better this way. At least now, I could pretend someone was listening.

"Forgive me, Father, for I have sinned. It's been . . . well, it's been a really long time since my last confession," I said, crossing myself. "I didn't mean for there to be such a large gap between these sorts of things, but, uh, something happened that made me mad at God. Well, actually, a lot of things happened. And I wasn't just mad at God. I was mad at everyone. Which seems kind of understandable. So many people could've stepped in and stopped him, and no one did, so I—" I caught myself. I hadn't meant to let the words out like a flood finally bursting through the gate so desperately trying to hold it back, but I did.

Tears pooled in my eyes, dancing delicately on the verge of drenching my cheeks. Before I left the house, I put my mom's rosary on. I gripped it tightly as I continued. "I know that God wasn't responsible for my father. But someone was. Maybe bad things happened to him too, and he didn't know how to deal with them, so he took them out on us. Or he always had a mean streak in him, and we were just easy targets. I don't know what it was. I don't think I ever will. But that part doesn't matter as much.

"He chose to hurt us—he shouldn't have, but he did. And . . . and I didn't know how to deal with that—with any of it—and no one was helping us, so I did something about it. I took everything he'd done to us and turned it back on him. I made sure he suffered. I made sure he'd never forget what he'd done."

I paused, letting out a shaky breath. I couldn't hold back the tears anymore. I wiped them away as they fell onto my face, the seat in the confessional, the floor. I couldn't control them anymore. They did what they wanted to.

"But what I still don't understand is why any of it happened in the first place. There were so many signs of trouble, but no one stepped in. No one wanted to help. And if God really is out there, watching us, why wouldn't they send anyone to stop him? Why were we left alone, forced to deal with everything he put us through? What did we do to deserve that?" I sniffled, using whatever courage I had to push the question out that'd haunted me for most of my life.

"What did *I* do to deserve that? He was my *father*. I was just a kid. He should've comforted me when I skinned a knee, instead of skinning the other one to match. Tucked me in and read me bedtime stories rather than forcing me to hide under the bed, terrified, worried that Mom wouldn't make it through another night.

"He should've loved me no matter what. Protected me from people like him. But he didn't do anything he was supposed to. And I just . . . I want to know *why*, Father. What was it about me that was so broken—so terrible—that I deserved to grow up with that monster?"

I choked back a sob, trying to hold myself together. I wasn't going to be able to keep this up for long, though. Everything that happened crashed into me like a train. I was exhausted. Completely worn out. And my eyes were getting sore from crying so much.

"I'm so scared, Father. I walk around every day completely terrified that I'll wind up like him. That one day I'll hurt someone so much—so deeply—that they'll be forced to do something they never thought they'd be capable of." I paused, swallowing back the bitterness that filled my mouth. "What if I'm a monster, too?"

I hadn't expected to openly sob in a confessional booth. But now that it was happening, the only thing I felt was relief. I'd bottled these questions up for so long that it was nice to say them out loud. Well, nice was absolutely an understatement. It was goddamn cathartic. Even if no one was listening, I finally got to ask the questions that weighed me down. Release them out into the world so they could haunt someone else.

Sniffles came from the other side of the window's slotted holes. Apparently, the questions didn't have far to go.

Nausea roiled in my stomach as I stepped out of the booth. That confession was only meant for me. No one else was supposed to be in here—but now someone knew what I carried around with me. The thoughts I was too scared to think about.

I threw open the door to the other side. A familiar face stared back at me. "Annabelle?" I asked, as she wiped away at her own tears. "How long have you been in there?"

"I came to get you." She gave me a weak smile. "Father Marcus is ready for you. I wanted to call out, but I saw you slip into the booth. I didn't want to stop you. It seemed like you needed to get that out."

Warmth rushed to my cheeks as embarrassment took hold. "I—"

"You don't need to explain, Cordelia," she said, sliding out of the confessional.

"I think I do."

She shook her head. "Family can be . . . complicated. But just because you have those fears—or think those thoughts—it doesn't mean you're a monster. Just human."

I chuckled half-heartedly. "I feel like that's worse."

"It could be." She smiled at me. The expression filled her whole face. There was genuine warmth in her light brown eyes—and a hint of sadness, too. "I'm so sorry that I didn't try to stop you. I meant to, but you just kept going, and I—I'm sorry. I really am. That was a violation of your privacy. I understand if you're angry or want to report me."

I sighed. "I won't report you. On one condition."

"Name it."

"Don't sneak up on me while I'm pouring my heart out ever again."

She nodded, holding her hand out. "Deal."

"Ah. We don't need to shake on it. We're fine."

The smile drifted off her face as she dropped her hand. "If you're ready, it's almost time to begin the ritual."

My eyes widened as the full weight of her words barreled into me. "Wait . . . you know what I'm about to do?"

Her gaze darted to the confessional before it settled back on me. "I've been studying exorcisms with Father Marcus for a few years now but have never seen a blessed weapon ritual. Is it wrong if I'm a little excited to see how it works? I've only ever read about them!"

Well, damn. It felt a little silly to admit that exorcisms and blessed weapons weren't things I thought nuns could do. But it made sense that she'd be involved with all of this. My mouth hung open. I closed it, clearing my throat.

"Sorry," she said, gauging my reaction. "I'll be there for moral support. And to observe. I've been forbidden from intervening. Not that I would—I'd never forgive myself if I ruined the ritual."

I nodded slowly. "Right. Well, we should probably get this thing over with before I change my mind."

"Oh, of course," she replied, almost skipping out of the room. "This way." She gestured through the doors that led out into the lobby.

"Hey, Annabelle?" I asked, as I followed her.

"Hm?"

"Thank you. For not judging me."

She paused, turning to look at me. "It's not my place to judge you. But even if it was—people aren't all good or all bad. It's our potential to be both that makes us so interesting." She turned around, heading for a door that led to a wide field behind the church. "I think you can do a lot of good in this world. You need to trust yourself in order to see that."

"If you say so."

"It's not something I say," she replied, holding the door open for me. "It's something I know."

I gave her a small smile as I stepped outside. Annabelle might be certain that I still had a chance of being good. But I wasn't so sure.

Especially once I killed my father. Again.

CHAPTER TWENTY-FIVE

IN WHICH I LOSE A PIECE OF MY SOUL. AGAIN.

I IMMEDIATELY REGRETTED WALKING OUTSIDE WITH Annabelle. The wind howled around us, tugging at my sleeves, pushing against me. Trying to drive me back to the church in a futile plea to get me to change my mind. I put a hand in front of my face, gritting my teeth together as I moved forward.

A branch snapped in half. I jumped back at the sound but regained my ground, stepping closer to the priest and his strange setup. A medium-sized metal bowl filled with what I assumed was holy water sat on top of the altar. The priest held a rosary in his hand. He moved through a silent prayer, passing each of the beads between his fingers. A long, slender dagger sat on the altar next to the bowl. I wasn't sure what I thought I'd find when I got close enough to make out the details, but it definitely wasn't that.

"Ah, Cordelia," Father Marcus said, from the top of a small hill. He was silhouetted in the dark, moonless sky. Stood at the makeshift altar still as a statue. "Nice of you to finally join us."

Annabelle cleared her throat. "That was my fault, Father Marcus. We had a bit of a heart-to-heart on the way here." There was a small bonfire to the left of the altar. Annabelle darted behind it, nodding meaningfully to the podium.

I sighed, relaxing a bit as the wind picked up again. Annabelle kept her promise. She didn't mention what I'd talked about in the confessional. And I wasn't going to give her a chance to. It was better for all of us if I got this over with as quickly as I could.

"Well, I'm here now," I said, waving my hands up in the air as I moved up to the altar. "Ta-da!"

"Ta-da indeed," Father Marcus said, putting on his Red Sox baseball cap. "Cordelia, in order to create a blessed weapon, you'll need to place your kalis in the bowl and take this—" He handed me an index card. "We have to do a call and response kind of thing. Unfortunately, my bit has to be in Latin, so it won't make any sense to you. Just wait for me to take a meaningful pause and then read your next line."

I squinted at the card. "This is in English?"

He shrugged. "Well, they never said anything about *your* part. Just mine."

"They?"

He gestured around us. "The powers that be. Whoever the hell they are."

Annabelle gave me an encouraging thumbs-up. "You can do this, Cordelia. We believe in you."

"Thanks?" It came out more like a question than I would've liked. Even though she didn't tell Father Marcus that I snuck into the confessional booth and poured out my feelings, she was still on my list. I was about to forfeit a piece of my soul and she was treating it like she'd just won free tickets to Disneyland. Her dark eyes filled with a curious hunger as she stood by the bonfire.

I shuddered, focusing on the bowl in front of me. "Okay. How do we start this thing?"

"You must place the kalis into the bowl," he replied, picking up the other dagger. "Use this to cut your hand. Once the wound is fresh, place it in the holy water and grasp the blade's hilt. That's when I'll start my bit, and when you read from that card."

"Okay." I walked up to the altar and gently laid my kalis in the water. I wasn't super pumped about cutting through my palm, but if that's what I had to do in order to take care of my demon problem, it was time to take one for the team. "Seems simple enough."

"Why wouldn't it be?"

"I figured there'd be more to it, is all."

Sighing, I picked up the priest's ceremonial dagger and sliced through my palm. The blade stung as it delicately tore open my skin. I closed my fist and put the other dagger back where I found it. Relaxed my bloody hand once it dipped in the holy water. The cold liquid met my fresh cut. I cursed, sucking in a pained breath as I met Father Marcus's gaze.

Annabelle cheered from the other side of the fire. "You're doing great, Cordelia."

Father Marcus nodded. "One last word of advice. Things might start to get a little weird during the ritual. You may see or hear some things that are a bit frightening, but they're not real. As long as you stay focused on the task at hand—merging pieces of your soul with this blade—the ritual will be successful. Your determination to see this thing through—your willpower—*that's* what's strong enough to wipe a demon out of existence."

I nodded. Maybe he was onto something. I hadn't been this determined since the first time I sent my father to Hell. Anxiety wound in my chest, coiling tightly around my heart. I wasn't going to enjoy this.

He gestured at the bowl. "Without tethering your blade to the essence of who you are, your kalis is nothing more than a very pretty sword dipped in blessed water. You have to believe, with everything you have in you, that you're capable of doing it." His brown eyes met mine. "*Are* you capable, Ms. Scott? Or have I just wasted my time?"

I took a deep breath. Squared my shoulders as Father Marcus held my kalis above the bowl. "Do it," I said, nodding at him. "I'm ready."

The priest bowed his head. "Then we will begin." He handed the dagger to me, gesturing to the bowl. Blood flowed out of my palm as I gripped the blade's hilt and slowly dunked my hand and the kalis in the water. It stung as soon as it made contact with my open wound. I winced as drops of dark red swirled around in the clear liquid.

The next words out of Father Marcus's mouth were in Latin. I did exactly as he said—reading aloud the words on the index card whenever he paused—and holding onto my kalis like my life depended on it.

The blood in the water wrapped around my blade and my hand, long strands of dark red ribbon tying us together. An eternity stretched on as he recited his part in Latin and I said everything on the card with the confidence and clarity of someone who'd finally figured out what they were supposed to do with their life.

Flames crackled around my feet, sending heat crashing through my body. Sweat beaded on my forehead. The air thickened around me, slowly covering Father Marcus and Annabelle in a layer of fog.

Father Marcus was right. This was *definitely* about to get a little weird.

I swallowed, focusing on the index card in my hand. I cleared my throat, speaking the ritual incantation as clearly as I could. Every muscle in my body shook. Fatigue tried forcing me to sit down. I wiped away at my sweaty forehead with my free hand. It was like I had a fever, but I wasn't sick.

"And with this blade, I will condemn all wretched beings who seek to test it," I said, once Father Marcus paused again. A shadow appeared in the water, turning it into a thick, inky black. The water bubbled like it was boiling. But it wasn't hot.

"Cordelia," my father's voice said, sending white hot pain searing through my veins. *"I'll see you soon."*

I closed my eyes, wishing him away. The priest said I would see and hear things that weren't real. That's all it was. A hallucination.

By the time I opened my eyes, the fog was too thick to see anything past my nose. Father Marcus chanted something in Latin. I tightened my grip on the kalis as long, clawed fingers snaked around my heart. It squeezed so hard that silver dots erupted in my vision. I doubled over, almost dunking my head in the inky black water. The priest's voice wavered at the sound, but he didn't stop. And I didn't let go of the kalis.

Father Marcus paused. It was my turn to say something, but a pale orange glow wove through the fog, parting it like stage curtains right before a performance. It was like everything had been filtered through the strange light. The trees and grass—even the people—were different.

The priest was still on the other side of the altar, but it was like he'd stepped out of a nightmare. Skin sloughed down his cheeks. Dragged from under his eyes by nails that were too sharp for their own good. It hung off his face in shreds, shaking a little as he spoke.

The air turned putrid, wafting around me as the wind blew. Father Marcus shifted. I stood there, frozen, as small bones protruded from the back of his robes. Bile rushed into my throat, but I swallowed it back down. It was the top of his spinal column. Something—or someone—pulled it out.

The orange glow faded, giving way to the fog once again.

If my heart had the option, it would've leaped out of my chest. Adrenaline mixed with heat, leaving my mouth sticky and dry at the same time. As soon as Father Marcus was out of sight, electricity jolted through the bowl, the water turning the same eerie shade of pale orange.

Something slithered under my skin. Snaked its way up my leg and wound down to the arm that held the kalis. My hand lifted out of the bowl, pointing the end of the blade at the center of my chest. I tried to let go of the dagger, but my movements weren't my own.

The blade danced dangerously close to my jacket. I opened my mouth to scream.

Nothing came out.

My kalis pierced through all of my layers way too easily.

The tip of the blade kissed my skin, bringing the sting of the night's cold air with it. Tears pricked in the back of my eyes as icy metal dug into my body.

The sword dragged down in a solid line, cutting from just right of where my heart was, all the way down to my stomach. Pain crumpled me down to my knees as I was finally able to scream.

"You're gonna die soon, kiddo," my father said as heat climbed up my legs. *"What a shame."*

I glanced down, suppressing a scream as flames rose up from the ground, swallowing the lower half of my body. My organs spilled out onto the ground, covered in way too much blood.

No. It wasn't supposed to end like this. I couldn't die. Not yet.

I pushed myself up off the ground, still screaming as I shoved the kalis back in the bowl.

Fire pulsed at my feet, burning up the pieces of me that lingered on the ground.

"Now, Cordelia," Father Marcus yelled, from somewhere in the fog.

I had to finish the ritual.

The water in the bowl bubbled furiously, turning ice cold as I recited the final lines. "My soul will act as a divine weapon," I said, barely able to get the words out. I swayed on the spot. Did my best to stay standing. Something reached out, grabbing one of my exposed ribs and breaking it. I screamed, silver stars erupting into blinding white pain.

In the bowl, blue slivers of light mixed in with the pale orange glow.

"It will protect me in times of peril," I continued, sobbing as my free hand uselessly stretched across my stomach, trying to hold both sides of me together. The light and shadows in the ritual bowl formed a hand. It reached over, clasping mine. I swallowed, choking back a sob as I said the last line.

"And vanquish my enemies, before they vanquish me."

The hand in the bowl—and the one around my heart—faded away at those words. The shadows and lights wove together, drifting out of the water and wrapping around me. The wind picked up, filling the world with screams and roars—until it stopped abruptly. The light disappeared. The sounds died. The fog vanished.

Father Marcus stood at the other side of the altar, watching me.

I pulled the kalis out of the water. Darkness and light wove around the twisted blade, jumping from it to the wound in my palm. My skin closed up, leaving nothing but the faint trace of a scar.

The fire that'd been at my feet was stamped out.

Air returned to my lungs as I sucked in a deep breath. My free hand—the one that tried to cover the cut I'd made in my chest—rested on my coat. I pulled it away, holding it up.

No blood.

I patted at my coat, brushing the part that'd been ripped open by the dagger—but there wasn't a hole. I dropped that hand, glaring at the priest as I held the knife up in the air. "You said things were going to get weird. *Not* that I was gonna hallucinate carving myself up!"

Father Marcus tilted his head. "Is that what you saw? Interesting."

Annabelle wasn't smiling anymore. Her fascination gave way to dread. My heart sank. She looked at me like I was a monster.

"That was terrifying," I snapped. "I can't believe I gutted myself, and also heard—" I paused. Annabelle seemed to be on the verge of throwing up, but Father Marcus hung on my every word.

"What did you hear, Cordelia?" the priest asked me.

I swallowed, choosing to answer with a different version of the truth. "Screams. I think . . . I think they were from Hell."

The priest nodded. "That's a common occurrence, I'm afraid."

"Common?" I asked, heat rising in my face. "How many times have you done this?"

"Enough to know that you're now in the possession of an extremely powerful weapon. I trust you won't take this responsibility lightly."

"I'll do what needs to be done," I replied.

"Excellent." Father Marcus smiled. "If you'll excuse me, I've got a lot of planning to do for your town's anniversary. There's much to be done. Novitiate Reyes will show you out."

"Right. Thanks," I said, as Annabelle beckoned me toward her. She swallowed, blinking back tears as I got closer to her.

"Oh, and Cordelia?" Father Marcus called out, after we made it a few steps away.

I stopped, turning to face him. Nausea roiled in my stomach as a brief glimpse of the skin sloughing off his cheeks flashed across my vision. "Yes?" I asked, my voice cracking way too much over one word.

"The blessed weapon will allow you to trap the demon. In order to seal the demon in place, you'll have to stab it through the heart. You won't have a lot of time to do it." His smile widened, pulling his skin taut across his cheeks. "Don't miss."

CHAPTER TWENTY-SIX

IN WHICH I DID THE MATH WRONG

ANY UPDATE? **FRED TEXTED ME SOMETIME DURING THE** blessed weapon ritual. Probably between Father Marcus's creepy transformation and when I stabbed myself with the kalis.

Got it, I shot back. *Home soon.*

I'd been too scared to ask Annabelle what she saw during the ritual, and she didn't try talking to me after. Did the fog roll in around her, making it impossible to tell what was going on? If she looked at me, was I as gruesome as Father Marcus? Spine torn out, face in shreds?

Maybe it was better if I didn't know.

Hopefully, the blessed weapon would be able to trap Jesse *and* kill my father. The priest wasn't clear on what, exactly, it could do beyond the whole trapping thing. But to be fair, I didn't exactly ask. I wasn't quite sure how to explain that my father was brought up from Hell and currently running around town as a half-demon, half-human hybrid.

A vulture screeched as I turned down onto the long, winding

road that led through the woods and to the residential side of Ruin's End. A giant gust of wind rocked my car. My knuckles paled as I gripped the steering wheel tighter. Nudged it a bit, so I stayed on the road.

Even though the wind was strong enough to shake my car, the trees didn't move. A chill raked down my spine, long fingernails scratching into my skin. I slowed down, not needing to tempt fate by going too fast when the next strong burst of air hit.

A pair of orange eyes flashed in my rear-view mirror. My foot slammed down on the brakes. Tires screeched, shrieking through the numbingly silent night air.

"What the—" I started to ask before something crashed into the side of my car. Heart pounding, I frantically reached into my bag for my kalis. I swallowed. My quick, shallow breaths fogged up the driver's side window as I peered out of it.

Nothing.

I exhaled, holding the kalis close to me. Maybe I was just seeing things. Some strange side effect from the blessed weapon ritual. A leftover hallucination. Those orange eyes might not be real. It could have just been the wind and not a person that smashed into the side of my car.

Well, not a person. Not anymore, at least.

I'd waited in one spot long enough. If this *was* real, I wasn't going to sit around and let my newly-minted demon of a father tear me out of my own car. I floored it out of there, tires squealing as they peeled onto the road. I'd be home in ten more minutes. And Veronica should still be following me. If my father tried anything, she'd see it.

She'd help me stop him.

"Cordelia," my father's voice said, so close he might as well have been in the backseat of my car. My heart pounded, frantically trying to leap out of my chest.

I eased off the gas, foot hovering above the brakes.

It wasn't just in my head. He was here.

"Cordelia," he said again.

It was closer, like someone screamed my name in my ear. My car swerved sideways as I hit the brakes. I clenched my jaw, doing what I could to make sure that it skidded to a stop rather than flipping over. Held my breath as the tires protested over the road one last time.

Once the car stopped moving, I let out a deep breath. My heartbeat pulsed through my veins. A quick, clipped rhythm. I took a few minutes to steady it, sitting in my car that was in the middle of the road, angled in the wrong direction.

"Okay," I said, once I'd managed to slow my heart down a little. "Take your foot off the brakes, Cordelia. And drive."

The sound of metal being torn away from itself filled the air with a scream. Cool night air barged into the car. My whole body shook as I bit back a scream. The same putrid, rotting smell from the blessed weapon ritual wafted around me.

"Hey there, kiddo," David Scott said, breaths ragged as he stood where my driver's side door used to be. "Nice to see you again."

I sat there, frozen. His voice was lower than I remembered. A sharp edge lingered around the ends of each word, waiting to cut into me as soon as I turned to face him. All I wanted to do was curl up into a ball. Cry. Scream. Run.

But I wasn't going to give him the satisfaction of seeing me scared. Not anymore.

Not when I gave up some of my soul to create the thing that could kill him.

He was the ghost that never stopped haunting me. Every day, he'd sink his claws deeper into my skin, tearing me apart until he thought there was nothing left. But what he didn't understand was that while he was destroying the person I could have been, I rebuilt myself into someone new. Piece by piece, I broke apart and slowly turned into what I never wanted to be.

He taught me how to become a monster.

And now, it was time to return the favor.

Without looking at him, I reached for one of my backpack's straps. Small glass vials clinked as I pulled the bag closer to me.

"Sounds like you're taking after me," he said. "What've you got in there? Airplane bottles, maybe? Kind of weak, but we all have to start somewhere."

If it was anyone else, I would've laughed at the assumption.

His pale hand reached into the car. Cold, clammy fingers slid down my cheek. He turned them sideways, digging his nails into my skin. I blinked back tears as icy, searing pain bloomed where his nails had been.

Warm liquid ran down the side of my face. I was bleeding.

"What's wrong, kiddo?" he asked, pulling his hands away. "You won't even look at me. I think I deserve that much, at least. Especially after what you did."

My grip tightened on the backpack's strap. I took a deep breath, finally turning to face him. His bright orange eyes glinted in the darkness around us.

"You're right," I said, not daring to look away from him. "I haven't given you what you deserved. But I will."

I grabbed the kalis from the passenger's seat with my free hand and swung my backpack forward. The two textbooks I had in there flew out, slamming in his face. He staggered back as my holy water-filled test tubes dropped to the ground. Thankfully, they were sturdy enough that they didn't break.

I pulled my sword out of its sheath. Pocketed one test tube and uncorked the other.

Blood sang in my ears—a pot about to boil over—as I charged at him. I screamed, throwing the holy water in his face. Steam erupted from where the liquid touched him, sizzling and searing into his skin. He cursed, staggering even farther back. I pressed forward, not really knowing what I was doing, but using whatever advantage I could take.

Lights and shadows danced across the kalis, growing more solid the closer I got to my father. A bird screeched overhead as my foot broke a branch in half. The sound that used to fill me with dread gave me the courage to push forward. Veronica was here. Watching. If I needed her, she'd be there.

But there were some things I had to try on my own first. I ran at the distracted demon. Held the second test tube up to my mouth and uncorked it with my teeth as I ran toward him. I threw the contents of the little glass vial onto his face. The hiss of his skin burning filled the air. As did the tang of rotten, crisped flesh. I gagged but kept moving, getting way too close to him for comfort. My screams mixed with his as I plunged the dagger into his heart.

Or, I tried to plunge it, anyway.

He pulled his hands away from his face, stopping me right before my kalis dug into his chest.

"Just kidding," he said, winking at me.

It was like the whole world slowed down. He grabbed my throat, lifting me into the air. His face wasn't burned. My eyes widened as I tried prying his frozen fingers off me. That didn't make any sense. The holy water worked on Fred, and Fred was a demon. Just like my father.

"I can see the gears turning, kiddo," David Scott said, squeezing my throat. Air cut off on its way to my lungs. I choked on nothing as he continued. "I'll make it easy for you. There are certain benefits to being fresh out of Hell. I guess I have you to thank for that. If you hadn't sent me there in the first place, I wouldn't be what I am now." He pulled me closer, so I could look him in the eyes as he said, "Powerful."

Stars erupted in my vision as the pressure worsened. I scrabbled at his hands, still trying to get him to let me go. But that only made his grip tighten. A vise around my throat that I had no hope of removing. I dropped the kalis. Distantly, it clattered down as it hit the ground.

My vision darkened. Panic fluttered in my chest. His bright orange eyes would be the last thing I saw before I died.

Wind rushed around us as a familiar scream burst through the silence. Veronica slammed into my father, swearing. She knocked into him so hard that he let me go. Pain bloomed in my ribs as I crashed sideways into the ground. I gasped for breath, sucking in much air as I could.

Veronica's bones cracked and snapped as she knelt. Beige fur—sprinkled with giant spots—sprang from her skin, covering her completely. She opened her mouth, roaring, as her jaw elongated and her eyes darkened.

The aswang could take many forms. This one happened to be a jaguar.

I would've cheered her on for being such a badass, if I wasn't still fighting for air.

The jaguar charged at my father, using its momentum to pounce and pin him to the ground. It roared again. Sank its claws into his chest. I grabbed my kalis. Pushed myself up. Coughed furiously as adrenaline rushed through my veins, propelling me forward, even though every muscle in my body screamed at me to stop.

"Veronica!" I yelled. The jaguar tilted its head, lifting a paw and shifting slightly so I could get closer to my father.

But the demon took his chance at the small distraction. His hands slid under the massive cat's torso, throwing it off him.

I screamed, changing course, needing to get to her. To make sure she was okay. But he reached out and grabbed my legs, yanking me back down to the damp ground. My chin slammed into the soft dirt. Pain shot through my jaw as my teeth sank into my tongue, and the warm, coppery taste of blood filled my mouth. I spat it out, scrambling to stand as my father strode by me.

He stopped once he passed me, turning back around. Picked up my kalis. Weighed it in his hands as I got to my feet. The lights and shadows that wrapped around the blade froze, marbled in strange patterns.

He winked at me again. "Thanks for this, kiddo." He moved faster than should've been possible, standing over the jaguar. He put his foot on the cat's neck, putting pressure on it. The world sped up around me as the jaguar's fur receded, leaving only Veronica in its wake.

David Scott lifted his foot from my best friend's neck. He picked her up and slammed her back against a nearby tree.

"Don't worry," he said, the smile in his voice sending a chill through my body. "This is going to hurt."

I screamed, rushing to get to them before he could do anything. But I wasn't fast enough. I wailed. Sank to the ground as the dagger sank into Veronica's skin, piercing the spot over her heart—

"What?" my father barked, drawing the dagger back. I blinked, staring at the blade's edges. They were clean. No blood.

Veronica's eyes widened. Her hands flew to the spot that should've been stabbed. "How—" she started to ask, but she didn't have time to finish her question. My father brought the kalis down on her again.

This time, I moved. Used whatever small reserves of energy I had left to get over to them.

The lights and shadows on the dagger began shifting and changing as I got closer to it. He pulled the kalis away. Still clean.

"That's new," Veronica said, right before she brought her elbow up and rammed it into his nose.

He swore, staggering back.

Pure, unbridled rage burned inside of me. He'd tried to kill me the same way he had seven years ago. He stole the weapon that held a part of my soul and wanted to use it to kill my best friend. All he'd ever done was take. He was never going to stop.

When he'd been alive, I was forced to give up pieces of myself just to pretend that I was whole. I let him steal them from me in order to survive.

He destroyed who I was. Who I could've been.

And it was all because he loved being a monster more than he loved me.

Now, he was doing the same thing. But it wouldn't last for much longer.

The dagger glowed; lights and shadows merged together, giving the blade a light blue tint. He screamed as the dagger seared into his skin. But this time, I felt it working. The kalis's energy matched mine, burning him. Hurting him in a way I wanted to but couldn't.

He gripped the blade, rage warping his features into the creature I'd tried to forget. "Nice try. But you're going to have to do better than that if you want to win." He escaped into the forest, moving too fast for me to stop him.

I stood there, helpless as he vanished with the only hope I had left.

CHAPTER TWENTY-SEVEN

IN WHICH I AM THE RECIPIENT OF A PEP TALK

GRAVEL CRUNCHED UNDER VERONICA'S FEET AS SHE walked up to my car. The driver's side door lay a few feet away, completely discarded. She picked it up. Threw it in my trunk as I sank down to the ground, putting my head in my hands.

I'd already cried too much tonight to make any new tears. My eyes were sore. Burning. But maybe more would come anyway.

I didn't know how much time had passed between my father's sudden departure and the soft, low sound of a luxury car slowly driving up to us, but it didn't matter. I'd carved off pieces of my soul and created a blessed weapon.

And, just like that, my father took it away.

I dragged my hands down my face. Winced as my fingers grazed the wounds that David Scott left on my cheek.

"Fred's here," Veronica said. She might as well have been talking to me from another dimension. Her voice was distant. Hollow. As empty as I felt inside.

I gave her a weak thumbs-up, not bothering to stand. She moved closer to me as Fred's car quietly drifted to a stop. He killed the engine. Popped open his door.

Our demonic guidance counselor sucked in a deep breath, exhaling as he asked, "What the hell happened here?"

"My father," I replied. Veronica held out her hand to help me up. I took it, slowly getting to my feet.

"And the blessed weapon?" Fred asked. Next to me, Veronica shook her head.

I tried swallowing some spit, but my mouth was dry as a desert. And still a little bit of blood in there. Perfect. "He took it." That was all I could get out before my voice broke.

Veronica slipped an arm around my shoulder, pulling me closer. Warmth radiated off her. It seeped into the cracks that fighting my father created in me, and I burrowed into her shoulder as Fred looked over at my totaled car.

"That one's gonna be hard to explain," he said.

Laughter bubbled up in my throat. I figured he'd try cheering me up. Or be mad that I lost our one advantage so easily. But I hadn't expected him to be so casual about everything. The only things keeping me standing were the thin line of tension snaking down from my shoulders to my legs and Veronica. Fred's calm reaction cut it in half. My knees buckled as it snapped.

Veronica caught me, holding me up. "We should get her home," she said, steadying me. "We don't want to be out here if . . ." Her voice trailed away. We knew what she was going to say.

If he *comes back.*

She was right. Even though we would've stood more of a chance with Fred on our side, I couldn't take seeing him again. Not tonight. Not after what he'd almost done to me.

"Right," Fred said, walking around his car and opening the passenger's side door. "I think it's best if Cordy rides with me. Veronica, you'll drive the ruined car behind us."

Veronica tensed, her arm wrapping tighter around me. "No."

Fred sighed. "Yes."

"I'm not leaving her alone," Veronica replied.

"You are," Fred said, crossing his arms. "You'll be following us the whole time. *If* we get any unwelcome visitors, I'm in much better shape to fend them off. I wasn't invited to your little fight, remember? And I've been dealing with demons for centuries. You've known we're real for, what? A few years? I have lifetimes of knowledge." Veronica opened her mouth to interject, but Fred cut her off before she could. "Besides, Cordelia and I have something to discuss. I'd prefer it just be between us. If you don't mind."

The last thing we needed was a fight to break out between Fred and Veronica. I reached up, gently pulling my best friend's hand away from my arm. "It's okay, Harmonica. I'll see you when we get home."

"Cordy—" she started to say, but she caught herself. Looked away as she blinked back tears. "I'll be right behind you the whole time."

I squeezed her hand and pressed my car keys into them. "I know. Thank you."

Dirt and rocks crunched under my feet as I moved away from her and closer to Fred. I ducked into his car, sliding into the passenger's seat. He closed the door and said something to Veronica that was too muffled for me to make out. She replied.

I closed my eyes, letting the heat in Fred's car wash over me. An engine roared to life nearby. Veronica shouted something else to Fred. He paused in front of his door and waved at her before getting into the car.

"Well," he said, closing the door behind him. "Looks like you had an interesting night."

I sank further in the chair, not daring to look at him. I wouldn't be able to take it if he was judging me. Or, even worse, if he pitied me. "That's putting it lightly."

"I suppose it is."

The car glided smoothly from the side of the road. Silence sat in the back seat, watching us as we drove down the long, winding path that led out of the woods.

"What did you want to talk about?" I asked, when I couldn't take it anymore.

"We'll get to that," he replied. "First, I'd like to know how you're feeling."

I scoffed. What kind of a question was that? "Not great, Fred."

"Obviously. But I want to dive a little deeper than sarcastic rebuttals."

I stared straight ahead at the small patches of night the headlights carved through. There were so many ways to answer his question. I wasn't even sure what to say until the words tumbled out. "I don't want to die."

My thought weighed heavy in the air around us. Silence shifted, drifting closer as the car's heat wrapped around me. Saying it out loud made it feel more real. True. Tangible.

It wasn't like I'd been hiding that particular sentiment from myself. It was always there, informing everything I'd ever done. That was why I sent my father to Hell in the first place. He wanted to kill me. I wanted to live.

It was one thing to experience that seven years ago—to tuck the fear and loathing away into a place that I never thought I'd need to see again. I'd done my best to forget about it. Tried to move past it. But there was no use in ignoring it any longer. My father hadn't changed. If anything, he'd gotten worse.

Now, he had new ways to kill me.

Not that I was going to let him. Thanks to David Scott, I'd become the monster he'd always wanted me to be. But I was something else, too. Something different.

He would always be a part of who I was. Small pieces broke off him and took root in my veins long ago. Poisoning me from the inside out. I carried them with me, along with the scars he left behind.

But no matter how much he tried changing me, at the end of the day, I was still me: a high school stage manager with *meh* grades, a caffeine addiction, and a best friend who loved me so much that she turned into a monster to protect me.

And *that* meant something. It had to.

"You're not going to die," Fred said, once it was clear that I wasn't going to add anything else to the conversation. "I won't let that happen."

"You shouldn't make promises you can't keep. Especially when my father is involved."

Fred winced. "If I had known that it was possible to bring him back—"

"Why didn't you?" I snapped, my voice rising to a yell. Part of me wanted to take it back—apologize for losing my temper so quickly. But I stuffed that bit of me away. He needed to understand what he'd done to me. What he'd taken away by creating a deal that was so easily bent and broken.

My voice cracked into a thousand pieces as I said, "You promised he wouldn't come back, but he did. And now—and now . . . ." I took a deep breath, balling the ends of my jacket in my fists. "He'll try to destroy everything. Including me. And I want to stop him. I *have* to stop him. But I'm scared. I know I shouldn't be, but I am." I laughed bitterly. "Have been my whole life."

"Hm," Fred said, as we finally got out of the woods and turned onto a main road. "Do you want to know what frightens me?"

"What?"

"Everything. This world is a terrifying place."

I frowned. "You can't be serious. You're a demon. That's pretty scary."

"Maybe. But I don't scare you, do I?"

"You haven't tried to." It was true. Sure, there were times when flames from Hell appeared around him and he antlered-up, but it never felt like I was in danger. If anything, it was like I had an extra layer of protection.

"Because I don't *want to*, Cordelia. The things that do—the people who want you to be scared—are only doing it because they want to prove they have power over you. They want to fool you into believing that you can't stop them. But you *can*. Even if that's hard for you to believe right now, I need you to remember that."

I thought I was out of tears, but they came anyway. I looked around wildly, blinking them back. "I'll try," I replied.

"No. You won't try. You'll succeed."

"But what if I can't?" I asked, letting the words come crashing out. "He took my kalis. I can't fight him without it. I tried tonight, and—and I almost died." I shook my head, staring out the window. "You're wrong about me. You think I can handle this. That I'm some badass who's brave enough to face him without the one thing that could kill him, but I'm not. I can't."

"You can—"

"No," I snapped, cutting him off. "I'm not ready to fight him again. Not after tonight." I let go of my jacket, fingers brushing my neck. My skin was tender to the touch. It would start to bruise soon. "I'm not strong. I'm scared."

Silence settled back between us, shifting around in such a small space. It pushed us closer together and pulled us farther apart as neither of us tried to break it. A few tears streaked down my cheeks. I sniffled, wiping them away as Fred cleared his throat.

"After Dolores changed," Fred said, turning down my block, "do you know what I did? Absolutely nothing. I should've tried helping her—discovering a way to reverse her transformation, or figuring out where she could be safe in the meantime. But I didn't. I sat there, terrified, and allowed that fear to rule my life. I still do, sometimes."

"This isn't very comforting," I replied.

"I know. I wasn't trying to be."

"Oh. Well. Thanks, I guess?"

Fred exhaled as he pulled into my driveway. "My point is that it's perfectly understandable to be scared. To feel like there's nothing you can do, and wallow in that for as long as you need. But you can't let it consume you. You don't have that luxury."

"You did."

"I had decades to recover. Centuries. You have three days."

"Great pep talk, Fred. I feel so much better."

He ran a hand through his dark blond hair. "You're up against things that you never should've had to face in the first place. But here they are. They think they have the advantage because they're bigger, stronger, ruthless. They're formidable opponents, certainly. But they're not you."

"Good for them," I muttered.

"No," Fred said, turning to face me. "Good for *you*. There's power in that. In who *you* are. All you have to do is believe it."

My hands twisted together. I looked down at the dash. "Enough power to stop a demon?"

"I'd like to think so." He turned his car off. Cool air rushed in as he opened the driver's side door. "Now, tonight we definitely experienced a small setback, but it's not the end of the world. Tomorrow I'll try hunting down your blessed weapon."

"I'll help."

Fred shook his head. "We still have no idea how to trap Jesse in that Maleficent. You must figure that out before Friday. There's no other way to stop him."

"Fine. If I can't go with you, take Veronica." I reluctantly opened my door.

Fred frowned. "Tempting, but Veronica was right. We can't leave you alone. She stays with you. You'll need the help more than me."

"But—"

"I'll be fine, little one. You have more pressing things to worry about. Don't waste a thought on your friendly neighborhood guidance counselor."

Veronica pulled up in my broken car before I could respond. She parked it, hopped out, and was at my side faster than I could blink. "You okay?" she asked.

I nodded. "I will be. Once this is all over."

"Then let's make sure we end this, shall we?" Fred asked, clapping his hands together. "Let's get some rest and deal with our rapidly building pile of problems tomorrow."

I let Fred and Veronica inside the house, but I lingered in the doorway, staring out into the night. I'd barely made it out of that alive. My father was out there, somewhere, ready to finish what he started. He'd changed so much. And it was all because he wanted to kill me.

I wasn't sure which was worse. Making a deal with a demon to get rid of a monster.

Or becoming one.

CHAPTER TWENTY-EIGHT

IN WHICH WE SEE REGINALD AGAIN

VERONICA AND I BROUGHT MY CAR TO THE BODY SHOP just as the sun crested in a red-hued morning sky. Neither of us slept much, which meant that we were both in dire need of caffeine. But we had more pressing things to deal with before we solved that problem.

I didn't want Mom to come back from her shift and discover that my driver's side door was currently sitting on the back seat—or for some well-meaning mechanic to call her and tell her what happened—so Veronica and I went to a place that'd fixed a minor bump in her fender without alerting her parents. All we had to do was bribe the guy with some of Mrs. Dominguez's homemade pancit and we were in business.

"Well?" Veronica asked, as I slid back into her car.

"He thinks it'll take a week," I replied.

"What're you gonna tell your mom?"

"That's assuming she notices."

"She could."

I sighed, leaning my head back against the seat. "Maybe I needed a new battery or something. It probably won't even come up. Anyway," I said, looking at her as I swerved around the subject, "I think I know what we should do next. But you're not gonna like it. I'm not sure I will, either."

"Comforting."

I winked at her. "I try."

She rolled her eyes, turning her key in the ignition. The engine roared to life. "Okay, Accordion. Where are we going?"

I closed my eyes and pinched the bridge of my nose. Fred left sometime in the middle of the night to track down my father, but before he went, he reiterated that our top priority was discovering a way to trap Jesse. As if I didn't know that.

We had two days left to narrow it down, and Wikipedia had way too many results for us to even try to sort through all of them. Even then, Wikipedia might've missed something. Open-sourced information could only go so far, especially when it pertained to demonic rituals.

Only one person in town knew more about this stuff than me who a) wasn't a priest, and b) wasn't a demon. Unfortunately, I couldn't ask him. According to the town's paper, he was buried in a quiet ceremony that only his brother attended. His parents were out of the country, otherwise, they *totally* would've been there. I didn't really buy that—Dustin's parents easily could've taken a flight home—but the Joneses owned the paper. And most of the town. So, nothing bad was ever written about them.

If I wanted to figure this out, I'd need Blake's notes. I knew who could help me get them, but I wasn't sure he'd hear me out.

I had to try, though.

“I never thought I’d say this,” I replied, slowly opening my eyes. “But we need to go to Dustin’s house.”

“You’re right. I *definitely* don’t like that.”

“There’s no way around it.”

Her jaw clenched, but she nodded. I figured I’d have to argue my case more. Lay out exactly why going to the Jones McMansion was the smartest move. But Veronica had seen Blake face down the demon, too. Jesse ordered the aswang to kill Dustin’s brother, but she flew away, refusing. And once she did—once she showed Jesse’s demon whose side she was really on—he brought my father back from Hell.

Maybe that was why Veronica turned onto the road without trying to talk me out of my decision. She understood it just as well as I did.

The only way out of this mess was how we’d gotten into it in the first place.

Together.

Veronica pulled up to the mansion’s front gates, slowing to a stop at the callbox. The window *whirred* as it rolled down. She reached out, fingers hovering in front of the button. “We’re really gonna do this, huh?” she asked, pulling her hand back in the car.

“Yep. Now or never, Harmonica.”

Her arm extended, finger hitting the button like a snake striking its prey. A high-pitched series of beeps came from the callbox. Then static. And, finally, Dustin’s sullen voice barked out, “What do you want?”

I leaned over Veronica, trying not to let the faint scents of lavender and vanilla overwhelm me. My fingers brushed the warm, bare skin on her arms. Veronica gasped. I swallowed, wishing away the warmth that rushed up my cheeks. A quick glimpse in the driver's side mirror confirmed my biggest fear: I was blushing.

I cleared my throat, hoping that the Joneses' callbox didn't have a camera installed. "Can we come in? We need to talk."

Static wove through the few beats of silence on the other end.

"Do you think he heard us?" Veronica asked, shifting. Her hand brushed my flaming-hot cheek. Well. That was embarrassing. I snapped up, jostling back into the passenger's seat.

"I heard you," Dustin shot back. "I just don't want to talk to you."

"You don't have much of a choice." I projected, just to make sure he heard me.

"Of course I do. Go away, Scott. And you too, Dominguez. I don't want anything to do with either of you."

"Dustin—" I started to say, but Veronica cut me off.

"We're going to make those assholes pay for what they did," Veronica said, so firmly that it temporarily wiped all my doubts away. "You can help us, or you can sit in your house and mope. What's it gonna be, Jones?"

The line clicked off. A few birds chirped in the nearby trees. My heart pounded so loudly in my chest that I was sure Veronica could hear it. That wasn't the approach I would've taken—not when he'd just watched his brother get brutally murdered, but then the gate slowly swung open, and Veronica smiled smugly as she drove through it.

"How'd you know that would work?" I asked.

"I didn't," she replied. "I just thought about what I'd do if—" She paused, glancing at me before she looked back at the road. "He just lost someone he cared about. I figured he might need a little extra motivation to get us through the door. Some creative goal-setting, if you will."

"Let's hope trapping a demon is creative enough."

Dustin walked out of his house right as we got to the front of it. He had on black sweatpants and a black crew neck. He stood there, watching us as Veronica parked.

My best friend nodded to him, opening her car door. "Oh, I think it will be." She greeted him, walking closer as I slowly got out. This was the first time I'd seen him since the paramedics separated us. His blond hair stuck up at weird angles, like he hadn't bothered to comb it. Dark circles burrowed under his eyes, leaving his pale skin bruised with rings that shouldn't have been there.

My hands drifted to my neck. I'd wrapped a scarf around it before I left the house this morning. The faint outline of my father's fingers had already turned my skin shades of purple and dark blue.

A sea of differences drifted between Dustin and me. But the scars we shared—the ones we couldn't see—would hopefully be enough to bring us together.

I owed him an explanation for a lot of things. And an apology, too.

"If you're killing them, I want in," Dustin said. It was probably the only version of hello he could give us.

Something rustled in the trees surrounding his house. It sent a flock of birds into the air, scattering and squawking.

Veronica's head snapped in the direction of the sound. "Not out here," she said, gesturing to the door. "Inside."

Dustin crossed his arms. "You can't just invite yourselves over."

"Too bad. We just did," Veronica said, pushing past him. She marched toward his house like a general getting ready to enter a war room.

"Was it something I said?" Dustin asked.

If our worlds hadn't fallen apart—if this was another normal, ordinary day—I would've given him some kind of snarky response. Or told him to shut up. But everything was different now. Including the three of us.

"Dustin," I said, searching around for the right thing to say, but falling short, "I—"

"No," he said, cutting me off. "I don't want to hear it."

Something like a laugh mixed in with a deep, low growl rumbled from inside the tree line.

"But I'm—" I started to say.

He turned away from me. "Your girlfriend is right. We should go inside."

Luckily, he couldn't see the blush that was definitely creeping into my cheeks. "She's not my girlfriend."

Dustin sighed. "You're really good at seeing what you wanna see. You know that?"

"What's that supposed to mean?"

"Nothing," he said, stepping away from me. "Why is she even here, anyway? She doesn't have anything to do with this."

"She does." Was all I could say, because Veronica's truth wasn't mine to tell.

"Whatever." Dustin tossed the word out like he was throwing

it away. He walked away without another word.

Veronica stood in the door. Her whole body was tense. Alert. She looked out into the trees like she was expecting something—or someone—to burst out of them at any moment. And maybe she was. Jesse and my father could be following us. Watching our every move. Waiting for the perfect time to destroy us.

I shook my head, trailing after Dustin. My blessed weapon was gone. It'd be the perfect time for them to try attacking us. But I'd already lived in the shadow of constant fear. When I was a kid, I'd always do everything so carefully because I didn't want to give my father a reason to hate me. In the end, he hated me anyway.

I was tired of feeling like I always had to look over my shoulder. That the slightest mistake would result in a new bruise, or a broken bone, or worse—my death.

No matter what I did, my father was going to find me. It was a fact that I'd accepted as easily as breathing. He could be in the woods, a hundred feet away, ready to strike. Or somewhere else in town planning his next move. He'd find me on his terms. In his own time.

Which was fine by me. The next time we met, I planned to be prepared. I didn't believe the nonsense Fred was spouting last night—that I had the power to stop David Scott. But I'd meant what I said. I didn't want to die.

If I did, I'd make sure I took him with me.

"Let's go to the study," Dustin said, closing the door behind me. The last time I'd been in the entryway, Dustin and I were running out of his house, away from the aswang.

Away from *Veronica*, as she tore through the house, leaving chaos in its wake. It even destroyed the huge glass chandelier that'd been hanging over the stairs.

It'd only been a few days since then. But now, it looked like nothing had ever happened. The chandelier was back. Everything was in its proper place.

"It's so clean," I said.

Dustin shrugged, leading us down the hallway filled with way too many taxidermized animals. "Had to cope with all this bullshit somehow."

Veronica's hand brushed mine. My heart raced a little as I asked, "You cleaned this all yourself?"

"Despite what my parents think, I'm not completely useless," Dustin deadpanned. He stopped in front of the study door, opened it for us, and gestured inside. "After you."

Veronica stepped through first, pausing as she got a look at the pack of dead, stuffed wolves crowded around the couches. "What the hell is this?" she asked, giving me a skeptical look as I moved next to her.

"I don't really know." I pointed to a reddish-gray wolf in the middle of the circle. "But that one's Reginald."

"I'm so glad you remembered!" Dustin said as he closed the door. Absolutely no trace of sarcasm in his voice. Damn. He really *was* glad that I remembered. He drifted over to the couches, sitting under Reginald. "He's my favorite one. Come on, sit down. I want to know how we're going to kill the demons."

"Sit down . . . under the wolves?" Veronica asked.

"They're not going to bite, if that's what worries you," Dustin replied.

I took Veronica's hand, careful not to lace my fingers through hers as I led her to the couches. I let go of her, sitting on the end of the one across from Dustin. I figured Veronica would sit on the other end, but instead, she sat so close to me that I felt warmth coming off her body. Our arms brushed through our jackets. She didn't seem to notice, but that small gesture sent a spark running through me.

Dustin's gaze drifted between us. An amused glint shone in his icy blue eyes. "So," he said, leaning back in the chair. Once again, he blocked the shadowbox with its quill from view. "You promised me a shot at revenge. How do I take it?"

"You're not the only one who wants revenge," Veronica said.

"Oh, yeah?" Dustin asked. "What did they do to you?"

"Turned me into this." That was all she said before her bones started cracking and breaking. Her brown skin lost its luster and warmth, fading into a cold, dead gray. A film of slime stretched out over it. Her jaw elongated. Eyes turned pitch black. Fingers stretched out and merged with her nails. Formed claw-like talons ready to cut. Or kill.

Dustin's mouth hung open for a few seconds. His face turned red as he snapped it shut, swearing as he jumped up from the couch. His hands balled into fists. "You're the reason Blake's dead." His voice dripped venom. He launched over the table that sat in the middle of the couch circle, pulling his hands back as he got ready to punch the aswang. But Veronica was faster. Stronger. She snatched him out of the air, slamming him down onto the table.

It didn't break, but it sure came close.

Dustin gasped from getting the wind knocked out of him.

"It wasn't her fault," I said, as the aswang transformed back into Veronica.

"It was," Veronica said. She still pinned Dustin to the table.

"At least a little. And I'm sorry about that, Dustin. I really am. If I'd known that leaving would—" She paused, looking at me. "I had no idea that was going to happen."

"You left us alone with a demon," Dustin snapped. "If you'd stayed, you could've fought the other one. Blake would still be alive."

Veronica shook her head. "No. I was a liability. I could already feel the demon trying to force me to kill your brother. If I hadn't left, I would've given in. I did what I thought was best in the moment. What would keep both of you safe."

"But we won't be safe," I said, interjecting before Dustin could, "until we trap Jesse and kill my father."

"How do we do that?" Dustin asked.

"We don't know," Veronica replied.

"We were hoping Blake found something, before . . ." My voice trailed away. "We need access to his things again. We have to find his research."

Dustin blinked, shifting his gaze to each of us. A few seconds of baffled silence filled the air before he burst out into a fit of delirious laughter. "You want me to help you go through my dead brother's things in the *hopes* that he's found the key to solving your demon puzzle?"

"Yeah," Veronica and I said together.

"And what if he doesn't have it?"

"What if he does?" I countered.

Dustin squinted at both of us. Chewed on the thought. And sighed. "I'll help you on one condition."

"Name it," I said.

He smiled. It was wild. Feral. And ready for revenge. "When you destroy those bastards, I get a front-row seat."

CHAPTER TWENTY-NINE

IN WHICH WE FIND A DIFFERENT PIECE OF THE PUZZLE

WE SEARCHED BLAKE'S ROOM FOR TWO HOURS AND found nothing. We'd almost given up when Veronica mentioned The Coffee Spot. Partly due to it being lunchtime, but also because Blake's office was there and, aside from Dustin and his absentee parents, no one else had access to it.

The three of us stood at the café's threshold, watching people coming in and out. They didn't really pay attention to Veronica and me. Not when Dustin stood beside us. He'd cleaned himself up a little and put on jeans instead of sweatpants. To anyone who caught a quick glimpse of him, it must've been like seeing a ghost. Even more so now. His brother's death dulled some of Dustin's sharp edges, molding him into something new.

"You ready?" I asked, nudging him with my elbow.

He exhaled, putting his foot on the café's porch. "Yeah."

The Coffee Spot closed for a few days after Blake's death, but after his funeral, his parents forced the manager to open it back up. Technically, the crime scene was between the café and the woods, so as long as no one went near the roped-off area, they wouldn't be tampering with anything. But it was the principle of the thing that got to me.

Robert and Olivia Jones hadn't bothered to fly back into town for their son's funeral. They were fine with carrying on as if Blake hadn't died tragically and expected everyone else to do the same. Even Dustin, who they hadn't bothered to check on at all.

I touched his arm. "If it's too much, you can always leave."

"I know," he replied, pulling away from me. "Let's get this over with."

Dustin walked through the door first. Veronica followed. I cast one last glance to the trees surrounding us—looming and leering as if spying on our every move—and then darted inside.

Heat filled the café, but it was the only warm thing about it. Normally, customers and baristas would be chatting animatedly, or sitting at tables furiously typing away at their laptops while they sipped various espresso drinks. Or teas. But now, the place was virtually empty. No discussions, debates, or laughter filled the air. Two people sat at their own tables, each at separate ends of the café. A lone barista stood behind the counter. She gave us a small nod.

Dustin waved at her, turning down the hallway to Blake's office. Once Veronica and I followed, and the barista was satisfied that we weren't going to order anything, she went back to arranging pastries in the display case.

Dustin held the door to Blake's office open. Veronica stood in front of him for a few seconds. Staring at him. When she'd sized him up enough, she went inside.

"I don't remember her being this intense," Dustin said as I walked past him.

Veronica cleared her throat. "That was before a demon turned me into an aswang."

"What happens when we trap the demon? Will you turn back into a person, or—?"

Veronica shrugged. "I have no idea. Maybe. Hopefully? I guess we'll see on Friday."

"We'd better start looking for a way to do it, then," I replied. No one protested. We all exchanged an uneasy glance before splitting up. Dustin took the desk. Veronica had the filing cabinets by the door. I had everything else.

Blake's office was the exact opposite of his room. The lighting was warm and cozy. There was an armchair that I could probably take a nap in, if I really wanted to. But it was also messy as hell. Papers strewn all over his desk. Post-it notes randomly stuck to the wall. Books stacked from the floor to above his desk. The only thing he was missing was a bunch of old articles and lots of red string to connect them.

I had no idea how we were going to find a trapping ritual—or if Blake had figured it out—but I was doing my best to will it into existence. It was here, somewhere. We just had to root through the chaos first.

I drifted over to a stack of books, flipping them open as Veronica rifled through filing cabinets and Dustin popped open the desk's drawers. He opened and closed them in a short, staccato rhythm. I pulled a large, thick book out of the pile.

The pages were worn. Old. Smelled like mothballs and regret. I leafed through it, coughing as dust rose through the pages and into the air.

The random page I landed on had a picture of a wolf standing on two legs. Diagrams of various moon cycles surrounded the creature.

Wasn't really expecting a whole encyclopedia entry on werewolves, but stranger things had happened during the last week. That wasn't all, though. Monsters from all around the world were in here. Onryō. Púca. Even the aswang.

"Oh shit," I said, finally finding the demon entry. Most of the stuff we already knew. Loves making bargains with humans, creepy powers, generally assholes. Not super helpful. But something scrawled in the top right corner of the page caught my eye. A number.

"What's up?" Veronica asked, taking her head out from the inside of the filing cabinet.

"One hundred," I said, looking up at Dustin. "You're sure it doesn't mean anything to you?"

He shook his head. "Other than that note in Blake's desk and the town's anniversary? No."

I stood up, accidentally knocking the pile of books over. They spilled onto the floor. "It's written on this page."

"So?" Dustin asked.

"So, it has to mean *something*," I shot back. "Maybe it was his favorite number, or—"

"Or a combination for a safe," Veronica added.

"Well, yeah, but there's not a safe in—" I said, as Veronica nodded at my feet. I looked down, finishing my thought. "Here." A small safe sat on the floor, tucked under a side table.

The pile of books that I'd knocked over blocked it from view.

Dustin scrambled out of his chair and down to the floor. I held my breath as he put in 1-0-0 as the combination. He tugged at the handle—nothing.

"Dammit," he said, pulling at it some more. It didn't budge. He tried a few more things—Blake's birthday, their address, the date The Coffee Spot opened.

Still nothing.

"Maybe we should leave it," I said, as Dustin pulled the small safe up from the floor and set it on Blake's desk. For a second, it looked like he was going to chuck the thing at the wall and try to break it open that way.

"No," Dustin growled, swatting me away before I could get close to it. "I need to see what's in here."

Veronica put her hand on his shoulder. "Statistically, you could be trying to crack this thing for years before you get it open."

"We don't have years," I said softly.

"I know," Dustin snapped. "But what if there's something in here that can help us?" He looked down at the ground, voice breaking as he said, "I need to see what he left behind."

Veronica and I exchanged a glance before she said, "Cordy and I will keep searching the office. You focus on the safe."

After ten minutes, we were back to where we'd started. Our office search hadn't turned anything up and Dustin still hadn't opened the safe. He hit it, screaming.

Even though Dustin thought he was living in Blake's shadow, his older brother had always been looking out for him. He wanted him to be better. Died trying to help him. Everything Blake had ever done—obsessing over demon research, becoming an amateur exorcist, even opening The Coffee Spot—had been about his family and the legacy they'd leave behind. Of course, that legacy was tarnished by one thing: the deal with a demon that created our town.

It couldn't be that simple—but maybe Blake's obsession with clearing his family name was the answer.

"Try our founding date," I said.

"What?" Dustin asked.

"When Ruin's End was founded. You know, the thing we're doing a whole musical about?" I deadpanned.

Dustin rolled his eyes, entering that combination into the safe. He pulled on the handle. Swore as it released and the safe clicked open.

Only one thing inside: a small, leather-bound journal.

Dustin's hand shook as he pulled it out. Age had yellowed and worn the paper inside. The ink was faded and dull, but still legible.

Ryeland Jones.

"Whoa," I said, looking over Dustin's shoulder.

"How did he find that?" Veronica asked.

"Does it matter?" Dustin replied. He was right. It didn't really. He turned to the next page. In the top right corner, fresher, darker ink marked it with a "one."

Ryeland hadn't numbered the pages. Blake had.

"Go to page one hundred," I said, nudging him with my elbow.

The entries we skimmed through were filled to the brim with words. Endless recollections of Ryeland Jones's daily life. The town's history museum would eat this shit up—but we weren't getting paid to read this whole thing. And we didn't have time to go on a ninety-nine-page-journey with Dustin's great-grandfather.

Page one hundred, though, was different. Three lines in neat, concise writing hovered right in the middle of it:

The daemon's undoing shall come forth
When the instrument that solidified our bargain
Is used once again.

Well, thanks, Ryeland. You could've been a bit more specific.

"What does that mean?" Veronica asked.

"It doesn't even rhyme," I quipped.

Dustin turned to face both of us. "You both made deals, right? How did you solidify your bargains?"

My hands flew up to my neck. I hadn't taken my scarf off. "I . . . uh, I nodded."

Dustin squinted at me. "What?"

"I wasn't really able to do anything else in the moment—"

"I signed something," Veronica interjected, saving me from having to stumble through an explanation. "He used a quill."

My eyes widened. The quill in the shadowbox on the wall of the Jones McMansion. "Dustin—"

"Blake *was* right!" he said, slamming the journal shut. "The one in my study really *was* used in the original deal. That's gotta be it!"

Veronica frowned. "How is a quill supposed to trap him? Isn't that what the blessed weapon is for?"

"No idea," I replied, shrugging. "Maybe the quill has to be in the same room or something. I'll tie it to the kalis if I need to. Once I get it back." Rage burned through my body. My father still had the kalis. Hopefully, Fred would be able to find him and get it before Friday. If he didn't, we could stand some kind of chance with the quill. If we figured out how to use it.

Maybe we weren't totally screwed after all.

"We don't know how any of this works," Veronica said. "It's like we have the ingredients to a recipe but no instructions."

"We have two days," I said, patting the bag where I'd shoved Blake's monster encyclopedia. "And now we have one more thing to use against them. We've got this."

CHAPTER THIRTY

IN WHICH WE PHONE A FRIEND

WE'D ALREADY SPENT MOST OF THURSDAY WATCHING paint dry. Literally.

We still weren't sure how to trap Jesse in the Maleficent, but Dustin found something useful in Blake's belongings: directions on how to make a sigil. We also spent the day hiding holy water and crosses in the theater, in case that was where we needed to make our last stand. We used blacklight paint for the sigil to ensure that no one knew it was there, arcing it across the stage.

It wasn't exactly a safe bet, but it was the only one we could make.

With school canceled and other anniversary events up in the air after Blake's death, opening night of *Our Demon Town* was the one place Jesse could make a big statement. If he truly wanted to kick off his grand plan of making more bargain hot spots like Ruin's End, maybe he'd use the show as a way to prove how well his concept worked. He seemed dramatic enough to try to win me over in front of a crowd. After all, it was what he'd done when he sang to me after rehearsal and at karaoke.

If we had to choose somewhere for a last stand, the theater was as good a place as any.

Dustin sighed, leaning against the side of Ryeland Jones's fake house. "Do you think we did enough? My back's pretty sore." As if to punctuate his point, he stretched.

Veronica shook her head. "We're prepping this place to take on a demon. I don't think 'enough' applies here."

Dustin waved her thought away. "You're a monster, right? Can't you just fight them? Why do you need us?"

"They're too strong," I cut in, before Veronica could reply. "Even if Fred was here, my father and Jesse would wipe the floor with us."

"Where is he, anyway?" Dustin asked.

"I wish I knew," I replied. I hadn't heard from him since he promised to track down my blessed weapon. A billion texts and way too many voicemails later, I had no idea where my demonic guidance counselor was.

Dustin frowned. "But the priest said he'd help us tomorrow, right? At least there's that."

I nodded. "Father Marcus said, 'Neither Heaven nor Hell could keep me from attending opening night.'"

Veronica chuckled. "You sure he wasn't talking about baseball?"

"He does love the Red Sox," I replied, "though this time, I think he was referring to our groundbreaking production and once-in-a-lifetime premiere of *Our Demon Town*."

"Can't wait to see the reviews," Veronica said, kicking her legs out as she sat at the edge of the stage. "The special effects were wicked! It really felt like they trapped a demon on the stage. Five stars."

"Still trying to figure out how they did that trick with the Maleficent," Dustin added.

I groaned, lying down flat on the stage. "That makes two of us."

With Fred MIA and Blake's research well slowly drying up, we were running out of options way too quickly. Father Marcus was looking into it, too, but he had more experience in exorcising demons. Not shoving them into cute porcelain Disney villains.

I put a hand over my eyes, exhaling loudly. "What if I break the damn thing's head off and stuff him in it? Like however they make sausage."

Veronica snorted. "I don't think that's how they make sausage."

"My family owns a factory that does that," Dustin said, yawning. "When this is all over, we could go on a tour."

I rolled over onto my side, squinting at him. "Your family really does have something for every occasion."

"Except when it counts." Dustin glared into the middle distance. He crossed his arms, his blue eyes storming. "Still haven't heard from my parents, by the way. They can keep The Coffee Spot open but can't be bothered to see how I'm doing with all of this."

"Parents suck," I replied.

"My mom will be in the front row," Veronica said quietly. "Do you think she'll be okay?"

Silence drifted through the air between us. If Jesse *did* decide to wait until the show started to get all demon-y, everyone in the audience would be in danger. If I couldn't figure out how to trap him before then, we'd all be doomed.

We weren't exactly in a winning position. But I couldn't let Veronica and Dustin stoop down to my levels of unhelpful pessimism. "The sigil will work. We'll keep Jesse confined until we figure out what to do with him."

"What about your dad?" Dustin asked.

It was my turn to glare into the middle distance. "I'll take care of him."

"You don't have to do it alone, Cordy," Veronica said.

I smiled at her. "I know."

Dustin raised a pale hand. "Does it bother anyone else that we don't have much of a plan beyond 'put demon in sigil cage and see what happens'?"

"You got any better ideas, Jones?" I asked, a little too sharply.

Dustin opened his mouth to reply, but something crashed backstage. I jumped up, getting to my feet. Veronica was quicker. Her bones cracked as she shifted into her jaguar form. The big cat roared, racing backstage.

"You ever think we'll get used to that?" Dustin asked. I shrugged. A scream followed.

"Help!" Sal yelped, while the jaguar roared again.

Sal?

I ran backstage, catching the edge of my elbow on a set piece. Pain bloomed in my arm as I found them. The jaguar had Sal pinned down and was slowly transforming back into Veronica. I stopped abruptly, doing a horrible job of not looking mortified.

Well. We're fucked.

"Sal?" I asked, when I finally moved a little closer to them. "What are you doing here?"

"I could ask you the same thing!" Sal replied, eyes wide as they shifted their gaze from Veronica to me. "What the hell is going on? And why is Veronica a were-cat?"

Veronica held her hand down, offering to help them up. "Not a were-cat. I'm an aswang."

"A what?" Their voice was two octaves too high.

"Shapeshifting witch-vampire combination from Filipino folklore," she replied, still waiting for them to take her hand. "And I'm sorry about tackling you. I thought you were—"

"Well, this just got interesting," Dustin said from behind me.

Sal blinked, looking up at him. "Why is Dustin here? Why are *any* of you here?"

"Long story," Veronica said, grabbing their hand. She hauled Sal to their feet. "And it's one that you don't have to worry about."

I nodded. "You should go, Sal. Forget you saw us here."

"Hell no," Sal said, crossing their arms. "You're hanging out with *Dustin* and not me? Full offense, Jones."

"Offense taken," Dustin replied.

"It's not like that," I said.

"Then what's it like?" Sal asked.

I took a deep breath and let it all out in one frantic wave. "So, demons are real, and your play is pretty accurate, actually, and tomorrow we might have to fight two of them. One of them founded the town and the other is my father, but we're not getting into that. I have to figure out how to shove the town-founding one into a Precious Moments Maleficent, otherwise he's going to make more towns like ours and lure more people into deals, stealing parts of their souls and condemning them to Hell. We're here to set up a few traps for the demons, just in case we need some extra help tomorrow and they decide to start shit on opening night because the other demon—the one who isn't my father—is Jesse. We have a priest lined up to help us, too, but he's not here at the moment. Oh, if my father *does* show up tomorrow, he'll definitely try to kill me." I glanced over at Dustin and Veronica. "Did I miss anything?"

"Guidance counselor's a demon," Dustin added.

"Right," I continued. "Fred's a demon, but he's a good one? I think? He's helping us, but we haven't heard from him at all. Anyway, you don't have a part in any of this. You should go. Preferably, as far away from here as you can get. Especially if opening night starts to get a little demon-y."

Sal's expression went through a lot of different micro-emotions as I spoke. But by the end of my rambling, they stood facing me with their arms crossed over their chest. Jaw clenched with determination. "Sounds like you need more help. I'm staying."

"What?" I asked, voice cracking so many times on such a small word. I expected them to run, but instead, here they were. Ready to face down two demons without a second thought.

"Honestly, Cordy, I'm offended you didn't ask for my help sooner. Weird shit goes down in this town and I'm *not* a part of it? Completely unacceptable!"

"You're serious?" Veronica asked.

"As serious as Barry at the Yankee Candle Semi-Annual Sale," Sal replied.

I wanted to throw my arms around them and pull them into the biggest hug, but I kept it cool and smiled instead. "Thank you, Sal."

They winked at me. "Don't leave me out of the weird shit ever again, Scott."

"You've got it."

"So," they said, tapping their chin. "You need to figure out how to trap a demon?"

"Yeah," I replied.

Sal pointed at Dustin. "Then I'm gonna need this one's help."

"Me?" Dustin asked, stumbling back a little.

"You," Sal said. "Your brother helped Barry and me with research for the play. Bring everything you have to my house in one hour. We're gonna figure this thing out."

Dustin nodded toward us. "What about them?"

Sal smirked. "Seeing as Cordy might die tomorrow and Veronica's a cool, scary monster lady, I think they can do whatever they want."

A few hours later, dishes clattered in the sink as Veronica hand-washed them. I sat at the counter, clinging to what little remained of my hot chocolate. She was determined to spend the night at my house again. I'd offered to take the couch so that she could take the bed. I hoped that one of us would actually be able to use it and get some sleep. But she turned me down, taking the couch instead.

I wanted to spend the whole night talking to her. Tell her how much I loved her, just in case things went horribly wrong and I died. Or she did. Not that I wanted to dwell on that possibility. If it came down to it, I'd do anything to save her.

It wasn't because I was trying to be noble. Or brave. It was a selfish thing, but it was a truth that I'd unraveled at some point during my sleepless night: a world without Veronica Dominguez was a world I was afraid to live in.

She made a deal with a demon to try to protect me. Hadn't run away when I told her what I'd done. Stood by me without a second thought as we got ready for a fight we weren't sure we could win.

She'd be there for me no matter what. And I was determined to do the same.

"What do you want to do tonight?" she asked, watching me as she dried the last dish. "Go for a drive? Watch a bad horror movie?"

Aside from confessing my feelings, all I really felt like doing was crying. But that wasn't a productive answer, and it would only make her more worried.

I took a deep breath. Exhaled as I slid back into my favorite chair at the counter. Something heavy lingered in the air around us. The question she asked wasn't so simple. It was like she wanted to know what the last thing that could bring me happiness was, just in case things went the wrong way.

If I didn't make it. Or she didn't.

I looked up at her, not bothering to plaster a fake smile on my face. When I spoke, my voice sounded as tired as I felt. "Can we just sit here? Together?"

She opened her mouth to say something but snapped it shut. Nodded. Slid into the chair next to me with a sigh. "Yeah, Accordion. We can."

And we did. We sat there, staring at the kitchen's yellow wallpaper in complete silence, until it was time to go to sleep.

CHAPTER THIRTY-ONE

IN WHICH WE DON'T GOT THIS

CONTRARY TO MY WORST FEARS, HELL DIDN'T OPEN UP and swallow our town whole while we slept. Or at any point during the day, for that matter. Despite the impending doom of Jesse's grand plan finally coming to fruition, the day seemed pretty unremarkable. It was sunny, bright, and not at all ominous. If we were in a movie, dark clouds would swirl overhead. The wind would pick up. Lightning would strike a tree and split it in half.

Instead, the few clouds in the sky drifted lazily above us as Sal, Veronica, Dustin, and I stood in the school's parking lot, looking at the auditorium's pale brick walls. We still had a couple of hours before everyone else would get here, and another hour on top of that before the show started.

"Have you heard from the priest?" Dustin asked. His skin normally didn't have a lot of color, but now it was almost as white as a sheet of paper.

I nodded. "He'll be there. Won't intervene until we give the signal."

"What's the signal?" Sal replied.

"I think that'll be pretty clear when we trap Jesse in the sigil," Veronica said. "You know, once things really start to get all demon-y."

Sal rocked back on their heels. "Right. Cordy, do you have the Maleficent?"

I dug around in my bag for Fred's figurine. Held it up in the air with an uneasy smile. "Yup. Still not sure how we're getting a demon in this thing."

"I've got some ideas," Sal replied, "but nothing solid. Might be a trial-and-error kind of thing."

"I'll take it. Thanks, Sal." I dropped the Maleficent into my bag, but I missed.

"Careful," Veronica shouted, diving for it. She caught it before it could hit asphalt. "Don't want to break it." She handed it back to me. Our fingers brushed as I took the Maleficent from her. Veronica's eyes widened. She pulled her hand back with a small gasp.

Dustin raised a brow, quickly shifting his attention from us to Sal. "I grabbed my family's quill, too," he said, without bothering to take it out of his backpack. "If we interpreted Ryeland's journal right, it could help us. Somehow."

"I still have so many questions," Sal said, with a frown. "And not enough answers."

I sighed. "We'll figure those out soon enough." I took a few steps toward the auditorium, turning to face my friends. "Worst-case scenario, it all falls apart and we do what we've always done best."

"Curl up into a ball and cry?" Dustin asked.

"Stress out about Shakespeare?" Sal added.

"Scream into a pillow while angsty music plays?" Veronica threw in.

"What? No!" I said, trying hard not to laugh. "We'll improvise."

"Oh," Sal said, while Dustin turned to Veronica and asked, "Can you share your angst playlist with me? I need some new music."

Veronica narrowed her eyes for a few seconds before her lips twisted into a smile. "If we live through this, we can trade sad songs."

Whatever color left in Dustin's face drained away at that. He looked over at me. "Do you think we're gonna die?"

"No," I replied, and I meant it. "But we can't rule it out. These demons are dangerous, so we'll need to be careful. What we're going to do isn't impossible. It's just really, really hard."

"Especially without Fred," Veronica said. "You haven't heard from him?"

I checked my phone, hoping it would be different this time. That he'd text, or I'd have five missed calls, and I'd have a voicemail waiting where Fred proudly shared that he found the answer we'd be looking for and he'd solved our problems on his own.

Instead, only a whole lotta nothing. "Crickets from Fred. But he'll be there when we need him."

Dustin cleared his throat. "He's a demon, Cordelia. What if he's been playing you this whole time?"

I hated to admit it, but Dustin had a point. Fred's radio silence was worrying, if not more than a little suspicious. Maybe he'd been working with Jesse all along, instead of against him.

If that was the case, Fred was a better actor than I gave him credit for. He seemed genuinely shaken after Jesse turned him into a clown. And apologetic that my father was brought back from Hell.

"Fred was trapped in the Maleficent before," I said, hoping everyone could hear the note of finality in my words. "If he's not on our side, maybe there'll be room for two demons in there."

"Three," Veronica pointed out.

"Hmm?"

"Your dad makes three. You really think we can fit all of them in there?"

I shrugged, turning away from them so they couldn't see my expression. "All we can do is try."

Hopefully, they didn't hear the lie in my voice. The uncertainty. The slight waver that betrayed my true intentions.

I meant what I said about Fred. I didn't think he was working with Jesse, but if he was, I'd put him in the Maleficent with his demonic business partner.

My father was a different story. But I'd face that harsh truth when I needed to.

"Come on," I said, without turning back around. "We still have a lot to do."

Their footsteps followed quietly behind me as we walked up to the theater.

One way or another, in a few hours, this would all be over.

"We're holding for five," I said into my headset.

"Copy that, boss," Leon replied.

"Got it," Ashley chimed in. A few seconds later, choruses of *Thank you, five* sounded from each of the dressing rooms.

"You ready for this?" Sal asked. They were standing next to my podium backstage, flipping through my script binder.

I grimaced at them. "We're about to find out, aren't we?"

"Barry's walking toward the stage," Leon said, over my headset.

"Great. Take the house lights down to 10 percent and go to pre-show cue three." From the gap underneath the two giant red curtains that covered the stage, the lights shifted. "Make sure the spot's on Barry as he climbs the stairs."

Applause started at the same time the spotlight clicked to life. I moved closer to the curtain, straining to hear Barry's footsteps. He picked up the mic that I'd placed before we opened the house. Reverb screeched through the air.

"Get it under control, Jeff," I said, putting my head in my hands.

"Sorry," Jeff replied. Whatever he did up in the tech booth worked. Barry's mic stopped imitating a banshee.

"Thank you all so much for coming," Barry said, once the applause died down. "Today should have been filled with celebration and merriment. Unfortunately, instead, it's a sobering reminder of the loss that we suffered only a few days ago. Blake Jones was an invaluable member of the theater community when he attended this school, and the support he continued to show us throughout the years was a light in some truly dark times. After speaking with the students, we've decided that tonight's performance of *Our Demon Town* will be dedicated to his memory. We hope that, wherever he is now, he knows how much he was loved."

Barry paused, waiting for the obligatory applause that followed a memorial speech. After a few awkward seconds of nothing, someone started to clap. The rest of the audience followed.

"Now," Barry continued, once it was quiet again. "I'd like to introduce you all to the student who made this entire show possible. Sal Rogers spent a whole year working with me to refine this script into the Broadway-worthy show that you're about to see. Sal, come on out and say hi!"

"That's your cue," I said, pushing Sal past the curtain. "Places," I hissed into my headset.

Somewhere backstage, Ashley and the other stagehands prompted actors to get into their positions for the top of the show. Normally, I'd walk around and tell everyone to break a leg. But I was too afraid to leave my podium. As soon as I stepped away from it, I wouldn't be able to keep the lie going. I'd stop being Stage Manager Cordy and turn into Demon-Trapping Cordy.

Maybe I was lying to myself. But I wanted to live in the illusion that I was a normal high school student for a little while longer. Even if it was only for a few more minutes.

"I'm so excited for you all to finally see *Our Demon Town*," Sal said. "When I say that we poured our blood, sweat, and tears into this production . . . well. I think by now you know that I mean it quite literally." Sal paused, laughing. "Okay, maybe not literally. But a lot of work went into this production and we're happy to share it with you on such a historic day. Ruin's End has seen a lot of shi—*interesting* things during the century it's existed. Hopefully, it'll be around for another one. But just in case it's not, I hope you'll enjoy my vision of what it might've looked like back then."

More applause—and a few whistles and cheers—rang out for Sal.

"I could go on and on about this show," Barry said, cutting back in, "but you didn't pay to see me. Nor did you pay to hear each other's phones ring or watch someone record the show while they were sitting right in front of you. Please take this moment to silence all of your electronic devices. And do not, under any circumstances, record this show. That's very illegal, and it's not nice."

A few nervous laughs rang out through the crowd.

"Standby cue three," I said, grabbing onto the rope that pulled the curtain back. My heartbeat quickened. It was almost time.

"Standing by," Leon, Jeff, and Ashley replied.

"The students in the cast and crew are a talented bunch," Barry continued. "So, without further ado, I'd like to present our spring production of . . . *Our Demon Town*."

"Go cue three," I said.

The lights went out. The orchestra started playing the show's overture. And I pulled the curtains back.

"Here we go," I said, to no one in particular.

Despite the looming fear that in a few minutes I was going to fight—and trap—literal demons, I was still proud of everything we accomplished with this production. Even if it was a hot mess for our very limited Tech Week run.

The blackout onstage faded, and an eerie red glow danced on top of the cast's heads. Anticipation fluttered in my chest, a brief respite from the anger that usually resided there.

The air in the theater was absolutely electric. Everything in the opening number went off without a hitch as the ensemble set the scene perfectly. Maybe that old theater superstition about a messy Tech Week leading to a stellar opening night was true.

Of course, that was discounting the fact that as soon as Jesse walked onto the stage and into the sigil we made, shit would hit the proverbial fan.

As soon as the ensemble ran out into the audience to exit, everyone was hooked. Applause roared from all sides in the house as we blacked out and brought the lights up for the next scene. I checked my clipboard, getting ready for the next set of cues, even though I knew we weren't going to need them for much longer.

Static filled my headset, making me jump. A croak mixed in with a growl wove through the sound. I almost lost the clipboard.

"Go cue eight," I said, determined to finish as much of the show as I could before Jesse stepped onto the sigil. The lights slowly faded up on the next scene. Veronica stood with her back to a bunch of fake trees, right at the edge of the boundary that we'd painted yesterday. Jesse walked out from the wings, decked out in his best *Great Gatsby* impression.

"There you are, Ryeland," Veronica said, relief coloring her features. "We've all been looking for you."

"I think I found a solution to our problems," Jesse, as Ryeland Jones, replied. My heart pounded frantically as he set one foot over the barrier, slowly lowering it to the ground. "All we have to do is—" He paused, looking over at Veronica. "*Oh.* That's clever."

The corners of Veronica's lips pulled into a smile. "We thought so, too."

"Cue nine, Leon," I snapped into the headset. "Now!"

"That's not what I have in my script," Leon said.

I pocketed two vials of holy water. "Forget the script. Just do it!"

One of the things I did while we were watching paint dry was re-do the lighting cues for this moment. Once Leon did what I asked, we went back to the opening number's red glow, with one exception: a bright light shone right above Jesse's head.

He sighed, stepping fully into the sigil. "Is this really what you wanted, Cordelia? You're ruining the show!"

I took a deep breath, holding the Maleficent as I walked out onto the stage. "It was already ruined when they cast a demon in the lead role." Murmurs and unease rippled through the audience at that. But I kept going. "For the past one hundred years, you've been stealing our souls. Feeding off our hopes and dreams for your own gain. That ends today."

I wasn't sure how Jesse was going to react to being caught in a sigil. Mostly, I'd hoped it would throw him off guard enough to give us some kind of an edge. Reveal the one piece of the puzzle we'd been missing. The last thing we needed in order to trap him.

Instead, the demon tossed his head back and laughed. "It's so cute that you tried this. Really."

"Cordelia," Barry called, from somewhere in the audience. "What's going—"

He didn't get to finish that question. As he asked it, Jesse raised his hand up, snapping. Flames burst out of the floor by the front row. Up and down the side aisles, too. Everyone in the house shot up, scrambling out of their seats. They raced to the emergency exits as cast and crew slowly trickled onto the stage.

"Everybody out," I roared, pushing them away from Jesse.

"But—" Ashley tried to say, as Leon shouted into my headset.

"Get them all out of here." I left no room for question in my voice. Ashley and the rest of the crew rushed the cast off-stage. Instruments clattered as the musicians in the orchestra pit climbed out, racing for an exit.

Jesse waited until the theater was quiet again. "I think we're alone now," he said, snapping again with a smug look on his face. The fire in the aisles and at the front row died.

Barry and Veronica's mom stood in the fourth row, looking at the stage. Sal *had* been in the audience, sitting next to Barry. But now, they were nowhere in sight.

"Ah, I spoke too soon," Jesse said, clicking his tongue. Barry opened his mouth to say something, but he didn't get the chance, as Jesse froze our theater teacher and Mrs. Dominguez in place.

"Mom!" Veronica raced off the stage to check on her.

"Let them go," I said, rounding on the demon. "They don't have anything to do with this."

Jesse shrugged. "They were foolish enough to stick around when they had their chance to leave. They're fair game, as far as I'm concerned. Oh, and speaking of—" He cleared his throat. "David! Would you mind bringing our next guest up to meet his adoring fans?"

Footsteps sounded behind me as my father appeared from backstage, grabbing Father Marcus and holding my kalis up to his throat. He winked at me, pressing the blade into the priest's skin.

Fred hadn't found him, then. Or maybe he had, and he was dead.

My hands balled into fists. I'd figure out what happened to him once we were done here. Now, David Scott had my blessed weapon. But he wouldn't for long.

Jesse paced around inside the sigil. "Now that we're all here, perhaps we can talk."

I glared at him. "Talk about what? How screwed you are?"

Jesse smirked. "Stop playing hard to get. Make a deal with me, and I'll scare all your monsters away."

My grip tightened around the Maleficent. I didn't like the sound of that. "No, thanks. I'm good." I glanced over at my father, still holding the priest hostage. I needed to separate them, somehow.

"You sure?" Jesse asked, sugar and venom dripping from his words.

I swallowed, nodding over to my father. "Yeah, tried the whole banishing. Didn't work out, thanks to you."

"But it can. You humans are so short-sighted, you know that? You can never see the bigger picture." Jesse raised his hand, imitating a beauty pageant contestant's wave. My father dropped the kalis and let go of the priest, doubling over. His screams filled the theater, bouncing around, splitting the air with his pain.

I ran over to the priest, grabbing the kalis and dragging him away.

Jesse snapped his fingers, and my father's screams stopped. He was still doing it—his mouth was open, and from the way he grabbed his abdomen, he wasn't okay. But no sound was coming out, no matter how hard he tried. "That's better," Jesse said, as if he'd just turned the volume down on some loud music and not taken my father's voice away. "You see, I can hurt him in ways your guidance counselor couldn't. I can make him truly suffer for what he did to you. For what he *intended* to do to you. All you have to do is agree to my bargain."

He sat down in the middle of the sigil. "So, what's it gonna be? We can do this the easy way or the way that ends in you dying. Your choice. But make it quick." He waved at the exits. Flames sprang up around them. "I don't have all day."

CHAPTER THIRTY-TWO

IN WHICH SHIT HITS THE PROVERBIAL FAN

FATHER MARCUS SHIFTED BESIDE ME. "YOU SHOULD DO what he says, Cordelia."

"What?" I squinted up at him. "Are you serious?"

"Yeah, *priest.*" Jesse spat the word out, the first hint of anything other than calm composure coloring his words. "Are you serious?"

"I am," Father Marcus said, looking down at me. "You don't know what's at stake here, child. You should listen to him."

David Scott groaned. He was still a crumpled pile on the ground. Whatever Jesse did, it was pretty effective. Making a deal with him was tempting. It would solve my problems quickly. Efficiently. Just like before.

Only, nothing had really been fixed after my father was sent to Hell. Even for the few hours I had my soul back, I hadn't felt whole. And Mom still avoided me as much as she could. It was funny, in a sad way. I spent so many years pretending not to be a monster. But I turned into one.

And maybe that was okay. There were different kinds of monsters, after all.

I tightened my grip on the kalis and the Maleficent. "Here's how it's gonna go, Jesse. I'm going to trap you in this cute little figurine. And then I'll deal with my father myself. So, now *you* have a choice." I held the Precious Moments statue up. "Take the easy way—go into this thing willingly—or we'll make this as painful as possible for you."

Jesse tilted his head as he watched me. "You and what army?"

"This one," Veronica said, from the house. She launched herself onto the stage, hurtling into Jesse. Her nails extended into razor-sharp claws as she changed into her jaguar form mid-air. It was impressive—if not a mistake. When she barreled into him, they both went crashing out of the sigil. I couldn't see it without a blacklight, but her claws might have scratched some of the paint away.

"Thanks for that," Jesse said, right before he threw Veronica into the side of Ryeland Jones's fake house. He looked over at me, brushing myself off. "It looks like we've both chosen the hard way. May the best monster win."

"Don't worry," I said, finally able to return his smirk. "I will. Hit it, Sal!"

If Barry's mic feedback was slightly annoying at the top of the show, it was even worse now. Sal—and, by the looks of the blond hair also in the booth, Dustin—turned all of the mics on at the same time. I ran backstage to where we stashed the wireless ones, shoving them all together. The mics screamed. So did Jesse. And my father.

Dustin turned on a spotlight, shining it in Jesse's face. The demon covered his ears and closed his eyes as a fire erupted on top of the tech booth. Dustin and Sal screamed—chunks of the booth's roof fell away. I ran to the stairs at the edge of the stage, bounding down them. Raced up the center aisle toward the back of the auditorium when sparks flew out of the tech booth. The feedback stopped.

For one bizarre moment, it was completely silent in the theater, like we were all holding our breath, waiting to see what would happen next. But then the sound system blared random selections from past shows, skipping around like a soundtrack experiencing technical difficulties, and pandemonium blew up the peaceful stillness around us.

Dustin and Sal raced down from the balcony, almost crashing into me.

"What the hell do we do now?" Dustin asked.

"We stick to the plan!" I said, holding the kalis out to him. "Give me the quill."

"I'm still not sure that's what Ryeland meant," Sal said with a frown. "You really think putting the feather on that Maleficent will help you trap him?"

I plucked the quill out of Dustin's hand, tying it to the figurine. "Let me know if you get a better idea. And don't worry. There's a plan, remember? It'll all be fine." I tried my best to sound more confident than I felt.

"I wouldn't be so sure about that," my father said. He grabbed my shoulders, yanking me away from my friends and back into the center aisle. "You can't win, kiddo." He tried prying the kalis out of my hand.

"Neither can you," I shot back. "Wasn't Jesse trying to kill you a couple of minutes ago? Doesn't seem like your team is pretty solid, *Dad*." I elbowed him and wriggled out of his grasp.

I backed down the aisle, getting closer to the stage.

Something heavy and metal flew into a wall above us. I winced at the loud sound. Sweat made my palms clammy and slick. I tightened my grip on the kalis. The skipping songs stopped, filling the theater with a calm, dead silence. I'd lost track of Jesse, but he had to be up there. He must've torn out our whole sound board.

"That was expensive, asshole," I yelled up at the balcony.

"Don't worry," Jesse called from above. "You won't be around when they need to replace it. We should burn this whole place down, really. It's so tragically pathetic. Wouldn't you agree, David?"

My father tilted his head, smiling at me. Flames burst up from the ground at his feet, stretching and climbing onto some nearby chairs.

Oh, hell no.

This theater had been my second home for four years. I knew every nook and cranny. Could walk around in complete darkness and not bump into anything. I was here when the whole place hummed with anticipation on opening night. Mourned and celebrated the closing of a show as we tore the set down. Got excited for new possibilities during each new round of auditions.

It was filled with so many emotions. Memories. Hopes, dreams, fears, promises—even heartbreak. Stories that we meant to tell and others that we fell into.

I loved this place more than I ever thought I would. I couldn't let these demons turn it into something terrible. This was my home.

They were going to pay for ruining it.

The theater wasn't the only thing they'd destroyed, though. Both of them had torn apart different pieces of me. Fracturing my soul in ways that I hadn't anticipated. They worked together to keep me rooted in the past. Held me back from building anything new.

Jesse and my father both used fear as a weapon. Worked together to make sure it coiled around what was left of my heart, injecting so much poison into my veins that I forgot living like that wasn't normal.

The same thing had happened to Fred—wherever he was. When he tried to confront Jesse, he froze. Almost stopped helping me because of everything the other demon had done to him.

I took a deep breath, adjusted my grip on the kalis's hilt, and then screamed as I launched myself at my father. I brought the blade back, ready to drive it forward with all of the force I could muster, right into his heart. He dodged out of the way. I stumbled a few steps ahead, grabbing onto the top of a nearby chair with my freehand.

David Scott laughed. A harsh, heavy sound that scraped through the air. It stopped me short. I hadn't heard that since I was a kid.

"Cordy!" Veronica screamed. I turned around, but it was too late. My father's fist slammed into my face, tearing open the wounds in my cheek that had only just started to heal over. Blood streaked down my face as I crashed into the edge of a row of chairs. Pain arced through my back as I rebounded down to the floor.

Veronica shouted again, her screams morphing into a roar. A jaguar pounced on him, knocking him down to my level. I scrambled up, trying to get to both of them. He used his knees to push the jaguar off him, tossing the big cat aside. He was on his feet faster than I could move.

He raised his hand, readying another strike. I flinched.

"David Scott," Father Marcus yelled from the stage.

My father froze, looking up at the priest. "Yes?"

"I command you," the priest said, crossing himself. "In the name of the Father, the Son, and the Holy Spirit, to return from whence you came—"

My father screamed, pushing past me and charging the stage. He picked up the priest, throwing him backstage.

I ran toward the stage, shouting a stream of curses as I moved. But someone's fingers wrapped around my arms, yanking me backward.

"No," Veronica whispered in my ear. "Don't fight him."

"Let me go," I shouted, trying and failing to get out of her grasp.

"You should listen to her," Jesse chimed in from the balcony. "Best to surrender now before anyone dies. We've been fairly patient with you, Cordelia. But that goodwill has a limit."

I took a few steps back so I could get a better view of the balcony. A shadow moved near the front entrance of the house, catching my eye. A quick glimpse of bright yellow was all I needed to know. Veronica was right. I shouldn't fight him. But I could stall him a little.

"Why is he still helping you?" I called out. "You just offered to kill him."

Jesse laughed, leaping down from the balcony. "You really shouldn't believe everything you hear." He advanced slowly toward me and Veronica, pushing us up the aisle and back to the stage. "David and I were curious to see what you'd do, if given the chance to get rid of him. I figured you'd take the deal. He thought you'd want to do it yourself." Jesse shrugged. "Looks like he knows you better than I thought."

Bile clawed its way up my throat. "He doesn't."

"You sure about that?" Jesse asked, waving to my father. David Scott disappeared backstage, dragging Father Marcus out by his collar. "Your father figured you'd run to this priest once he came back. Seek guidance from a servant of God." Jesse continued to press Veronica and me onto the stage. "But you failed to realize one thing, *kiddo*."

Veronica growled as I asked, "Oh, yeah? What's that?"

Father Marcus wriggled out of my father's grasp, running toward us. "Give me the figurine, Cordelia. I can trap him."

I nodded, tossing the Maleficent to him. It tumbled through the air, doing a few flips as it sailed into his hands.

Or, at least, it should've sailed into his hands.

Father Marcus stepped away at the last possible second, letting the Precious Moments Maleficent crash into the ground.

It shattered.

I staggered back. Would've fallen over if it wasn't for Veronica. She reached out, grabbing my arm, steadying me as I looked at Father Marcus.

"What did you do?" I asked him, tears pooling in the corners of my eyes.

"What had to be done," Father Marcus replied. His expression turned to unfeeling stone as he shifted his attention to Jesse. "A deal's a deal. Am I done here?"

"Of course," Jesse said, clapping him on the back. "You were such a good distraction. Maybe *you* should consider a future on the stage."

I squeezed Veronica's hand. "Distraction?" I asked, trembling with rage.

"Oh! Yes! I should catch you up." Jesse skipped toward us. "There's no such thing as a blessed weapon. I had the priest plant it in Blake's head. And yours. It took a little bit of work on my end to make that ritual convincing—and the meddling nun provided an unforeseen complication—but Father Marcus handled it all perfectly. He had you fully reeled in, hook, line, and sinker."

Panic fluttered in my chest. If the blessed weapon wasn't real, then I hadn't given up part of my soul. I had all of it. But I still didn't feel whole.

To make everything worse, Father Marcus lied to all of us. And he didn't care. No remorse. Apologies. Just the smug satisfaction that came with lying to a bunch of teenagers.

And, now that he'd shattered the Maleficent, he took the only advantage we had against Jesse.

"You're all pieces of shit," I snapped. My outraged words echoed around the auditorium. "You gain our trust. Find ways to break us. Turn us into monsters. Do you regret any of it? Do you feel bad at all?"

Jesse tucked a hand under his chin, imitating *The Thinker*. "Not really. Ruining lives is a perk of the whole 'being a demon' thing."

"Fuck off, Jesse," I yelled at him. Not the most elegant expression of my feelings. But it was honest.

Looks like you're in a bit of a mess, Fred said, in my head. *I can help you with that.*

Dustin screamed, charging up the stage left steps before I could reply. He rushed the priest, tackling him to the ground.

"You lied to Blake," he shouted, trying to punch Father Marcus. "You got him killed!"

The priest dodged the hit, scrambling away from him. "What happened to your brother was unfortunate," Father Marcus replied, "but casualties were inevitable."

I ran over to Dustin, pulling him away from the priest. Sal darted up the steps, standing with us. "This still part of the plan?" they muttered.

"Wait for it," I replied.

Whenever you're ready, Princess, I screamed in my mind.

You don't have to be so loud about it, Fred said.

Relief almost made me collapse. But Dustin, Sal, and Veronica pressed in closer, helping me stand.

I cleared my throat, looking at Jesse, my father, and the two-faced priest. "You're right," I said, as smoke rose out of the orchestra pit. "Casualties *are* inevitable." Bright yellow eyes—and the silhouette of antlers—shot toward the priest. Tendrils of smoke wrapped around him, pulling him down into the pit. His screams filled the air until they didn't.

"What a shame he had to be one of them," I said, separating from my friends. I swung the kalis around in my best impression of a Jedi getting ready to fight. "Who's next?"

CHAPTER THIRTY-THREE

IN WHICH I DECIDE WHO I WANT TO BE

JESSE BLINKED, GAPING AT FRED AND ME. "DID YOU just kill my priest?"

Fred nodded. "I did. And there's more where that came from." His voice wasn't shaking, but his hands were. Still, he was doing a good job of putting on a show. I had a million questions for him. The first was, definitely, how the *fuck* did he just do that? The second, where the *hell* has he been?

There'd be a time and place for our intense Q&A, though. Facing down both of our demons wasn't it.

Annabelle scrambled out from the orchestra pit. "Sorry we're late. Fred had some trouble finding me."

"And then we hit traffic on the way," Fred added.

Jesse's shocked expression warped back into pompous smuggery. "Look who finally decided to do something with his sad, pathetic life," he said to Fred. "Didn't know you had it in you to take initiative."

You're going to need to run now, Fred said, in my head.

No, I replied. *I'm helping.*

You're so stubborn, he shot back.

I scoffed. *It's like looking in a mirror.*

Even though Fred's eyes were fully bright yellow, and he had no irises, it still felt like he was rolling them. *Fine. Have it your way.*

The same tendrils of smoke that killed Father Marcus curled around Fred, wrapping around his legs like vines. They climbed up his body, and as they did, any human remnants of him fell away. He grew a few feet taller. Not counting the antlers, which arched out of his head and wove into themselves until they made something that looked like a crown.

His skin cracked and peeled into pieces of bark. Small green leaves sprouted out in the gaps between them.

"Holy shit," Dustin said, scrambling up from the spot where he'd tackled Father Marcus. He ran over to my side, shoving Veronica out of the way. "The guidance counselor really *is* a demon."

"Why would I lie about that?" I snapped.

Dustin shrugged, leaning in close to me. "Off-topic, but do you still keep spike tape in your podium?"

"Yeah. Why?" I asked, but he ran backstage before he could answer my question. "Weird."

Veronica sighed, moving into the space he'd left behind. "Seriously."

Jesse launched himself at Fred, wrapping his arms around the Nightmare Deer's torso as he pulled him down into the orchestra pit.

I screamed, running for the edge, but a clawed hand yanked

me back. My sword clattered down onto the taped-up marks I'd spent weeks placing as I was thrown downstage. I hurtled toward a fake brick wall, putting my hands around my head to soften the blow.

I didn't crash into it.

Instead, I was pulled up into the air and placed softly back on my feet a few steps away from where I should've fallen. A giant vulture landed in front of me, screeching.

"Thanks, Harmonica," I said. The vulture cooed in response.

My father swore, moving closer to us. "Your little friend won't always be able to protect you."

I glared at him. "Not if she has anything to say about it."

As if to punctuate my point, Veronica the Vulture flew up to my father's face and tried gouging his eyes with her talons. He barely turned out of the way; she scratched his face up instead. Blood pooled out from a gash in his cheeks that was in the same spot where he'd cut me a few days earlier. My hand went up to my cheek as his did.

Veronica charged him again. I scrambled out of the way, searching the stage for my discarded kalis. My heart pounded as a high-pitched ringing, like mic feedback, screamed in my ears. I couldn't find my kalis.

Again.

Something glinted in the house. I ran to the edge, shielding my eyes to look out into the theater. Sal stood in front of Barry and Veronica's mom, both still frozen. They held onto the kalis like it was a baseball bat, ready to swing at whoever came close.

I gave them a thumbs-up, even though I wasn't sure they could see it. Even though blessed weapons weren't real, the kalis could still do some damage if it needed to. If I didn't have it, I was glad Sal could use it to protect the adults.

Dustin burst out from behind a curtain, holding spike tape in one hand and a blacklight in the other. "Buy me some time," he said, ripping a piece of tape off.

I nodded, trying to figure out how in the hell I was gonna do that.

Sounds that could only be described as decidedly unholy came from the orchestra pit. I wasn't sure what was happening down there, but until they resurfaced, I was fine with letting Fred handle that one.

Veronica grappled with my father. They tore down one of the giant red velvet curtains as their fight transitioned backstage. Sal stood guard in the house and didn't need much help there, as the demons were occupied. Annabelle was nowhere to be found.

My hands tightened around the vials of holy water in my pockets. Would she betray us, just like Father Marcus? She was his apprentice, after all. Maybe the secretly-working-for-a-demon apple didn't fall far from the proverbial tree.

Veronica screamed. It wasn't a vulture's screech, or a jaguar's snarl. It was a human sound. My throat turned to sandpaper as I swallowed. I couldn't worry about Annabelle now. Veronica needed my help.

Uncorking one of the vials, I raced backstage, throwing the holy water onto the demon formerly known as my father. Just like a few days before, it hadn't really burned him—but it distracted him enough to let Veronica get a good hit in. She tore off some of the town hall set piece and smashed it into the side of my father's face.

I grabbed a nearby broom, sticking it out behind him as he stumbled a little. He tripped on it, hitting the ground with a pretty satisfying *thud*. Veronica brandished the set piece as she ran up to him. It ended in a very sharp, very fine point. She thrust it down, aiming for his head. He rolled out of the way. She slammed it down with such force that it wedged into the stage.

David Scott whistled. "Not too bad."

Veronica cracked her neck. "I know."

"Wait!" I yelled, stepping between them before they could fight again. "Have we maybe thought about . . . trying to talk things out?" They both looked at me like I'd said the most ridiculous thing possible. Which, to be fair, I probably had. But it did what I wanted it to do. My father's attention shifted from Veronica to me.

The corners of his mouth curled into a smile. "I think we're past that, kiddo. Don't you?"

I shrugged. "Can't blame a girl for trying." Then I turned around and ran upstage. Burst through the curtains like the little alien that shot out of that guy's chest in that one Sigourney Weaver movie. "I hope you're ready!" I said, kicking Dustin out of the sigil. I stood in the middle of it, waiting for my father to follow.

For once in his life—well, afterlife—he did something I wanted him to. Unlike Jesse, he didn't realize what he'd done until he was a few steps in. I winked at him, hurrying out of the circle as he screamed. He ran at me and slammed into one of the boundaries.

Dustin's eyes were wide. "I can't believe that worked."

"Same," I said, patting him on the back. "Nice job, Jones."

Dustin beamed. That might've been the first genuine compliment anyone had ever given him.

"One down," Sal said, jogging back up the steps. "One to go, right?"

"Something like that," I replied as they handed my sword back to me. "Thanks, Sal."

"Oh no, thank *you*," Sal said. "I felt like a badass holding that thing."

"You *are* a badass."

"You flatter me—"

"Enough," Jesse roared from the pit. Flames crackled as the sharp sound of bones breaking snapped through the air. Somewhere below us, Fred whimpered.

Fire shot up, blanketing the top of the orchestra pit. Veronica pulled me back from the edge of the stage. My father—who'd been aiming a stream of curses our way—fell silent.

The fire parted in the middle, slowly peeling back.

Two cat ears poked out of the flames. Jesse's true demon form—probably a mountain lion, by the looks of it—rose into the air above the pit.

Fred's Nightmare Deer was pretty impressive, what with the bark skin and the antler crown and leaves sprouting from his skin. I figured Jesse would be more detailed—more intimidating—than a mountain lion standing on two legs.

"That's it?" I asked, unable to stop myself.

"What do you mean, 'that's it'?" Jesse asked. His normal voice was layered with a perpetual growl. "It is I, Marbas, Great President of Hell, governor of thirty-six legions of demons. And, once you agree to our bargain, Cordelia Scott, I will be unstoppable."

Sal burst into laughter next to me. "I think you're a few months early for the Furry convention."

"What a cute little kitty," Dustin managed to get out before he cracked up.

"You *dare* mock me?" Jesse—Marbas—said, voice sharp. "I'm more powerful than any of you will ever be!"

Veronica shrugged. "Maybe. But at least we don't look like a big house cat."

"Oh, come on," I said, not bothering to hold back a smug smile. "He's a mountain lion, Veronica. Very scary."

"Looks a little like the school mascot," Sal said, wiping their eyes. They were laughing so hard they started to cry.

"Wally the Wildcat," Dustin chimed in. "Is that you?"

Marbas roared, shooting through the air, right toward us. Veronica got in front of us, ready to take the brunt of his attack—but he was yanked back by shadowy tendrils.

"Fred?" I asked, moving to the edge of the stage.

He didn't reply. Instead, Annabelle walked out slowly from one of the wings, chanting. Fred wasn't holding Marbas in place. The tendrils came from the book held in Annabelle's hands.

"Whoa," Dustin said, as Sal said, "She's on our side, right?"

"I hope so," I replied.

"I call upon the strength of those who came before me," Annabelle said, as she stepped closer to the demon. "Marbas has taken power from the powerless. Help me level the playing field a little." She paused, adding a very thoughtful, "Please and thank you," after a few beats.

A light glowed between Annabelle's hand and the book she held—which, interestingly, wasn't a Bible. It was Ryeland Jones's journal.

I wasn't sure what—or who—Annabelle was talking to. But it didn't seem religious. More like she was asking for some non-divine intervention.

She turned her attention to us for a brief moment. "Whatever you're gonna do, do it now."

That small second of distraction was all Marbas needed. He broke through some of the shadows holding him in place. More shadows burst out of the journal's pages as she started chanting again.

"What are we supposed to do?" Dustin asked.

Without the Maleficent, I didn't have an answer. But there were still things I needed to know. I glanced at my father, still trapped in the sigil. Marbas brought him back to torture me—and it worked.

But not anymore.

Marbas struggled against his shadowy restraints. "Are you sure you wouldn't like to make that deal? Your father in exchange for my freedom?"

I stepped forward, steeling myself. "You really think I'm going to help you after everything?" I asked. "Why? Why me? You could've made a deal with anyone in this town, and you're still trying to win me over."

Marbas stopped fighting. He smiled serenely at me. "You made a deal with someone who wasn't me. A pathetic excuse for a demon. I had to prove that I was better than him. Simple math, really."

Here was the thing about the orchestra pit that Marbas was being dangled over: the only way in or out—other than toppling down the twenty-foot drop off the stage—was to use doors that led under the stage and into a hidden door in the auditorium. So, when Fred figured that out and crept down the side aisle behind, I knew I had to keep the demon—formerly known as Jesse—talking.

"That's very Greek Tragedy of you," I replied.

"Lotta hubris in that one," Veronica added. She reached back, squeezing my hand as her shoulders tensed. "Don't know how I feel about pride as a motivation, though. You turned me into an aswang because you were insulted that my best friend made a deal behind your back? That's a little petty for an evil mastermind. And *then*, to top it all off, you agreed to my condition: you can't harm her. Rookie move, Jesse."

I nodded. "Especially one who's supposed to be some big, bad, all-powerful demon. Fred wanted me to trap you, but there's not much of a point, is there? You can't even break free of those shadow tentacle things. You're pretty useless. Besides, what kind of an alias is Jesse Smithe anyway? That's like, the most basic generic name. Pretty sketch, if you ask me."

"I thought the *'e'* made it more unique." Marbas bristled. "You *wish* you had the power to trap me. They tried that a hundred years ago, too, and it didn't work. And do you know why?"

Sal grabbed my arm. "I do," they breathed. "What did the journal say? Something about an instrument?"

"The daemon's undoing shall come forth when the instrument that solidified our bargain is used once again," Dustin replied. "But the quill didn't work."

"That's because it's not the quill," Sal hissed. "Think about the play. What did the demon do to the people who made the deal?"

Dustin squinted. "Drained their life force for power."

My mouth dropped open. "Do you think that'll work?"

Sal shrugged. "Got any better ideas?"

We didn't. I broke free of the group, moving toward Annabelle. "Say we needed to juice up a demon. Could you help us with that?"

She nodded, not breaking her chant.

I turned back to Marbas, crossing my arms as I faced him. "You're right, you know. The math was pretty simple. You spent all this time talking about how you're a better demon than Fred. And maybe you are."

Ouch, Fred said in my head.

Brace yourself, I warned.

I continued as if he hadn't interrupted my thought. "But you didn't plan on one thing."

"Oh?" Marbas asked, amusement somehow shining through his feline features. "What's that?"

I pointed to my father. "All both of you have ever done is take. You needed to prove you had power over others, so you forced them to give you pieces of themselves. But not Fred." I took a few more steps toward the edge of the stage. "I wonder if it's different to give a piece of yourself willingly. I guess we'll see."

What are you planning, little one? Fred asked.

What you've wanted me to do all along, I replied. *Except you're gonna do the honors. Not me.*

I raised the kalis above my head. "I call upon the strength of those who came before me," I said, parroting Annabelle's invocation from earlier. Some of the shadows from Ryeland's journal wrapped around my arm. "Help me give my energy freely to the demon who wields this sword."

The shadows slid down my arm and into the sword's hilt.

It pulsed with light and darkness. I passed it to Veronica, who repeated the invocation. She handed it to Sal, who did the same. The light show happening on the kalis's blades grew more intense as Sal gave it to Dustin. Once he finished his invocation, the light and shadows swallowed the kalis completely.

Marbas screamed, freeing one arm from Annabelle's hold. In the corner of my eyes, she stumbled, dropping the journal. I ran over to her side, helping her up. Sweat beaded her forehead. Her eyes widened as the shadows were torn into tiny pieces, fading away into nothing.

"Run," she said, pushing me out of the way.

Marbas lunged toward us, claws elongated as he pulled his paws back, getting ready to strike. But Fred was faster. He appeared in front of Annabelle, shoving the kalis into the spot where Marbas's heart was supposed to be.

Silence rang out loud and clear across the auditorium. No one dared to breathe as we waited to see what would happen.

Marbas's eyes—which widened when he was stabbed—filled with mirth as he started to laugh. "You really thought that would work?" He cackled. "You fools! You can't defeat me! I'm the Great President of—"

Light erupted out of his wound, wrapping around him like a vine. It split off into a bunch of different branches until he was restrained.

"What?" His voice cracked on the word.

"It's simple math, Marbas," I said, putting my hand on Fred's shoulder. "We won. You lost."

"Happy Deal Day," Fred said, shoving the kalis in even further. The light around Marbas glowed so bright that I had to shield my eyes as it swallowed him up.

He screamed as he was pulled into the blade.

And then, Marbas the deal-making demon was no more.

"Well," Fred said, turning to me with a relieved smile. "I don't know about you, but I could use a nap."

"Don't call it a day yet," my father said, before I could reply. He dug his hands into the stage's floorboards and tore them up. Well. That was one way to get rid of the protective sigil.

David Scott stepped out of the barrier, tossing the piece of the stage aside. "The fun's just beginning."

CHAPTER THIRTY-FOUR

IN WHICH I FIGHT MY DEMON

MY FATHER AND I HAD DIFFERENT DEFINITIONS OF THE word 'fun.'

To me, fun was the thrill of opening night. Celebrating a show after it closed. Monday Night Karaoke with Veronica. Finding new shows to love with Sal, and, hell, even hanging out in Dustin's McMansion, when an aswang wasn't chasing us.

To David Scott, fun was tossing Dustin and Sal aside on his way to get to me. Throwing Annabelle into the house like she was some kind of rag doll. Ripping a chunk out of Fred's shoulder because he dared to stand in front of me. Grabbing Veronica's vulture form by the talons and swinging her so hard into a nearby wall that she crumpled to the ground, unconscious.

It was like watching a movie play out in front of me. Someone else's life presented in super high-definition for an audience to enjoy. But this wasn't something I could turn off and walk away from.

One by one, my friends tried stopping my father from reaching me. And then, one by one, they fell.

When wounded, Fred dropped the kalis. I caught it before it hit the stage and held it as tightly as I could as he slowly stalked toward me. In some other universe, we were in a nature documentary, and he was the lion trying to take over a preexisting pride. I was the lion cub he needed to kill in order to win everyone else over to his side. Some neutral British narrator would talk about how sad it was that a cub's life was taken so soon, but that it was as inevitable as the sun rising and falling each day. Male lions, when trying to establish dominance, would always kill cubs that weren't their own.

So, what did it say about my father, who was so determined to kill someone who *was* his child?

"Let's go somewhere a little more private," David Scott growled, as his hands wrapped around my throat. He lifted me off the ground, bolting to the edge of the stage. Didn't hesitate as he bounded up to the balcony.

He landed close to the tech booth, loosening his grip. I kicked at him, bringing the kalis up and slicing through his arm. He recoiled. Light burst out of his wounds instead of blood as he let me go.

I scrambled back, skirting up the aisle and toward the tech booth, sparks flying out of it every now and then. I winced. Caught my bearings. The kalis hurt him now. It could've been another trick, like how he'd pretended to get hurt a few nights ago in the woods. But this felt like something different. Power surged through the sword and into me.

Blessed weapons weren't real. But maybe trapping a demon in my kalis had its benefits.

"You think you can win," my father snarled. "But you're nothing without your friends. It's just you and me, kiddo. The way it was always supposed to be."

"No," I said, but he continued on as if he hadn't heard me.

"No?" he laughed. "Come on. You're trying to tell me you haven't spent the last seven years wondering when we'd meet again? Thinking about how we'd make up for all that lost father-daughter time?"

Fire burned in my veins. "I did the opposite, actually. All I ever wanted to do was forget you. But I couldn't."

"Guilt is a helluva thing. Isn't it?"

"What do you know about guilt?"

For a brief moment, all the hatred in my father's features faded away. He looked at me the way I always wanted him to. Like I was someone he loved.

"I know it can eat you up inside. Turn you into something you're not. Someone you don't recognize. That's why it's important to let it go."

I loosened my grip on the kalis. "How?"

He took a step toward me. "By finishing what I tried to start all those years ago. Do you know how much easier life would've been without you in it? Your mom and I would be happy."

Tears pooled in my eyes. My hands shook as I took another step back. He said the things I'd always been afraid to wonder about. What if it had been me and not him that day? Would things be better for everyone?

David Scott smiled. For a second, it was the exact kind of charm that had gotten him out of every report Mom made against him. The thing that convinced everyone else that he wasn't abusing us. "But you can change things now," he said, compassion coloring his words. "You've spent so much time running from me. From yourself. You don't have to do it anymore. I can end all of your suffering, if you let me."

He had a point. It was exhausting to keep pretending that I could get away from it. That I didn't have to face any consequences for my actions.

I sent my father to Hell out of desperation and the need to survive. It was a decision driven by fear and anger. And I'd hated myself for it ever since I made it.

But I was so worried I could become him I hadn't bothered to check and see if it was really happening. He made choices to hurt people, just like I had. That was where our similarities ended. David Scott died alone and unloved. No one remembered him or cared that he was gone.

I had a theater full of friends who all tried to get in his way. Hurt him before he could hurt me. What did my father have? Marbas? Sure, Fred's former mentor was powerful, but he didn't care about the creature he'd brought back from Hell. To Marbas, David Scott was just a means to an end. But my friends all chose to stay. To help me, instead of running away.

Maybe I wasn't as horrible as I'd always imagined myself to be.

Only one way to find out. I needed to see who I was when I stopped comparing myself to him. I couldn't keep living in his shadow, carrying the weight of what I'd done to him around, afraid that the poison in his blood seeped into mine. He was right, in a weird way. I had to let him go. Free myself from the guilt I'd carried around for way too long.

And I would, as soon as I took care of my little demon problem.

David Scott shook his head. "I can see those gears turning, kiddo. It doesn't take a genius to do that math. Your friends are all too hurt to help you. Too far away. You can try to get me with that sword, but I'm faster than you. Stronger. I don't care if I hurt you. But I know you. I know my daughter. *You* care if you hurt me."

I swallowed as he took a few more slow, deliberate steps closer to me.

His smile curled into something feral as he continued. "I'd tell you I'd make it painless, but I've already lied to you enough, don't you think?"

He lunged for me. I braced myself, getting ready to swing at him with the kalis.

A vulture screeched again, popping up from the edge of the balcony. It launched at my father, shifting into Veronica as she crashed into him. She knocked him down to the ground, getting back on her feet and pulling him up with her. She pinned his arms behind him, holding him as still as she could.

"Do it, Cordy," she said, turning him toward me.

I nodded, slowly walking up the aisle.

My father chuckled. "Oh, you don't want to do that."

Rage boiled inside of me as I asked, "Why not?"

"It's okay to have second thoughts," my father said. "Just means you're a decent person. Not a monster like me."

Of all the things he could've said to me, that one was the worst. Whether I was a monster or not wasn't up to him. Not anymore. He might have made me into a version of himself, but it was up to me to choose to be something different.

And I did.

The absolution I needed wouldn't come from him. Or from the tear-soaked insides of a confessional booth. I hadn't forgiven myself for what I'd done. Not yet, anyway. But I wasn't going to hate myself for it anymore.

That was over now.

And so was David Scott's hold on me.

I walked up to my father, standing closer to him than I ever thought I'd choose to be again. I met Veronica's eyes. Anger burned bright little fires in them. But there was something else, too.

Pride.

Love.

And a subtle nudge for me to get the damn show on the road.

"You were wrong, you know. I'll never be like you," I said, smiling. "It was never just me. Even when you think you've gotten rid of my friends, they'll still be there for me. More than I can say about you."

I put one of the kalis's curved edges up to his throat, digging it into his skin. He tried pulling free, but Veronica tightened her grip. I dragged it across his throat in a straight line. Light pooled out of it. I leaned in close as he gasped for air. "But you were right about one thing. I'm not running anymore."

I took a step back, watching the light spill down from his throat and onto his shirt. I let the tip of the kalis rest right over where his heart was. "I'd tell you to go to Hell," I said, as I slowly pressed the dagger into his chest. "But you were already there. Where do demons go when they die, I wonder?"

Veronica let go of him. I used all of my force to shove the blade all the way. "Bye, Dad."

David Scott screamed as I pulled the kalis away. Father Marcus was right. It really *did* do more damage on the way out than it did on the way in.

He tried staggering back, but Veronica was faster. She knocked him down to the ground.

Flames sprung up from the theater's old dark blue carpet. They wound around him, covering him completely in a few seconds. The smell of burned skin wafted into the air as he writhed and cursed.

Veronica moved to my side. She wrapped her arm around me. I put my head on her shoulder, leaning into her. We both stood there, watching as David Scott became nothing but a faint burn mark on the carpet.

Again.

CHAPTER THIRTY-FIVE

IN WHICH THINGS WRAP UP NEATLY

IT TOOK LESS THAN A MINUTE FOR MY FATHER'S BODY to burn away into nothing.

"That was fast," Veronica said, burying her head in my hair.

"Demon sword fire," I replied, shrugging. "Guess it's hotter than we thought."

Veronica pulled away from me, laughing. The sound curled around me, blanketing me in warmth that I'd never been able to feel before. Soon, I joined her. Veronica shifted so that she stood across from me, tucking a piece of hair behind my ear as our laughter slowly died down.

"Cordy, I—" she started, but I interrupted her.

"I'm sorry," I said, looking down at the ground. "I never wanted anyone to get hurt. Especially you."

I wasn't sure what else to say. I'd been so afraid to make a mistake—so terrified that I'd hurt someone—that I didn't really allow myself to live much of a life in the first place. Even though I tried my best, bad things still happened. Blake died.

And Veronica was forced to turn into a monster.

"I'll find a way to change you back," I said, pushing away Fred's story about Dolores. History wouldn't repeat itself. Not this time. "I promise."

"I know you will," she said, tucking her hand under my chin. She tilted my head up, making sure I met her gaze before she spoke. "I would've turned into anything to keep you safe—but I'm glad I had some say in it." Her eyes flickered down to my lips.

I swallowed, warmth rushing up to my cheeks. Okay, so maybe I was wrong before. She wasn't looking at me like I was just a friend.

Veronica laughed again. She laid on a thick southern drawl as she said, "Why, dear, sweet Accordion, are you blushing?"

I swatted at her shoulder. She caught my hand, lacing her fingers through mine. Red crept into her cheeks as she stared at me.

"Veronica," I said, bridging the gap between us before I could make sense of what I was doing. I reached up, brushing her lips with my thumb. She closed her eyes. A smile stretched across her face. "Veronica," I repeated, her name a song as it drifted out of my mouth. "I—"

"Don't get me wrong," Dustin bellowed from the ground level. "I'm happy for both of you. Really. But we've got multiple problems down here. Can you get all sappy with each other *after* we've figured out how the hell we're going to explain any of this?"

Veronica and I jumped apart, both still blushing as we moved to the edge of the balcony. We peered over it. Dustin stood in the center aisle, arms crossed, as he looked up at us. Sal helped

Annabelle stand—she winced in pain. It was hard to tell from far away, but it appeared her arm stuck out at an unnatural angle. Fred was about halfway through a row of chairs near the stage.

I grimaced at Veronica. She winked at me.

I sighed, looking down at Dustin. "You heard all that?"

"Yeah," Dustin shot back. "The acoustics in here are wild. It's almost like we're in a theater."

Barry and Veronica's mom unfroze a few minutes before the cops burst through the theater's door. Thankfully, they hadn't been aware of anything that happened. The last thing they remembered was me calling Jesse a demon and everyone else in the auditorium running for the exits.

After we'd all given the cops our statements—and gotten the all-clear from the EMTs— Veronica, Sal, Dustin, and I sat in the lobby, not really sure what to do next.

Dustin cleared his throat, wiping away at the tears that pooled in his eyes. "Blake's gone," he said, as sobs racked through his body. "He's really gone."

"We couldn't have done it without him," I offered. I didn't know if it was helpful at all to hear. But it was the truth.

"Those sigils saved us," Veronica added.

"How'd you hold my father for so long?" I asked.

Dustin smiled through his tears. "I superglued the tape to the stage."

My mouth hung open. ". . . You . . . super . . . glued . . . ."

"Five layers," Dustin cut in. "Would've been six, but then you rushed out."

I blinked a few times. The absurdity of my father peeling away at five layers of superglued spike tape was too much to handle. I laughed, pulling Dustin into a hug. His tears soaked through my shirt, making my shoulder damp. A week ago, I wouldn't have let him this close. But there were worse things in this world than Dustin Jones.

"What do we do now?" he asked.

"I don't know," I replied.

Silence hung over all of us. Veronica laced her fingers through mine as we looked out through the glass doors and into the uncertain night in front of us.

"You should go home," I said, to anyone who was listening. "Get some rest. I'll send you updates."

Dustin sighed. "I don't think I can drive."

"I'll do it," Sal chimed in. "Come on, Jones. I could use a little sleep after all of that."

"Thanks, Sal," Dustin said, standing up. "And thank you both, too. For everything." He nodded at Veronica and me as Sal led him away.

There were only a few people scattered around the lobby after they left. Veronica and I sat together, leaning against each other as paramedics and cops moved in and out of the theater. Dustin would be okay. We all would, in time. But dealing with everything wasn't going to happen overnight. Things weren't going to magically get better just because Marbas and my father were gone.

Seven years ago, when I sent him to Hell, I wasn't prepared to deal with what that actually meant. How long the road to moving on from what he'd done—to healing—really was.

Footsteps slowly approached us. Veronica and I looked up

at the same time. Mom stood next to us, watching me.

"Cordelia?"

She'd barely noticed me before, and that was when it was only the two of us at home. For her to see me when there were other people in the room—it was nice.

Different.

Veronica squeezed my hand. "I'm gonna go check on my mom. Be back in a bit."

"How are you?" Mom asked, sliding down into the seat across from me.

"I'm tired," I replied, letting the words weigh me down. "But alive."

"That's what counts," she said.

Silence took its familiar spot between us. An ache shot through my heart. I didn't want things to go back to the way they'd been before.

"So, I've been thinking . . ." Mom started, before her voice trailed away.

"Yes?"

"I have the weekend off. We should spend some time together. If you're free."

Tears pooled in my eyes as I looked up at her. All I'd ever wanted was for her to spend time with me. Treat me like I existed. "I'd like that."

"What's wrong?" she asked, handing me a napkin.

All of the emotions I'd held back for so long came rushing forward. I let the tears fall down my face, dabbing at them with the napkin. "I'm not okay, Mom," I replied, holding her gaze. "I know you always wanted me to be, but I'm not."

She blinked back her own tears as she said, "I'm not, either.

But I hope we can be. One day."

I nodded. "I think we can." I paused, not knowing if I wanted the answer to my next question. But I needed it. So, I asked, "Do you wish it was me?"

"Hmm?"

"Do you wish it was me who disappeared, instead of him? Would things have been better with him around? Would you be happier?"

"Oh," Mom said, looking down at the ground. "No, Cordelia. If I ever said anything that made you feel that way, I'm sorry."

"Really?"

She nodded. "Really. Whatever happened—it was never your fault. I hope you know that."

Some part of me did. But it helped to hear her say it.

Mom sat with me until Veronica came back and promised to talk to me once she got home. It wasn't a huge step forward, but it was a start. And that was all that mattered.

"You okay?" Veronica asked, taking one look at my tear-soaked face. She waited until Mom walked away to ask her question.

"No. But that's okay, isn't it?"

"Yeah, it is."

"We're all gonna need therapy, huh?"

"Probably. Gonna be a weird few days to try to explain, though."

"Maybe we leave the demons out."

"Yeah. That's probably a smart move." She laughed, but it died down too quickly as she looked at me. "I'm sorry about almost killing you a few times. And all the other stuff, too."

I tucked a stray strand of hair behind her ear. "We both

made mistakes. And I'm sorry, too. I shouldn't have run away from you in the woods."

"Or at karaoke."

I chuckled. "Or at karaoke."

"Maybe we can start over?"

"No." I shook my head. "I don't think we can do that."

She looked down. "Oh."

I lifted her chin up, so her gaze met mine. "We can't forget about what we've done. But we can move forward. Together. If that's what you want."

She smiled. It was the most beautiful, dazzling thing I'd ever seen. "Of course, it is."

I pulled her close to me. Our noses touched as I whispered, "I love you, Veronica Dominguez."

She closed the distance between us, pressing her lips into mine. Fire surged through my blood, spreading through my body. Someone nearby cleared their throat, and we sprang apart. The kiss was over too quickly—which was probably fair, since we *were* about to make out in the school's lobby. But that didn't matter. It was the first of many, many more.

We laughed, touching our foreheads together.

Veronica kissed me lightly. "And I love you, Cordelia Scott."

I pulled away from her, winking. "But, like, as a friend, or—"

She rolled her eyes, still laughing. "If you don't know the answer to that question, you really haven't been paying attention."

CHAPTER THIRTY-SIX

IN WHICH THIS STORY ENDS . . . AND ANOTHER BEGINS

JESSE—AND HIS FATHER'S—MYSTERIOUS DISAPPEARance still made waves through the town months after our opening night fiasco. When we eventually *did* open *Our Demon Town*, Dustin wound up taking Jesse's role as Ryeland Jones.

After our last performance, Dustin's parents opened up The Coffee Spot for our cast party. It was part of his apology tour for being such an asshole for four years. Rumor had it that he was trying to sweet-talk his parents into letting him take his brother's business over once he was ready.

It would take a lot of business school to get him to that point, but he was willing to put in the work.

Barry stood in front of the barista counter, clinking a glass filled with carbonated apple cider—only the best fake champagne for the most legendary cast to ever perform in our theater.

Everyone involved in the show crowded into the main area where a karaoke stage once proudly stood. Family and friends hovered nearby, spilled out into the side room, or basked in the vaguely humid mid-June air.

Barry cleared his throat. "Can I have your attention, please," he said. The room fell silent. "I would be remiss if I didn't start out by acknowledging the devastating loss that shook our community at its core. Blake Jones was a true thespian who only ever wanted to support everyone who called the theater home. He shall be missed. So, first and foremost, to Blake. May he find peace in the great beyond."

"To Blake," everyone said. Aside from Jesse's disappearance, Blake's murder was our town's biggest unsolved mystery. There were already stories of a winged, shapeshifting monster haunting anyone who was unfortunate enough to be walking around alone at night.

What they didn't know was that Veronica and I went on routine patrols, just to make sure other demons didn't try to move in on Marbas's old territory. Since we shoved the demon into the kalis before he could make his last deal, his dream of creating more towns like ours came to an abrupt halt. But that didn't mean a place like Ruin's End wasn't alluring in its own right. To keep everyone safe, Veronica, Sal, Dustin, and I went to St. Gertrude's every Wednesday and Sunday to learn how to cast out any more demons that decided to wander into town.

Annabelle also volunteered to give me demon-weapon lessons. I still had no idea how to fight, or what my kalis could really do, but I was excited to figure it out.

As for Fred—

"Cordelia," my guidance counselor said, gesturing to the front door. "Can we have a word outside?"

Barry was still in the middle of a long-ass speech about the show. He choked up and took another sip of carbonated apple cider as he talked about how producing *Our Demon Town* had always been such a dream of his and how perfect everyone had been.

And he was right. Nothing went wrong during the entire run. No dropped lines. Fumbled transitions. Technical difficulties. Each of our eight performances had been flawless.

"Did you make a deal with Barry?" I asked, as the front door closed behind us.

"Now, why would I do that?"

"Because the show was *too good.* Suspiciously good."

He smirked. "Demon-Human Confidentiality, little one. Even if a bargain *did* happen, I couldn't tell you."

"Yeah, yeah." I sat down on The Coffee Spot's front steps and looked out into the woods. "So," I said, as Fred sat next to me. "What happens now?"

"I keep looking for a way to reverse Marbas's curse," Fred replied. "I don't know where Dolores is, but the next time I find her, I hope I can change her back."

I nodded. "I want to help you."

"Are you sure?"

"Yeah," I replied. "Veronica needs to be de-aswanged. And, if I've learned anything from this whole weird ordeal, it's that you don't have to do it alone." I shrugged. "Besides, knowing more about how all this demon stuff works could make me a better exorcist."

"Is it really an exorcism if you're not driving them out of a human?"

I winked at him. "The devil's in the details, isn't it?"

"I suppose so." He chuckled. "Thank you, Cordelia. I'd love the help."

We sat there in a comfortable silence. Eventually, Barry's speech ended, and happy voices filled the air as everyone went back to their conversations.

"Hey, Fred?"

"Hmm?"

"Thank you. For everything. Lots of people knew about my dad, but you're the only one who ever did anything to help me."

"Oh, that's not true, little one." He nudged me with his shoulder. "You decided to help yourself before I even came into the picture. *You* demanded that something be done. I was nothing more than a vessel for your righteous anger."

"Righteous, huh? Someone sounds a bit like Annabelle."

Fred rolled his eyes. "For what it's worth, I'm . . . *um* . . . proud of you."

I looked away from him. "For becoming a murderer?"

"No. You were faced with a difficult decision, and you made a choice. You did your best. And now, I think—I hope—that you're finally moving on."

"I am," I said. It wasn't a lie. "And I'm proud of you, too. I think Marbas's fate is a lot more . . . fair isn't the right word."

Fred chuckled. "How about 'fun'? It's nice to have him tucked away for safekeeping."

"And it makes the kalis look sick as hell," I replied. Wolves howled in the distance as I smiled at him. "Makes me seem kind of intimidating."

"My dear girl, you're intimidating enough on your own. You don't need a demon shoved into a sword for that."

"You mean that?"

"Of course. You faced your demons, and you won. Not many people can say that."

"Not literally, at least."

Fred smiled, nudging me with his elbow. "You're a monster, Cordelia Scott." For the first time since I could remember, that word didn't hurt.

"I know," I replied, setting the sword down next to me. "But only when I want to be."

He nodded, looking out into the woods. We sat there for a few minutes in a comfortable silence before I finally broke it.

"You wanna talk about my feelings, don't you?"

"It *is* my job as your guidance counselor to discuss these matters. I just want to make sure you're okay."

"I'm starting to be," I replied, as another wolf howled in the distance. I wasn't sure what was going to happen next. But I had people who would stand by me no matter what. And I knew we'd be able to face anything. Together.

"How do you feel right now?" Fred asked.

I turned the question around for a few seconds before I replied. "Whole. Loved."

"Those sound like good things to me."

I smiled. "They are."

"Damn, what a party," I said, grabbing a few discarded cups and tossing them into a trash bag. "I wish everyone knew how to throw things away. This is ridiculous."

"You're telling me," Dustin whined. "They've completely

wrecked my coffee kingdom. This is why I can't associate with theater kids after graduation."

"*That's* why?" Veronica and Sal asked at the same time.

The four of us stared at each other for a moment before bursting out in laughter. A wolf howl joined us as the sound slowly died down.

The back door opened. Fred stuck his head out of it. "Did I hear *fun*?"

I threw an empty cup at him. "You did. Either help us or get the hell out, old man."

He rolled his eyes. "I'd rather leave. Barry and I are going to watch *The Bachelor*—"

Another howl joined the first, cutting him off. More chimed in, until a whole pack was calling out in the woods. But something was wrong with the sound, like human screams were layered underneath.

"Wolves?" Dustin asked, his voice cracking at the end of the word.

And that was when one word broke through the darkness.

"HELP."

"What the hell is that?" I asked, as something rustled through the nearby trees.

"A problem, little one." Fred sighed, dragging his hands down his face. "A very, *very* big problem."

I groaned. "Ruin's End seems to be full of those."

"Must be Tuesday," Veronica said, with a shrug.

Fred cracked his knuckles. "This will probably be quite dangerous," he said, with a smile. "Who's with me?"

Veronica transformed into a vulture, soaring into the air. Dustin grabbed a nearby folding chair, while Sal took the knife we used to cut the cake. I held the kalis up to the moonlight. It glowed red, bathing the area around us in an eerie glow.

"Let's do this thing," I said.

We all rushed into the woods, ready to face whatever was coming for us. Together.

THE END

ACKNOWLEDGMENTS

This book wouldn't exist without Hannah Fergesen. Thank you for being an awesome friend, and an expert at figuring out what this book was trying to be—even if it took a billion drafts to get there!

To my incomparable editor, Lauren Knowles, whose enthusiasm for Cordy, Veronica, Fred, Sal, Barry, Dustin, and Annabelle rivals my own—thank you for taking a chance on me (and on this book!). Your empathy, guidance, and brilliant notes truly elevated DAMNED to a level I never dreamed of and I'm so glad we'll get to keep working together on lots of fun future projects!

To Cas Jones, my awesome Managing Editor, thank you for herding the million cats (and schedules) that it takes to turn this book into a real thing people can hold!

To the Editing Team, Tamara Grasty and Krystle Green, thank you for your awesome thoughts and insights, and for helping to make this book the best version of itself! And Cass Costa, my wonderful copy editor—thank you for helping me figure out when to use a comma! A thank-you to my awesome proofer, Aimee Lim, as well.

To the Design Team, Laura Benton and Rosie G Stewart, you are all ridiculously talented and I'm so grateful for the care you took with DAMNED's cover! And the book's layout is gorgeous! Thank you!

To Lizzy Mason and Lauren Cepero, my fantastic publicists—thank you for supporting me and getting DAMNED out there!

Will Kiester, you've been the best first publisher a girl could ask for. I'm so honored to have found a home at your imprint and to bring more Filipino American stories into the world with you and your awesome team!

Sara Fairchild (and, by extension, the other Fairchildren—Duke, Liam, Eloise, and Grace)—thank you for always believing in me and never giving up on me, even when I did.

Justine Pucella Winans—Fred thanks you for being the President of his fan club and I thank you for being the best critique partner/roommate/salt friend a Depressed™ Writer could ask for.

Leanne Yong—thank you for becoming one of my first friends in AMM. I'm so glad we could share the same debut year and I can't wait to hype up everything you do!

Tamar Shani, Raquel Brooks, and Miranda Miller—thank you for being my IRL LA friends who aren't involved in publishing at all! You keep me sane!

Christine Calella, your notes helped shape this book into what it is today. I'm so excited that we're pub siblings and can't wait for your debut to knock everyone's socks off!

Shelly Page, I'm honored to be co-editing *Night of the Living Queers* with you and am so excited for it to be out soon!

Tori Bovalino, where would I be without you and *The Gathering Dark*?!? Living a sad, folklore-less life, probably.

Elle Tesch and Andy Perez, thank you for your keen

thoughts on early drafts of DAMNED and for being your awesomely talented selves.

To C.H. Barron, thank you for your excellent notes and making the lumpia scene even more delicious! And a billion thanks to Cath Liao, for your beautiful note that made me cry a lot.

Caris Avendaño Cruz, Pamela Delupio, Rosiee Thor, Birdie Schae, Wen-yi Lee, Clare Oscongo, Brighton Rose, Sophia Hannan, and Colby Wilkens, thank you for your endless support, sage advice and scream-a-thon celebrations. And to Ann Fraistat, thank you for being an awesome '22 Debut Buddy, and for letting me panic in your DMs!

To my AMM and Pitch Wars family—Mallory Jones, Trang Thanh Tran, Chloe Lauter, Mary Feely, and Crystal Seitz, it has been an honor to be your mentor. Thanks for trusting me with your words, and for sending me everything you write from now until the end of time!

To Skyla Arndt and Kara Kennedy, thank you for your friendship and for letting me scream to you about Cordy's journey. And to the rest of Hex Quills—you're simply the best!

Rebecca Mahoney, thank you for being the best podcasting partner ever, and for our haunted adventures together. The Tater Tot Incident still terrifies (and inspires) me to this day.

Courtney Gould and Jessica Lewis, your haunting queer stories make the world a better place.

Sandra Proudman, thank you for always being there for a celebration or venting session.

Harper, AJ, Shannon, Camille—I'm so glad we all met through Sandra and you're all amazing!

Grace Li and Laura Southern, I wouldn't have been able to

make it through the past few years without you. Thank you for shouting with me every step of the way.

Garrett Pereda and Shane Frank, thank you both for reading an early version of DAMNED and for giving me awesome notes! Celine Robinson, your friendship, advice, and thoughtfulness are everything! Tara Knight, Lindsey Villareal, Justin Lee, and Kerry Williamson, thank you for being awesome!

To my Supernatural group chat—Meghan Fitzmartin, Talli Buchanan, Casey Hammonds, Emily Russell, and Emma Peterson: I hope we can all work together again someday.

Michael Gordon, Dane Anderson, and Chris Zatta, thank you for your support as I navigated working on two shows at once while writing a book!

Andrew Dabb, you taught me so much about how to tell a kick-ass story. Thank you for your wit, humor, compassion, and for being the best boss in the biz!

Artemis, you can't read this because you're a cat, but know that you're the best cat and I love you—even if you're a pain in the ass. Baby Bright Star, you're also a cat and can't read, you little destructive bastard. Please stop tearing everything up.

To Chris: We've shared many wins and losses already, and there's no one I'd rather figure out life with—even if you ate the mac and cheese I was saving for lunch that one time. One day we'll make rich people money and afford a house in LA.

And finally, if you're reading this, thank you so much for making it all the way to the end of these acknowledgements and for picking up DAMNED IF YOU DO. I hope you enjoyed it and found a little bit of yourself in these pages.

ABOUT THE AUTHOR

ALEX BROWN (SHE/HER) is a former theater kid (and occasional stage manager) who spends her free time bringing productions to life, both on-stage and off. When she's not pretending to live in a musical, Alex writes stories about monstrous girls and the people who love them. Alex is also the co-creator of *The Bridge*, a haunting, folklore-filled narrative fiction podcast that's had over 1,000,000 downloads to date! She has a story in the indie bookstore bestselling YA folk horror anthology, *The Gathering Dark* and is co-editing *Night of the Living Queers*, a YA horror anthology. Alex lives in Los Angeles with her partner and their two chaotic cats. As far as she knows, she hasn't made a deal with a demon . . . yet.

Damned if You Do is her debut novel.